AEROVOYANT

#52/87

Summer 2020

The official Little Free Library Book
Tour, "Year of the Quarantine"

Kanorado, Kansas

Enjoy!

P L Tavormina

AEROVOYANT

THE INDUSTRIAL AGE
VOLUME ONE

P.L. TAVORMINA

AUTHOR'S NOTE

This is a story about climate.

Ever since it became obvious to me decades ago that some forces actively suppress climate science, I've felt that science itself is under attack. The seed of an idea for a book was planted. Two characters—a young woman who is targeted because she perceives atmospheric chemistry and a young man who is essentially a walking history book—sprouted in my mind. Their families, their lives, the choices each of them makes, and their interconnected cultures began growing too.

The goal of this novel is to frame science and history within a climate story. It's a methodical story. Some readers describe the pacing as slow; others do not. But sacrificing the science and history—the nonfiction part of the fiction—to "speed things up" would detract from why this story exists in the first place.

So yes, this is a story about climate science. But it's also a story about family, and courage, and how each of us has part of the answer to the global challenge we face. It's a story about hope.

ACKNOWLEDGMENTS

I couldn't have contemplated a project like this without the loving support of family and friends, and professional feedback from editors and artists. My heartfelt gratitude to all the Tavorminas and Boedigheimers who bounced ideas around with me and read through early drafts. Thanks to Vicki McGough for story guidance and Leah Brown for copy edits. I thank Michelle Argyle for the beautiful formatting and James Egan for the fantastic cover.

Also, many thanks to local and online writing buddies, including members of Conejo Writers, The Inklings, the Ventura County Writers Salon, and Absolute Write. To personal friends, thank you for listening patiently when I told you the novel was finished—and then went back to wrestle through another draft.

I so appreciate the help from all of you.

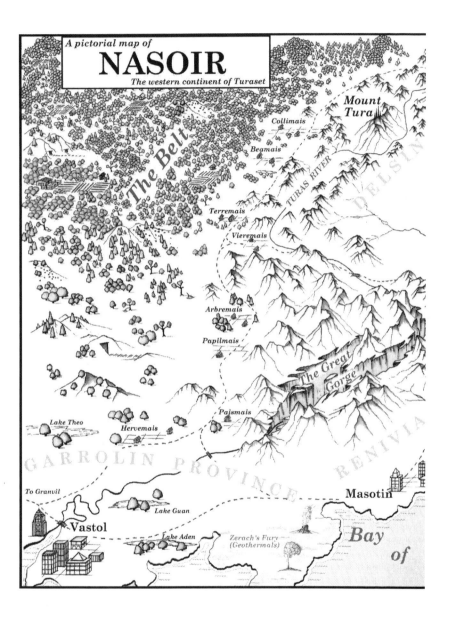

A pictorial map of

NASOIR

The western continent of Turaset

Mount
Tura

Collimais

Beamais

The Belt

DELSIN

TURAS RIVER

Terremais

Vieremais

Arbremais

Papilmais

The Great
Gorge

Pajsmais

Lake Theo

Hervemais

RENIVIA

GARROLIN PROVINCE

To Granvil

Masotin

Vastol

Lake Guan

Lake Aden

Zerach's Fury
(Geothermals)

Bay

of

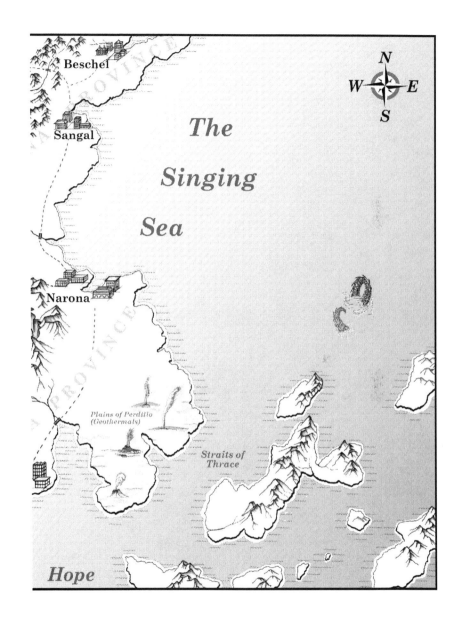

Prologue

"Why did they all die?"

Alphonse had curled up next to his grandfather, whose shoes were off for the evening. The familiar smell of leather and too-warm socks was starting to fade.

His grandfather's eyes crinkled. "They didn't, or we wouldn't be here."

Alphonse gave a small, frustrated sigh at being handed yet another logic puzzle. "I mean, why did *most* of them die?"

At that, his grandfather laughed. "Very good, Grandson. Very good indeed. Most of them died because they came from another world."

"Called Ert." Alphonse scooted closer, right up against the old man's side. Snug.

"Earth. That's right. Our ancestors wanted to live on Turaset, but the air made them sick. The radiation from our suns was like nothing they'd seen before."

"The radi . . ."

"Ra-di-a-tion. The breath of fierno."

Alphonse ran his finger along the back of his hand. His skin had gone mahogany again, because of fierno's breath. "They didn't change color?"

"No, they didn't. None of the colonists had purple skin tones like your friend Matiya, or blue ones like the little girl next door."

"Because there wasn't feerno on Ert?"

His grandfather's face went smooth, and his lips curved in a small smile. It meant the storytelling could last forever—all the time in the world, as long as Alphonse wanted—and he smiled back. "Fierno, Grandson. Earth. That's what we think, but we don't know all the details."

"Because they died."

His grandfather squeezed him gently around the shoulders. "Again, not everyone died, but yes. They needed to survive. And they believed some things *should* be left behind. They saw what happened to Earth and took it as a lesson. And so, they brought some things—"

"Like grapes."

The man laughed. "Yes. Grapes. And destroyed other things."

"*. . . destroyed other things.*" Alphonse wondered what those things were. The room fell quiet in a middle-of-the-night kind of way. The kind of quiet Alphonse knew from waking up in a drowsy pocket of blankets and reaching about for his stuffed lion. Still and deep, where any small house-sound might cuff away at his ears. It was like that for a minute.

"The Precepts say it's important to live in a simple way."

Alphonse didn't care about the Precepts. "But how come we turn colors?"

"Because of the breath of fierno."

"No. How *come*?"

"Ah. How did it come to pass." His grandfather lifted him onto his lap, and Alphonse leaned onto his chest, where the steady thump from his grandfather's heart pulsed into his cheek. "It's hard to know the truth after so long. We think the scientists changed our cells."

Alphonse scrunched his face.

"They say the founders took the different colors—pigments—from Turaset's byantun trees and quiver-fish, and from other plants and animals too, because those creatures survive fierno. And they gave the pigments to us, into the part of us that gives us our shape." His grandfather held Alphonse closer, and his voice dropped to a whisper. "They even say, Alphonse, that there are *more* gifts inside our cells. Waiting to be unlocked. Gifts to help us avoid the mistakes they made."

"On Earth."

"That's right! And you said that exactly right. On Earth."

Chapter One

The last time Alphonse wore this tie had been to his grandfather's funeral seventeen years earlier.

He remembered playing with it during the service, twisting the too-long tails around each other in one direction, then the other, then back again, while the funereal deacons watched with disapproval. There'd been eulogies, and embraces, and other things he probably should have held onto over the years, but in truth the only crisp details he remembered were the glaring deacons and this thin, black tie.

Tonight, he found it in the copperwood chest on top of a few suits his mother had put away. Tucked between his grandfather's wallet and spring-driven pocket watch. Traces of sandalwood cologne drifted from the suits—ghosts, the past wrapped up in this little chest. The memory of his grandfather, Councilor Stavo di Gust, saying Alphonse too might sit on the city's Council one day.

A seat had opened, and with his mother's connections, Alphonse had a shot. A tingle of nervous anticipation spread down his arms. Pushing a tie clip over the tails, he muttered, "You should be here." He headed downstairs, where his mother was speaking into the distavoc.

"Into the joint account, tomorrow." As she spoke, Ivette Najiwe fiddled with a carved ring on her index finger. The color matched her dress, both white. She met his gaze and pointed to a jacket laid out across the sofa. "We need the money by mid-morning. Yes, I know the limits."

The jacket was white as well. He walked past it to the hallway closet.

"You don't need to record the transfer at all." She snapped a finger and gestured at the jacket again.

He pulled a brown one out, mouthing, *Matching clothes?*

She exhaled loudly. "Why do you need the name? Fine. Zelia Naida."

The funds she was transferring had to do with the combustion industry, the interprovincial conglomerate of energy production, which meant this call would take a while. Alphonse stepped outside to wait.

Bel and Letra, the twin suns of Turaset, were climbing down the western sky. Two identical drops of liquid gold. Dusky light from both carpeted the Martire Arel range, and his breath caught. The *glow* out there. One peak in that great swath soared over the others, Mount Tura and its crowning pinnacles, the Prophets. His grandfather had once said they'd climb those together.

Anticipation and anxiety tossed around inside of him, along with a little self-doubt. Sangal's most influential lawmakers would be at the gala tonight, and he'd need to convince them he was the right choice for the Council seat.

Relax.

Behind him the door opened and his mother stepped out, reached up, and flicked something from his shoulder. Her eyes landed on the tie, and her expression froze. "That's Father's."

"Yes."

She regarded him, unspeaking, frown lines starting on her forehead.

"I'll change if it upsets you."

"It doesn't upset me. It concerns me. The Council's different now. He has no place in your thoughts."

No. She was wrong. If ever Alphonse needed an anchor, it was tonight.

"I thought you wanted this."

"Yes, of course I do. Yes. It's the means that bother me. Grandfather wouldn't stand for appointment by acclamation."

"You don't know that."

"Mother. Think about the laws he wrote; the ones he fought for and the ones he let go. Whoever's named has zero mandate from the people. Acclamation—it just isn't a good foot to start on."

"Alphonse. You are an excellent candidate."

He blinked. This was a departure from their normal argument. His chance at success had always been pinned to her connections, her job with the industry and its influence up and down the coast. Quietly, he said, "Thank you. I'm sorry. I'm a little nervous."

A hired automobile pulled up, and gesturing to the aut's back door, she dropped her voice. "You have no reason to be. Listen, I understand how you feel. I do. It's possible nothing will come of tonight. I'll do the talking. You be agreeable."

Agreeable. She meant he needed to keep his head together around the Council leader, Lesteri di Les. "The man's a crook," he muttered.

"The man is necessary. Just hold your temper."

Alphonse had often thought campaigning for a council seat would be the political equivalent of scaling the perfect cliff. There'd be plenty of challenges along the way. Building a platform, finding support.

An opponent and debates. Each step, a pitch up the face.

Reaching the Council through acclamation, well. That was different, wasn't it? But the destination was the same. At its heart, acclamation was a different route to the same clifftop. Nothing more.

When they arrived at Governance Hall, Alphonse held the door and followed his mother in and upstairs to the banquet chamber. Narrow windows, lavish drapes. Waiters with trays and politicians with drinks. A few other political funders. Same as a dozen times before.

"Councilor di Les," she murmured. "By the far wall."

Yes, there he was, speaking with a councilwoman. As head of the ruling caucus, di Les could line up the votes to give that seat to anyone. Alphonse swallowed against his nerves. He'd bet good money that if di Les picked him, there'd be some string attached. He might be asked to swear a loyalty pledge of one sort or another.

His mother took a flute of sparkling wine from one of the waiters. "Try to enjoy yourself. He'll be free soon enough."

"Yeah," he breathed.

Outside, first sun was down. Evening light had deepened, and the view of the Prophets was clear. Immutable, monolithic giants, standing guard over the Martire Arels.

So old.

Those great cliffs would have dominated the western skyline even before humanity claimed Turaset as its new home. Legends, dozens of them, had been built off those hills. One said the ghost of a colonist, Arel, haunted the pinnacles. Find Arel and steer fate, that was the legend. It had become the family joke, too, that Stavo had written his environmental laws to keep Arel safe.

His mother leaned over. "The councilor's free."

"Right." Alphonse's hope and fear focused into a point. Once seated, the new councilmember would help steer law. He started toward di Les.

His mother pulled ahead at the last moment. "Lesteri!"

"Ivette."

All massive bulk and calculation, that's how di Les came off. His hair looked like snow that had seen too much exhaust, shoved off to the side in clumps, and his complexion was a ruddy gray, but that part was temporary. Everyone's pigmentation shifted when Bel and Letra aligned.

"Alphonse. That's a sharp look. New suit?"

"Good evening, Councilor." Alphonse ran his hand down the tie. "In a manner of speaking, I suppose it is."

His mother locked eyes with him, seeming to know exactly where his thoughts were. This was a climb, he reminded himself. He needed the next grip. "I understand Sangal has sent a delegation to Beschel. Something about off-shore mining?"

Di Les's eyebrows went up and he grinned. "You follow energy policy. Yes, there's archaic carbon under the shelf. More than we thought."

His mother smiled. "Alphonse loves policy detail."

Di Les studied her. "Ivette. Alphonse is young. Etta di Low is not, and she makes a stronger case for the seat. She's been my aide for a long time."

"I wonder if she shares her father's views on donation caps."

It grated that his mother would bring money into

a discussion that should more rightly focus on qual-
ifications. From the scowl on the councilor's face, it
seemed he agreed.

Di Les tapped a ciguerro out of his pack. "Frankly,
I'm in no rush to fill it. I've been more preoccupied
with my bill. Getting it through committee. You and I
had an understanding."

"You'll get your votes." She gestured at a group
sitting a few feet away, and wine dribbled over the side
of her flute. "Clumsy."

But that move wasn't clumsy; it was calculated. Get
a small thing—say, help with a spilled drink—then go
for the prize.

She took the napkin di Les held out. "Thank you,
Lest. I've funded half the councilors in your caucus
and pulled strings for a few others. I'll make some
calls."

Di Les was appraising him now. Standing taller,
Alphonse anchored his thoughts into the issues he'd
like to work on. Besides expanding the boundar-
ies for wilderness protection, which in all likelihood
would take years due to claims the industry made for
the land, factory workers were paid a bare fraction
of what they deserved. The combustion industry said
cheaper oil would solve poverty, but there were other
possibilities. Changing tax law might free up a little
revenue.

Ivette handed her glass over. "I need this freshened."

What she wanted was privacy with di Les. Alphonse
took the flute and nodded. "Councilor."

He worked over to the bar, handed the flute to the
barista and turned to watch his mother. She was eyeing
di Les now. Di Les leaned toward her, said something,

and she laughed. He said something else, and she whispered into his ear.

Alphonse swallowed and turned back to the bar. *Different route, same clifftop.*

Down the bar, two councilors, both women, were discussing trade. The older of the pair had gone on record opposing interprovincial commerce, and Alphonse didn't understand her reasoning, since other parts of the economy weren't constrained in that way. It seemed opening trade might spur innovation. If he was seated, he'd have the opportunity to speak with her—

"Let's talk about that seat."

Startled, Alphonse found di Les next to him. "Sir, thank you. I'd like that. Discussing it. I'd very much like that."

"It's a representation, son. The seat is a symbol. What I'd actually like to go over with you is the importance of strengthening City Council."

"Sir?"

"Making it stronger." Di Les leaned onto the bar and faced forward; he didn't look at Alphonse at all. There was no sense of judgment from di Les's eyes, no tension. The man's face was simple contemplation. Maybe his bland expression was supposed to put Alphonse at ease, but the last thing he'd expected was for di Les to behave as though the seat held no consequence.

"Picture a tree. Think of my colleagues and myself as a tree."

Alphonse adopted the man's stance. "Um. All right."

"It needs a strong trunk, that's fundamental. The trunk is the center of the tree, but it's not enough to make a tree grow. It's just a trunk. The tree also needs a healthy canopy to harvest the light."

"Uh, yes. That sounds right, sir." Nerves pricked away at Alphonse's chest. He hadn't expected a botany lesson, either.

"Those parts are important. The tree certainly needs a robust trunk. It needs a canopy. When a child draws a tree, those are the parts they draw. The visible parts."

Bewildered.

"Do you know the most important part of the tree, Alphonse?"

"I'd say . . . I suppose the branches, sir, to connect the trunk to the canopy."

Di Les shot him an affable smile. "That's not a bad guess. Not bad. Most people say the leaves. Most people, they get ahead of themselves and compare councilmembers to individual leaves. Etta, she said leaves. Some people say flowers."

Flowers made as much sense as anything, as much sense as this conversation, which was to say not a whole lot.

"No, it's not the branches, and it's not the flowers. It's the roots. The toes, sinking into the dirt. The part no one ever thinks about, but I want you to think about it. A byantun tree can burn right down to the ground, and a person might say it's dead and gone. Then spring rolls around and so does the rain and those roots send up new growth. Same tree! And do you know why? Because of the *roots*, Alphonse. They remember the past. They wait for things to be just right, and they make their move. They regrow that tree."

The councilor stood there, like a massive tree trunk himself in the middle of the gala, and after a few moments Alphonse said, "The past had a few nice things going for it."

"Mm. That it did. That it did. And it stretches back a good long way. Do you know another interesting thing about roots?"

"I'm afraid I don't, sir."

"Roots *dig*. As deep as they need to. For anything they can find to make the tree stronger."

"I see."

"We are the tree."

"Yes."

"And each of us, Alphonse, has our role. Now, regarding the Council, what role do you see for yourself?"

His nerves surged. "Sir. I'd like to do something about factory wages."

Di Les chuckled. "I'm afraid the labor committee's full."

"Sorry, that wasn't clear. I meant if we look at revenue streams—"

"Tax law?" Di Les gave a heartier laugh, and the two down the bar paused and turned. Di Les quieted. "I applaud your career goals, young man. You have some real brass in your spine, but I do suggest walking before running."

Flushing, Alphonse looked down. Some other issue, then. Probably too early to mention wilderness protections—di Les's stance on archaic carbon was clear. "Well, I've also wondered about starting an exploratory group on public services."

Di Les still wore a friendly smile. "I'm not sure you understand the tree, son."

Obviously. Alphonse said quietly, "It seems you're looking for a 'yes man.'"

Di Les regarded him more carefully. "Let's dispense

with the metaphor. There's a reason sitting on the Council is called 'service.' We're a body, and we *serve* to improve lives. I need a nominee who understands the advantage of a cohesive block."

"I do," Alphonse said, hearing the eagerness in his voice. "Absolutely. Our strongest and best laws are built from common ground. Grandfather said a healthy debate—"

"Your grandfather nearly destroyed Sangal. I have an empty seat. Do you understand what I need or not?"

"*...nearly destroyed Sangal.*" Heat flooded Alphonse's chest. His grandfather had been one of the best councilors this city had ever seen. "People depend on the Council—"

"People *depend* on energy. There's oil in the Martire Arels, but the land's off limits—your grandfather's work—and that's got to change. If you want to serve, Alphonse, you'll open up those ranges."

Undo Grandfather's laws. The barista set his mother's flute in front of him, and he fixed his eyes on it, willed his temper to settle, smooth out, go the way of those bubbles disappearing into the air.

"You'll vote to prospect. To drill. You'll work to get that archaic carbon out of the ground fast and hard. Do that, every time, and someday we'll talk about exploratory groups and public services."

"You want me to undo Grandfather's work."

"I want our citizens to have the fuel they need. Do you understand me?"

Alphonse held his tongue and threw a glance across the room. His mother's eyes were granite hard. *Take the seat.* Her message couldn't be plainer.

Time sliced through him, and he was a small boy again with laughter filling the family home.

His grandfather's bill had passed, and he swooped Alphonse into his arms and promised a camping trip.

Alphonse pulled a napkin from the stack on the bar and blotted his palms. "I do understand. You want me to dig up the Martire Arels and sell them off piece by piece."

Di Les looked over to Alphonse's mother, who appeared to be following the exchange as easily as if she'd been standing next to them. Her eyes pleaded with di Les over some point, but whatever that point was escaped Alphonse. She had no real respect for the man. She worked with him, or against him, as suited the needs of the industry. With a sharp start, Alphonse realized she might see him that way too.

Di Les turned back. "Your candidacy carries a few advantages."

Advantages. His heart plummeted—she'd offered money. He threw a harder glance over. In all their discussions, he'd been clear he wanted to earn his place. It had always been a point of conflict, her ongoing insistence that holding a seat was worth sacrificing a little integrity, and his rejection of that position. Now, with the seat in reach she was selling him out wholesale. She might even consider it some sort of bizarre gift, although more likely she hadn't thought past raw numbers. He slammed his fist down. "If you want to rape that land, and you're willing to sell democracy in the deal, count me out."

Alphonse strode off in a blind fury, hot. Before he knew it, he was at the window. In the distance, the Martire Arels lay velvet black on gray, jagged and hard. Completely indifferent to di Les, to him, to his mother. Alphonse's rush of emotion sank. He couldn't do a thing to protect that range as a private citizen.

And he couldn't weigh in on any other issue, for that matter.

His mother was with di Les now, panic and disbelief on her face. As their voices rose, other conversations in the room trailed off. Everything was unravelling. Then di Les stormed out, and Alphonse's mother waved him to the door.

Once in the aut she pulled a bottle from the liquor supply. Her voice was venomous. "How can you be so stupid?"

Utter disbelief. "He wants to strip the protections. He wants to repeal Grandfather's laws."

She grabbed a glass tumbler. "You had one job."

"One job? What are you saying? Look, every year the Council does more for the industry and less for the city. Grandfather understood—"

She clubbed him, the bottom of the glass hitting his jaw squarely. His cheek hit the window and he cried out, "What is your problem? I'm your *son*."

"We need the seat, and I handed it to you on a platter."

"You handed yourself on a platter." He blanched at his words—that was her style, not his. "Pull over," he ordered.

The driver slowed and rolled to the curb. Alphonse pushed the door open. "I'm walking home. Then I'm packing a bag. Don't come after me."

"Come after you? Fierno," she swore. "I know you, Alphonse. I *raised* you. You're not going anywhere, and if you do, trust me, you'll be back."

Chapter Two

The aut rumbled away.

Alphonse turned to a darkened storefront and slammed his palm into the brick. It hurt. He slammed the other hand, grunting with each strike.

Above him a window squawked open. He paused.

"Do you need help, mister?" A young man hung across the sill. Second-level apartments sat atop all the stores in this part of Sangal, most of them with their lights out for the night.

Alphonse slumped back against the wall. "No. Sorry, I should've been quiet."

"Those bricks ain't much for helping. Do you want to talk about whatever it is?"

There was such honesty in the offer. "Not really, no."

"Well, all right. Good night." The man pulled back in and shut the window.

Things had gone so horribly wrong. He'd never even considered she might offer a bribe. He didn't want the seat, not if it meant buying his way. Not if it meant voting for any piece of garbage legislation put in front of him. He pushed off the wall and began to walk.

Certainly not if it meant undoing Grandfather's work. His grandfather would've understood why Alphonse had lost his temper. There was comfort in

the idea that Stavo di Gust might have lashed out at
the bribe, as Alphonse had.

Back at the family home, he slipped in through a
side door, went up to his rooms, and turned on the
light. The air purifier down the hallway clicked on at
the same time. The pulse of that purifier, switching on
and off through the years, filtering the stale city air
with its faint odor of petroleum—that pulsing whisper
of affluence had always felt like the house itself breathing. Some nights when Alphonse couldn't sleep, when
his chest was too tight, he'd lay awake wishing for a
device like that to help him breathe.

Right now, his breathing was fine. Alphonse
changed and grabbed his pack out of the closet. He
took the training weights out and pulled supplies
down from the shelves. Rod and reel, climbing gear.

He took his time, double-checked each piece. The
water skin had a crack—he'd need a new one. His
lines were tangled. After sorting and packing it all, he
looked around the room, at the old school awards on
top of his dresser, the dusty stuffed lion next to them.
The fading note from his grandfather tucked into the
mirror frame. *See you tonight.* Alphonse had found it
the day they arrested him.

Tucking the note into his pocket, he whispered, "I
won't be back."

Alphonse walked. The air was salty and breezy, and if
he closed his eyes, it was almost enough to imagine he
didn't live in a city at all. When he reached the edge
of Sangal, the suns were rising and businesses were
opening for the day.

He stopped at an outfitter's shop. "I need rations."

"Where you headed?" The woman squinted up at him.

The Prophets. Maybe Arel really was out there, dispensing wisdom. Didn't matter; climbing the Prophets had been in the back of his mind ever since Grandfather promised it years earlier. Of course, the outfitter would tell him to take a partner. He slung his pack to the floor. "Did you ever need time away? You know. Do something different, clear your head."

The woman chuckled, "Doubt I'd'a gone into business like this otherwise."

Alphonse returned her smile. "Yeah. It's like that. I'm heading out for a while. Maybe a long while."

"Most a person can carry lasts about three weeks, Mr. Najiwe."

He suppressed a flash of annoyance. Everyone recognized him. It came with the family history. "How much weight is that?"

"Sir, it's 'bout thirty pounds dry."

Alphonse ran through the numbers. He'd trained up to fifty but not over any real distance. The pack was already twenty. He'd need water.

"You ever packed in deep before? It ain't no party."

He glanced around the little shop. The things on the shelves were familiar, most of them anyway. The others he could probably figure out. "Grandfather taught me."

The shop owner's face gentled. "Shame what they did to him. Let's see what we can do. Get the weight down."

She replaced Alphonse's tent with a lighter one and made a few other suggestions. Water skin, rations. Information on foraging. Alphonse hauled the pack up with a groan.

"Yep. It sure adds up." Doubt filled the woman's eyes.

"I'll be fine."

"All right. Those canisters, each is six meals. The lid's the bowl; just add water. You got ten. The tent, machete. All of it, all what you got there, it's all standard." She glanced up at Alphonse again and pursed her lips.

"What?"

"You're wanting time alone, Mr. Najiwe, but it's early. Wait a few weeks, there'll be other folks out. Safer, in case you hit trouble."

"I'll be careful."

"Yes, son. Please do."

The trail into the ranges began at one of the geothermal fields dotting Nasoir's coast. This one was Autore's Drummers. Someone or other had named the field, called it a "percussive tribute to the divine" with its geysers and fissures.

Alphonse had last been here after his twenty-second birthday, with a girl. Her eyes were amber, and he'd wanted to lose himself in the color, get trapped in those eyes. And her hands were delicate, soft, like music in their way. It might've been love; he thought it probably was. But in the end, in tears, she'd said it was too difficult to spend time with his mother. That lovely girl had stood here, by this red mud pot he wanted to share because its steady plops matched his pulse and might match hers too. She ended the relationship that night.

He put her out of mind. The sky was azure, breezes

blew down the slopes, and Alphonse filled his lungs with the rush of sage and creosote.

After a few hours of hiking, he reached the campground where he and his grandfather used to stay. Shimmying the pack off, Alphonse picked up three smooth stones at the entry post and started down the loop to the first site they'd used. Dark ashes filled the fire pit, and Alphonse placed a stone in the middle. "I was five. We found spiceberries, and I ate too many." He'd been so sick from the berries he remembered little else.

He went further down, to a nearly-horizontal copperwood tree that marked their second trip. He set a stone on its trunk. "I fell. You made me a splint." That muffled crack of bone, like the snap of a wet wishbone, that sound had shocked him even more than the pain. And that night in the tent his dreams had been vivid, filled with prisms, with sounds, not-quite words, like someone calling from a great distance.

The third site they'd used, back in the shrub, here they'd stayed two weeks. He placed the stone on the flat patch of ground where their tent had stood. Late nights, drifting to sleep on his grandfather's lap, the memories rushed back with aching clarity.

"You told me about service." He recalled so clearly his grandfather saying that one man, and one argument, could shift the hearts of an entire body. He remembered his grandfather's words. *Call me Stavo*. Speaking to Alphonse as though they were equals.

Why didn't his mother speak like that? Even now. She was the old man's daughter. She'd been kind when Alphonse was small, he was certain, but at some point she and the Council had wrapped into a contorted thing. It had been a slow drift to a different perspective, and Alphonse had been carried along too.

On that third camping trip, Alphonse's dreams began to change. They were more sensate, tactile, almost like travels, and it had felt like the moment of comprehending a second language. Those fractured dream-prisms coalesced into a perfect spectrum of light. He'd stood, lucid, inside a great library.

The library held all of history, each piece recorded in a hundred different ways, like a letter or a film. Like the pulse of a planet, or geology or music, layers and harmonies fitting together. History was vibration through time, Stavo had said, and the library held pure experience of the past.

That night in the library, Alphonse and Stavo had stood on Turaset at its founding.[1] They had seen their planet as it had been, before the men and women arrived with their genetically-modified seed and embryo banks. They'd seen Turaset's strange, intensely-colored sessile beasts anchored into the ground. Creatures that flew in a jumping, bounding way. Plants, vibrantly-pigmented ones, undulating across the landscape. Everything was so brightly colored, and those pigments protected Turaset's creatures from what the colonists called fierno's breath.

They had seen the metal ships land. They'd seen the code writers who engineered those pigments into the human genome. The authors of humanity's survival.

Autore.

He and Stavo had watched as, over the centuries, Turaset was terraformed to become more like Earth.

Alphonse had awoken confused and afraid. His grandfather had pulled him close. "Don't worry,

---

1   The history of Turaset, including its colonization and regression to pre-industrial society, is described in Appendix 1. Appendices, world maps, and additional in-world stories are also available at pltavormina.com.

Grandson. Everything through space and time is connected."

His visions continued but were often forgotten, as
though the library couldn't hold him *there* and mani-
fest as memories *here*. He would wake knowing only
that his sleep had been disturbed again. Occasionally,
knowledge slipped through and he'd ask his mother
later and she'd be irritated and say her father had been
delusional. Alphonse learned not to speak of the travels. Eventually, he convinced himself they hadn't happened.

Now, aching for the past, he brushed his hands
together, went back to his pack, and continued on.
Other than the crunch of dirt under his boots and the
babble of the trailside stream, the world was silent.

My world. He breathed it in.

Near mid-afternoon, he left the trail and forced
his way through shrubs up to his training cliff. Resting chest-first on it, he spread his arms wide, dry heat
against his dampness. So musty. So good. Surely he
could become stone itself if he sank deeply enough
into the smell. Releasing his breath, he took in more.

My rock. I am rock.

That afternoon, Alphonse took four practice
climbs along four different routes. Every grip and hold
came back; he shifted and pushed up with the memory
of muscle. Afterward, he sat on top of his rock and
looked westward, where the Prophets peeked over the
ranges like two fingertips beckoning.

On the third day, the trail turned away from the stream
and switched back and forth more steeply toward the

first pass. A pair of courting raptorfowl screamed overhead, bounding and soaring, fierce and free.

Alphonse was further into the ranges than he'd been before, and Turaset's twin suns grew into points of heat as the day whiled away. The pack cut into Alphonse's shoulders, sweat dripped from his hair, and old memories stirred with the breeze.

You'll come tonight, Alphie. Tell Delsico's donors about Marco leaving.

Puzzled, he'd said, *No, Mommy. I don't want to talk about Daddy.*

They'll have cakes. Come, you won't need to say anything. I'll tell them.

I don't want to!

Oh Alphonse, don't fuss.

He'd gone, and she'd told the industry donors that Marco didn't want the burden of raising a son. The pain of that evening still stung, and he yelled into the slopes, "I was *six*. Why would you *say* that?"

Hiking through the afternoon and into early evening, he lost count of the switchbacks. As the first sun dipped behind Mount Tura, Alphonse closed on the easternmost pass, huffing the last eighty feet to the saddle. The terrain beyond rose into view and he stopped.

Awe. There was no other word. Before him lay a massive, virgin landscape. Peak after peak fell into the distance, with Mount Tura standing proud, centered in grandeur spanning the horizon. Snow on the higher slopes balanced the lush valley below, and the twinkling thread of the Turas River ran north to south as far as he could see.

Starkly beautiful flinty outcrops peppered Mount Tura's ridgeline. Alphonse sat suddenly on the trail and stared. His mother, she was like those great cliffs— hard and rimmed in cold, protruding into his world. Refusing to yield yet oddly fundamental to life.

An ache started high in his chest and passed down, through his core and into the ground, and with it, Alphonse lost himself to the view. If he'd been different, if he'd stood up to her ideas sooner, things might be better now. Their lives might have gone differently if he'd shown more integrity, been a force, defined the landscape instead of allowing her to do so.

It would have required him to be some other person long ago, during those chaotic years after his grandfather's death. The awareness he would have needed then, to see the course she was laying—impossible. It was too much to expect of a child.

Like those protruding granite fins, etched in time, the past was written.

Wilderness. The thought offered itself. Endless ranges lay ahead, and the outfitter's doubtful eyes sparked in Alphonse's thoughts.

He could die out there. No one would know.

Tura's Prophets wore mantles of cloud; they were dark, draped in white. They watched over the folding glory of syncline and anticline, over the layers of rock stacked like books in a library. The Prophets stood shoulder to shoulder, facing him, silent, like funereal deacons knowing what lay ahead for a child too small to understand.

Light faded as second sun crept downward, and shadows from distant peaks stole across the valley. A

cooling breeze swirled up, bringing new scents, pine
and cedar.

I could summit. I could stand with Arel.

The thought pulled energy up through him, warming and immediate, at odds with the cool evening
breeze turning suddenly chill.

He stood. "I see you," he yelled at the Prophets.
"And I'm coming for you."

The words echoed.

Chapter Three

Myrta de Terr hoisted a second pail of milk onto the table and thwacked Lavender's rump, sending the nanny goat out of the shed. Nothing on all of Turaset could possibly be any more revolting than squeezing a dirty goat udder, one gripping fist at a time.

Milk on her hands, her clogs, splatters of it on her clothing. There were even drops in her hair. She drowned in a vile, endless sea of the stuff. It was like a second skin. If she had to empty one more nanny, she'd probably up and turn into a kid herself.

She arched her back. At least it was done for the morning.

Outside the shed Terrence and Nate, Myrta's papa and oldest brother, crouched in one of the nearer fields. Papa Terrence stabbed his field-blade into the ground and jerked it through the dirt.

With conjunction over—Bel'letra having joined and split again—the men were ripping through the topsoil. That leathery crust from fierno's breath was why her brother Nate said she wasn't suited to fieldwork, but a sea of dirt would be just as bad as the milk anyway. Myrta pushed the milking stool to the wall and set the stack of empty pails on the table next to the full ones.

Her mama, Celeste, came into the shed smelling of griddle cakes. She'd been boiling maple water. She handed a piece of candy over. "Is this all the milk?"

Myrta nodded and sighed, half-expecting the sound to come out as a bleat.

"Mm. I'd hoped for three pails anyway. We need more cheese for market." Celeste pulled a broom from the corner and began sweeping.

Working with Celeste—Myrta was supposed to address her parents by name now that she was of age to marry—was one of the nicer parts of the day. They could talk or not as suited their moods, which usually lined up like shadows. They finished cleaning and started toward the cheese house.

"You're very quiet this morning, Myrta."

She'd been thinking of the cheesemaking, or rather selling. "I hope there are more market days this year."

"We expect fewer."

Myrta pulled up short. Milk sloshed onto her clogs. "Fewer?"

More grimly, Celeste said, "Well. There's no point if there's nothing to sell."

Yes there was—escaping the farm. Taking a break from chores. "Mama. The *horses* leave more often than me."

The dourness in Celeste's eyes faded, and her tone softened. "Oh sweetheart, I know. If the droughts end, we'll have more reason to go."

Myrta felt, quite suddenly, as though an endless line of udders pressed toward her, forcing her thoughts into the march of weeks and months ahead.

"Managing the stead comes first."

Myrta blinked at the moisture in her eyes. Somehow or other, she would leave this farm one day. At times like this, it couldn't come soon enough.

Celeste began to walk, and Myrta followed, trying to imagine a summer with even fewer market days than last year.

"Why don't you join Terrence and the boys when they visit Reuben?"

"It's not the same."

"You'd be away from your chores. You might have fun."

Reuben was a logger. There'd be one family. One. Nothing to buy, nothing to sell, no music, no dancing.

"I'll ask Terrence to take you along. He hopes to find you a suitable match, and that's easier to sort if you spend a little time on other steads. He asked again about the cotton grower's son."

Myrta gripped the pail handle harder. She'd met *that* man twice, both times at market. He seemed much like Papa, tall and imposing, and he'd gotten her name wrong both times. "I don't know, Mama."

Celeste smiled. "Exactly my point."

They entered the cheese house. Along one wall was a stove and a workbench with mounted drawers. The facing wall held an icebox with rennet and cultures, and fresh rounds hung in a room off the back. Myrta put her pail on the workbench and pulled out a cheese press. "The press is warping."

Celeste brought finished curd from the back. "Work around it." She went back to the adjoining room.

Myrta tied her hair into a rough knot and got to work. She'd always thought finding her own path made more sense than matching, on the other hand her brother Nate had a match and would marry soon enough. He seemed content about it.

But even if she stayed in the belt, claiming her own piece of land seemed better. Running a stead as she saw fit, coming and going as she chose. Yet again, things were easier with a second pair of hands, which marriage provided.

She put the curd in the press. Maybe matching with

the cotton grower's son would be all right. She'd be somewhere new, and he might like for her to carve out her own place on his stead.

Tightening one side of the press, she pictured him as she'd seen him last—carrying a book. She tried to remember what his voice sounded like and wondered how it might be to sit with him in the evenings and read. Possibly they enjoyed the same stories. She tightened the other side of the press, and whey trickled out between the boards, cool and pale on her hands. Cotton growers always dressed well. That seemed to be part of their business.

As she tightened down, a pungent aroma—the sourness of curdling; the smell she loved because it was the very end of milk—drifted up. Myrta leaned forward and breathed deeply.

Tightness shot through her temples. She dropped the press with a clatter.

Not again.

She put her hands to her face. Warmth circled her eyes and crawled behind them, back to her ears. The room began to spin; the stool tried to throw her off. Steadying against the bench, Myrta pushed on her temples and hummed a little tune.

Her mama dashed in. "How bad? Does it hurt?"

She gave a shake. There was never pain, just vertigo and this sensation, like hot, angry worms coiling under her skin. Her concentration narrowed.

"Here."

Her mama's shaking hands held chips of ice. Myrta pushed the ice against her forehead. The air around the curd—that swirled too. Ripple, ripple. She closed her eyes, breathed in, counted to three, then out.

"Not just the breathing. Relax. Imagine you're falling asleep."

Myrta kept her tone level. "It's a little hard with the ice."

Celeste said more strongly, "Focus, Myrta."

She did as she was told. She imagined emptiness. An endless expanse of cold sky. No worms, no dizziness, just calm.

After a few minutes the vertigo passed, and the rippling warmth too. She dropped the last bits of ice into the tray with a sigh.

Celeste still gripped the edge of the workbench. "The exercises are important. Have you done them?"

"Of course. Yes." Myrta took a fresh cloth from a drawer and dried her face.

"You need to do them. Every night. Every single night." Celeste wiped the spilled whey, her hands still shaking. "At least you didn't faint."

That evening Myrta took a basket of eggs to the farmhouse and kicked her clogs off at the door. She stepped into the washroom to clean up, and as she did the side door squeaked open and back. "Teams'll need extra grain."

That was Nate's voice.

"You got it."

And that was her other brother, Jack. As children, she and Jack would escape chores together and run off, pretend to be anything but farmers.

She dried her hands. Evening contentment spread through the farmhouse with the smells of baking bread and vegetable stew. Myrta took the eggs to the kitchen, where Celeste was ladling up. Papa Terrence had a forkful from the pot. Celeste leaned onto him.

Sometimes it puzzled Myrta, their affection,

because she could easily count the number of long conversations the two had ever held. Celeste called Terrence's silent acceptance a blessing. She'd grown up in the foothill town of Collimais and spent time at the central university in Narona City, a place so busy she said a person couldn't think straight.[2] Terrence had farmed from childhood out here in the belt. Their backgrounds were nothing alike, and yet somehow, they wound together like two plies of yarn.

Celeste's eyes fell on her. "Oh good, you're in. Put these on the table."

Terrence went to the table's head. "Lookin' well, Myrta. Keepin' up with chores?"

"Yes." She sat. He'd ask about the goats next.

"How're the goats? Are the kids thriving?"

"Yes." Every evening when he probed like this, she felt like a lump of butter forced into his idea for her future. Married off to the cotton grower's son—What was his name? Everett? No, Emmett.

Emmett, the cotton grower's son, she reminded herself.

Everyone had a role in the belt. Most everyone was matched. She could demand a different life—it happened sometimes.

"And the nannies? Milk comin' strong?"

"Yes." Talking chores, every day, with a man who looked like a farm, with eyebrows sprouting out of the furrowed acreage of his forehead, arms and legs like fenceposts, it felt like signing a lifetime agreement.

There was no good reason *not* to claim her own piece of land.

Nathan strode in with Jack right behind. Nate's

---

2   Celeste's university years are described in the novella *Sisters*, at pltavormina.com.

horse mane of hair was tied back in a thong, and he had a strong nose like Terrence. Jack was taller with high cheekbones, like Celeste. He kept his hair short, kept a folding razor handy, sometimes shaving himself bald. Anything to keep the dirt down, he said.

He leaned over and whispered, "Stay strong. He gave it to me outside."

She resigned herself. "The nannies are fine. The younger mothers are giving more milk, but the older ones are gentler. We pressed cheese today. A *lot*. Enough to sell at market."

Celeste brought the pitcher over. "She works hard. It's not always easy."

Terrence glanced at Myrta. "Nathan carries his load."

Well, so did she. And Nate had permission to leave. He went places all the time, talking with growers, planning out the crops.

Celeste sat. "Nathan is Nathan. Jack is Jack. And Myrta's Myrta."

Jack's eyes twinkled. "Mama, your insight is inspiring."

Myrta ate without saying a word, neatly and quietly.

After a few minutes Terrence said, "Good stew, Celeste." The gravel in his voice was like a carriage rumbling down a washboard road, like he had somewhere to get to but couldn't be rushed about it. "There's only the five of us fall to spring. We have near a hundred acres. We all pitch in."

"Yes, and the children take more work every year. Five is more than it used to be."

Jack began to comment on the difficulty of five equaling any number other than five, but Celeste silenced him with a glance, took a warm roll, and handed half to him. Nate devoured his stew.

Nate always ate like that. He was always hungry.

Celeste set her fork down. "Terrence. About your plans to see Reuben's irrigation system—"

"Amount he paid for that thing. If it's worth half what he laid out, it's worth a look, but it'll be a fool's purchase when the drought ends."

Nate mopped up stew juices with a roll. "Could be useful after. We could grow corn. It's a short season. We could double plant."

Papa grunted. "Half-baked idea, pullin' water against gravity."

Celeste straightened her knife and fork, making parallel lines out of them, which meant she was building up to something. Myrta sat straight and popped a blueberry into her mouth. She glanced back and forth between her mama and papa.

"Why don't you take Myrta along?"

Myrta held the blueberry on her tongue and sat perfectly still.

Terrence stopped eating and looked at Celeste. "D'you think that's a good idea?"

"I do."

He seemed to turn it over. "No. She has chores here. Makin' the cheese."

Celeste set her spoon next to the fork, next to the knife. All three pointed straight across the table. "Terrence. Neither she nor I have been off the farm in half a year."

Myrta looked down into her lap. It was a common holding, here in the belt, that daughters were strong in ways that sons were not. Farm wives, they were the strongest of all.

During the silence, Terrence worked through the

rest of his stew. Then he lifted his eyes to her. "Myrta has naught to do with irrigation, and we're countin' on that cheese. Reuben's stead is a half morning away. I'm sorry Myrta. Answer has to be no."

She exhaled. In truth, she did understand. His worth was all tied up in how the farm got on, and the droughts had taken such a terrible toll, the yields half what they'd been. The goats were more important than ever. Still, for him to decide so quickly hurt.

She'd stay. They'd leave, see other people, and she'd stay. Jack was trying to catch her eye, but she ignored him.

Celeste stood and began clearing dishes. "Myrta needs to learn more about other steads. She needs more time with children, too, before bearing her own."

Frowning, Myrta wondered why Celeste had gone there.

"Irrigation's got nothin' to do with that."

Myrta kept her mouth shut. Her mama was still trying. She rose to help with the dishes, rolling the blueberry against the roof of her mouth.

Celeste took a cobbler to the table and said with a smile so slight that Myrta thought she might be imagining it, "Reuben has babies. Take Myrta. She'll keep them out of your way."

Myrta picked up a dirty bowl and scraped the last bits of food out. No one was talking anymore, but she didn't dare look. She wasn't nervous, she truly wasn't, but the idea of nervous was ready to pounce if she let it. She bit into the blueberry, her teeth slicing into its meaty middle. She washed the bowl, set it in the drying rack, and reached for another. Why wasn't anybody saying anything?

After another long moment, her papa finally spoke. "Myrta. This is a working trip."

A flutter rippled through her. "I know, Papa. I mean, I know, Terrence."

His face was like a crust of soil, and his eyes were green, same as her own, but on him they looked like bean sprouts. They looked like springtime. "How'll the goats get by, daughter? Milk dries up quick."

Her heart beat faster. It wouldn't be market, not nearly, but it would be somewhere else. Her words spilled out. "I'll leave the kids with the nannies. We'll lose one day, that's all."

After another long pause, he smiled and nodded.

Jack grinned, pushed back from the table and joined her at the sink. He gave her a squeeze around the shoulders and murmured, "Away from farming."

She smiled, straight out the window. "Off the stead."

Chapter Four

Alphonse stood next to his grandfather on a windy cliff overlooking a surging and violent landscape.

"Our history, Alphonse. Back to the very beginning, recorded in rock and code."

"I won't remember this, Grandfather."

"Don't worry. The day will come when you hold all of history in a thought. Mark my words."

The molten sea below him churned. Alphonse grew warm. Then hot—unbearably so.

"We stretch back to the beginning of time, atoms cycling into structure. Then formlessness, then structure again. Complexity and dissolution, Alphonse, pulsing and breathing like the landscape below."

Fireballs crashed from above. Radiation seared the planet's surface.

Alphonse gasped and fell to his knees. His shins burned and dissolved. His legs, his torso, his entire self. He melted into the Hadean Sea.

"The story is a gift from the founders."

"I don't want it," Alphonse tried to scream, but not a sound escaped as he melted into nothingness.

He woke in stages. The air here was good, so unlike his neighborhood in Sangal with its ever-present smell of fishing canneries.

The worst city funk was in the northwest octant, where his friend Eduardo lived. Eduardo managed an extraction rig for Delsico, part of the combustion industry, and said often enough that his rig workers tolerated the stench because of the pay.

But here, the suns were rising and the air was crisp, laced with cedar and pine. Invigorated, Alphonse struck camp.

He started along a ridgeline footpath, rutted and crowded with overgrowth. Barely a path at all. His pack caught on bramblethorn, and he grew irritated as the morning passed.

At mid-day, still on the ridge, he stopped to eat. Water turned the powdered rations into a pasty meal, a stiff batter with grains and nuts. Edible. Definitely welcome.

But the water skin was lighter than it should be, and a thread of unease worked into his thoughts. Resolving to make better time, he got underway.

The path grew more crowded as the afternoon passed.

Evening rations took most of the remaining water, which really should have lasted longer. He patted around his pack, and after a moment, found a wet patch. "Fierno," he swore, then ran his fingers on the water skin's seam and up to the neck. There it was, the dent that kept the lid from sitting tight. Groaning, he slapped the skin onto the pack.

The next morning, Alphonse woke to a throbbing headache. He took the last swallow of water and started onward, hacking his machete through the scrub.

The suns blazed, but he didn't sweat. He pushed through more brush when, without warning, the ground lurched, or maybe he did. He was down, his forearm and left cheek stinging from a patch of spinebark. He stood, but everything twisted again.

Alphonse came to awareness in the dark with a tongue like cotton and his head splintering. Every part of him throbbed.

He bushwhacked off trail, straight down toward the river. Twice he fell. Dirt and burrs worked into his boots and trousers, and he was in another patch of spinebark and numbing from the needles, but he pushed up and stumbled on. Every whack of the machete matched by a dull thud at the base of his skull.

At last, as the stars faded into dawn, he saw it—the massive Turas. It barreled down the canyon, white and frothy, churning and rushing. With a croaking cry he slipped and scrambled the last two hundred feet, dropped his pack, fell to the bank, and scooped up a handful of frigid water. Ice shot into his blisters and down his throat. He took more, and more, two hands splashing onto his face, hair, neck. His fingers numbed from the cold, his mouth too, but he scooped as much sweet, beautiful water as he could manage, and at last, sobbing, he pushed out of the spray and collapsed against a boulder. He'd made it.

Alphonse faded in and out of consciousness as the river crashed by, until near mid-day, the pulsing stab of his headache began to ease.

The sky was brilliant. Around him lay blanketed slopes of unspoiled, wild, stunning beauty.

Alphonse worked his way southward along the

river, forcing his way through tangles of saplings and undergrowth. Eventually the river widened and slowed, and as the heat was peaking for the day, he came to a spillway bordered by a steep cut.

"A bath." Mirth bubbled up as he said it.

Bathing. Being clean. Alphonse laughed outright and dropped his pack.

He stripped naked, plunging his clothing in piece by piece to work out the dirt and muck. His spirits rose, and before long, he launched into an old sailor song. He threw himself into it, his voice filling the air with tales of sea-maidens and nanquits.

Alphonse washed himself next, gasping at the ice-cold water. He splashed his torso, waded deeper and howled, and finally dunked his whole body to scrub every sore and scabbed piece of himself.

Shivering, he clambered back out and sluiced off.

That evening, warm and dressed again, he settled in. Outside the tent, breezes murmured through the trees like voices, promises. He drifted, at peace.

Hours later, pelting thuds and a dull, ominous roar woke him. "No. No, no, no!" Alphonse shoved his boots on and bundled the blanket. The roar grew louder. He crawled out of the tent where his pack sat, soaked.

Sheets of rain chilled him with spikes of fury. He grabbed and collapsed the tent and stuffed it into the pack and scrabbled toward the bank cut. The roar grew louder. He climbed up the cut and threw his arm around a willow.

The floodwaters crashed and knocked him back into the surging crest. He went under, took a lungful of water, and fought his way up. By some grace his hand connected with a root, and he held.

Stay firm. It felt like a memory of his grandfather.

"I *am*!" Throwing his other hand forward he missed the root, threw again and got it.

Rain yowled and the water surged in angry peaks. The clouds were gray, heavy, sodden wool, barely lightening in the dawn. His muscles straining, both arms burning, he fought to get his footing underneath him, where the mud kept washing away. Another crest raced at him, hurled debris against him, and a rage welled up in him.

There it was, the next trough, and yelling, he was in it, pulling and grabbing hand over hand up the root. Another crest was hurtling toward him.

Alphonse slammed the toe of his boot into the bank. He slammed the other toe in, higher, and threw his right hand around the willow trunk again. When the water crashed against him, buoyancy aided him up, and he threw his left arm around the trunk, his wrist scraping. "Ow!"

The surge passed, and he was in another trough but higher than before. With another mighty roar he pulled up and lunged his torso onto the top of the bank. If he could get one leg up, he'd be out.

He threw his knee over.

Alphonse scrabbled up and away. He fell to his side coughing, slipped out of the pack and spluttered for air. Above him, the sky was turning to glaucous ash, and a seed of euphoria sprouted within. He was safe. He pushed to stand and whooped. Logs whipped by in the current below, and Alphonse yelled, "Take that," at the river. Then to the sky, "Yes, *I* win!" He threw his arms out, the rain softening in the morning light, a thousand cool slaps of acceptance. Every piece of himself cried out, straight to the mountains. He fell to the ground laughing and crying as the current hurtled by.

Chapter Five

Their carriage rattled along toward Reuben de Reu's logging stead. In the back, Myrta grinned so hard she thought her face might crack in two, and Jack kept chuckling at her good spirits. In the front, Terrence and Nate argued about how much rye to distill into whiskey.

They arrived mid-morning. Reuben's house was larger than theirs and had a stone foundation. Two automobiles sat next to it, like metal boxes on wheels. Her papa looked at the auts as he reined the horses in. "Those Renico folk sure do love their mechanation. Needin' two auts to get here." He shook his head and helped Myrta down. "Unhitch the horses, put 'em to pasture, daughter. And keep them babies away." Then he left with her brothers.

Myrta walked up to the auts. These city people, they'd be somewhere else tonight. They weren't left on a farm for months on end. She rested a hand on the closer one. It had a front seat, no rear seat at all, and a funny smell came off it, a smell she couldn't place, but it wasn't a farm smell.

There were rolled up papers inside, they looked like charts, and a tool case of some sort. The whole thing seemed cramped and uncomfortable, nothing like the carriage, but still, these people could speed back and forth from one place to another whenever they liked.

The nearer horse, Rennet, pawed at the ground. He

was chewing on his bit, working his jaw around it. She went over to pat his neck and the soft skin under his throat. "Those auts sure aren't very personal, are they?"

He tossed his head.

Rusty, the other horse, stood solid. He never complained, never fidgeted like Rennet did. She went to him and scratched behind his ears. He was sweatier than Rennet too, probably pulled more of the weight this morning. "You're happy in the belt. It suits you."

Maybe it was wrong to want to be somewhere new. Everyone she knew, just about everyone, lived in the belt. They enjoyed it, steading. Her mama always said the cities moved too fast. Even her uncle in the foothills, who'd grown up in a city, said life was better when things went slower.

Still, steads, they were all the same. A piece of despair shuffled around in her heart.

She pulled the horses to the pasture, took the cheese basket from the carriage, and walked up to the home. Georgie de Reu, a few years older than Myrta and with a mop-top of hair, opened the door. A small boy hid behind Georgie's legs, and a pudgy-cheeked baby girl, a year or so old, sat on her hip.

"Myrta! So nice you could come today. Come in. Come, come in. No, no, don't worry about your shoes, dear. Leave them on. We have so much traffic in and out today I'll need to wash the floors either way. Come in."

With her free hand, Georgie took the basket and led the way to the kitchen, where windows looked onto a small field and vegetable patch. Georgie set the basket down. "Oh, these cheeses look delicious. We'll put them out later. Would you like a cup of camsin? I can pour two as easily as one. We don't have honey. Have a seat dear, just clear a spot."

"Yes, please."

Georgie set her daughter down, and the baby girl began pulling drawers open. The little boy had found a crust of bread somewhere and peered at Myrta from behind his mother.

Georgie wiped a bit of jam from his face. "They're dears but a handful. Reuben wants a third. Of course, that would be lovely, especially another little girl, but he'd like a second son of course, and—oh!"

The kettle had simmered over, water hissing on the stove. Georgie took it and began steeping the camsin leaves. "Can I get you something to eat? Eggs? There's bread on the table. Little Rudy likes bread. Rudy, be a good boy and sit at the table when you eat."

He ran out of the kitchen.

Georgie sat and handed over a steaming cup. "How are you, dear?"

It was just all so very *much*. Myrta took a sip to focus her thoughts away from the chaos in the kitchen, everything about it so completely unlike the disciplined de Terr kitchen. "Fine . . . thank you."

"How long has it been? Was it when baby Rosa was weaning? That must be right. I remember we couldn't carry on a conversation because she fussed the whole time, she wanted to nurse, and of course I hated saying no, and my breasts felt like they would burst from the milk, but Reuben wants another baby so it had to dry up. Oh. I forgot the milk."

"Last summer. At market."

"That's right. Market. What good cheese you had. Are these the same? I'm so glad you're selling. You're selling this year, yes? The same ones? They look delicious. We'll have some when everyone comes down for lunch."

The baby girl wandered off to the front room where her brother was playing.

Georgie continued, "You're in charge of the animals, aren't you? That must be so lovely, working with the animals. It would be so nice, being with the baby goats all day, and of course goat milk is delicious. I hope you don't get too attached. Is that hard? When it's time to slaughter one of the animals? But what am I saying? Forget I asked. I'm just glad trees don't scream."

Myrta was unsure how to respond, or which question might be most important, or if any of them mattered at all. Georgie seemed happy to simply have another person around and would probably carry on talking no matter what Myrta said. "I tend the animals and help Celeste inside."

The baby girl cried from the front room, and Georgie's attention went to the door. "Oh, that boy. He loves to knock over her blocks. Please excuse me." She hurried out.

Myrta took another look around the room. Her chair was sticky, and some of whatever it was had gotten onto her skirt. Stacks of dishes lined the counter. Somewhere nearby, dirty cloth diapers needed attention, and the baby's inconsolable cries blasted into the kitchen. The boy ran in and through, to a back room. He slammed the door.

"Where were we?" Georgie said, returning with Rosa on her hip. The baby girl's eyes were puffy, and she held a block next to her chest.

Goodness. The thought of being matched and having babies? No. "We were talking about cheese."

Behind the closed door, the little boy was pounding

something hard against the floor, over and over again. Myrta didn't know if she should go comfort him, grab a tissue for the baby, clean the kitchen, straighten the front room, or drink the camsin. "Can I help with anything?"

"Oh, no. No. Don't worry about the mess. The children are just so happy to have company today. Would you like to hold Rosa while I clean up?" And a squirmy moist package of babyhood was plopped into Myrta's lap.

She hadn't held a baby before. The little girl seemed to have more limbs than was right, and her diaper possibly needed changing. Yes, it did. Mucus oozed from Rosa's nose, drying into a crust on her lip. She threw her block to the floor and began wailing.

Myrta leaned over to grab it. "That's okay, we'll just pick it up." The baby howled.

Georgie called from the sink, "You're doing great," but did not even look over. "So nice to have help with Rosa. Isn't she dear?"

The babies at market were never this loud. Myrta found herself handling the girl as she might one of the animals, making shushing noises and stroking her head.

Georgie came back to sit, dishes in the sink and counters wiped. "What she'd really like is to be outside. Why don't we take her outside? Little Rudy needs to sulk, and a quiet house will be just the thing."

But the men were outside, and Myrta's job was to keep the children away. "Maybe the woods?"

"Oh, the woods are a bad idea. Baby Rosa will run off and be out of sight before you know it. They're always running into the woods and coming back with scrapes and bugs. I don't want little Rudy to feel left behind either, when he decides to come out. Let's see what the men are up to, and Rudy can find us if he wants."

Surely the two of them could watch one little girl, even in the woods. "I could hold Rosa. In the woods. And then we won't bother anybody."

"What, a little visit from us? Reuben won't mind."

"I think Terrence and Nathan want to focus on the irrigation." She was supposed to keep the babies away.

"Oh, we won't talk to them. Not a peep. We'll just watch."

Myrta said with more force, "We could play with Rosa in the front room—"

"I mean, so many visitors today! The big business people with their fancy auts, and your family as well. It's very exciting, and it's good for Rosa and Rudy."

Georgie had decided, and it wasn't as though Myrta could lock her up and keep her away from her own husband.

They walked up to the fields, the ground sighing underfoot with each step, releasing the scent of good soil. Reuben's land adjoined another steader's, and a small irrigation system stood on the fence line between their properties.

Terrence's gaze fell on them. He glared at Myrta, and she tipped her head at Georgie and gave a little shrug.

He and Jack stood next to a large tank with Reuben de Reu—a thin man with straw-straight hair sticking out from under a hat. Gesturing at a metallic box next to the tank, Reuben spoke with a serious-looking older woman.

A second businessperson, a man, leaned hip-level against the box. He had thick dark hair shot through with gray. One of his ears tilted oddly and had a narrow map of scars around it. He flicked something to the ground, twisted it with his foot, and flashed a grin straight at Myrta. His eyes were deep brown, his teeth straight and even, and two dimples came out when he smiled. With a flush of warmth, she looked down.

Reuben said to the woman, "It's not the flow. Pump shuts down 'fore the field's half done. Happened again yesterday."

"Mr. de Reu, please understand. If the pressure's too high, the system turns off. When you increase demand, everything heats up."

"Now hold on, Carmella. You said it'd handle high demand. We got two steads here."

"The system's adjustable. You have options. You can ration—"

"The point's pullin' water when we want it." Little bits of spit flew from Reuben's mouth as he spoke. Myrta had seen him angry plenty of times—he always let his feelings straight out. He never held them inside as Terrence did.

Carmella continued, ". . . or you can install the larger pump—"

Reuben seemed even more frustrated by that. He spluttered, "We ain't puttin' more money in. You guaranteed a working system."

"Or," the woman said patiently, "You can learn the settings."

Her papa spoke up. "Reuben, that's good sense. You don't buy a tool y'can't work. Nathan'd know how to use it if we put one in."

Nate looked up from the knobs on the box. "It's sensible. Pressure dial says when you're pullin' too hard. There's gauges to keep track. This is worth somethin'."

"Nathan, quiet now." Terrence turned to the

businessman, the one with the misshapen ear. "People'd be more inclined if you dropped your price."

"We'll work something out. We want your stead to be as productive as possible. Believe me, it's good for you and it's good for us too." The man interlocked his fingers and held his hands forward like that. "We depend on one another. We rely on the food you grow, and you can rely on our technology."

The man's voice had a strange quality, like it hit multiple notes at the same time. Myrta risked another glance. He was giving her papa his complete attention.

The businesswoman, Carmella, said to Reuben, "Why don't we run the system and explain the settings as it warms up." She adjusted a few dials, explaining the reason for each and every one. Reuben seemed annoyed by that too, but he paid attention. When everything was ready, the woman pulled a cord on the box, and a sound like a swarm of locusts blared forth.

The baby squawked and wailed. Georgie held her close, shouting pet names at her. Terrence glared at Myrta again and stabbed a finger toward the house.

"Should we go back?" Myrta hollered into Georgie's ear.

"Oh no," Georgie shouted. "Baby Rosa doesn't like it, but Reuben wants them to get used to the noise."

"I think we should go back," Myrta yelled. "I don't think they want us here." As she said that, little Rudy ran up from the house. Terrence hollered again in Myrta's direction, but she couldn't make out the words over the noise.

"Rudy," Georgie cried in delight. "Such a big boy. Mama's so proud." She turned back to Myrta and shouted, "I don't think we should go back."

Jack walked over mouthing something, but the racket muffled his words too. The man with the funny ear flashed another of his warm-eyed grins, and the little boy pelted toward him.

Feeling she'd failed her only task, Myrta ran after the boy through a plume of acrid smoke.

With ferocity more intense than anything she'd ever experienced, a wrenching sensation surged through her temples, and she sank to her knees, then crumpled completely, palms to her face. Warmth blossomed around her eyes, a tugging pressure, angry worms coiling. She curled up, begging the world to stop spinning.

"What's wrong?" Georgie cried.

Jack reached her. "Myrie, what is it?"

"Make it stop. My eyes!"

They were pulling in their sockets, inward and outward at the same time, and something deep within her roared awake, feeling as natural and innate as her own monthly cycles.

She opened her eyes, but everything tilted crazily. The man with the ear was staring at her with a fierce intensity. The air around the fuel pump shimmered like plumes of a fine blue silk, streaming outward. If she didn't feel so horrible she might wonder about it, but instead she rolled over, moaning, and closed her eyes again.

"We'll take you back," Jack shouted. "We'll find somewhere for you to lie down." He put an arm under her shoulders and helped her up. With Jack on one side and Georgie on the other, they made their way down to the house.

Jack settled her in a bedroom and pulled the drapes. "Just lie still. Does it hurt?"

She shook her head.

He took her shoes and pulled up a blanket. "What do you need?"

"Ice. Get ice." She pushed on her temples and took measured breaths. "I might throw up."

Jack left and came back with ice and a bowl. "What's going on?"

She mumbled, "I get dizzy." The room spun again. She grabbed the bowl and threw up, and Jack fetched a towel and a glass of water.

"Go back up, Jack." Groaning at how badly things had turned, Myrta sank into the pillows. "I'm in trouble. If you're here, it's worse."

He did, and after a long while, she slept. When she woke, the room was steady again. Dishes clattered on the other side of the home, and she went to the kitchen.

Georgie looked up. "Oh you sweet thing, how are you? Better, I hope? The children have so much energy, they make me dizzy too. They're napping now. It's so peaceful when they nap. Would you like a carrot?"

Myrta sat. "No, thank you. I feel awful. I came to help, and I made problems for everyone."

"Oh, heavens no. Oh stop. Carmella and the boys figured the whole thing out. It's always like that with something new, isn't it? All's well that ends well. They're still up there, buzzing like bees around all the tubes and dials. Your brother Nathan keeps talking about how much it could help your crops, but Terrence keeps saying the droughts will end sooner or later."

"Was he angry?"

"Who, Terrence? Why, of course not, why would he be angry? Oh, I suppose he is quite stern and that must be something to live with, but he wasn't angry. No, not at all." Georgie cocked her head for a moment, seeming to think. "He did seem annoyed, now you mention it. With Melville."

"Who?"

"Melville. Oh, right, you weren't introduced. I forgot in all the excitement. Melville and Carmella are the business folk from Renico, you know, that big company that makes all the devices. Carmella told us they have a log miller! Can you imagine? Think how quickly Reuben could slice boards if it was mechanated. Anyway, where was I? Oh. Melville. He's the one with the dimples. Terrence called him Mr. di Vaun, but Reuben just calls him Melville. Is that rude? You must've noticed, the one with the horrible scar around his ear. Poor man, I wonder how that happened. I wanted to ask, but that would be rude too, wouldn't it?"

Myrta sorted through the words. "Why was Papa annoyed with Mr. di Vaun?"

"That's a good question. Well, let's see. Melville was so quiet all morning. Just standing there and smiling. Oh! I remember, it was after your dizzy spell. That's why I forgot, because we weren't there. Jack and I helped you down to the house, and Rudy wanted to see the irrigation machine again, and I walked the children back up, and of course they loved being with the big business people and the mechanation. And Melville was very talkative, asking all sorts of questions. Where did Terrence farm? Had he ever lived anywhere else? But Terrence, he just wanted to understand the irrigation. He finally snapped, telling Melville to mind his own business, only using stronger language if you take my meaning."

With a flash of guilt, Myrta thought Terrence might have been annoyed because the children had returned.

The front door opened, and voices spilled into the kitchen. "Sure pulled water quick," Terrence chuckled.

"Told you. This'll change things." Reuben clapped Terrence on the back. "So long's it works."

The serious woman, Carmella, stayed close to Terrence. "We have a larger system, Mr. de Terr. It's better for farm steads."

He guffawed. "Course you'd say so. Better profit for you."

The kitchen crowded as everyone filed in. Easing out of her chair, Myrta went to help with the meal. Georgie handed her a loaf of bread and she started slicing. Soon, she felt eyes on her. She glanced up. Melville di Vaun was watching her, and he crossed over.

"You had a bit of a rough spot up there." His eyes were kindly. Brown and warm.

"I'm sorry, sir. I'm fine."

"You collapsed in the exhaust. Were you dizzy?" His voice seemed to hum its way under her scalp.

She stepped toward Georgie, flushing. His gaze was so very intent, as though she was the only person in the room. "It's fine."

The men at the table were joking about yields, and the baby began to cry from the back of the house. Then the little boy too. Georgie hurried out of the kitchen.

"You should have that looked at." He walked around her, coming close enough that his breath fell on her.

Smoker. She leaned away from the smell. "It's nothing. I'm better." She pushed past him, heart pounding, and went to the other counter, the one nearer the table, and set to work slicing the cheese. It felt as though the man's gaze had riveted to her right temple. She bit her lower lip and shook her head. Why was he watching her? She pushed the knife through the cheese again and imagined it severing the space between them.

Georgie returned with the children and sent them to play in the front room. She went back to the salad.

The man said, his voice calm, so at odds with Myrta's pounding heart, "I've had my fair share of medical training. Your dizzy spell looks like something we call precipitous vertigo."

She wasn't supposed to talk about it. If he had any sense at all he'd see how nervous she was.

He tilted his head, and his eyes moved between her temples and eye sockets and back again. "And I'll wager you had no headache at all."

At that, she snapped her attention completely to the man. Celeste always insisted the spells must be giving her a headache, no matter how many times she explained otherwise. This businessman understood. He hadn't even asked first.

He smiled. His cheeks dimpled. "I could check your eyes. Do a few exams. You don't want precipitous vertigo to progress. We'll take you with us when we leave."

What? She must have misheard, but his eyes were still warm. He stepped over to her again, and she pulled back, the knife shaking in her hand.

"Renico's doctors are the best on the continent."

Jack looked over from the table, and Myrta shot him a terrified glance. He nudged Terrence, and the two stood.

Melville took Myrta's wrist. His palm was moist. She jerked her arm away. He said in a low voice, "There are surgeries that can help."

She didn't mishear *that*, and even Georgie cocked her head and stared.

Melville said, so quietly it sounded nightmarishly like it came from inside her own head, "There's room for you in Carmella's aut."

Terrified, she pinched her eyes shut, her heart thumping harder. "Stop it," she managed.

Terrence bellowed, "Let her be. Jack, take Myrta, gather the team and hitch up."

The mood in the kitchen soured, good cheer gone like pollen on the breeze. Melville looked over to Terrence. "I meant no offense, Mr. de Terr, my words came differently than I intended. Your daughter's health is as important to us as your stead's. I'm sorry for hitting a bad note there. I crossed a line, but I truly didn't mean to."

"Out here, di Vaun, we don't pester others as you seem overly inclined to do."

"You're right. Please forgive me. Sit. Enjoy the meal, and let's put this misunderstanding behind us. Carmella and I would like to arrange a visit to your stead to price out the equipment."

Her papa's eyes blazed. "If you're expectin' to do business on my stead, di Vaun, you'd ought learn some propriety. Nathan, come now. We're leavin'."

Chapter Six

"You survived the flood."

Deep satisfaction filled Alphonse. "I did. Where are we, Grandfather?"

"We witness the dawn of life."

They stood on the seafloor. Superheated liquid spewed from a giant black chimney, and as the liquid cooled, crystals formed into lattices, growing the sea vent taller.

"It begins with the chemistry of the vent. Be the chemistry, Grandson. Be the chimney."

Alphonse shrank to become a crystalline cavity inside the seafloor vent. Within him, chemicals dissolved, rushed outward, and collided with others. The kinetic energy of that mad diffusion spurred new reactions.

Carbon atoms bonded and formed chains. Some sealed into a membrane bubble. More chains, more rings, more branched compounds—molecules folded and configured in countless ways.

"I don't understand," Alphonse cried.

"Simply experience the chaos."

Eons passed, and the complexity around him grew. Molecules began to interact. After another timeless stretch, one even copied itself.

Now there were two inside a bubble, and in a burst, the cell split.

"Reproduction. Life! Alphonse, it is the emergence of order."

After the flood, Alphonse kept small goals. He cleaned his things and hung them to dry, straightened the dent in the water skin and re-packed his gear. His mother's words flitted about in his thoughts. *". . . trust me. You'll be back."*

No. He'd survived dehydration. Flood. She was wrong.

That evening, Alphonse turned in early. His awareness blurred toward unguarded fog, and years fell away. He was fifteen.

It's simple, Alphonse. We run Luca di Vern, Delsico's safety officer, for the seat. He'll back the reforms Father wanted.

As she spoke, she wrote strings of numbers on a pad. Calculations, finances, dealings.

Mother. Luca doesn't do the job he already has. Eduardo says things could be safer at the plant, but Luca ignores the rules he was hired to enforce. Half the workers can't get medicine—

Eduardo's a salesman. He knows nothing about it.

He's more than a salesman.

She summed up a column and crossed a name off a list. *It's an easy race. The industry will fund it, and Luca will win.*

The next morning, dew coated the grass. First sun broke over the eastern forerange, and he stood and stretched. Primal satisfaction rippled through him.

He continued south along the riverbank and found the trail and the footbridge that crossed the Turas. He was back on course toward the Prophets.

As the days passed, he worked up slopes and along ridges, deeper into the ranges. The solitude of spring-time mountainsides filled him with awakening, like the hills themselves. Some afternoons he'd do no more than sit by a stream with his fishing line, cleaning his gear amidst fields of wildflowers. Some nights, no more than lay under the stars near the warmth of a small fire and listen to the wilderness.

Cricket. Owl.

As he lay to rest each night, he felt the energy of his life pulse into the planet. The heat of his body sank into the vastness of Turaset. His breath was the air, every inhalation the breeze overhead, every exhalation a caress on the ground.

I am the mountain.

He often slept outside the tent, where against the darkening sky, silhouettes surrounded him. Above him, multitudes of stars. One night, one blazed across it all, and the towering ranges shrank. The universe held him.

He wandered higher. The cedars were gone, only sand-sap and pine remained, the ground carpeted with their cones and the cones full of sweet nuts. Then, even those trees grew scarce and everything was rocky with scattered lakes rimmed in lichens and thick with quiverfish.

He was closing on Tura's Prophets.

One afternoon Alphonse lay on a warmed slab of granite. Mount Tura filled his view, pushing space to the side. The trail to the spires zig-zagged up, and he contemplated the top of the pinnacles where Arel was said to wander.

What wisdom would I seek? I want the Council as it used to be, dedicated to the common good. I want Mother to want that too.

A chill breeze blew along the peaks, and the hills purpled into evening.

Early the next morning he traversed a rocky saddle and started up Tura's switchbacks. By mid-day his breath came in huffing gasps, and his head was light. He arrived at the base of the spires that evening, sweaty and exhausted.

They rose, all the more beautiful for their solid immediacy under his hands, and warmth from the suns flowed out from them, through his palms, through his cheek.

The Prophets were sheer, straight, proud spectacles into the sky, stabbing straight into the blue. Snow draped the upper pinnacle, the heights he'd stand on tomorrow, and water trickled down the face and across the trail.

Alphonse fell asleep that night facing the Prophets.

Three established routes existed on Tura's greater pinnacle. The easiest hugged a thirty-inch split at the bottom and again at the top, broken by a four-hundred-foot run of bare face. That was his climb; it was

simplest, and he'd only need rope for the middle section, which had permanent eyebolt anchors drilled in.
Alphonse donned his gear.

Lesser peaks surrounded him, covered with pockets
of snow. Glistening pearls. Mountaintops were everywhere; he couldn't turn without seeing dozens, ocean
whitecaps, he was floating on them here under Mount
Tura.

"Hello!" The sound fell into quieting echoes. Grinning, Alphonse looped his rope, clipped it to his harness and started up.

Pinches and handholds were everywhere. The climb
was not technical, not at all. At twenty feet he pivoted
into the fracture and jammed his right toes in front
and left heel behind.

It was the focus he loved. The immediacy. Everything else fell away as he found the next grip, foot
placement, pressure, twist. He thrilled in the balance,
his balance, rotating around his center, he tucked and
pushed up inch by inch, working through the puzzle
of vertical motion.

At fifty feet the crack widened to a three-foot chimney. It was easy to breach the gap, jamming hands and
feet on either side. He looked down, straight down the
narrow chute, struck by the beauty of rock and fissure.
The world cracked open below him.

I am the chimney.

'*Simply experience it.*' Again, the thought felt like
his grandfather speaking to him.

A hundred feet up, the cold drove Alphonse out
of the split. He swiveled, grabbed a frag on the face.
More trickles of water. Straddling the corner, one leg
in the crack and the other out, he gripped, shimmied
to the next hold, and the next.

I am the cliff.

This was the zone.

His thighs burned but his knuckles were stiff with cold, and he stopped to clench his left hand a few times, then his right. Sangal lay on the distant coastline, his home, his past. He recalled days when he was young and some small pain, a child teasing him or a split lip, would bring his mother running, and she'd cry, "Alphie, be strong. You're all I have."

Such truth in her words then, and she'd raised him, true enough. Why were they so different now? He spun the question round and round, like a shell on a musing string. Surely his mother understood her own father's idealism. He remembered her agreeing with Stavo. Had it been sincere?

The crack was pinching off now, and he needed his rope. He hooked the end to an anchor, spooled out a length, and clipped it to his harness.

A tricky spot jutted ahead. Part of the route navigated a small buttress, and he studied it. Then easy, exuberant, he held the rope and leaned back from the near-vertical cliff, planted his feet on its face and cried out in joy. A warm wind swirled up from the trail, caressing him. He yelled again, straight up.

Water streamed freely down the face, and the glare on the spires was bright. Ice. The morning suns lit it afire, but this route ended on the southern face. Yes, that was clear.

Three hundred feet. His right foot found a two-inch ledge, and a toehold for the left was there, a narrow crack that hugged his foot. His grandfather had protected these ranges, this very climb. Stavo would've done more but for a group of councilors who struck back, saying his laws threatened economic advancement throughout the provinces. Those councilors had

P.L. TAVORMINA

58

seen to it that Stavo served time. Alphonse had never gotten a straight answer on why, from anyone.

A powerful popping erupted above. A sheet of ice broke and hurtled down. Alphonse screamed and hugged the cliff as blocks and shards of ice careened past him, glancing off the face, shattering and spraying apart in slow motion.

They hit the ground; the crash resounding through the cliff and into his chest. His focus shot upward. He held still, barely breathing. "Miere," he muttered. At this distance the sheer volume of ice above was impossible to gauge, or whether any loose rock sat up there too. Fingers cramping, he thought again that if he died out here he'd have no one to blame but himself. The thought chilled him.

But I know how to climb. Three feet or three hundred, physics didn't change. This cliff was not technically challenging. *Find the zone.*

The rock, rough and damp, smelled of moss and sulfur. He fused his thoughts into it, imagined he was the cliff, timeless. It felt for a fleeting moment that he was. And with that stretch of unbroken being, his chest relaxed. Then his arms, his legs.

Alphonse took the next toehold and clipped into another anchor, attached another length of rope to the harness and held quiet, finding ledges, pushing on. Soon he'd meet the buttress and could swing around it.

He reached for the next anchor.

The hook slipped, and his heart leapt upward. He overcompensated, grabbing too quickly with his right hand and gripping too hard with the left. "Miere!" The frag came free and his foot slid. Alphonse was in free fall. "Miere! *Autore!*" His harness caught, he swung out, time slowed again, then sped up as he swung toward the cliff. He cushioned the impact with his legs.

The next anchor pulled out of the face with a second sickening lurch. He was in free fall again, yelling. The harness caught him. It yanked up against his buttocks and the rope's contortions threw him away from the face, again.

Alphonse careened back toward the cliff, and with his arms over his head, he twisted sideways and rammed into it. Something cracked. He howled at the impact. Something had sliced into his right thigh, but whether the cracking had to do with another anchor above, the rock, or one of his own bones, he didn't know.

Yelling still, in raw rage, on the next inbound swing he caught himself with his good leg, clamped his hands around frags, and held fast. Breathing hard with tears drying on his cheeks.

Three hundred feet above the trail and seven hundred feet below the summit, Alphonse clung to the rock with a shooting pain in his right thigh and warmth seeping down his leg. Hugging the cliff, he screamed, wordlessly, into the Martire Arels.

Finally, he looked down. The front of his thigh was gashed, four inches, a ragged hot slash. His trousers were drenching red.

Alphonse's focus narrowed in. He needed to descend before another anchor failed or more ice broke off or the red patch soaking his trousers grew too large. He clawed over to his mounted line on the cliff face. The new goal . . . back where he started. Down. His thigh throbbed, moist and hot.

Swearing in agony, Alphonse lowered himself one-footed, his right leg awkwardly held out. At the chimney, he unclipped, left the rope, and jammed back down. At fifty feet the chimney narrowed, and he came out of the chute twenty feet off the ground.

He eased down and hobbled from the spires, choking on his breath. He grabbed the pack, pulled it over, and worked the tent out. Pitched it and crawled in. Found bandages, a tube of ointment. Blood everywhere. He pulled his blanket around himself, sweat chilling on his face.

The immensity of what he'd left in Sangal. Everything back home, the machine grinding onward, the industry, his mother.

Alphonse choked on his breath. Summiting Tura—gaining wisdom? His sobs came harder. Nothing had changed, except now he was badly hurt.

A wrenching realization, his stupidity for throwing away a council seat, turning his back on a path that could have led to real power. If he'd had more time to think about di Les's terms, he might have found some way to live with them. The man had been so clear that Stavo's work must be undone, but there might have been some way around that.

Daylight returned. The bandages had stiffened, and his wound throbbed. Alphonse limped to the trickle of water running down the spires and wetted the strips. He teased them off, swearing as they pulled free. The wound was shallowest near his knee, and deeper into the meat of his leg.

He needed a doctor.

It was over eighty miles to Sangal, but Nasoir's western settlements were no more than twenty. He struck camp and hobbled down the Tura trail, switching back and forth, and back, and forth, eventually taking the western fork heading further inland. Further west.

Alphonse managed several miles that day and several more the next. He curled into his blanket each night, dizzy and feverish, and his thigh swelled larger and hotter.

On the fourth day he started down the final flank. If he made the tree line, he could boil water.

Chapter Seven

Terrence and Nathan argued the entire way back to the farm while Myrta sat with her eyes closed, trying to steer her thoughts away from the visit altogether. It had gone so horribly wrong, the whole day, and the memory of that man's hand on her wrist felt branded into her thoughts.

That night in her room she lay under the blanket her aunt, Ardelle, had sent her. When Myrta was small, they'd visit Ardelle and Uncle Ephraim in Collimais. Ardelle always gave Myrta gifts, and she told stories Myrta hadn't heard before. That Myrta had been born at the inn, same time as cousin Odile. "The other girl," they used to call one another when they were little.

Myrta pulled into a ball under the blanket. That man, at the de Reu stead, the one so different from any steader. His words kept repeating in her thoughts. *"We'll take you with us . . ."*

She couldn't curl any tighter. "Stop, stop it!"

Below, the front door creaked, and Terrence and Celeste's voices sounded up the stairs. Celeste spoke. "The system must have been impressive."

"Ain't convinced."

"We don't need it, Terrence." Chairs scraped on the kitchen floor. "Why was everyone in such bad temper tonight? Were there problems at Reuben's?"

"Good system. Not perfect, mind, but it'd see us through drought no problem."

"Love. I'm not asking about the irrigation, I'm asking about the children."

Terrence grunted and there was a pause. He sometimes took a while to answer Celeste's questions, especially if it was something he might think she didn't want to hear. "Myrta collapsed. Jack tended her."

"Collapsed?" Celeste's voice rose. "Did she faint?"

Myrta rolled onto her pillow and pulled the blanket over her head.

"I said collapsed. Her color went off, and Jack took her t' the house. One of those Renico folk got close, set me off."

Celeste's voice rose further. "Renico? Renico was there? At Reuben's? I thought the system was installed. Why were they there? They shouldn't be there."

"Settle down, Celeste, it's maintenance. 'Sides, we've no reason to worry. That fella stepped over a line, is all. I set him straight."

"They shouldn't be there," Celeste repeated. After a long moment she said tensely, "I'm sorry. I'm sorry, Terrence, you're right. We've no reason to worry."

The next morning, taking the milk to the cheese house and still plagued by the memory of that man's voice, Myrta startled at seeing Celeste already there working on the warped press.

Celeste's face was taut. "Terrence tells me you had a spell yesterday."

She gritted her teeth and set the pails on the workbench. This was the last thing she wanted to talk about.

Celeste folded her arms across her chest too tightly, like her face. Where she gripped, the knuckles on her hand stuck out in little anxious knobs. "He said people from Renico were there. What happened?"

Myrta busied herself. "Nothing."

"Did they bother you?"

"No." The man had looked at her so intently, like she was more important than even her papa, and he said things a steader would never say.

After a few moments Celeste turned back to the press, unscrewed the rods, and slid them to the side. Myrta tied her hair back, washed her hands, and went to the next room to pull down the curd.

When she returned, her mama had lined up the threaded rods into parallel lines, one right next to another. "We need to discuss this."

Myrta threw the curd into a bowl. "I don't want to talk about it." She clanked a pot onto the stove.

"Myrta—"

"Georgie liked the herbed cheese. I think we should make more of that." Myrta poured milk into the pot and some of it splashed over the other side. "Less of the plain. We can try dill. We have both. Chives and dill." She pulled a cloth from a drawer and wiped the spill.

Celeste's voice grew gentle. "Dear child—"

"I'm fine." Myrta scrubbed at a stain on the workbench. It had been there for years and wasn't going anywhere. She scrubbed at it anyway. "I'd like to go to first market. We have cheese. I think I should go. I think I could sell all of it. Please."

"Was the spell as bad as that?" Her mama's brow had knitted into a hard lump.

"I'm *fine*."

"No, you're *not*."

Myrta threw the towel down. "All right, yes, it was bad. I threw up. I thought I'd have to ride home like that. Yes." She turned away. "I don't know what I did wrong. I'm doing everything you said to do." Myrta choked on her breath. "What if I'm getting sicker? What if I need—?"

"You aren't."

"You weren't there. Papa was so angry—"

"Don't worry about him."

"—He'll never let me go anywhere again. Everything was spinning. I threw up!" Tears ran down inside her nose, and the view outside smeared into a mess of farming and dirt.

Her mama tried to hug her, but she shook it off. Quietly, Celeste said, "Why don't we try something new?"

Like Myrta was a recipe. Change the dill to fennel, maybe that's better. Like that warped press, fixable if they took the bad part out and put in a different part.

She wasn't a recipe. She was sick.

"You've done your exercises?"

"Yes, Mama. Yes. Every day."

"Maybe the irrigation was louder than you expected. Maybe, with the excitement of travelling, it was too much. Maybe you didn't sleep well the night before, and it all added up."

"That's not it!"

The leaves outside quivered in a breeze so light it touched nothing else. That's what her spells were like, they were like that. "If I get sick from such little things, how can I go anywhere? Anything might set me off, a tired child or a loud aut. If Papa installs a system, will I get sick here?"

"Let's not get ahead of ourselves. You're better today. I believe if you take ten minutes to relax in the morning—"

"Morning exercises too? They don't help."

"The exercises certainly *do* help. Doing them when you're at risk, any time you leave the stead, we can stay ahead of this."

Through her teeth, Myrta said, "I can't spend all day rubbing my temples, thinking quiet thoughts, and imagining that I'm falling asleep. Think about it, you're making no sense at all."

"One step at a time." Celeste's voice grew firm. "Morning exercises, and nighttime, and any time you leave the stead."

Lips pressed tight, Myrta turned to the stove. Her breath shuddered through her, and she poured more milk into the pot and blinked moisture from her eyes.

"Myrta. Those city folk from Renico. Did they say anything?" She was fiddling with the press again. "About your spell?"

"No."

Celeste had once called it a family trait, said it could get worse and would have done so years ago if not for the exercises. That staying relaxed kept it in check, like how some farmers kept turkeys in little pens so they would stay weak. Whole seasons would pass without a single spell, so she'd always believed the exercises mattered. But now the spells were coming more frequently and getting worse too.

"They didn't say anything? Are you sure?"

"I'm sure." It wasn't true. That man hadn't taken his eyes off of her. Blinking furiously, she stirred the pot. Why had he paid such attention to her? She didn't want to think about it.

As the milk started to steam, she muttered, "And I didn't like the babies either."

Celeste laughed, nervously at first, but it soon gave way to an easier sound. "I knew if we waited long enough, we'd find something you and Terrence agreed on."

Unable to help herself, Myrta smiled.

"The exercises are very important, Myrta. You simply must keep on top of them. Promise me."

She nodded, and Celeste left.

Myrta finished setting the cultures. Outside the window, rows and rows of tilled soil filled her view. Soon, beards of sprouts would appear, turning the fields to green, matching the maple and oak leafing out. She stared at the brown and green and blue in balance. Nature taking care of itself. Like a song or a story.

More exercises. But they aren't helping, not anymore.

Nature in rhythm. Unfolding on its own.

Maybe I just won't do them at all.

Chapter Eight

Alphonse stood on a barren cliff. The sunlight was brighter than before. The ocean held a greenish patch.

"We've watched for a billion years," Stavo said.

"I can't breathe." It didn't distress him.

"There's no oxygen."

The spot of green drew Alphonse in, and he shrank as before. This time he became a simple cell, a blue-green bacterium in the ocean. "Grandfather. Why does this happen?"

"The best way to learn history is to live it."

Alphonse did, as a cyanobacterium in ocean waters. He used carbon dioxide for food, and sunlight gave him the energy he needed to turn it to sugar. From the sugar he grew and divided, becoming two, then four, then eight. As he turned the carbon to sugar, he felt a searing pain through his membranes and molecules. "It hurts!"

"The pain is oxygen—your waste. It is reactive. You must expel it."

He did, and the oxygen diffused into the water. Over time, the oceans became replete with it, but the air did not. And yet his waste oxidized the others, the simple cells that were

not like him, and as it did they died. "Grand-
father, I'm killing them. All of them. I . . . I'm
killing everything."

"You're simply growing. You don't mean
for your waste to change the chemistry of your
world. It's a simple lesson, but one we don't
always learn."

His thigh burned with a searing pain. Alphonse hiked, if one could call it that, down the trail toward the western foothill towns. His knee didn't bend properly, and he needed to roll onto the out-side of his foot to keep on. He probably looked like a drunkard, with his scraggly beard and filthy clothing.

Alphonse distracted himself by humming. Dredging up old memories. Anything to keep moving.

When he was five, his mother wanted him to go with her on a trip to the eastern continent, Deasoir. He'd been once before, and there was something . . . a ritual with snakes? Something to do with one of the Deasoirian religions. He'd begged to stay home, and she'd gone alone.

He tried to recall school lessons. Economics. Politics. Geology.

The same forces that built Nasoir's oil reserves made for poor soils up and down the coast. Only the capital city of Vastol, on the Turas River delta, had any decent fertile land. The landlocked agricultural belt ahead of him was essential to the continent. It fed Nasoirians and provided lumber for their homes.

Alphonse unbuttoned his shirt and shuffled along on his makeshift crutch. At mid-day he sank against an oak, groaning and hot. Dozing, he dreamed of his grandfather, in prison years earlier when Alphonse was only six.

Alphonse, you're too young to have come here. So impetuous—it will be your undoing. The guards must take you home.

No! You're sick. I want to be with you. He'd left school without permission and found his way to the detention center alone.

The scent of machining oil from the bars pervaded the air, and a coughing fit shook Stavo's frame. *It's no place for a child. Your mother needs you.*

Alphonse cried, a frightened childish noise. *She should get you out.*

She will. Go home, be with Ivette. You are a very smart little boy and a very strong little boy, and we have years ahead. But I need rest. Go. You must take care of yourself too, Alphonse. Go.

Alphonse roused, and the memory spurred him on. He came to a stream and splashed water on his face, took his shirt off and dunked it, draping it around his neck.

Eventually, oak and sycamore dotted the hills again. He didn't remember stopping, but he must have, for then it was morning and he was flat on his back.

Thick greenish pus smelling like sewage dribbled from his wound.

I smell like miere. He was weaker too. Taking only the water skin and crutch, he stumbled onward. As

first sun lit the distant foothills below, he saw what
might be squat buildings, maybe a road.

Around midmorning Alphonse heard an aut back-
firing, the most welcome sound imaginable. His cheeks
grew wet, and he staggered on. Some time that afternoon he reached the edge of town. He slapped against
a door and blacked out.

Alphonse's leg was numb, and the bedsheets smelled
of antiseptic, crisp and sharp. A breeze blew in from
windows on the far wall.

Alphonse closed his eyes and released a long sigh
before sinking into his pillow, into the mattress. He
rubbed his face and ran his hands through his hair. *I'm
alive. I'm shaved and tended.*

A woman's voice woke him sometime later. "Let's
see how you're doing, mountain man."

He pushed to sit, more alert than before "How
long have I been here?"

"Three days." The matronly nurse pulled the sheet
down.

His leg was no longer swollen. Instead, it seemed
wasted, with a fat dressing from his hip to his knee.
She removed the dressing and he took a sharp breath.
His thigh was roughly half the size it should be. A port
had been inserted at the site of the gash.

"What did you do?"

Another nurse bounced in holding a tray with tubing and syringes. She had freckles and curly red hair.
"Ready for your treatment?"

"What treatment? What's going on?"

The redhead laughed. "We're on your side, honey."

She placed the tray on the table next to him. "I'm Cordelia. You might not remember that."

He pushed further back in the bed, up against the head rail.

"It's time for your injections."

"I don't remember you. What are you doing to me?"

The nurses exchanged a patient look. Cordelia said, "That's the amnesion, honey. Doctor removed most of the muscle, and trust me, you don't want to remember *that*. But today's a big day. You only need the regeneron. We re-growing that tissue as fast as we can. Doctor cleared the amnesion and anestheton. You can have them if you like. I think you should."

These were city drugs. They'd taken his thigh muscle? His alarm grew. "I don't want amnesion, Cordelia. I want to remember. This." He wanted to bolt straight out the door. "Cordelia," he repeated, more loudly, determined to keep her name.

Her eyes danced, and she rubbed his forearm. "That's fine. You're going to be just fine. Just the anestheton and regeneron then."

She prepared the medicines while the heavier nurse swabbed down his thigh and the port. He looked back and forth between them—they tried to make idle talk with him, but he didn't know these women. His thigh was *gone*?

Cordelia laughed again. "Mountain man. We're your friends. Imagine you're back on that spire, not holding anything. We're your harness."

Another wave of anxiety flooded him. "How do you know—"

"You told us."

That didn't help him feel better.

"All right. Let's start the anestheton." Cordelia

attached the tubing to the port in his thigh and smoothly injected the liquid. It was a cool pressure that spread outward and inward. He'd thought he had no feeling there, but the pressure was unmistakable. Then his leg was gone. Not numb, but gone.

Cordelia detached the tubing and syringe and smiled again. "See? Not too bad. So. What about your name?"

"Where am I?"

She laughed. "All right. You're in Collimais. Maybe you'll remember this time." She prodded his thigh with a pencil. "Feel anything?"

He couldn't. His leg was gone.

"That's good. Let's grow that muscle." She cocked her head. "Honey, this is your last chance for amnesion."

"It won't hurt."

"Oh honey. It'll hurt either way. The amnesion lets you forget how bad."

"But I've had anestheton."

"We're growing a new *muscle*. Anestheton helps— but you still get pain. The amnesion lets you forget that part."

And this conversation. And anything he might say—his name, his background. Anything he'd said in those first days was already gone. "No."

"All right. On to regeneron." Cordelia attached tubing to the port again. She took the second syringe and injected the contents.

He didn't feel anything. It wouldn't be bad; he'd had anestheton. She disconnected the tubing from the port.

A pinpoint of warmth took hold, spreading out and down, like drinking warm cocoa on a cold day. It didn't hurt. After a minute, the sensation grew from warmth to heat. The heat quickly transformed into an itch. Slight, really. Not painful.

The first nurse had returned. She and Cordelia stood on either side of the bed and each took one of his arms.

"I can handle it."

The nurses exchanged a smile.

The itch spread inward somehow and intensified. He wanted to scratch it away, it began to sear at the inside of his thigh, like a swarm of wasps, stinging him, pins and needles deep inside his leg, a thousand of them. He tried to sit, wanted to grab the port.

"Hang on," Cordelia said.

He wanted to claw the skin away, scrape open his thigh, release the swarm, but the nurses had clamped his arms down. The pain grew, and he groaned.

The nurses' faces were stony, determined, and both had broken a sweat. "It's going to burn, hon."

His femur shattered, like glass, a thousand toxins attacking bone, muscle, nerves, his leg fragmented, his skin dissolved, all his tissues were on fire, and he kicked downward with his good leg. His back arched. He tried to pull his arms free again, but the nurses were too strong.

In a sing-song voice, Cordelia said, "Almost over."

He wailed, kicked the sheets, and slammed his good foot against the bottom rail.

Finally, the mad frenzy of wasps slowed, and gradually, the stinging ended. They were crawling again, trapped inside. He panted, sweaty-wet.

The wasps were quiet. They were gone.

He opened his eyes, still breathing hard.

The first nurse propped him up by his shoulders and placed a new pillow underneath him. She took the damp one away. Cordelia dabbed a cloth at his hairline.

"What the fierno was that?"

"We're growing a new muscle. See?"

The depression in his thigh filled in as he watched. *Miere.*

"The old one was rotten."

He stared at his leg. "Thank you, Cordelia." After she left, he lay back into the fresh pillow and reached for the medical pad. He'd had a dose of antimicrobion, the surgery, some stitches, and these treatments.

The accidents at the plants. Those people could be treated. Sometimes they were, but not often. What was the difference between their situation and his? It couldn't be wealth, unless he'd said more about his family than he should have, which he hoped he hadn't. The line workers deserved this level of care. Any sane person would agree. His mother had to agree.

The next day Cordelia came in, set the tray on the table, crossed her arms, and smiled as though she had a secret.

He pushed to sit. "What?"

"You're walking today. Put that muscle to work." She tilted her head. "It doesn't seem right without knowing your name."

Relief washed through him. "I'm ... look, Cordelia, I'm nobody."

"Oh, come on now. Everybody's somebody."

True, and he might've been a councilman. But he wasn't, and he needed time away from all that to regroup. Time away from his mother and the past. "I mean it, I'm no one Cordelia, but my name's Alphonse. Alphonse di Anton, from Masotin."

She perked up at his words, hair bouncing as she nodded. The smell of citrus floated from her. She filled in a line on the chart. "All right, Mr. di Anton. Let's try a few steps."

She put an arm around him and lifted his leg over the side of the bed. He pulled himself off the rest of the way and fell onto her with a heavy grunt. She lowered her arm to his waist. "Take it slow. Try a step."

He held to her shoulders and lurched his right leg out. It felt like a log of clay. His foot landed with a thud. Dismayed, he stared at it.

"That's good, try the other leg."

He gripped her shoulder harder and lumbered the left leg forward, but his right knee buckled and she caught him.

It was as though he'd never known how to walk.

"Let's take another."

In a stuttering mess, falling and lurching, Alphonse worked around the bed. Cordelia called it a good first try.

The next day he took more steps with her help. Then he managed a few on his own, and a week into recovery he tottered up and down the hallway by himself, grinning the entire way. Back in the room, Cordelia was bathing his neighbor. "Doctor says your new muscle's all there, Mr. di Anton. There's just payment."

Payment. "I don't know how to cover this."

"Maybe your family?" She wrote something on his neighbor's chart.

Even out here they'd know his mother's name, his grandfather's work. "I don't think so."

Cordelia tapped a finger on her elbow. "Some patients wash linens, clean bedpans, that sort of thing. They work the bill down."

Bedpans? Doubtful. "Could I work in town?"

"Yes, I've seen that too." She gave him another encouraging smile. "Think about what you might be good at. I'm sure we'll find something."

Chapter Nine

Myrta pulled on a thick pair of socks, some old work trousers and a cableknit sweater from her aunt, Ardelle, who'd sent it to the stead after last fall's Caravan. The sweater still smelled faintly of the lavender it had been wrapped with.

Downstairs, the rest of the family was eating. Myrta joined them, and Terrence glanced up from his eggs. "That's no look for market. Get on a dress."

He had a point. Other women would be in dresses, although none of the children wore them. Besides, the sweater reminded her of Ardelle, and she didn't get many chances to wear it. "Papa, please. It's cold. I'll bring a dress and change after suns-up, I promise." She pled with her eyes, and after a moment his expression shifted from stern to endearing, as though he saw the cusp she stood upon, between childhood and womanhood. He nodded curtly and went back to his eggs.

The stalls went up on the market grounds, dozens of them, next to a permanent paddock and an open-air theater.

Jack took the team to the paddock while Terrence and Nathan helped Celeste and Myrta set up the cheese booth. Narrow tables front and back covered with brown cloth and a pair of low stools between. Nathan stowed crates of cheese on the back table.

Myrta greeted her neighbor. "Happy market, Mr. de Clar."

The man, a copperwood fiber weaver, was setting skeins out on a richly-dyed table runner. He greeted her, and Myrta offered a piece of cheese to his dog, who was all heavy and warm. The dog snuffled for more. Laughing, she knelt and scratched around his ears.

At least a hundred people would be here today. Myrta glanced around, wondering if she might meet some nice young man, perhaps from one of the towns. So far, only steaders had arrived.

The dog licked her hand again, and laughing, she rubbed his head harder. That set his hips wagging, and his breath hit her face, all dog-smelly.

"We need a puppy, Mama." She grabbed him around the shoulders and he gave a loud woof.

"Myrta, the dog can wait." Celeste was unpacking a crate on the front table.

"If we wait too long, I won't be home anymore." But she stood and helped. She said to the fiber artist, "Are your sons here today?"

"No."

The way he said it, hard without meeting her eyes, surprised her.

"They're lookin' for work in the cities."

Myrta felt her smile freeze, and after a moment forced a nod. Terrence sometimes said steading meant freedom but that the numbers didn't always work out.

They sold throughout the morning, and after lunch Celeste left to see the other stalls. Myrta was sorting through the cash box, setting reblas to one side and coinage to the other, when Jack walked up. "The cotton steaders came. Your match is here."

"Emmett's not my match." Still, maybe that was why Terrence wanted her in a dress.

Jack hadn't been matched. Not yet. He wasn't taken with girls, so the prospect of children, or rather the lack of good prospects, complicated the whole thing. He seemed happy to stay single indefinitely, and Myrta understood completely. Matching with Emmett? He was nice enough looking, she supposed, but older even than Nathan. Still, if Terrence was willing to send her off with Emmett then he didn't need her on the farm at all. She could do what the weaver's sons had done and look for work somewhere else, even in a city. She frowned, wondering if she ought to suggest it to Terrence.

Jack was laying out fat slices of cheese. "Oh, stop with the face, no one's talking matches right now. It's all irrigation."

There'd been no rain in weeks.

"Reuben said Mr. di Vaun's coming, so I thought I'd stick close."

Myrta blinked and sat too quickly, almost missing the stool. "He's coming *here*?"

"Yep. I think Reuben is helping him sell. They probably give him a kickback."

The words barely registered. That man's dimples, his hand on her wrist and his voice. He'd be *here*?

Jack leafed through the bills in the box, put some under the divider and closed it again. "It's not just irrigation, either. Renico sells an aut that plows fields. Nathan wants them to come out, price it all."

Nathan wanted that man on their farm? If he came, he'd be smiling at her in his warm-eyed way, watching her like he'd done before. "I don't think that's a good idea."

A child ran up, grabbed one of the slices, and pushed it into his mouth. A woman hurried after, offering to pay, but Jack handed a second piece. "Free samples."

Myrta's head buzzed. *'Renico's doctors are the best on the continent...'* She put her hands flat on the table and tried to think past that man's voice. He was selling a machine that pulled water, that was all.

A cheery voice called, "Myrta! Yoo-hoo! Rudy, there's your little friend. Now don't be shy. He's a nice boy. Go on, Rudy. Go say hi." Georgie came up to their stall and said to the other woman, "Hello again, Janette. Myrta this is Janette. Don't you love her dress? What a pretty color." She shifted the baby on her hip.

Myrta nodded at Janette, but her thoughts stayed on Mr. di Vaun. His attention on her had been so focused.

"Janette's from Beamais. She came all the way to our little market. All the way from Beamais. Isn't that nice? How are you, Myrta dear? Better from your dizzy spell, I hope. That looked so unpleasant. Have you had any more? Oh Jack, hello! I didn't see you, and you're sitting right there."

Myrta told herself to settle, even as she pictured that man on their stead, walking around their home, maybe finding her in the cheese house, maybe speaking to her. *'We have room for you,'* like it was perfectly normal to up and leave with a stranger.

Georgie continued, "I miss dressmaking. So many patterns. Reuben always brings fabrics after Caravan. Of course, I have no time with two little ones, and then Reuben wants a third so who knows when I'll be free to sew anything." She gave a slice of cheese to baby Rosa. "Oh! Janette. Tell her what you said. Remember? What you told me. Myrta, did you hear? About that young man in Beamais? And the lake? It was awful."

Janette picked up her son and held him close. "One of our neighbors—their boy's missing."

This finally pulled Myrta's thoughts from Melville di Vaun.

"We think he might have drowned." Janette's face emptied as she spoke, as though her words made the young man's absence more real. "We aren't certain of anything. They might find him any day. Today."

Georgie added, "And besides not knowing what happened—I mean, of course, he could be fine, like you say, right Janette? It just sounds like one of those old stories about people disappearing in the middle of the night. Can you imagine?"

Myrta had no experience of tragedy, not of any serious sort. The closest thing was the baby goat that escaped the pen years ago. They'd found it days later, dead in the creek, tangled in vines and bloated. She remembered being inconsolable, imagining it dying there, bleating for its mama and no one to help. But this was market, it was supposed to be neighbors and stories, dancing and pretty dresses, not people gone missing and memories of dead goats. "I'm so sorry." She was. What else could she say?

Janette thanked her and left with Georgie and the youngsters. Jack started talking again about the other growers. He was going on about drought and irrigation and Mr. di Vaun, which set her heart racing again. She couldn't think straight. Should she tell Celeste about the man's offer to see a doctor? It didn't feel right. She wanted to leave the farm, but by Bel above, not by climbing into an aut with a stranger. Of course, matching made no more sense than that. Climbing into a *life* with a stranger.

And then, as if her thoughts had summoned him, Melville di Vaun appeared at the end of the row and began talking with a seller. She sucked in a breath. The seller pointed at her, and Melville's eyes, so warm and brown, locked onto her own. She took a step back and nudged Jack. "I don't know what to think about him."

Under his breath, Jack said, "Nothing's going to happen. It's fine."

"Don't go anywhere."

Melville di Vaun strode up wearing a friendly smile. "Ah. Myrta and Jack. Good afternoon."

He sounded polite and kind and perfectly concerned, and she swallowed. "Hello."

Jack stood straighter and pressed forward against the table. "Nice to see you, Mr. di Vaun."

"Jack. I hope you're well. Myrta, I wanted to check after you. Be certain you've recovered."

"I'm fine."

"Good, good. I've given it a little more thought."

His eyes, still locked onto her own, held that same focus as before. As if Jack wasn't standing right there. "There are two different procedures, either of which might help your situation. Both are very straightforward, quite simple. Quick."

Her heart was thumping, and she gripped the back table with both hands. Jack sounded perplexed. "Mr. di Vaun, procedures?"

Mr. di Vaun was looking at her, intent on her, and she couldn't make sense of it. Her thoughts went all jumbled. Her health couldn't matter to him, not like this. Something was wrong. There he was, composed and confident, in his well-cut suit and cologne mingling with his breath. She was a farmgirl. Why would her health matter to him?

The scars by his ear made white traces, fine lines. She wondered if those scars were due to some accident.

Celeste hurried up, came between the tables, and dropped some packages. "Good afternoon. I'm Celeste, Terrence's wife."

Myrta stared at her mama's terse voice.

"Wonderful to meet you. Melville di Vaun."

"With Renico?" The edge in Celeste's voice was the same as it had been in the cheese house when she kept asking if these men had paid Myrta any mind. And even though nothing bad had happened, even the fiber artist was standing now, and his dog too.

Jack said, "Mr. di Vaun's worried about Myrta collapsing at Reuben's."

"That's kind of you," Celeste said. "Frankly, more kind than we'd expect." She put an arm around Myrta.

"Mrs. de Terr, I mean no disrespect. Myrta's condition is something we see from time to time in the cities, and it's treatable. It's called precipitous vertigo. It can become debilitating if untreated, but there're two medical options to correct it. It seems to me that as long as we're trying to help your stead, we might help in other ways too. Your entire family could come to Narona, meet the physicians. Afterward, she wouldn't be bothered by dizzy spells anymore."

The dog growled. Celeste said, "It strikes me odd that you're so very interested in a girl you've just met."

Myrta thought maybe it was a city thing, his forward manners, but Celeste was nervous too, and she had lived in Narona. Why did the combustion industry need doctors anyway? Myrta swallowed, focused down at the leg of the table where it sank right into the ground. She was safe. Nothing bad would happen.

Melville laughed. He put his hands in his trouser pockets and rocked back on his heels. "It seems I've created another misunderstanding. Cultural differences, I suppose."

Celeste said forcefully, "Myrta's fine. I need you to leave. You're blocking our customers."

Myrta looked up at that.

His dimples were fading, and he fixed her with another intent gaze. She shrank, everything pounding inside.

It's how a rabbit feels.

The man nodded and left.

Beads of sweat dotted Celeste's hairline. "Myrta. Was that the man Terrence told me about? Was he at Reuben's? Was that him?"

"Yes." And he was several booths down already, walking quickly and not speaking with anyone. He was supposed to be selling irrigation. Why wasn't he talking to anyone?

"Why didn't you tell me he was here? What did he say before I came back?"

Myrta heard the panic in her voice. "I didn't know he was here until now. He just kept asking after me."

Celeste took a long look at her. "You're shaking." She folded Myrta into a hug. "Stay away from him."

"We should go home."

"We can't. Terrence is working. No, stop worrying. We're safe. We're surrounded by friends." She blinked rapidly and took a deep breath. "Myrta. Another businessman, also with Renico, is here. He's with Reuben. Stay clear of both of those men."

Of course she would. Of course.

Once the selling wound down, Myrta and Jack headed to the open-air theater where folk stories were getting underway.

Myrta pulled Jack to a bench near the back. Jack looked around, probably for some of his friends. He had his own reasons for wanting off the farm, and he'd given her most of his day.

"Thanks, Jack."

He smiled and shook his head.

On stage, young people lined up. These were the players, leading traditional stories, a way for each generation to teach the next.

Chants broke out, and Myrta joined those nearest her, calling for the tale of Old Steader Elige. The players hushed the crowd and told a different one, the tale of the magical orchard that bore fruit all year. One of the players mimed a steader, eating apple after apple and finally falling down, rolling back and forth with his cheeks puffed out.

The benches continued to fill.

For the second story, the players pointed to a young boy and called him up. Myrta sent up a whoop—it was the tale of Old Steader Elige.

The boy ran to the stage and people called, "Get rid of him, get rid of Elige!"

The players threw their hands in the air and called back, "We'll try."

They began the story, with three players standing back in the shadows. The boy, in the role of 'Old Elige,' pointed at the stage's dark pockets and said the couplet, "I see you all from far away, your breath is clear, as clear as day." Then he pulled them back into view. Myrta booed with the others and called for Old

Elige to be sent away from the belt altogether. A player lifted the boy and threw him over her shoulder, carrying him off to the side, but the boy cried, "You say I bear a wicked mark, but I can see you in the dark!"

Another player led the boy to the back, into the shadows, and declared that Elige would never bother them again. The audience called to send him further yet. "A hundred miles, two hundred," they shouted.

The boy knew this cue too. "Your chimney smoke is plain to see, you cannot yet be rid of me." He ran back to center stage.

And then, Myrta's eyes fell on Melville di Vaun. Still at market, still with his raking gaze, standing past the benches with a younger man and scanning the theater.

She shoved Jack. "Look." Ducking her head, she pushed out and away, toward the paddock, heart pounding. She crammed between a wagon and the paddock fence. Jack was soon beside her.

"Why is he still here?"

"Myrta, he won't do anything, not in a crowd like that."

She threw a glance around the wagon to the market grounds. "All the booths are down. He's got no reason to be here anymore."

"Come on, he's probably just enjoying the show."

"He wasn't watching the *show*. The only reason he's here is because of me." Myrta called in to the paddock, "Rusty!" She climbed between the fence rails and a few of the horses ambled over.

"What are you doing? Terrence expects us here. We can't just ride off."

"Use your brains, Jack. That man's like a wolf that's caught scent." She grabbed Rusty's halter, pulled at the gate, and climbed onto the horse's back. His coat was rough and thick, and he nickered and sidestepped. She pulled on his mane and steered him through the gate.

"Myrta, stop. We need the team fresh."

In disbelief, she stared at him. "You're worried about the *horses*? For the love of all above, are you out of your *mind*?"

A man yelled. Mr. di Vaun, out of the theater and in clear view, was gesturing his partner to an aut. Myrta kicked Rusty into a trot.

"Holy heavens, Myrta stop!" Jack was getting onto Rennet. The engine on the aut rumbled.

She squeezed harder and kicked again. "Gid up!" The horse broke into a canter, hoof-falls pounding up through her seat. Myrta grabbed handfuls of mane, and the horse snorted and whinnied, ears flicking.

The aut was gaining, and Jack was still yelling at her but she didn't care. She needed speed, or to get off the road. She kicked and yelled at Rusty to pick it up. He brought his head up, shied to the side, snorted again, hooves striking the dirt. Her view narrowed into a tunnel, and waves of adrenaline surged in her head.

Myrta held the mane tighter, her fingers tangled in it, she kicked harder and harder, yelling at Rusty to go, go, sending the horse into a full gallop. She wobbled to the side. She was falling and Rusty was galloping with his ears flat back. She pulled on his mane to heave back up.

Jack yelled again.

She was upright. She kicked the horse. She kept kicking.

The aut caught up, Rusty shied from it, neighing and snorting. Melville's partner leaned out of an open window and grabbed at her shoe. He had her ankle.

Someone was screaming—it was her. She yanked as hard as she could and pulled her foot free.

Jack navigated Rennet between her and the aut and swung wildly at the man's arm. Rennet was frothing at the mouth, and his eyes were wide. Jack yelled again and she heard him say, "Get off the road!" The aut swerved and the man in the window nearly fell. He swore into the aut. It edged closer.

Myrta yelled back, "I have to get out of here!"

"Get *off the road*," Jack called back.

She wheeled Rusty around, prodding him behind the aut. Jack followed. The aut tried to turn, but the road was narrow and rutted.

As the horses crossed behind, exhaust hit Myrta full on. Pounding vertigo rushed over her, and she screamed, clutching at her forehead with one hand and Rusty's mane with the other. "Jack, help," she cried, listing again. The horses plowed up the hill, through scrub and brush.

"Can you relax it?" he yelled.

"No," she cried. Her head was oddly wrenched, parts within her skull pulling and pushing against each other. Rennet and Rusty slogged up the steep hillside, and the aut tried to hold even below. Something hot crawled under her skin.

Jack took Rennet higher. Rusty followed. On the crest of the hill, the vertigo pummeled away at her. She held on.

And then, a cool pressure washed over her eyes and back through her temples. The vertigo vanished as if it had never been, and a sensation like water flooded her skull. Myrta regained her balance between one breath and the next, she opened her eyes and righted herself. Her white-knuckled fist clenched Rusty's mane. Her balance was fine, and Rennet plowed on ahead.

Looking back at the road, Myrta saw the aut crawling along and almost fell off the horse again, for she saw more than an aut. A stream of brilliant cobalt blue, like lightning from an angry god, gushed from a pipe on the vehicle. Around the angry streak of blue, pale shades of red and green washed the air. "Jack, what's happening?" she cried.

"Come on," he called back. "The roads don't go this way."

Chapter Ten

Alphonse, now a blue-green bacterium, flourished in a boundless sea. He pulled carbon dioxide from the water and made sugar. He excreted oxygen—so much that it escaped into the air. The oxygen reacted violently with the methane in the air to create more carbon dioxide, which diffused back into the ocean, giving him even more to eat.

"You've generated a feedback, Alphonse."

He hummed happily. "There are many of me."

"The oceans are filled with you because of the feedback."

Time passed and more carbon diffused into the oceans, and the air grew rich with oxygen. After many millennia, Alphonse grew sluggish. "The water is cold."

Ages passed, and ice crept forth from the north and the south. "There's too much ice," Alphonse cried. "The water's freezing."

"An atmosphere with no carbon cannot hold heat. You've taken the carbon from the air."

And as the ice advanced, Alphonse slowed and stopped, suspended in a frozen sea. Ice covered the planet. Far away, as in a dream, Stavo said, "The world is entirely covered in snow. The blue-green bacteria did this seven hundred million years ago. The story of our world is one of change."

Alphonse wiped the sweat from his eyes and wrestled with the shim again, forcing it into the hinge.

No good. The door still scraped the frame. He swore.

There had to be a better way to pay his medical bill than by doing odd jobs at an inn. A woman's voice called up the stairwell. "Do you need help?"

"No," he grunted back, bracing against the frame and trying again.

"Sounds like you need a little help."

"I'm fine," he called, wedging the shim a third time.

The woman was Ardelle Vonard. Solid. Serious. This was her inn, and it was homey, in the way an old pair of shoes might be. Slumped and faded but comfortable.

"All right. When you're done, Ephraim needs you out back."

"Got it."

He stood to wrangle the door from a different angle, because by any mathematical analysis the shim should fit fine. Without warning, his thigh seized, and gasping, he grabbed at the jamb. These spasms! Cordelia had said they'd smooth out, but his leg was exactly like that door. All the parts there and still not working.

He kept at the job, and at last, when the door cleared the frame, Alphonse stood with a heavy sigh. He lumbered down the stairs with the tools, toward the back of the inn, down a little corridor, and out to the yard. Ardelle's husband Ephraim would be here, doing some odd task or other for her.

A stable stood to one side of the yard, and about thirty plum trees grew past it. Beyond the trees, a trail led into the mountains, marked by an old copperwood stump. Everything about Collimais was beautiful, and it was nothing like Sangal.

Ephraim was on his back underneath a carriage. He pulled out as Alphonse hobbled over.

"Al. I can use a second pair of hands."

The man spoke with a city accent, his words taking no space at all, like Alphonse's own clipped speech. Some people said it matched the pace of the cities. Alphonse wouldn't have noticed the man's accent back in Sangal, but here in this little foothill town it was as unexpected as the occasional sound of an aut back-firing. Ephraim seemed kindly, though. "Leg holding up?"

"It's fine, sir." Alphonse pushed against the ache in his thigh.

Ephraim watched in a detached, almost clinical way, and Alphonse wondered if he'd been a medic once.

"Newly regenerated tissues take a while. Yours is probably in the cellular proliferation stage. Don't worry, it'll get there." Ephraim took the hand tools from Alphonse and set them with a few others, then gestured at the carriage. "Any experience with these?"

"No, not at all. We use auts, of course." There were hardly any horse-drawn carriages in the cities any more.

"Of course." Ephraim seemed to study Alphonse more closely. "Have you worked on those?"

"Sure, but they're not..." Alphonse gestured at the old carriage, with its wooden wheels, its seat sunk

in the middle, and the whole of it faded from expo-
sure. "You know."

Ephraim handed a jack over. "They're close enough.
Front axle's bad." He set a second jack under his side
of the carriage.

They began working. Ephraim called across, "So
tell me, Al, what's your family's business?"

When Alphonse had started at the inn, he'd assumed
the Vonards would be a simple family. Provincial, with
a back-woods type of sensibility.

They'd been anything but simple. They'd piled
questions on him, especially their daughter, who
seemed fascinated by him in an almost adversarial
way. Ephraim, at least, kept a friendly tone.

"My mother's a teacher." It was true enough. She'd
taught him pragmatic cynicism after her father's death.
She'd taught him plenty over the years, most often
about people and their pressure points.

"And your father?"

"He left." The only thing Marco had given Alphonse
was his absence. It didn't matter. They barely knew
each other.

"That's too bad." The underside of the carriage
was easy to see now, and a split in the axle rod ran
along its length. "What took you from Masotin?"

The Vonards had thrown this particular question
at him more times than he could count, and in annoyance, Alphonse cranked the jack harder. "I told you a
few times now. Remember? I was looking for Arel."

"Ah, right. Seeking wisdom. You hiked to Tura—
from Masotin no less. You know, Al, I can almost picture it from Sangal or Beschel. But to walk there from
Masotin? That's impressive. How did you cross the
Great Gorge?"

Alphonse swore under his breath, cursing the man

for his smugness. There was no good way to cross the Great Gorge, the massive canyon cut by the Turas River south of Sangal. It was flanked by three-thousand-foot vertical cliffs. "I went around it."

Ephraim came over to Alphonse's side of the carriage, smiling. "That's quite a distance."

If his story had any truth to it, yeah, it would be. Alphonse yanked on the wheel. He just wanted to pay his bill and leave.

"Careful. Watch the frame." Ephraim eased the wheel off, examined the edge, and muttered, "It needs a new rim."

Ephraim's daughter came out then. Odile. She was a few years younger than Alphonse and looked a bit like Ardelle. Her eyes were gray with dark flecks, and something in the way she held herself reminded Alphonse of a girl he'd dated years ago. Confidence, he thought, that's what it was. Her hair fell like water, like a veil. It was closer to blond than either Ephraim's or Ardelle's.

She stood there with her hands on her hips, staring at him. At his nose, to be exact. His crooked nose. His off-center nose, broken years ago and crooked ever since. That's what she stared at.

"Al. You left oil on the door frame. Can you wipe that down?"

Her tone was chilly, had been ever since he'd opened his mouth, and off-putting didn't begin to describe it. She didn't know him, yet she seemed to distrust him on sight. Of course, confronting her about it was out of the question. She was Ardelle's daughter, and Ardelle had hired him. "Yes, ma'am."

He stood, brushed the dirt from his trousers, and limped back inside. Odile and Ephraim watched him without speaking as he crossed the yard, but as soon as he pulled the door shut, he saw through the little window that they were talking again, quite animatedly.

"Thank you, Al." He startled and turned to find Ardelle. "For fixing the door. You were right, you did that without any help at all, even with your leg. Would you mind wiping the frame? There's a bit of oil on it." She handed him a cloth.

"Of course, Mrs. Vonard."

He went back up and wiped the door, grabbed the oil canister, which he'd also forgotten, and went down and out again. Odile turned to him and said sourly, "Do you want to see the rest of town?"

No, not with her. He threw a glance at Ephraim, but the man's face was set. No easy out there; no extra line.

"Go, Al," Ephraim said at last. "She'll show you the hardware store."

The hardware store? In a town so small he could find a hardware store without a guided tour. "The nurse told me to take it easy on the leg."

"Cordelia said no such thing. Go on the walk with Odile. I'm not giving you a choice."

They went after supper, Odile ahead and him behind. Every twenty or thirty feet she'd stop and, clearly exasperated with his pace, wait for him. When they reached the main street she said, "Thoroughfare."

The shops were mostly closed for the evening. They passed one, an eatery, that was open and smelled of grilled meats. Different culture here; different kind of life. Everything from Odile's self-protective attitude to the smells and sounds and the rough-hewn planks underfoot.

Different, but appealing.

They passed another shop, a grain merchant. This little town probably had no more than a few hundred people. Of course, it was a between-point, where the goods of the belt were sold for transport to the cities. Merchants lived in these foothill towns, and each fall wagons assembled here before bringing their harvest to the cities.

A few families were out.

"So," Odile said with that same impossible cliff of expression she'd worn all week, "how do we compare to . . . Masotin, was it?"

"It's smaller." He heard his displeasure, and in truth she didn't deserve that. After a while he looked over. The tightness between her eyebrows was unmistakable. "I'm sorry. Why don't we try this again, Odile. Your town is nothing like Masotin, it's smaller of course, and I'd genuinely like to know more about it. How are the jobs here?"

"Fine."

She said it without missing a beat, and her pace quickened. He pushed to keep up. A stab of pain shot from his knee. He lurched onto a railing and grabbed his leg. His heel began hammering the ground.

"Is that the regeneron?"

She was staring wide-eyed at his foot as it slammed into the boardwalk. He kneaded his thigh until it settled, pushed off the railing and tested his weight. "Yeah. It's supposed to get better."

Her face zipped closed, her moment of openness gone.

"Anyway," he said, still testing the leg, "it's nice to see families out. Kids."

He was being conversational, but he was also curious. In the cities, children could work as young as twelve. Out here, with the tradition of apprenticing into a family business, they started younger. "Do they take work?"

She crossed her arms and looked at him icily.

"What? It's a simple question."

"Yes. We work."

"Here in town?"

"Yes. Or in the belt, when we're older."

His leg seemed to be working well enough, and he paced back into a walk. The muscle worked, just not smoothly. "Okay. Well, what if someone doesn't want either of those? They have to go somewhere."

Her eyes flashed. "You're very interested in how we do things. Is it so different in Masotin? That's where you're from, right? Or was it Narona?"

He forced a smile and resolved to make it through this walk one way or another. "I'm from Masotin. Sunny Masotin. Home to the greatest fishing fleet on Nasoir. How many workers—"

She grabbed him by the arm and yanked him around to face her. "Let me be clear, Mr. di Anton. We do not call our neighbors 'workers.' We know one another by name. We grew up together. We don't want city folk, especially deceitful ones, here. We're content. You can leave. I can't imagine anyone would ever want a job anywhere else. *Especially* in the cities."

Astonished. Her attitude toward him boiled down to his city roots. She disliked him for no other reason than that.

She started walking and he followed. They passed a grassy area, the street splitting on either side. "The Grand Square," she said.

'Grand' was the wrong word, but it was pleasant and more or less square-shaped. A few families were out here as well.

"Weddings, naming ceremonies, conjunction festivals. Those are held here."

Conjunction—when Bel and Letra aligned to create the illusion of a single sun—occurred twice yearly. Turaset's orbit brought it closest to Bel'letra during conjunction, and brutal radiation bathed the planet. Everyone's pigmentation shifted. According to the history books, most of the original colonists died during their first conjunction because they didn't have protective pigmentation, and that was a major challenge of colonizing Turaset. Now, in the cities, electrical lines were kept buried as a protective measure. Here in the foothills, of course, electricity was dependent on individual fuel-powered generators. There were no lines to bury.

Squeals came from the children on the green, the pure happiness of childhood. Alphonse wondered at times how much more of that he might have had and whether he'd be different now if his grandfather hadn't died and Marco hadn't left. "Are the festivals nice?"

"I wouldn't know," she replied. "I'm not superstitious."

True, these country traditions were rooted in superstition. The suns, according to one of the religions, symbolized twin gods, one ruling the body and the other the spirit. To be outside when the gods met was to risk losing the soul. Conjunction festivals were held after dark to celebrate escaping soul-death.

Odile had led him most of the way through the town now, and she stopped in front of another little shop. Fuel-powered tools and devices sat inside the window.

"So. The hardware store." She slapped the window frame. "This is it. The place where everyone buys their tools. And the fuel, and the service for the motors and engines."

It looked standard, if small.

Her eyes grew hard. "Masotin, yes? In Renivia Province? Tell me, Al. Why do we need fuel-powered tools?"

Maybe he'd misunderstood her. His eyes roamed down the street and fell on a building that looked like it might be a public bath. Past that, a schoolhouse.

He looked back. "Why do we *need* them? Well, look. You must have learned it in school. You grow food; we build things." He rapped the pane with his knuckle. "You'd have trouble making *glass* out here."

Odile crossed her arms. "Hmm."

"You would." He pushed the heel of his palm down his thigh again. They must've walked over a mile, and the soreness in his leg was deep and aching, like he'd just spent the afternoon climbing. In a sense this whole conversation had been an exercise in finding holds and pushing onward.

He could, he thought, take charge of it. Put on a charming smile, like his mother would do. Flirt a little. They'd walk back to the inn, and he'd convince her he was interested in her dreams. He knew how to do that well enough, had been raised by one of the best. He'd pretend to care about Odile and her ideas. That might be better, actually, than this hostility they seemed to feel toward one another, and certainly would be easier.

But as he considered it, he saw too much of his mother in it and not enough of the man he was trying to be. "Odile. I don't know what you have against me. I don't know why we're getting off on the wrong foot." Something heavy in his chest, some hard part of himself, loosened at the admission.

She frowned and looked straight into his eyes. The

flecks in them, dark and light, reminded him of mountaintop granite. "Why are you here?"

He slipped on her words, her forthrightness. This candor!

Why are you here?

Why. Because the Council was unworkable. His relationship with his mother too. That was why. He stared at the dusty planks. "I think I'm just looking for a little solid footing."

The words might sound cryptic, but they felt honest. He looked back up.

After a moment, her shoulders relaxed, and her face smoothed out. "Thank you. Your leg's had enough. Let's go back."

Back at the inn, two carriages stood in the lane, and once inside he heard voices coming from the back office. Alphonse didn't give it much thought. He bid Odile good night, went up to his room, and opened the window. The scent of sage blew in, good mountain sage. He lay on the bed, closed his eyes, and listened as he'd done before.

There it was. Cricket.

He imagined himself by a burbling stream with the spread of stars above. His breathing slowed and deepened, and the ache in his thigh smoothed out.

Frog.

Then glass clinking on glass, and a voice. "Is he with the combustion industry?"

Alphonse startled. That was Ephraim, his voice barely audible. He concentrated.

Odile's voice. "No. He's a dishonest boob. He's

not . . ." Alphonse flinched at her words and strained harder, ". . . Masotin."

"Desisters . . . those people . . ."

". . . the network."

He heard mumbles of other voices, two or three he didn't recognize. One was loud and had a shrill edge, like a peevish old man. "They want to drill the ranges. They've roped in di Les, over in Sangal."

Ephraim's voice. "Provinces . . . restrictions . . ."

Odile's voice. ". . . not *my* friend . . . Renico."

With a jolt, Alphonse stopped. This family tracked the actions of the combustion industry. He stared at the window, wondering where he might go to hear their words more clearly.

His stomach twisted hard. No. If they'd wanted him to join their conversation, they would have asked. They hadn't, and if he was honest with himself, he would have said no. There was little chance this family could teach him anything he didn't already know about combustion. More to the point, eavesdropping, like deceit, seemed like another bad habit to leave behind.

He closed the window and turned off the light.

Chapter Eleven

The horses plodded in the early morning suns. Jack and Myrta did too. The events at market—di Vaun chasing her, the bizarre stream of blue from his aut's rear pipe. Maybe a procedure *was* what she needed. She was so tired it was hard to think straight.

"Tell Papa about di Vaun." Under the exhaustion in Jack's voice was the sound of grim determination. "Promise."

Yawning, she nodded.

The barn came into view. Nathan and two field hands were in the wheat field talking about something. He was pointing toward the far end. Then he saw them and strode over, clearly upset and plainly tired, looking them both up and down. "Jack."

"Sorry, Nate."

"Save it." His voice was brusque. It was the tone he took with the hands when they hadn't done what he'd told them to do. Nathan ran his hand along the horses, down their withers and legs. He looked at their eyes and pulled their lips back to inspect their gums. "Team's thirsty. They're no good today. Myrta, take 'em to the trough, then stable 'em."

She pulled the horses away. Another pair of horses, not theirs, grazed in the pasture, and her heart sank. Terrence must have paid to get the carriage home. That meant money lost from sales. She could see it playing out, Mama and Papa and Nathan finding Rusty and Rennet gone, Myrta and Jack nowhere to be found.

She and Jack had run off now and then as youngsters, but for Papa to pay to get home from market, that had never happened.

She lingered by the fence. If she was sick like di Vaun said, that would cost money too. Brooding, she stabled the horses, made her way to the house, and eased the front door open as quietly as possible. Celeste and Terrence's angry voices spilled out from the kitchen.

They never argued, except about money. She'd go upstairs and change, give them time to settle before telling them about Mr. di Vaun and his aut.

Celeste's frayed voice carried into the hall. "You've always worked *with* nature, not against it."

"Why're you arguin'? You've seen the numbers same as me. We need water." His voice sounded like a distant storm, threatening and deep.

Myrta crept up the stairs. The fifth one creaked, and Celeste rushed into the hallway, her eyes bloodshot and her nose red, like she'd been crying. "Myrta, oh thank the heavens, Myrta." She ran up and hugged her. "Where did you get off to? You're safe. Sweetheart." She held her tightly and didn't let go.

In the kitchen doorway, Terrence said, "We need words. That's twice, against my better judgment, you came when you oughtn't. Past time to grow up, Myrta."

"Terrence, she's been out all night. Your lecture needs to wait. Myrta, come to the kitchen. Is Jack all right?"

"Yes." She followed Celeste and sat, looking at the table, trying to think about something besides this moment. The goats, anything. After a minute, she whispered, "I'm sorry, Papa."

He loomed over her. "What got into your head? Runnin' off like that?"

She didn't know how to answer. She needed to say something, be brave. "I . . ."

After a minute he rumbled, "I'm waiting."

Myrta sat very straight. This wasn't the first time Terrence had demanded answers from her. She had plenty of practice. "Mr. di Vaun was following me. He was *chasing* us. He drove his aut right up to me and tried to drag me inside it. He did. It's why we took the horses. I know it sounds crazy when I say it, but he was in his aut, trying to grab me, and . . ." She began choking on the recollection, because as frightening as that had been, the air turning into colors was worse.

Doctors cost money.

Terrence leaned back against the counter and heaved a sigh, looking for all the world like a man who'd long since considered himself done with children and expected his own to look after themselves or maybe him even. Myrta felt she'd disappointed him, this man facing a tiresome chore. Her. Terrence said, "He wasn't chasin' you. He's got no reason to."

Myrta took a breath, preparing to launch into what she'd seen, but before she said anything, Celeste set a bowl of warmed grains in front of her. "Sweetheart, eat. Terrence. That man came to the cheese stand asking after Myrta. He's dangerous. She has nothing to do with irrigation."

Terrence stood, still and expectant. "What happened?" He looked back and forth between them.

Her stomach hurt, and the food was a lump in the back of her throat, stuck there. Myrta put the spoon down and swallowed, but the lump remained.

"It seemed like Mr. di Vaun was after me. Maybe I shouldn't have, but I ran, and Jack stayed with me. I know we could've found you, but the paddock was right there, and I thought I'd just leave and come back. And," she stole a quick glance at Celeste, but her mama was watching Terrence, "I think something's wrong with my—" Try as she might, she was unable to say it. "I'm sorry."

Celeste was looking at her now. "With your what? What's wrong?"

Myrta forced the words out. "I think it's my eyes."

Celeste took a step backward. "Oh. Oh, dear heavens. Terrence, please leave."

He looked at Celeste. She didn't meet his gaze. His face stilled. "Celeste?"

She turned to the stove, took a hand cloth, and began wiping. "I'll see to Myrta. You needn't worry."

A look of suspicion came over him, and he thundered, "What is goin' on with Myrta's eyes?"

Stunned, Myrta stared at him. He had turned red, and Celeste faced him squarely. "Terrence, get a hold of yourself."

"I'll do no such thing," he boomed. "Tell me what's going on!"

Celeste was reddening now too, and her voice no longer shook. "These are *children*. They are the fruit of our love and our labor. All the work we do is for nothing if not to raise them well and safely."

"Why didn't you tell me Myrta has the Elige trait?" Terrence roared.

"Because you would not have allowed her to *live* here! That man tried to *take* her! You weren't there! He's with Renico!"

Myrta shrank into her chair. Celeste had a wild look; her self-discipline bled clean away.

Terrence bellowed, "You waited *years* to tell me my daughter has the trait?"

"*Your* daughter *doesn't* have it!"

Myrta looked at Celeste in astonishment, but Celeste had pulled back, eyes wide and mouth pressed shut, her face the image of shock. Her words hung in the air.

After a long moment, Celeste took a breath and her face smoothed out. She said with resolve, "Your daughter lives in Collimais with Ephraim and Ardelle. Myrta is our niece. She has the Elige trait. When the girls were born, Ardelle believed Myrta would be safer here."

The air in the kitchen lay still, like an oppressive summer afternoon. Terrence and Celeste faced off motionless, while Myrta tried to make sense of what she'd just heard.

A lifetime of memories flooded back. Celeste not speaking of Myrta's spells with anyone. The times Terrence would simply put up a hand to stop her from talking. That hand, with dirt etched into the creases like a field, like a map of his life. And Celeste would say to let him be and she'd keep Myrta apart.

Myrta saw the blanket from Ardelle, knit in the linked hearts pattern. The sweater, in a twined cable pattern. The letters and gifts all smelling of lavender.

Something cracked inside, pain or bewilderment, and through that shock a feeling of unbreachable distance.

She wasn't Terrence's daughter. Her biological father—Uncle Ephraim, holiest heaven—he was from a *city*.

Celeste had raised her under a lie. She stared at the woman, still facing off against Terrence, holding firm against his gale.

An inarticulate howl screamed out of Terrence's mouth, and there was movement again.

"What were we to do?" Celeste cried. "Leave her in the town? She wouldn't have survived five years."

Terrence slammed his fist on the table, its leg cracking from the power of his blow. Myrta jumped out of her chair and backed against the wall.

Celeste said, "Terrence, we never know what next *season* will bring. Keeping Myrie here was the only choice." She leaned into her argument with each proclamation. "It was the right step. We need to *protect* her until circumstances change."

Rage flashed across his face again and again like a tornado ripping through the house.

Celeste stood firm. Myrta stood, trembling.

She'd been raised under a lie.

Terrence stormed out of the kitchen, slamming the front door of the house as he left. Celeste's breathing—the only sound in the kitchen—came rough. After a moment, Celeste sat, the chair shaking as she pulled to the table. "Oh," she said, trembling, "I've messed up."

Myrta shut her eyes. She'd been given away as a baby and raised under a lie. She would have been given away in marriage, but she'd expected that. She couldn't stop shaking.

"Sweetheart?" After a long moment, Celeste whispered, "I've truly made a mess of things." Standing again, she busied herself about the kitchen. "Myrie?"

"I can't," she managed.

Celeste tipped her head. "All right. Go, lie down. I'll take care of the animals."

That evening, after a tense meal, Myrta crawled back into bed, under the blanket from Ardelle. Her eyes stung, and dried tears crusted her lids. She held her mind in its numb place and stared at the dresser across the room, at the dried lavender in a vase. The lavender from Ardelle.

There was a tap on the door. It was Celeste. "Can I come in?"

Myrta pulled her blanket tighter but didn't answer.

Celeste came into the room and sat on the edge of the bed. "I'll leave if you need."

Myrta pulled a pillow to her chest and silent minutes passed. The light outside darkened to deep pink. Myrta held herself as small as she could, a little puddle of nothing, all she'd heard that day and all she'd seen the night before too big to take on at once.

Celeste put a gentle hand on her knee. "Do you remember when you were small I would read to you?"

She did. They'd sit on the porch in the evenings, and Celeste would read to her and Jack. Fantastical stories with bizarre creatures, people seeking adventure, all sorts of tales from a stack of books Celeste had bought years and years ago in Narona.

"There's a true story I never told you. It might be hard to believe."

Myrta squeezed her pillow closer. Shafts of down poked through the casing and pricked her arms. She nodded once.

Celeste's eyes unfocused. She took a deep breath and rubbed her thumb back and forth over a tomato stain on her skirt. "When you and the boys were small, we would visit Ardelle and Ephraim and Odile every year. We'd stay a nice long time. Do you remember those trips?"

Myrta blinked hard and nodded again.

"And we had a little tradition. You and me and Odile and Ardelle, we'd go for a walk every evening away from the boys. Do you remember that too?"

The walks had been the best part. Just her, her cousin Odile, and Auntie Ardelle. And her mama too.

They'd stopped visiting years ago.

"Do you remember," Celeste's voice caught on her words, "that when you were very small, Ardelle would carry *you* on those walks, and I would carry *Odile*, and—" Celeste stopped for a moment. She wiped her eyes. She looked away. She sank a little bit, and then sat up again and continued, "that we would each hug the girl we held so tightly, and cover that girl with kisses, and tell them just how very much we loved them."

Myrta began to cry again.

"Dear child, Ardelle loves you so much. We both do. She's told you—in kisses, and letters, and special gifts, so that you would always have something to look at and remember . . . You must know that keeping you safe comes first."

Celeste sat a little straighter, but her voice was still weak. "Your great-grandpapa had a vision trait. Ardelle and I don't. But you do, and so you've grown up here, far away from anything to do with the combustion industry. Grandpapa said people from Renico, he called them discerners, he said they find people with it. Mr. di Vaun . . . I don't know. He's a very wrong man. I feel I should know him, that I've met him, perhaps when I was young. Oh, Myrta, I should have told you all of this long ago."

Yes.

"Ardelle and Ephraim . . . Ephraim knows the details best. I've ignored this, pretended your ability isn't real, told you to relax and not think about it."

Celeste gave a small, strained laugh. "As if that would make it go away. But Ephraim knows, he knows more about it than any person should. Myrta, I'm so sorry I didn't handle this better. I hope you can find it in your heart to forgive me."

Chapter Twelve

The world thawed, and the oceans came alive. Bacteria and archaea tumbled about.

"Volcanoes, Alphonse! They put carbon back into the air. Isn't it marvelous?"

Alphonse was a bacterium again but no longer a blue-green one. He was a proteobacterium, and he spun about in the water, scavenging for food. "I'm hungry."

Stavo laughed. "You're the trash collector. You are hungry for the waste the other microbes expel. Collecting the trash is a very important part of the story."

Pyruvate was the waste he lived on. Alphonse found a morsel and made a burst of energy. He searched for more; he found a trail; he could not get enough of it. He grew frantic, trying to find the source.

And then he did, he found the archaeon that excreted the pyruvate. Alphonse thrust himself against the archaeal cell. "There's so much inside!"

Ramming again and again, trying to get at the source of it, he finally breached the membrane. "I'm in!" Pyruvate surrounded him, he floated in the beautiful food—the other cell's waste.

"You've done well."

Alphonse ate it in a frenzy, he did not let one molecule escape to the ocean waters. He ate, and grew, and divided, over and over, inside the archaeal cell. He generated more energy than even he could use, and he shared with his host, so it too could thrive.

"The first complex cell. Many times, Grandson, cooperation is the path to success. Remember that."

After working at the inn for the better part of a month, it occurred to Alphonse that the Vonards lost money because he took a room. In fact, Ardelle had turned away travelers only a few days earlier. And if she was losing money, she might be paying him less than she would otherwise.

He went to the back office with a proposition and found Ephraim there.

Shelves cramped the room, stacked with a manic collection of books and papers. Alphonse ran a quick glance along the spines. Historical texts, plant and animal sketchbooks. Chemistry books. Economic forecasts. Surgical manuals. A book on the ancestral modifications—the genetic engineering said to lie at the root of the founders' success colonizing Turaset.

A table with a few city newspapers took up the middle of the room. Against the far wall sat a desk with ledgers, loose receipts, and a bottle of whiskey.

Ephraim was leaning against the desk, engrossed in a textbook.

"Excuse me, sir."

The man read for another moment then looked up.

Alphonse stepped up to the table and considered his words. Direct might be best, that seemed to be how things were done out here. "I'd like permission to sleep in the hay loft."

Ephraim frowned. "The inn's not rustic enough?"

"No, sir, the inn's fine." Better than fine, especially since the questions had dropped off. Life was pleasant here, with a day-to-day rhythm about it. The meals and the chores, the guests and the carriages. Bucolic, all of it. Even Odile had been friendlier, almost congenial.

Ephraim set the book on the desk with an expression somewhere between puzzlement and consternation. "Son, why would you want to sleep with the horses?"

But in truth, sharing space with this family throughout his waking hours—under the same roof, during the work itself—there was still too much of them throughout the day.

He couldn't say that of course. Easier to frame his request as a financial matter, which was true enough. "Mrs. Vonard didn't have a free room a few nights ago, so she took a loss. I thought if you had more reblas coming in—"

"Aha. I begin to infer your intent. Are you asking for a raise?" The corners of Ephraim's eyes crinkled.

"No, sir." Not a raise, just a mutually beneficial arrangement. "It's better if the room's free, and I thought—"

"Do you know what Ardelle would say if you slept in the barn?" The man seemed to be holding back laughter, his mouth pressed shut while his eyes crinkled further.

"Truly, I was thinking about costs. Forget it."

The laughter won out. "Actually, Al, I think I

understand. You strike me as an independent sort and sleeping under a roof with eight or ten other people, well. It's different than a mountaintop, isn't it?"

Yes, that summed it up well.

"Tell you what. Build a bed frame; we'll find a pallet. We won't give you a raise, but we can add a bonus whenever the inn's full."

In the evenings, Alphonse walked through the orchard and up into the hills. After ten or fifteen minutes of hiking, he'd reach a spot overlooking the town and sit on a smooth patch of soft dirt. He'd close his eyes and listen. He'd muse back through his childhood, trying to discern the moments his mother had so fundamentally changed. If he could work through that, find the pieces of her that were still warm, still loving, he might see a way to salvage their relationship.

This evening on his way back, he found Odile on the orchard bench making notes in one of the office manuals. She looked up, smiled briefly, and turned back to her book.

He'd made efforts to be pleasant since their walk, and the space between them was slowly defining itself. "I didn't expect to see you out."

She kept writing. "It's quieter here."

Plum branches heavy with fruit hung around the bench, and a faint smell of spices, cinnamon and cumin, came from Odile. She must've helped with supper. Alphonse said, "I'll leave you alone. Enjoy your evening."

"No, Al, wait." She turned to face him, and her eyes landed briefly on his nose, again, before she looked him in the eye. "Why do you say you're from Masotin?"

"Because I am." They somehow knew he wasn't, which perversely made him dig in deeper. If they knew his family background, Ephraim might pull him into their meetings, which seemed to be some sort of coalition of butchers and bakers opposing combustion. If Ephraim knew who Alphonse's grandfather had been . . . Alphonse laughed out loud at the thought of being drawn into a country squad of rabble rousers. Ridiculous.

Odile looked at him in a puzzled way, but he couldn't help it. He shook his head, still laughing. "Born and raised on the sunny coast of Masotin. Worked a trawler the last three years."

She eyed him warily. "No."

The color of her hair was like honey and her blouse had a grease spot, but she never seemed bothered by stains. She stared past him, down the orchard path toward the yard, then she lifted the manual by its spine and thumped it onto the bench. The book was worn, the front cover ripped and scribbled upon. *Combustion and Mechanation for Continental Advancement.* She looked down at the thing. "We don't need their tools."

The manual was from Renico, headquarters of the combustion industry in Renivia Province. Renico powered both cities in Renivia and oversaw the combustion subsidiaries in the neighboring provinces.

"When you go back to Masotin, tell them we don't need Renico—or Delsico, or Garco, for that matter. Or their manufacturing." Odile's voice took a startling note of fear. "They're changing Collimais. They're changing Turaset."

But her passion made little sense. Foothill towns

weren't part of any province and didn't fall under provincial law. The industry held no sway here. It couldn't make demands, and only sold to foothillers who wanted to buy. "They have no rights in Collimais. It's hard to see how they're affecting you."

"It's not a matter of *rights*. They pollute the air and the water. They change the weather."

"The weather?"

She exhaled loudly. "Why do I try? You don't even smell right. You're not from Masotin."

"I don't *smell* right?"

She didn't respond to that, and he shook his head. This woman was a puzzle all her own, and as much as he might wish to untangle that puzzle, it had to take second seat to his more pressing goals.

She shot him a look of determination. The strength of her gaze and the straight, forceful way she sat, it defined her. "You asked me what people do for work."

"Right. And you said there's plenty of work and people are happy. Happy little town."

"I lied. There's not enough work. So, on top of polluting the planet, Renico knows there aren't enough jobs here, and they recruit us into their factories."

"I've never heard that." If it were true, he should have. He put his right foot up on the edge of the bench and dug his knuckles into his thigh.

"Well, they do. It helps their profits, see, because foothillers," and she was gesturing past the inn, toward Collimais, "work for less than provincial wage."

"Hold on. So, why did you say everyone's happy?"

"I thought you were a handler."

"What's that?"

"You know, a scout. To recruit foothillers." With a look of disgust she lifted the book and threw it to the ground. Its front cover bent under its weight.

The resources of the belt—including people. That would fit Renico's profit-driven philosophy. "Miere," he muttered. "They hire kids out of the foothills."

"Yes. Like I said less than a minute ago. Do you even listen?"

He'd never heard such a thing, but it was possible. The lowest paying jobs, on the assembly lines—it made financial sense. "Do people come back?"

Odile leaned forward onto her knees and stared straight ahead, unfocused. "No. Maybe they make a good life." She looked up at him, her eyes lit again, like a campfire on a chilly mountaintop drawing him in. "We need information. We want access to their records. When you said you were from Masotin, and you've clearly had a decent education, we wanted to know if you knew anything useful about Renico."

He couldn't admit his mother was Ivette Najiwe, one of combustion's top political funders working in Delsina Province. Any hint of his past would be enough. Odile was clever. She'd figure him out. Ask more questions. Pressure him to join them.

He needed to stay cool, pay his bill, and go home to mend whatever was left of his family. A snatch of lullaby flashed through his mind, *and the birds with feathered kisses . . .* One of the songs his mother used to sing. Where had that woman gone? Did any part of her still hold Stavo's values?

"I, no. I don't know anything about Renico."

Odile pursed her lips and looked back to the mountains.

That evening in the hayloft, he lay on the pallet, recalling too many political events at the family home. Disconnected conversation about profit margins and accidents at the plants. The woman who lost a finger from an unguarded blade. The man killed by a falling crate. Alphonse tossed and turned, unable to sleep.

The next morning, two guests breakfasted with the Vonards in the dining room. Alphonse didn't recognize them, but they were very plainly city men.

Ephraim sat at the head of the table, with Odile to his left. She wore the white blouse that gathered at the sleeves, the one that reminded Alphonse of the jasmine blossoms out front. She stared straight ahead with her jaw set, like she had an opinion about whatever they'd been discussing. Ardelle, ashen-faced, sat across from her.

A middle-aged man with a scarred ear sat at the foot of the table next to an anxious-looking man who was possibly no older than Alphonse.

They all looked up. Ephraim said, "Al, good morning. This is Floyd Namoja and Melville di Vaun, from Renico."

From Renico.

Ephraim continued, "Mel's an old friend." He said to the visitors, "Al's helping with repairs."

The older of the two, Melville di Vaun, the one with the scarred ear, acknowledged Alphonse with a curt nod.

Alphonse looked back and forth between Ephraim and the visitors. Renico funded his mother to aid her efforts at shaping Sangal's council. He might actually learn something useful for his own goals if these men connected in any way to his mother. A long shot, but worth his time to listen. He sat to Melville's left.

Ephraim shot him a puzzled glance, and in truth Alphonse rarely ate with the Vonards. He ignored

Ephraim, who, after a moment, turned back to di Vaun. "Where were we?"

"The steads. Our maps are incomplete."

Alphonse kept his eyes down, listening to the inflections in the words, one of the things he'd learned over the years, the layers of meaning in conversation, the text and subtext. His mother had told him often enough to listen to a person's tone, that it said more than the words themselves.

Ephraim's tone was patient. "We're not a province, Mel. You're talking about steaders. Think of their perspective, escaping the reach of government, making independent lives for themselves. If Renico needs oil, look in the eastern ranges."

Di Vaun pushed his cup away. "We will, as soon as they're opened."

Alphonse looked up at that. Did di Vaun know di Les? Ephraim and Odile snapped their attention to him, and flushing, Alphonse stared back at the table.

Di Vaun leaned onto his elbows. "This tradition of claiming any piece of land without reporting usage." He slammed his fist on the table. "Resources in the belt are wasted. We need maps. Frankly, I don't care about the legality here, steaders have a moral obligation to cooperate."

Ephraim's gaze lingered on Alphonse before returning to Melville. "They keep to themselves. Let it go."

"Let what go? Progress?"

"Let the *mapping* go. Whatever your goal is, be it finding new reserves or, perhaps, people."

A barely audible whimper came from Ardelle, and Ephraim patted her wrist as he continued, "Renico has everything it needs on provincial lands. Leave the belt alone. And mind the camsin. You spilled."

"No. This is simple economics. If we don't expand,

we die. You, Ephraim, know as well as anyone that the standard of living has increased throughout Nasoir, tenfold at the very least, because of combustion. Yet you'd wish us back into the dark ages, back to the struggles of our ancestors, with your woodfires and livestock."

It did seem that Ephraim and this guest were speaking at multiple levels. It felt, to Alphonse, very much like the councilors back home, discussing budgets and laws while in truth discussing their own personal interests. Dealing with one another and planning short-and long-term items at the same time. Alphonse leaned forward, watching both men more closely.

Di Vaun continued, "Mobility. Steady supplies of electrical power. Technical advancements in medical care, agriculture. Combustion defines the *root* of opportunity. My work, *our* work," he said, indicating Floyd, "improves lives. You understood this once."

Floyd's gaze darted to Ephraim, then fixed on di Vaun again, and he swallowed. Melville gave the man a glance, and it was the sort of expression that Alphonse's mother might put on if she wanted Alphonse to follow her lead.

He's teaching him.

Di Vaun said, "Not to mention, mapping the belt can help reduce crime."

Ephraim laughed outright. "We don't have a whole lot of that."

"You're naïve. Any city boy yenning for adventure can come out here and run roughshod, take what he wants without any fear of reprisal."

Ephraim raised his eyebrows, leaned back in his chair, and said with heat, "If anyone's running roughshod, it's you. And Renico. Buying council votes, taking resources better left alone. We deal with dust-ups just fine, Mel, and the marshals are available in any rare case where things get out of hand. By the way, they never ask for maps."

The guest pulled his cup back, dumped sugar into it, and stirred noisily, splattering more camsin onto the table. Ardelle passed a napkin down, her lips pressed.

But Ephraim's eyes were still cool despite his tone. These two clearly had history. "In any event. How's Narona? I hope the storms weren't too bad."

Cyclones blew along Nasoir's coast each year, usually in southern Renivia and Garrolin Provinces.

Di Vaun drilled an angry gaze into Ephraim. "Our primary generator took a direct hit. Narona's lower wards flooded. We had no way to pump the water over the seawalls."

Ephraim paled. "Flooded, Autore. Are your parents all right?"

The man's face contorted. "No. My father contracted cholera. There was no power for twelve days. He's dead."

"Mel. Oh, Mel, I'm so sorry."

"My family, your family, a stranger's—what difference does that make? Twenty-eight people died, Ephraim, and if we'd had power, all of them would be alive today." He gestured around at the trinkets in the room. "You set out these ridiculous candles and lanterns as though they add charm, instead of reminding us how backward you are. How backward any of us would be if forced to survive with wood stoves and horses."

The space between Odile's brows creased further. Ardelle sucked in her breath and said, "Excuse me. I'll just check the muffins." She went to the kitchen.

Di Vaun glowered. "We need more oil. It's time for

steaders to recognize their responsibility. We need to map—"

"Let it go." Ephraim's eyes had turned chilly.

Silence hung in the room, and Alphonse recalled again when he was small, when councilors argued policy on the lower floor of the family home. His grandfather had railed at the short-sightedness of opening the ranges to drilling, even then.

Odile looked back and forth between the men at the ends of the table. "Al, come with me to the kitchen."

He hesitated. This conversation was more interesting than Ardelle's muffins.

Odile tipped her head at the door. "Now."

He pushed his chair back and followed her. Once through the door she hissed, "Do you know them?"

"No. Of course not. Do you?"

She glared and didn't answer.

Ardelle's hands were shaking as she removed a tin from the oven. Odile went to her and said in an undertone, "They'll leave soon."

"Thank you, dear," Ardelle whispered back, her breathing ragged. "Oh, Al, hello." She transferred the muffins to a platter. "Would you please take this to the table? I need a private word with Odile. We'll be there in a moment."

Ephraim was stirring honey into his cup, seemingly content. Not content, it was closer to say the man was comfortable, like an old jacket. And despite the arguing, di Vaun seemed comfortable too, although his associate, Floyd Namoja, looked green.

Ephraim said, "It's unfortunate you're only with us for one night. Something of a surprise to see you at all, of course. Business must be good."

Di Vaun inhaled deeply, seemed to want to say

something more about the belt but then perhaps thought the better of it. "Indeed."

"You're finding customers?" Ephraim sipped his camsin, relaxed and focused.

"The benefits are obvious. Sales are robust."

Ephraim smiled, but it didn't reach his eyes. "We look forward to more visits then. What products are moving?"

Di Vaun looked at Ephraim with skepticism. "Kind of you to take an interest. The market's wide open. We'll move fieldauts soon."

Odile and Ardelle returned, and as she sat, Odile said, "Do steaders need field automobiles?"

Ephraim shot her a glance.

Di Vaun fixed his eyes on her, and she gave him her steadiest gaze. She was so cool under pressure! Alphonse expected composure from young women in the city, but not from a country girl. Melville said to her, "Fieldauts will improve a farm's productivity five-fold or more."

"You have real vision. I would never imagine a machine to grow food."

"We'll feed the continent on a bare sliver of land. Fieldauts will wipe out hunger."

Di Vaun seemed to believe it, and the argument held merit.

"They'll also put more carbon into the air." Odile's voice had taken on its own heat. Ephraim placed a hand on her arm.

Di Vaun gave her a hard look then turned to Ardelle. "Your sister, Celeste, makes excellent cheese."

Ardelle's expression remained tight. "How nice. Where did you see her?"

"First market was yesterday. We expect Terrence to buy irrigation."

Ardelle dabbed her forehead with a napkin. "Well. Yields have been low."

"We could gauge his needs better if we knew where to find him."

Any last bit of color drained from Ardelle's face. "Heavens. I'm no good with directions."

Di Vaun studied her for a long moment. She sat still, and he said, "All right, Ephraim, let's put it to you. Where is the de Terr stead?"

"Aha. And so it comes out. There's one and only one location on this hypothetical map of yours that interests you. Mel, let me be clear. We're happy to see you. We'll feed you, and visit, and share every diversion in Collimais. But I'm certain of one thing—if Terrence had truly wanted to look into your products, he would have given you directions to his stead himself. My advice is to ask him when he comes through. During Caravan."

After the guests left, Alphonse went out back to clean the carriage harnesses. Odile was there, pounding a rug with a length of pipe. Her thumping whacks reminded him of Stavo's final speech to the Council.

Mother took me. He kept pounding the podium.

For a split second, time shifted and he was there, in the past. He heard Stavo's voice as clearly as if the man stood next to him. *We hold the future.*

Odile stopped pounding the rug. She panted and wiped damp hair from her face. "What? What do you want?"

"I—nothing. Are you upset?"

"Me?" Odile took another ferocious whack, dust puffing from the rug. "Upset?"

"Never mind." He didn't need her problems. What he needed was to itemize his mother's choices on a timeline, try to see her reasoning, why she'd abandoned her father's ideals.

Odile was talking and pounding. His awareness came back when she imitated di Vaun's voice. "'The benefits are obvious.'" Odile looked at him expectantly. "Al! Everything they do—the resources, polluting—their only goal is money."

Combustion was all this girl thought about. It defined her, like her determination, here in this little inn with its one ridiculously small generator. "You really hate Renico."

Punctuating her words with three ferocious whacks of the pipe, she said, "They. Ruin. Everything." The carpet swung back and forth like a sheet in a storm.

But they didn't. The industry provided jobs, goods, services. None of the cities could run otherwise. People depended on the industry for work. "That's debatable, but you obviously think they do."

She hit the carpet again, this time with her balled-up left fist, grunting, twice, three times. She slugged the carpet and it fell into the dirt; then she swore and kicked it.

He stepped over to clip it back up. "Have you ever visited any of the cities?"

She glared at him and threw the pipe to the ground. "It's not about the *cities*. It's what Renico does to people. To families. They destroy families."

"They what? How?"

Odile opened her mouth but paused. "I'm done with this conversation." She stormed into the inn, and he watched the door slam.

The problems were complex, that much was true, and if passion like hers could ever be channeled onto any of the city councils, what a difference it might make. Democratic ideals. Fair pay and good health. Families, clean air and water. No one of these could be separated from any other without threatening order itself.

The Vonards spoke to resources in ways he'd not considered, ways his mother had never discussed. Maybe she'd never thought about the greater impact of combustion; possibly she'd never thought past her own goals. Whatever his mother was after, Alphonse didn't know. That was the question that nagged the most.

Chapter Thirteen

Celeste refused to say any more to Myrta about her Elige trait, only that they'd travel to Collimais as soon as work was covered on the farm to discuss it with Ephraim and Ardelle. Instead, every morning and night she said that in all the ways that mattered they were still mama and daughter.

Nathan took to calling her Cousin Myrta. Jack was oddly withdrawn.

Two weeks later Celeste told her to pack, and Terrence saw them off before dawn. In the barest morning light, Myrta climbed into the carriage wrapped in her blanket.

Celeste and Terrence stood inches from one another. Terrence's eyes seemed to drink in Celeste's face in one of those unspoken moments they shared. Then he looked at Myrta, his eyes crinkled in worry. "Be safe in town. And Celeste, don't be taxin' the team."

"Terrence, if that man shows up, pay attention." Celeste climbed into the carriage. Terrence patted Rennet, then walked back to the house.

They started down the dirt road. Light filtered through the trees, bathing everything in morning greens and yellows. They'd be riding all day, and that meant a sore bottom. Myrta shifted on the seat cushion and pulled up a leg to sit on.

Once they were out of view of the stead, Celeste patted Myrta's knee. "Terrence should have been angry with me, not you." She said it as if it were something she'd thought about, like one of her math problems, and she'd figured out the right and the wrong of it. "But the anger he felt, it goes both ways. He loses sight of that from time to time. How different we all are. How our expectations of one another don't always fit as they should. We're all so different. In Narona, the years I spent there, I saw how fast everything moved, and I came to see how very different we all are. I met Terrence on a home leave."

Myrta knew the story. There'd been a harvest festival in the Grand Square in Collimais. Ardelle and Celeste had gone after dark, when the dancing had started and lanterns lit the green.

"When I met Terrence, the first thing I noticed was how solid he was. Is. He's as steady as they come. He's grounded."

That was a good word for it.

"He was nothing like the city men at school. Terrence loves nature, all of it, and I fell in love with that. I wanted to be that to him, steady, like nature was to him. But for all the things that nature is, one thing it isn't is fearful." Celeste brought the team up to a trot. "Still, I couldn't tell him about our family trait because it comes with a stigma. You saw how angry he became when he learned about your eyes. When I met him, I thought that if he knew our family carried it, he'd have nothing to do with me."

They clopped along, the wheel nearest Myrta creaking softly on each revolution.

"Nathan didn't have the trait," Celeste said after a few minutes.

"How did you know?"

"Because of Ardelle. She asked Ephraim to examine Nathan. I was never so frightened as I was that day. Here he was, this beautiful baby. I needed to know, but it terrified me. I couldn't tell Terrence, but Ephraim was part of the family now, and he and Ardelle were expecting a baby of their own. He agreed to check Nathan during our winter visit. Ardelle took Terrence outside to plan the orchard."

The suns were higher, and the ruts in the road easier to see. Celeste steered the team around the deeper ones. Myrta pulled her other leg up to sit on for a while, and dewy dampness from the cushion seeped into her trousers.

"I thought if we were lucky, Terrence would never need to know."

On some of those visits to Collimais, Uncle Ephraim would look at her oddly, frowning at her temples. In a way, it was the same look Melville di Vaun had given her at the de Reu stead.

Celeste continued. "I remember the windows in the office were open. Terrence was outside, telling Ardelle to put in pears, but 'Delle said no, just plums. Ephraim and I were inside," she repeated, "and he hated doing the exam, and he hated the instruments too."

Staring straight ahead, Celeste's face remained distant. "I held Nate. Such a big voice. He didn't want to be held, but we forced him still. It wasn't easy. It wasn't easy for any of us. We had to know."

Myrta could never imagine Nathan forced through anything.

"Nate made it through the first part, the eye exam with the bright lights. We thought we'd just keep going. I remember Terrence was outside telling Ardelle how much water plum trees needed."

Celeste seemed completely caught in the past. Her gaze was unfocused, like it had been in the bedroom that night. "The second part of the exam, he sprayed air at Nate's face. To see if there was an instinctive response. Nathan screamed! I thought that meant he had the trait and I screamed too! But Ephraim, he wasn't done, he hated the whole thing, but we needed to know. Ephraim yelled for us to hold still. The window was open!"

Myrta saw it, Uncle Ephraim raising his voice at Celeste. Terrence outside with Ardelle.

"Terrence rushed in, thinking Nathan had been hurt or Ephraim was abusing us. He saw us in the office like that, his son fighting with all his little strength. Ephraim struggling with us, trying to finish the exam. Me screaming."

Myrta had never seen Nathan fighting anything like that, afraid like that, like Celeste was describing.

"The fury on Terrence's face. He punched Ephraim so hard he knocked him out. And Ardelle came in, and she was pregnant, and she always had trouble carrying to term. The exam, all of it, she put it together, and she started crying out of fear for her own unborn babe."

Celeste's eyes had gone wide through the story. Myrta waited, but when it became clear she wasn't picking up the story again, Myrta said, "What happened?"

Celeste's words came out in choking bits and pieces. "Terrence and I—we fought. I, I told him what Ephraim had been doing, and that's how Terrence learned our family . . . has the trait. He felt he'd married a coward, for not telling him, and so, of course . . ." She stopped talking, and her tears streamed freely.

"It wasn't your fault."

"Not telling him was. And not telling him about you—not telling him the reason I went to Collimais to help Ardelle deliver you was because she and I both knew you might have the trait as easily as Odile might, and she was born then too. But how could Terrence not *see* it? You are so very clearly Ephraim's daughter, and . . ." Celeste's voice quavered, as though her strain was more than this, more than the vision trait. Myrta put a hand on her knee and squeezed.

Celeste continued softly, "I've told myself all these years that he *did* know, deep down, he *must* have known you were not his. That in some way he agreed with our decision. But what kind of husband—father—what kind of *farmer*—wouldn't see the stamp of nature in his own child's features? He didn't," she wailed. "He never *questioned* that you were his."

For all of the difficult details of living as a de Terr child, that part rang absolutely true. He'd accepted her, in his way, if not encouraged her as he did the boys, and he always trusted Celeste. "Because he loves you, Mama."

Celeste took a long, shuddering breath. She wiped her eyes, sniffed, and patted Myrta's hand. "Myrta. Remember something for me. Terrence's anger was at my decision. He's not angry with you. Terrence has kept you fed and clothed and safe, and he's done so your entire life. He loves you, Myrta. In his way."

Chapter Fourteen

They stood on a strip of beach, and the world held depth and color, a vibrancy like those occasional dreams from his childhood that had broken through to Alphonse's waking life.

A green clump of stringy ooze washed onto the shore and back.

"Why are we watching slime?"

Even his voice was more resonant. Alphonse inhaled good sea air.

"Four billion years. Ninety percent of Earth history. It took that long for the land to become habitable. The oxygen you made in the ocean— that oxygen created an ozone shield high above us. Now life leaves the sea."

Alphonse shrank and became an algal cell full of chloroplasts and mitochondria, the organelles that drove the biochemistry of his life. He washed in and out with other algae, to the beach and back.

In the ocean he was buoyant and plump, making sweet sugar from carbon dioxide. But when he washed onto land he shriveled. Limp, stranded, and hot, he cried, "I need water!" and waited for another wave to carry him back.

Stavo laughed. "It's another challenge to overcome."

Alphonse was nothing, a speck on the dry shore. "I'm dying!"

The waves swept him out and in again, higher, in a clump with some others. They were so high that the water surely would not reach. Frantic, the algae made a crust out of some of themselves, and the rest huddled underneath, staving off dehydration and collecting what water they could from rain when it fell.

After many generations, some extended themselves into the soil to plumb water from the ground. Others created strong walls to hold upright.

Roots and stems.

"The first land plants are born. Adversity, Alphonse, spurs progress. Remember this."

Ephraim jogged down the steps to the yard. "Al. How's the leg?"

Alphonse stood straight and leaned on the rake with a yawn. He didn't think about his leg at all anymore, although if he ever tackled Tura again, he'd take a partner. "It's fine."

His problem was poor sleep, ever since the visit from Melville di Vaun and Floyd Namoja. Combustion had its fingers everywhere, even here in Collimais, and it ate at him.

"Sometimes those new muscles don't work quite as we hope."

Alphonse's battles with insomnia always came hand-in-hand with tightness in his chest. Like how he'd get after political functions or after his disastrous fall on Tura.

Ephraim pointed at a section of roof tiles. "Ardelle reminded me we have bad shingles. She wants those pulled. Start there on the lower eave and take off the split ones, but let me know if your leg acts up."

"Where will you be?"

Ephraim frowned. "She also wants the plums picked. Every last one. I'll be in the orchard."

Alphonse grabbed a hammer and pulled up to the lower roof section. Some shingles barely hung together at all; they warped outward and fell apart in his hands. Most were intact.

It was a decent job as these things went. It required focus, effort. Given the size of the job, he might get a good night's sleep tonight.

Overhead, the suns rose higher and the roof began to bake. He took off his shirt, tossed it to the ground, and worked through another row.

It was hot, like the beach back home. No, it wasn't like a beach at all; he was on a mountainside. Had he dreamt of mountains last night? He'd barely slept.

Another row. Alphonse jerked alert. This hillside was parched. There'd been too little rain. Shaking himself, he focused through another row. Three bad shingles.

He huddled with the others like him, stranded on the beach, waiting for rain.

Alphonse startled alert again and found himself slipping toward the eave. He caught it and lowered down, then grabbed his shirt and went inside.

Ardelle sat at the kitchen table. She looked up from one of the ledgers. "It's nice to see you, Al. Sometimes I think you forget to eat. Can I make you a sandwich?"

"No, thank you ma'am. I need a little water."

"Are you sleeping? I wish you were in a proper bed."

This she said daily. "Yes, thank you." He finished the water and went back to the roof.

The shingles rattled against each other as he pulled them off, rattled again as they hit the ground. Sweat dripped off his hair and hissed on the roof.

Rattle and hiss. It was too hot on this mountain. He pulled another tile; it slithered away. If the waves reached him, he'd float back to sea. Shingle, rattle, hiss. If he made the river, he'd survive. Alphonse worked toward the valley, back and forth down the switchbacks. He pulled snakes from the ground whether they'd split their skins or not.

Ephraim was helping him down, saying something about electrolyte balance. Alphonse's hair was plastered to his cheek, and patterns of roof shingles decorated his forearm. Ephraim led him to the front room.

He floated in the cool of the room, cold ocean water. He lowered himself onto the sofa and pushed the heel of his hand into his forehead, right between the eyes. Ephraim left for the kitchen, and Odile must have been there because she said something about plums. Ice clinked, and Ephraim said a job started was better than nothing. Then he returned with two tumblers of water and handed one over. "How's the head?"

Alphonse was exhausted, but his head was all right. "Fine."

"Any muscle cramps?"

"No." Condensation rimmed his glass. He held it to his face, closed his eyes, and the heat drained from his skin. Wet, like a river. His head lolled sideways. Cool glass. Beautiful, cool water.

"You look terrible. We'll put you in a guest room."

"No. Thank you." *No.* He rolled his neck.

Ephraim sat in a cushioned armchair on the other side of the low table. "Son. You passed out on the roof. Something's going on with you, and it's more than you needing a bit of solitude. Let's back off the work and put you in a guest room."

"No. I'm fine. Working helps."

"Helps *what*? You're unwell."

Ephraim was waiting for him to say something, but he was simply glad to be back in the sunlit waves.

"At the very least we should get in touch with your family."

"No." The word burst from him, and Alphonse shook his head again, this time in apology for the outburst. He drank more water. Every cell in his body sucked the wetness into itself. His thoughts bobbed. He forced them back into the room.

"Al. What's going on?"

He put the glass on the low table between them, pushed the fingertips of both hands into his forehead, and massaged. Not a word about his past.

After a few moments, Ephraim's chair creaked. He was leaning back now, watching. "Why did you cross the ranges, son?"

The sudden, forceful expulsion of air from his chest surprised even Alphonse. "I'm sorry, sir. I thought we were past this. I'm here to pay my bill."

Ephraim crossed his arms and studied him. "Yes, and you've been quite guarded about everything else. Frankly, you seem to be running from something, and let's be clear, whatever it is potentially puts my family at risk. We've given you meals, a roof, and a paycheck. You're collapsing, and we deserve to know why." Ephraim sat quietly, his eyes fixed on Alphonse. "Have you had enough to drink?"

"I'm fine."

Standing, Ephraim went to the fireplace. He ran his fingers along the mantel and examined the tips. "You know, sometimes talking helps."

The words hung in the air. The man simply didn't need to know.

Ephraim knelt and swept stray ashes from the hearth, then hung the brush. He rearranged the poker from one side of the caddy to the other, then back again. Then he straightened the shovel and checked the mantel for dust again. "I'm waiting."

"I'm not certain for what. May I leave?"

The man turned. "No, you may not. Your debt's not clear, and you collapsed on my roof. You've avoided conversations about your past. And at the risk of repeating myself, you passed out on our *roof*. Something is weighing on you. That much is clear. Are you in trouble with the law?"

Alphonse shook his head again and kneaded the back of his neck.

"Then I really can't imagine why you insist on being so secretive."

There must be some quick way to satisfy the man. Maybe a small concession would be enough. "I'm not from Masotin."

Ephraim took a few moments before responding. "You don't say." He crossed and sat in the chair again. "Young man. I'll ask again. Why did you cross the mountains?"

"Look, why would anyone? There's no mystery. I needed time away."

Ephraim leaned forward, his gaze chilling Alphonse. "You've had time away. But you're in worse shape now than when you arrived. It feels to me as though something has caught up with you." He picked up his glass of water and swirled it idly. "Family?"

Alphonse startled. "Why do you say that?"

Leaning back, the man smiled. "You're a young man. You left home. It's a good bet your family figures into this."

Alphonse was at the room's back door, as though he'd been swept there, without any awareness of standing or walking.

Focus.

Was it exhaustion confusing his thoughts? Alphonse held the jamb, blood surging in his ears, weakness replaced by growing annoyance at this man who pulled at him with aid and then adversity, between a welcome paycheck and a fraught sense of imbalance. Any misstep might reveal his background.

Odile was down the hall, banging on something in the kitchen, like this man's questions, hammering, hammering. His thoughts wavered again, and he was stranded high on the beach with the others.

Ephraim said calmly, "We can sever the job contract."

He'd be cleaning bedpans at the hospital. Bedpans! Alphonse turned in a fit to face Ephraim. His aggravation overwhelmed him. He hefted the end table next to the sofa and made to hurl it across the room, but Ephraim was grabbing the other side.

"Settle down!" Ephraim wrestled it out of Alphonse's grip.

What the fierno's wrong with me?

Alphonse stared at Ephraim, his rage subsiding like a wave back to sea. He worked back through the conversation, tried to find where he'd lost the thread.

Young men *did* leave home, all the time. There need be no mystery here, and the more he thought about it, the truer it felt. Ephraim was trying to understand Alphonse, and to be so guarded held too much of Ivette in it and not enough of Stavo. "I'm sorry, Mr. Vonard. I did leave home. Yeah, I wanted some time away, that's all. I'm not in trouble with the law. You're right, it's family. It's my mother. She comes on strong."

"That's unusual for an educator," Ephraim said quietly.

Alphonse sank to the sofa. If Stavo were here, he'd simply come out with it. "She's . . . she's not an educator. She's a funder."

Ephraim's eyes were as sharp as a winter chill. "Politicians?"

He didn't answer.

Ephraim's voice grew distant and unthreatening. "Where did you grow up?"

Alphonse heaved a mighty sigh. "Look. Why don't you tell me *your* story? I haven't needled you—not once. Not about your history, not about the guests that come through or the meetings you hold."

He picked up a book from the low table, another manual from Renico, and flipped to a random page. "Look at this. '*Infiltrate the refinery.*' Are you out of your mind? Sir? Who the fierno are *you* to badger me like this?"

Ephraim stood there, frozen and staring. Alphonse didn't care—this man couldn't even keep up his wife's inn without help.

Then Ephraim relaxed. "Oh, dear Autore. You're right. You're absolutely right. You've been nothing but courteous, despite your secretive way. You're right, Al. It never occurred to me to tell you about myself, as a sort of, let's say a transactional arrangement . . ." Ephraim looked straight up to the ceiling and laughed. "I'm getting old."

His laughter settled, and he picked up his glass, swished it back and forth. Remnants of ice chirped, and he drained the last bit of water. "You could have fallen off the roof today, son. Could've been seriously hurt. None of us want that."

Ephraim rubbed at his palm and said absent-mindedly, "A machine can't ever be killed." Then to Alphonse, "I believed in combustion when I was young. Because machines can improve lives, and they can't be killed."

That was too simplistic. Mechanation relied on mining archaic carbon. There was lung rot among the miners, explosions on the gas lines, not to mention the accidents in the factories. There were too many risks. "Combustion isn't safe either."

"That's right, Al. That's right. Still, when I was young, I thought there was no question. Oil and gas, mechanation. On balance these seemed better."

The moment between them felt like an open vista spreading out in Alphonse's mind, fold after fold, peak after peak of life here—everything he'd seen since he'd arrived coming into focus. Odile reading the manual in the orchard. Ephraim's friendliness toward di Vaun. The books, the internal documents for the industry lining the office shelves.

With complete certainty, Alphonse said, "You worked for Renico."

Ephraim's face fell. "It's no secret. I developed . . . certain protocols." His voice trailed softer. "I was young. I operated under a framework, a set of ideas, and I trusted that all of us shared those ideas. I trusted we all kept the public's well-being front and center."

He walked to the window and faced outward. "Yes. I worked for Renico. I *trusted* Renico. The first time that trust, that *public* trust, was broken I made excuses. For my friends, for my mentor. The second and third times I made more excuses." Ephraim tapped his finger against the glass in a steady tempo. "After a while, I found I had a habit of excusing others while I held to the notion that we worked for something pure and good."

Pure and good. The industry's goal had never been that. They made city life possible, but their goal was profit. Even Odile saw it. Ephraim must have known the business end.

"Al, I need this to be quite clear. I wrote protocols to improve public health and safety. I brought these to my superiors and was told . . . was told they'd be considered. But they weren't. I revised and improved and modified and redrafted the proposals, always to improve public health. To improve the industry. My *part* in the industry. I spent years—" his voice caught. "Years. I finally gave my supervisor an ultimatum. I said our treatment of people needed to change, or I'd leave. It was the only bargaining chip I had! I was . . ." his voice grew faint, and Alphonse barely heard it under the blood still pulsing in his own ears, "I was very good at my job."

Even in the cool of the room, Ephraim's shirt clung to his back, a moist spot growing in the middle. A shudder passed through the man's frame. He kept tapping the window like a drumbeat.

"What did your supervisor say?"

Ephraim whipped his head around and belted, "He said our *only* goal was to expand operations." Ephraim pushed his hand against his face and sank down onto the sill. "And every action fit *that* framework perfectly. I left."

The anguish on the man's face was plain, a page of his life laid out for Alphonse to see.

"Al," Ephraim said quietly, "where exactly are you from?"

Alphonse exhaled heavily, the weight of Ephraim's confession pulling him to answer. He could still refuse. He'd lose the job, wash a few bedpans, pay off his bill that way. But he planned to return to Sangal anyway, set things right with his mother, and there wasn't much Ephraim could do that would change any of that.

"I'm from Sangal." His chest relaxed.

Ephraim looked up. "Your mother's a funder in Sangal?" The man's expression lit with realization. He stood and crossed back to the chair. "There are only three women who raise political funds in any serious way in Sangal. One never married."

Miere. Ephraim was right.

"One is the dearest soul a person could hope to meet."

I made a mistake.

"And the third—your name is Najiwe."

Autore. He's fast.

"You . . . Al, Autore. You come from a long line of influence." Shaking his head, Ephraim began to pace. "Good heavens. I had the grandson of Gustavo di Gust fixing our roof."

"Look, I had to get away from all that."

"Stavo di Gust's grandson almost fell off my roof and died," Ephraim said, again to himself.

"I didn't fall." Alphonse dug his knuckles into his leg.

"I hired Councilor di Gust's grandson and paid him below minimum wage."

No, the foothills didn't have a minimum wage, and

Ephraim knew that. The roaring in Alphonse's ears grew louder. It was too late to take the admission back.

"And the reason he didn't say anything, is because he didn't need to know the wage."

Panicking, and at some level aware of the irrelevance of his words, he said, "Collimais doesn't fall under provincial law." It was a meaningless statement, noise, nothing. He'd just laid his entire history out for this man. His chest seized.

"This changes everything. Your mother moves money for the industry. She supported di Vern. She's lined up candidates for the courts."

"Drop it," Alphonse managed, now pounding his fist onto his thigh. He was standing. "She's not someone you'd want to work with. Everything... her deceit..." he pulled in a breath, a whisper of air.

"I *wouldn't* work with her." A glint lit Ephraim's eyes. "You left something very powerful back in Sangal. If you're running from Ivette Najiwe, if you oppose her goals, then you certainly have a place here."

Alphonse straightened to his full height. "Don't look at me like that. *Drop* it."

"You have leverage with her." Then Ephraim smacked his forehead. "You have leverage with Councilor di Vern. We can craft your words, tell you what to say. You can shift his votes!"

Alphonse's chest seized again. "No. I won't go back. I'm not ready. No."

"Why in heavens' name *not*?" the older man cried.

Alphonse gripped the arm of the sofa with one hand. He dug into his thigh with the other and gulped for air. "I can't... I refuse." *Autore.* "No!" He fell to his knees and his hands hit the floor. He was gasping, couldn't get air. What had he done? Why had he thought he could share with this man? This old man with ideas of revolution? His body was near convulsing. He couldn't get air.

Ephraim's hands were on him, and he was murmuring, "Autore, what's wrong with me. Forgive me, son."

Alphonse panted, "What matters, the only thing that matters, is restoring the Council." Somehow through the torture of saying it out loud, he added in a whisper, "And I'd give anything to have Mother see it that way too."

The breath that came from Ephraim was long and slow. "Oh, dear boy. I see." He helped Alphonse to stand. "Son. You need rest. But I promise you, I see what you're saying, and if you're looking for some way to make things better, I promise you we share a vision."

A vision? No. In this moment he felt only despair.

Chapter Fifteen

The kitchen light shone warm and inviting through the back window. Myrta arched her back and sighed in relief, done at last with bumps and jostles and bounces and ruts and rocks; done with the limp cushion that had done nothing to protect her rear side. Celeste asked her to wait with the horses. Her *mama* asked her to do that. The only mama she'd ever known.

Truth be told, Myrta was nervous more than anything.

A moment later, Ardelle ran out. Her aunt, or her mama. She hadn't made sense of it yet.

Ardelle grabbed her and hugged. "Sweet, sweet Myrta. I'm so sorry."

She didn't hug back. She was in a closed-off place and it didn't seem to matter, because Ardelle had enough squeeze for both of them.

"I'm . . . hello, Aunt Ardelle."

"Let's get you inside. No, don't worry about the horses. Ephraim will see to them."

In the kitchen, a cobbler steamed on the counter. Her uncle, or her papa, was speaking to Celeste. He stopped midsentence and met her eyes. His were moist. "Sweetheart. It's very, very good to see you."

"Hello."

"She's overwhelmed," Ardelle said quietly.

"Of course."

Ardelle hovered about. "Would you like something

to eat? A glass of water? Anything, what can I get you?"

"I'm okay." The dessert on the counter smelled like plum. It was probably a plum cobbler.

"Myrta and I have had a long day, and all of it in the carriage. We're tired."

Ardelle and Ephraim kept looking back and forth between them, and the way Ardelle fluttered about, like she wanted to hug Myrta again, touch her, make sure she was real, that part at least made sense. They both looked older than Myrta remembered, their faces more lined, their eyes pulling down, the skin on their necks loose. Like Celeste and Terrence. In her memory they were younger.

It was mostly Ephraim who took her attention though, because he was crying, without making a sound; his tears simply falling. He stood there, stock still. But now he took her hand, and his was warm and strong. The way he held hers was like a hug, a kind one, one that refused to impose upon her.

She squeezed.

In a troubled voice, he said to Celeste, "We should discuss—"

"Tomorrow."

He exhaled softly and nodded. "Of course."

Myrta woke to the sound of laughter from downstairs and stretched, creaking her muscles into limberness. She held the moment of newly-waken clarity, the moment of welcoming the morning light before the day's work settled into view.

The same lace curtains from childhood hung in the window. The walls had once been white and now were blue, and they blended into the sky outside, where the mountains sat. Bigger than she remembered, and without a single field or silo in sight.

She dressed and found the others downstairs in the office. "Good morning."

"Good morning, sweetheart." Ardelle poured her a glass of juice.

Odile was sitting next to Celeste. Their cheekbones were the same, and their hair. Myrta stared. Odile was in the wrong family too. She wasn't laughing.

"Hello, Myrta."

Maybe she should apologize. She felt she'd ought, because none of this was right, but before she could, Odile turned and started talking with Celeste again.

Ephraim came in and shut the door. "Al's cleaning the stable. That'll keep him busy for a while. Myrta, Celeste told us about market, and Mel's aut, and that you saw the air in color."

Odile and Celeste looked over. Everyone was staring at her, and no one was speaking. She hadn't expected this. She thought they'd have breakfast. "No. I imagined that."

"You didn't. You absolutely did not. You saw colors in the air. Each of those is a different chemical."

All eight eyes were planted squarely on her. She sat suddenly, realizing that she hadn't had supper yesterday either.

"Your ability to see gases is a genetic trait. It's been written into our DNA since before Turaset's founding."

Myrta was hungry. She tipped her head down, where four parallel grooves were gouged into the surface of the table like little trenches, filled with brown gunk. She wrinkled her nose.

Ephraim was still talking. "Ardelle and Celeste's

grandfather had the trait. He could measure gas concentrations by sight."

She ran her finger back and forth over the grooves. Someone should clean this table. It was disgusting.

Ephraim kept talking and talking, and with a sinking feeling, she stared at her lap and wondered if the horses might like a visit.

"Nitrogen, oxygen, he could measure those of course, and others too, argon, nitrous oxide, carbon dioxide, all of them."

She folded her hands and studied her left thumb. Her nails needed filing.

"Transition metals, inversion layers—"

"Ephraim," Celeste said at last, quietly. "You might try a different approach."

The room grew still, and after a moment, Myrta risked a glance. Ardelle was resting her forehead on the back of her hand and had closed her eyes. Celeste pulled out a handkerchief and passed it over. "Delle . . ."

Ardelle took it, sniffled into it, and looked out the window. "I wish . . ."

Odile said stiffly, "You're very calm, Celeste."

"We had no choice. The only way to keep you both safe was to exchange you."

"You had a choice! At least Ardelle sees it. Excuse me." Odile stood and crossed the room, stopping in front of Myrta. "Whatever you want to know about what they did, you need to demand it from them." She left.

Myrta looked up at Ardelle, who had blanched. A moment later the back door of the inn slammed, and outside, Odile crossed to the stable. Celeste, too, followed her with her eyes.

Odile had one thing right—Ardelle and Ephraim

had been asking questions instead of the other way around. Myrta said, "I don't know anything about what's happening, and you do. All of you do. You're staring at me like I was born wrong. What is this thing I have?"

Celeste came and sat next to her, and Ephraim closed the door again. His gaze fell on the desk, on one of the drawers.

"The last thing you need right now is a drink."

Surprised, Myrta looked at Celeste. She didn't remember Ephraim as a drinker, but apparently Celeste did.

He nodded and walked to the window, facing away. "Let's start at the other end. We sent you to the belt to keep you safe, and Celeste is right—we had no good alternative."

Ardelle took a shuddering breath. Myrta reached over and took her aunt's free hand in her own. Ardelle looked at her with hollow eyes. "I'm so sorry."

"The Elige trait, it's natural." Ephraim rested his hand flat against the pane. "And no one has it in the cities. For years now, it's not there at all; it's been culled out of the population. There are still plenty of cases out here."

Alarmed, she said, "Do they want to 'cull' me?"

He turned back. "First things first. We sent you to the stead. We knew you'd have normal vision for years. Celeste suggested the exercises. What was it Celeste, turkeys? In little pens, to stay weak?"

Celeste reached across the table to add her own hand to the other women's. "Does it make the slightest difference where the idea came from? Look at your daughter. Look at your wife."

He did, and his face froze. He blinked, went to the desk, and opened the top drawer.

Fraught, Ardelle said, "Don't start on the whis-key."

At the same time Celeste said, "It's not even mid-day."

Jamming his hands into his pockets, he began to rock back and forth on his feet. "Your ability is a gift."

Myrta looked away. The air was too still; the room too much a receipts-and-books kind of place. Nothing about this moment felt like a gift.

"We expected your vision to change when you were ten, maybe eleven. It didn't, and we thought those exercises had kept everything dormant. We hoped your secondary tissues wouldn't develop at all."

"To protect you," Ardelle whispered, her face red and puffy. "To protect her," she insisted to Ephraim.

By sending her to a farm and not telling her about her eyes or her parentage? That wasn't protection. She'd been isolated and living with the wrong family.

Ardelle's voice broke. "If we'd had the courage to tell you, you would have known before the discerners found you."

Myrta pulled her hands back, staring at this group of people who by their own words knew the danger they'd put her in. "I don't understand. Why is the belt safe? Why did Odile grow up here? What exactly do you mean by *culling*?"

"Mechanation. The combustion industry—"

"I have nothing to do with that!"

The lines in his face deepened. "Just give me a min-ute. When you were born, these devices weren't popu-lar out here. Renico—well, that's how we bought the generator. There was nothing in the belt, no mechana-tion at all. It's too far out, the roads too poor."

Celeste sounded closer to terrified than Myrta had ever heard before. "The crops will fail without irrigation, Myrta. The stead—Terrence's whole life is that stead. Our *family's* life is that stead. We can't live without water. We need the irrigation to survive."

Ephraim sat. "We wanted your trait dormant. But by keeping it weak, we've created an obstacle."

The anxiety in his voice came close to matching Celeste's. Myrta stared at him, then Ardelle, then Celeste. All of their faces were drawn in pain, more pain than she'd imagined any of them could feel, as though they were the weak ones.

He was still speaking. "Your eyesight, when used properly, can protect you. You could be strong enough, with your trait, to follow the movement of anything you choose from a great distance. But, Renico knows about you now, and you don't know anything about the danger they pose. You grew up in the belt! We need to reverse everything, absolutely everything, we've done."

"I must be safe here."

Glancing at the desk drawer he muttered, "They think you're on the stead."

Celeste stood and went to the window, made to pull the curtain, but stopped and stared. In the yard, Odile was speaking with a tall man. They were laughing, easy, having a good time.

Myrta inhaled the dead air of old books and dirty rug and thought she'd rather be outside, with them. "Odile knew all about this." The way her cousin was behaving—so comfortable out there—the only explanation was that Odile had known.

"Yes. She sorted through it." Celeste closed the curtains and said to Ephraim, "You have four months until Caravan."

He leaned forward onto the table and looked intently at Myrta. "The discerners will try to find Terrence's stead. You're safe here for the time being. But, they'll sweep the foothills when Caravan arrives. Our decision has stunted you—"

"To keep her safe," Ardelle cried. "To keep you safe. Oh sweetheart, what have we done?"

"Done is done."

Ephraim said more forcefully, "Myrta, you must learn to use your trait, and more than that, to fully control it."

Celeste said, "Four months."

After supper, Celeste said she and Odile needed to discuss plans for Odile to return to the farm. Ephraim, Ardelle, and Myrta went down the hall to the back office. Myrta fiddled with a button on her blouse and braced herself. "Odile said I can see air pollution. Is that true?"

Ephraim was closing the door and stopped mid-pull. "Yes."

"She said that's why Mr. di Vaun's so interested in me. Why he keeps saying I need to go with him. Is that true too?"

Ephraim closed the door, crossed to the desk, and pulled a bottle of whiskey out. He poured a shot of liquor into a glass, sat, and drank it in one smooth action.

"Is she right?"

"Yes, she's right."

Ardelle stood and took the shot glass.

"Ardelle . . ."

"Ephraim. I'm taking this to the kitchen." She opened the door and Odile's voice drifted in. "No. Not ever. I don't belong on the stead, and I won't *ever* go." Ardelle pulled the door shut behind herself.

Ephraim said, "Sweetheart. We've spent seventeen years pretending your trait doesn't exist."

"I know."

He looked down. "All right. Yes, Myrta, it's the pollution. Not from his point of view of course; Mel thinks he's doing a great service, moving us as quickly as possible to a more advanced society." Ephraim paused and said more quietly, "And there was a time when I shared that thinking, even admired his dedication to what I saw as a noble cause."

"You *admired* him?"

Ephraim's face grew contemplative. "He and I were friends once. And think, if Mel could be turned from the path he's on, you'd be safer. He'd be more whole. Good all around. And not every lost cause is lost forever, after all."

She knew so little of Ephraim, this man who'd fathered her, only that he was from Narona. When they used to visit, he'd stare at her in a strange way. She didn't know much else about him.

He sighed. "But yes, for our purposes, it's best to think of his goals in terms of your ability. You can see air as discrete components, gases. Nitrogen and so on. Burning archaic fuel, like coal and oil, puts carbon dioxide into the air, which you can see, and it harms Turaset. Renico is cycling all of the buried carbon in the ground into the air, and it's killing our world. Quite simply, your ability to see that carbon creates a financial inconvenience for them."

Ardelle came back, sat next to Ephraim, and took his hand.

"Combustion is becoming so central to our lives that soon we'll depend completely upon it. To Renico, this is a waiting game. They want us dependent on them, and your ability to see carbon gases shifts the balance a bit."

That blue streak from the aut was seared into her memory, and Ephraim's words locked her comprehension into place. "So, the air. The changes to it, that's why they care about me."

"Yes."

"Even though I have nothing to do with them. What happens if they catch me?"

Ephraim clenched his jaw and looked around the room, settling his gaze on a cabinet mounted above the desk.

"It's been a long day," Ardelle said. "Sweetheart, you just got here."

"What would they do?" Myrta insisted, leaning into the question like Odile had said to do.

Ephraim shook his head. "We need to focus on the matter at hand, which is you learning your ability and undoing seventeen—"

"He tried to *pull me into his aut*. Tell me what he'd do."

Ephraim reddened. "I don't *know* what he'd do. It's Autore's own truth, Myrta. It could be anything. What I know is Renico exists to turn profit. Their protocols change to suit that need. I don't know what he'd do, only that it would be for Renico's ends, not yours." He pushed away from the table, stood, and paced.

"You know something. You're not telling me anything."

He wheeled around and said with heat, "At one time, yes, I did know a thing or two. And telling you how discerners operated, years ago? Using protocols that likely aren't even in place today? That would do far more harm than good. Ardelle's right. We're done for the day."

Chapter Sixteen

"Alphonse." The voice flickered in his awareness like a moth fluttering about. "Grandson."

He opened his eyes. He lay in a bed of ferns, mosses, and liverworts.

Stavo said, "These little ones, they were first, but look at all that's come along."

Yellow light dappled down. Trees towered upward, bark-covered columns thrusting into the sunlight.

Alphonse stood. He rested his hands on a tree fifteen feet across. The trunk was rough against his palms, the bark red and hard and good, and he could feel the water surging through the capillaries within to the leafy boughs above.

The only sounds in this forestland were the wind through the branches and distant thunder.

They walked. The plants went on, and on, and on.

"When is this?"

"Three hundred million years in the past. It is the age of lignin, the age of carbon, the age of plants."

The trees and ferns took the carbon from the air into themselves. From that they made their

bodies—leaves, branches, trunks, and roots.
Enormous insects flew overhead, and in nearby
swamps, frogs and salamanders thrived.

"Why am I seeing this?"

"These trees that cover the land become the
fuel our cities rely upon."

"The cities? There are no cities. There are
only giant bugs and frogs."

Stavo laughed. "Yes. But coal and oil
require planetary time scales in order to form.
It's crucial to understand this time scale."

Alphonse strode up the trail past the orchard. Ever since his family name had come out, the Vonards spoke of nothing but the ways Alphonse might move their foothill agenda in Sangal. They offered different ideas every day. Return home and give their arguments to di Les or to di Vern. Bring his mother *here*, for some bizarre intervention they thought would move her. Run for his own council seat—which he privately thought he might do someday, but on his schedule, not theirs.

Ardelle sometimes left the room when the topic of combustion came up. Odile gave impassioned commentary on obscure points of the industry's practices. That morning she'd gone on about the discharge of refinery waste and how pollutants entered the water supply. Lately, she always seemed to have a book in her hands.

The emotional state of the whole family had leapt into a register he'd not seen before, and living there now felt like walking a tightwire. This was the price of revealing his background. He kept as far from the Vonards as possible.

He reached the overlook, planted his feet wide, and looked west to the belt fading into the distance. Green forested hills dotted with steads. Hardly any people out there at all. The concept of neighbors probably didn't even exist.

Taking that council seat—it wouldn't have made any difference and certainly not in the short term. He would've been under di Les's thumb, and under his mother's too. What was it she was truly after? It couldn't be money—she had plenty. At least, now she did. Thinking back, though, she hadn't always. She'd come to it through her own determination during those early years, raising him alone. That was the first piece of the puzzle—her father dying and Marco leaving. It was the anchor for Alphonse to work from, to figure out her goal.

An endless expanse of trees lay in front of him. *Bark-covered columns, thrusting toward the sun* . . . The thought flickered in and out of his mind as from a dream. With the light shifting on the landscape, he thought that out there he might find the peace to work through her puzzle. The peace that eluded him here, with the Vonards.

Calmer, Alphonse went back down the trail, trying to recall the first change she'd effected on the Council. She'd started with industry fundraisers. Formed an alliance of sorts with di Les and another councilor named di Gof.

He rounded the bend at the bottom of the trail. Thinking back, she'd been interested in the makeup of the Council even before her father had died.

Odile was in the orchard with another manual. She'd braided her hair, pulled it back, and wrapped it in some elaborate style. It made her look older. She glanced up and smiled. "You know, Al, I was thinking. You've never told us about your friends."

Odile really was beautiful. Strong-willed like his mother, but in a way that focused on issues, not people.

She patted the bench. "I'd love to know all about them."

But this felt like flirting. Disingenuous. Something in her tone sounded duplicitous, or maybe it was the way she looked at him with a gauging sort of assessment, like she wanted an entry point into his past. Under other circumstances, spending time with a passionate young woman like Odile, one who cared about the same things he cared about, would be welcome. But after the incident with Ephraim, revealing any more about his past was out of the question. "Why?"

She smiled, almost coquettishly, and stood and came close to him. Inches from him. And her gaze lay on his face, her eyes to his. Her very presence seemed to still the breeze around them.

Then, as though she too was bothered by her behavior, the smile fell from her face. She crossed her arms, and it was just her again, standing there. Odile, her voice flat and driven. Normal. "Ephraim thinks you have connections who can help us, since you won't. He told me to ask."

There it was, their agenda. At least she'd been straight about it. "Autore, no. I don't have any friends." He turned and started down the path.

"Well it's clear why," she called out. "You only think about yourself."

He pivoted.

"Al, look at your mother. Who she is. Your contacts. You have an opportunity, but you're pretending to be a nobody. Look at everything you're throwing away."

"You don't know the first thing about it."

"I bet I do. And if I could be in Sangal, I can tell you this much—I would be. If I could get at Renico's records, I would. If I was *you*, I'd be *there*, doing anything I could to keep Turaset from becoming any more damaged than it is already."

Unbelievable. He didn't know what was worse, her thinking she had any kind of chance to change anything about the industry or the idea that she cared more about the whole mess than he did. "Look, I'm pretty sure if we put our heads together we can get you to the big city. Let's see. You could go with the handlers. I could hire you an aut. You could *walk*. Fierno, I'll draw you the map."

She made a wordless sound of frustration and strode up to him. "You're connected! I'm *nobody*, with nothing, in a nowhere town. If you go back, you can change things, make it so that everything, the records, *something* gets released!"

"You're delusional. You don't know the first thing about cities, let alone the combustion industry."

She was inches away, her hands balling up, undercurrents of something on her voice. "I know all of it. Everything they do; everything they hide."

He scoffed. "You know? You know what's in their vaults? At your ripe old age? And you know this how, because you grew up here?"

Her knee landed in the middle of his thigh before he saw it coming, setting off a massive contraction in his leg. He grabbed at it. "Odile!"

"It doesn't matter how I know. You don't even listen. People need your help. Turaset needs it!"

He pushed at his thigh. She'd gotten him right

where the muscle connected to tendon, and his leg was convulsing like it hadn't done in weeks. "Autore, Odile, this is a new muscle."

"Renico's killing the planet. And you could stop it, Mr. *Najiwe*."

"Oh for . . . they're not killing the planet."

Her fist landed in his stomach and he doubled over groaning, then stumbled back against a tree. He grabbed a limb. "What the fierno!"

Her right fist landed hard on his left eye, pushing his head back into a branch. He fell down against the trunk. "Cut it out!"

If he'd been seated on the Council, they'd have detained her already. But she didn't look concerned— why should she? People handled their own problems out here.

"You could make a difference. But go ahead, pretend it can't be done. Pretend you don't even exist." She made another disgusted noise and left.

The next morning, Ephraim came out to the barn with a carafe, a basket of muffins, and some tools. He called up the ladder, "I've got breakfast for you."

Alphonse hadn't shared meals with the family in over a week. The inn had been empty; the only guests a pair of women, one older and one younger, who'd arrived a few days earlier. The older one had a strength to her face, rather like Odile. The younger one was small. Easy to forget.

He rubbed his face and winced at the pain throbbing out from his left eye. Odile had really connected with that punch.

"There're some bad planks down here by the doors.

Ardelle wants those replaced. If you need anything, I'll be in the office." He turned to head back, but added in a hopeful voice, "If you change your mind about helping us out, you can find me there."

"My answer hasn't changed." Alphonse lay back on the pallet.

After a while, he climbed down and ate. The suns shone into the yard, light catching on motes. The smell of horses hung in the air, and an aut drove past. Under other circumstances, living here would be perfect.

Some of the boards framing the door crumbled as he pulled, others were impossible. He was wrenching at a stubborn piece when Odile came out for the basket.

"It's by the ladder."

She picked it up and stopped in the doorway. She leaned against the frame and stared at his eye. It had to be bruising. First time he'd ever been socked by a girl.

"I'm sorry."

He studied her. She *was* sorry. The hint of a crease between her eyebrows, the way she looked away now. She regretted hitting him.

Her skin was almost glowing, the morning suns angling off her forearm and cheek. He pushed to stand. "For what?"

"Insisting you see things my way. You were right."

"Excuse me?" He grabbed the carafe, which she'd missed, and set it in the basket.

"The truth is, I don't know what I'd do in your place."

There was a smell of baking about her, like she'd been making plum jam again, or helping with the muffins. A faint scent of sweetness and spice from her hands. He wanted this, this life. "Odile, look. I appreciate the gesture, but it isn't necessary."

"I know. I'm sorry."

She stood there, weaving a piece of cane back into the basket, focusing on it. Everything had an order with her, a place it belonged. Not to him; he didn't see it that way. Things didn't have a single place to be. But for Odile? Nothing bothered her so much as things out of place.

That was it, he realized in a flash, what so compelled him about her, her certainty about where things belonged. The cane in that basket. Him in Sangal. Archaic carbon in the ground. Herself, maybe she felt she belonged somewhere too. The way she looked about the inn, past it, there was a restlessness to her gaze.

Her hair had fallen over her shoulder, and he felt like pushing it back, not because she seemed annoyed, but because on any normal day she would have done so herself.

She said in a rush, "I've made a decision. I'm going with the handlers to work at Renico."

"What? You can't."

"Of course I can. You even offered to hire me an aut. I think going with the handlers makes more sense, because they'll take me for free."

It took a moment to get his mind around the teasing tone in her voice. She was making a joke, like she thought it was funny that she'd work in the plants where a woman had lost her eyesight in a chemical spill. Eduardo had stories every time Alphonse saw him.

"Odile, no. The danger in the factories—that's truly the one thing you and I agree on."

"I'll be careful," she said wryly.

"People are hurt all the time. You can't go. Do your parents know?" They'd never allow it, especially

Ardelle, who barely allowed Alphonse to sleep in the hayloft.

Odile looked away, not meeting his eyes. She hesitated. "Yes. Everyone knows, even the neighbors know. You're the *last* person to know."

He tried to catch her eyes, but she refused to look at him. "I don't believe you. You were the one who said foothillers don't have a chance, that the industry's too powerful. They'll put you on a factory line, and you won't change a thing."

"Wow. A sensible reply. Congratulations."

He grabbed her by the shoulders, wanted to shake her. She looked at him with alarm, and he pulled back. What, was he going to slug *her* now? "This isn't a joke. They'll say you have an eight-hour shift and make you work a double, back to back. Your partner gets the flu but can't call in sick. The whole line goes down, productivity's off, and they dock your pay. Nothing's reported. Don't do this."

Odile stared at him for a moment, which turned into two, then three. A whisper of morning breeze, like a kiss, stirred the dust around their feet.

"How do you know all that?"

She was so exasperating, confrontational one minute and vulnerable the next. He took a long look around the barn, the horses swishing their tails, flies buzzing near the manure. The inn and the gravel lane that needed smoothing again.

The highlights in her hair.

"I have a friend," he admitted.

"You? You have a friend. Yesterday you didn't, but now suddenly you do."

"That's right. Do you want to know where we met? How often we see each other? Whether we send letters back and forth?"

"No, of course not." She softened, held his eyes with her own, held him steady, like an anchored line. "Don't worry about me, Al. I'm serious, don't. I know how the handlers place people."

"I don't believe that for one minute."

A small smile played on her lips. "What do you think those meetings are all about, that Ephraim holds in the office? Al, we have contacts inside Renico. I'm going to be fine."

She took the basket to the inn. He watched her go, his chest growing tight.

Chapter Seventeen

"Tighten the muscles along the front margin of your temples. It's a matter of tension." Ephraim sat against the windowsill, his eyes closed and arms crossed. He was offering the same vague advice he'd given her for days. Myrta's goal, apparently, was learning to see air, an idea that seemed more impossible by the minute.

Backed up against a bookcase, gripping one of the shelves with both hands, she dredged up every scolding from Terrence, every time she and Jack hid in a closet or silo. Rammed every recollected terror from her childhood into the sides of her forehead.

Nothing. "All this is doing is giving me a headache."

He opened his eyes and sighed. "Sweetheart. You are capable of this. But you've kept your trait relaxed your entire life. I wouldn't be surprised if your anterior auricular muscles have deteriorated. Perhaps the middle ear tensors too. That would explain the vertigo."

She pressed her lips together.

"Don't give me that look. If you understood the physiology, this would be easier. Your eyes have duplicated tissue groups. The second set of extra-ocular and ciliary muscles shift the globe and lens into the alternate configuration. First as a matter of instinct and then with intent. The shift of the globe activates the photoreceptors."

Did he expect her to understand that?

"It's actually quite fascinating."

No, it wasn't.

"You've kept the key muscles weak. At this point they're probably quite spindly."

Her head throbbed. She stared at the top of the desk.

"Keep at it."

She tried again, but there was no vertigo and no sensation of hot worms coiling anywhere near her eyes. She pulled out a chair and plunked down. "I imagined the whole thing."

"Myrta!" For a moment Ephraim looked as though he might launch into another anatomy lesson, but then he stopped and said, "I diagnosed you myself, when you were born. You have the trait."

He came over, stood behind her chair, and placed his fingers along the sides of her face. "Do you feel anything if you clench your jaw and move the sensation of pressure upward?"

Sensation of pressure. Great. She tried and shook her head.

Ephraim exhaled forcefully through his nose right onto the top of her head. "I don't feel the extra musculature either, but it's a bad diagnostic to begin with." He paced back to the window, facing out, hands in his pockets, shoulders back. Looking irritated.

The lengths her family had gone to, leaving her on the farm for seventeen years. She pushed away from the table. "Can I be excused?"

He said out the window, "No. Getting you up to speed is not straightforward. There are levels to stimulating your tissue development, first turning the infernal thing on. You'll need to practice each stage before advancing to the next. We're already behind schedule—" He turned to her. His expression faltered. She knew why. When she felt the way she did now, all failure and frustration, she looked like a tusked moarab. That's what Jack said, anyway, that she turned into fury and spikes. She definitely felt like a moarab, ready to gore something.

"All right," Ephraim said. "Yes."

Myrta left, went to the kitchen, grabbed a plum from the bowl, and tore into it. Ardelle was tightening lids on another batch of plum jam. Pits and peels spilled out of the garbage pail. "How was it?" Ardelle asked this every time.

"Nothing. It was nothing. There was *nothing*."

From the office came the sound of a desk drawer slamming. Ardelle stopped mid-twist and looked down the hallway. Then came the sound of glass on glass. Ardelle pinched her lips and looked straight at Myrta. "Sweetheart. We need a break. And I'm dying to see you smile. Just once I want to see a smile on that beautiful face of yours."

"It's ridiculous. I sit there, and he says to think about tension. It doesn't *mean* anything." Myrta scrunched her face around her eyes again.

Ardelle smiled. "You're right, I don't think that's going to do it." She shoved the jars to the back of the counter. "Let's go shopping."

"All right. I don't care."

They left and walked the few blocks over to the thoroughfare, and Ardelle opened the door to a women's dress shop.

Myrta pulled up short. Racks of clothing crowded the little store. Sturdy dresses, gauzy ones. She drew her fingers down the sleeve of a blouse; the fabric rippled, light as a baby chick. She whispered, "Celeste always made our clothes."

Ardelle pulled a green and yellow sundress from

the rack and held it up to Myrta. "Well. You can buy them too, sweetheart."

That evening, Myrta sank into the office chair as she had done every morning and evening now. Ephraim was rifling through receipts on the desk. "I have a few ideas."

She barely heard him. His shoulders had gone all slumped, like the mashed potatoes at supper. She'd go back to the kitchen later for leftovers.

"I could examine your eyes while you're trying. I could look for the tissue changes around the orbit or within the lenses. The inferior rectal muscles relax before the medial musculature tightens. I might see that, or the ciliaries, if we're lucky."

"I literally have no idea what you're talking about. Would it help?"

He was fiddling with the pencils, like he thought they'd be sharper if he stared at them one by one. "It wouldn't hurt." He looked at the cabinet on the wall above the desk, and his shoulders fell further. "No."

There'd been gravy with the potatoes. Maybe there was leftover gravy.

His voice fell. "Or we could expose you to gaseous carbon. The exhaust from Mel's aut," he examined one of his fingernails and mumbled, "may have triggered an instinctive response."

She wasn't listening anymore. Odile had overcooked the green beans, but the caramelized onions made up for that. If she mixed the onions with the gravy, if there *was* any gravy, and put some potatoes on top . . . "Wait. What?"

He rubbed his thumbnail, not meeting her eyes. "I could expose you to gaseous carbon."

"Like the exhaust?"

His face creased in pain. "It would hurt."

"But it could work." It *would* work. It was the first useful thing he'd said. They could've tried it weeks ago.

"Children normally mature into this painlessly. Using gas would force it."

He stood there, so shrunken. But what he said made sense. Gaseous carbon explained everything—why she'd had a spell at Reuben's irrigation, and another behind the aut. She found herself standing. "I don't care."

He glanced at the cabinet over the desk.

"Uncle Ephraim."

He squinted.

"Sitting around is pointless. Nothing's worked, and Aunt Ardelle keeps saying how unsafe I am."

"If we get you up to speed before the Caravan wagons roll in, you'll have nothing to worry about." Ephraim looked at the cabinet again, muttering, "We could have worked on this years ago, but telling Terrence about you was out of the question."

"*Years* ago?"

All the lectures from Terrence, the daily chores, Nathan's endless torment, always feeling out of place—she could have been spared that years ago? "What, would you have just switched us back?"

His voice rose. "We never wanted to 'switch' you in the first place. We love you. I know it doesn't feel that way but try to understand—your safety had to come first." He faced down, looking shamed, and added softly, "I suppose, yes, we would have switched you back."

It was so entirely and utterly callous. She was no more than a *thing* to these people, but then, with a chill, with the idea of losing someone she loved, perhaps a child, she saw the possibility of making the same choices they had.

"Myrta, try something for me. Some of the muscles are behind your temples. Just, just think about the back of your temples, and push forward there with your fingers."

She did; nothing happened. "I want the gas."

"I know. We'll try a little—"

She planted her hands on the table. "Uncle Ephraim, we've been trying for weeks. I want gas."

"And *I* don't want to hurt you. Again. When I sprayed you as a baby you cried for over an hour."

"Why does that even matter? You left me on a *farm*. And I've been thinking about 'ideas of sensations of pressure' forever."

Ephraim leaned forward, his eyes sharp. "We will try a bit longer. If we fail, we'll consider the gas."

This was unreal. First market was over a month ago, and if he would simply agree, they could get on with it. But he refused to back down, and so Myrta endured another hour of failure and arguments. Ephraim said she wasn't trying, she accused him of hiding behind medical words. He said she should at least try to understand how her body was put together, and she said that wasn't the problem.

In the end, he yanked a case out of the cabinet and slammed it onto the table. "To be clear, this will not give you any control."

He pulled a handheld scope from the case, and his face blanched. Pursing his lips, he inserted a small canister into the handle. He sat across from her. "Whenever you're ready."

"I'm definitely ready."

"Keep your eyes open. This will certainly hurt." Pointing the scope toward Myrta's eyes, he pushed something on the back, and a "poof" of air shot at her.

Tugging tore at the sides of her face. She slapped her hands to her temples. The world started spinning.

"Don't fight it," Ephraim shouted above her cries.

She wanted to hurl.

"Make the muscles contract," he shouted.

Muscles? Her dinner was coming up.

Ardelle rushed in. "What are you doing? What's going on?"

"Ardelle, let her be."

The chair tilted sideways. She was on the ground groaning.

Ardelle ran over and squatted next to her. "Ephraim, what have you done?"

Myrta twisted away. The tugging had a will of its own, something insisting this *happen*, this contortion through her temples, around and behind her eyes, all on its own, more strongly than she'd felt before, deep and primal like a beast waking. "Make it stop!"

Ardelle cried, "Did you hurt her? Is that your *scope*?"

"Not *now*."

The urge to do the old exercises drove through Myrta like a spike, years of Celeste demanding that she relax. She rolled back and forth on the floor, slamming against the chairs and shelving.

Books fell down. Ardelle was yelling. Ephraim was yelling. Years of practice pitched battle against this strange biology gripping her. Waves tore through her skull. She needed to wrench her thoughts *away* from relaxing. She needed a distraction.

"Keep fighting," she cried.

Ardelle exclaimed, "Ephraim, what have you done? She wants us to *fight*."

"Then we fight!"

"Are you out of your mind? You want to fight because a sick child is asking you to?"

He shouted, "Because *our* sick child is asking us to."

Somehow, through the ensuing screaming match, Myrta focused on a task opposite her lifelong practice. And a few minutes later, the curious pressure washed over her again, through her eyes, through her temples, relieving the vertigo. Between one instant and the next, the world steadied. The floor was solid. She lay still, with her eyes closed. "You can stop."

Ardelle was in the middle of a rude observation about Ephraim's bathroom habits.

Myrta repeated, "I said stop."

Ephraim was beside her now. "Can I look?"

That pressure, that feeling ... it was the same as before. She cracked one eye.

Rainbows filtered into view. Reds, greens, faint streaks of yellow like the trails of shooting stars. Silver flecks drifted in the air.

Both eyes flew open. Cobalt blue hung like clouds around her parents' faces and in front of her own, swirling in and out with their breath. Color surrounded her. Everywhere. Everywhere there was color mixing, settling.

"It's the same," she whispered. Only this time, they said it was normal. The chemistry of the air, Uncle Ephraim had said.

It was beautiful.

Smiling gently, Ephraim examined one of her eyes and then the other. "Now, Myrta. Now do you believe me? You were *not* imagining things."

The next morning the bedroom was bright. Outside, the handyman was harnessing Rennet and Rusty.

Myrta pulled on a dress and found Celeste and Ardelle in the kitchen.

As she came in, Ardelle said, "Good morning, dear. After the excitement last night, we thought you should sleep as long as you wanted."

Celeste's lips were pressed together. She fussed with a basket of plums, arranging and rearranging them. She seemed to be putting them in parallel rows, but they kept jumbling back together. Without meeting Myrta's eyes, she said, "I'm going back to the stead. You'll stay here."

"What? No. How will I get home?"

Celeste swallowed. Her chest rose and fell, and she covered the plums with a corner of the little towel. "Myrta. You *are* home." She blinked a few times, then set the basket on the counter and put her arms out. Myrta ran into them.

"Oh, Myrta," Celeste whispered into the hug, "the stead is also your home. Always."

Ardelle said softly, "Sweetheart, you can live in the belt just as soon as your trait is developed."

The ground seemed to move. This wasn't right. "I—"

Celeste pulled away and picked up the basket again, wrapping both arms around it and holding it hard against herself. "Terrence is shorthanded. I miss the boys."

"But Mama . . ."

Celeste blinked. Tears fell to her cheeks. "Oh, dear daughter of mine, you'll be all right. You will. And we'll see you at Caravan."

Chapter Eighteen

Buried in swampy soil amid fallen trees.

Buried in deep ocean sediments amid phytoplankton.

Which of these, or both, Alphonse was never sure, only that he and those like him, cold and dead, were lost into oblivion.

Days turned to years, to centuries, to epochs. Alphonse awoke gradually over the final millennium. The soil and granite around and above pressed upon him. Compressed smaller and smaller in his tomb of death, he grew warm.

The bacteria and the archaea took their morsels of food and left behind the pieces they could not consume, and Alphonse suffocated in the hot, pressured subsurface.

"It is an important part of the story," Stavo said.

And over this great span of time, Alphonse became petroleum.

"We must understand the time scale."

Alphonse's medical debt was cleared with enough money left over to buy fishing gear and a notebook at the small general store on the thoroughfare. He left Collimais. He left without saying goodbye. They'd try to stop him otherwise.

He walked, this time north, on the rutted dirt road leading into the belt.

As Alphonse walked, he turned to his earliest childhood memories. The happy home, councilors visiting into the night, voices drifting up the stairs to the bedroom where he would curl up with his stuffed lion while his mother sang to him. He remembered the voices from below, the discussions of rules, and safety, and wages. He remembered the lullabies too.

When did that pattern change? Was it before Grandfather died?

Shortly after he died, di Gof took Stavo's place through the rarely-used process of acclamation. Di Gof wanted di Les on the Council, and when Alphonse's mother first started with the industry a few years later, she began working with di Les. That's when she'd first met Zelia Naida, the financier at Renico. The woman his mother had spoken with on the distavoc, the night of the gala.

Those four had worked together years ago.

When Alphonse was eleven, di Gof and di Les wrote a bill requiring full employment to vote. Five of Sangal's most progressive councilors—twenty percent of the Council and voices for the poorest residents—lost their seats that year.

He walked deeper into the belt, past mine shafts and cotton fields growing green and red. He was alone again, passing time with Turaset. Each night he pulled out his notebook and added new recollections. He noted the years. The cities. The payouts, not always with Zelia involved, but often enough. He pulled the pieces apart and pushed them together in new ways, trying to find the core of his mother's drive.

He remembered a day when she said something about the Council changing more quickly at last. Had it been on a birthday? Had she called it a gift? Di Gof and di Les—they'd written a law to permit councilors to swap between cities. How such a thing had passed in a representative democracy baffled Alphonse, but they'd managed it, and Lydia di Cur moved to Beschel in northern Delsina Province.

Mother started working at a provincial level when I turned twelve.

A few years later, she funded candidates in Narona, in Renivia Province, which had very little to do with Delsina Province otherwise.

Deep in the belt, Alphonse's notes grew longer by the day. They pointed to the industry and they pointed to the economy. His grandfather had once said that agriculture underpinned the economy more broadly than combustion ever had, but now combustion sold in the belt.

He needed to know more about the belt, how it worked and its economic needs, and any risk combustion might pose out here.

So, Alphonse made his way to a pair of neighboring steads. On one, pigs snorted in the morning air. The other looked to have something to do with logging. A smell of pine hung in the air and sounds of sawing and yelling came from an outbuilding. Alphonse walked up to an open-air barn where two men and a woman worked a log by hand, arguing back and forth about sharpening the blade.

He was at the entrance before they noticed him.

The thinner man, who had hair sticking sideways

from under his hat, waved the other two down and strode up to Alphonse. "Get off my land."

Alphonse blinked at the tone and took a step back. "I'm sorry. I'm looking for work, and I heard steaders hire. My name's Alphonse di Artur."

He held out his hand. The man ignored it. "Y' don't just walk up."

Alphonse stood straighter, thinking three people couldn't possibly pull down very many trees, especially if their blades were dull, but this man didn't seem to be hiring. He lowered his arm. "I'm sorry. I'll leave."

"Hold on. You from the cities?"

Even with a scrub of a beard, Alphonse didn't look like a steader, and his accent was a sure giveaway. "Yes."

The man measured him up and down. "You *walk* here?"

"I . . . guess. Yes."

The two others, over near the sawing braces, had watched the exchange. The man looked surly, but the woman seemed content. Relaxed.

Still aggressive, the thin man said, "Why'd'ja walk all the way here?"

It was a good question; it must look ridiculous. Alphonse jammed his hands in his pockets and met the man's eyes. He said, almost hoping the steader would disagree, because an argument suddenly sounded fun, "I like walking."

The man harrumphed at that and circled him, as though Alphonse was a workhorse for sale. "All right," he said. "I'm Reuben de Reu." He gestured at the other two. "That's Fred and Manuela. She goes by Manny."

Fred, the surly one, was bald with a heavy mustache. His shoulders were thick and muscled, reminding

Alphonse of some of the line workers Eduardo managed. Manuela seemed young despite her height—
maybe younger than Alphonse—with dark hair and
complexion similar to Alphonse's own. She smiled like
an old friend might.

Lines of determination surrounded Reuben's mouth
and eyes. "I claim land to the top o' that hill yonder.
You see them dyin' trees? That's drought. Those gotta
come out on account of the fire risk. That the sorta job
you want?"

"It sounds like good work."

"All right. Trial basis. Two weeks. If it don't work,
you'll be on your way. Understood? Hands sleep in
the bunkhouse. Paid five reblas per ton o' board, meals
included."

It was less money than Alphonse expected, but
there'd be no taxes on it, and he wasn't here for the
money anyway.

"You can start by stackin' those boards."

After supper that night, Alphonse, Fred, and Manny
walked back to the bunkhouse, which looked a bit like
the utility shed behind his family home. It was small
and cramped. A three-room cube. Reuben had said
it was the original quarters his father had used, back
when he claimed the land. It was left for the hands
after the larger house was finished.

There was a cot in the front room, a table and lantern next to it, and a small wash basin. The floor was
bare.

"G'night," Fred said, taking one of the back rooms
and closing the door.

Manny laughed. "He's not a talker." That much
had been obvious at supper. Reuben's wife, Georgie,
had gone on at such length, though, that Alphonse had
wondered if Fred's silence was simple politeness.

But Manuela, she was a city girl, a breath of familiarity. Alphonse said, "Do you hire out every year?"

"No. No way. This is my first season. I want to get into construction."

"You don't need to work out here for that."

"Maybe. But I want to build something new. I figured I'd start by learning the basics. Lumber's a basic." Manny took off her work boots, set them next to her cot, and went to the basin to wash up. "Narona's crowded. You know? We need to build out."

"I've never been."

"It stinks. Like a sewer. When you breathe that all day, you're sick all night."

Narona was known for its stench, due in part to the annual storm flooding. Most of the stink traced to petroleum seeps. The oil reserves throughout Renivia Province were the richest on the continent.

"I carried packages for a few years. Every time I carried out of Narona, the air was better. Just a few miles out the air's better. I delivered up to Beschel and down to Granvil, and there's lots of room. There's good air too." She sat on her cot and took off her socks. A ring of sawdust marked her ankles, and she rubbed it off and slapped her socks against the cot frame. "I figure Reuben's a connection. If I do a good job, maybe I'll get a break on lumber and order the cuts I need. So, I'm here for the money but the contact too."

Manny had a route. She had a foot planted in a solid toehold and had started her climb.

"What about electricity? You can't just build anywhere you want. There's no generators."

"Renico's laying cable between the cities."

Alphonse shook his head. "The ground's too rocky. Exposed wire, sometimes it's damaged at conjunction, and the ground's too hard to bury anything."

The young woman was shaking her head, laughing as Alphonse spoke. "No, I'm telling you they figured it out, how to bust rock. Burying the lines is going to be easy." She drew out the last word like a kiss.

"I don't believe it."

"It's true. Cities won't need central generators anymore. We can spread out."

Alphonse saw it, new cities on the coast, no oil extractors, no refineries, no generators. No city-level power at all, just lines from the existing generators.

"So, you want to build that?"

"You'd better believe it."

That night, Alphonse lay in his cot in the third room and stared up into the darkness. Almost daily he'd remembered more councilors that his mother had helped onto their seats or into new cities. She seemed to be thinking past a provincial scale. She seemed to be thinking at a continental scale.

He ran through the numbers. Councilors congregated at the provincial level into assemblies, and each provincial assembly elected ten senior councilors to serve on Nasoir's Continental Congress in the capital city of Vastol. This body of thirty, the Congress, elected the prime chancellor of Nasoir, who ordered the agenda during session. The chancellor also commanded the marshalry, which kept order during natural disasters and other emergencies and conducted the annual census at Caravan. And the marshals kept law in the foothills, but as Ephraim had said, crime wasn't much of a problem.

The chancellor had two powers—ordering the congressional agenda and commanding the marshals. But the chancellor also relinquished any voting rights, leaving the congressional block at twenty-nine. There was no obvious reason for Ivette to try and influence the chancellery itself, given its limited power, so it must be simply the Congress, but that didn't make sense either. Congress voted on continental tax law and managed some aspects of trade between the belt and the provinces. It settled disputes and provided oversight of the belt. But most laws, including city tax law, were handled locally.

Alphonse lit the small lantern next to his cot and pulled out his notebook. He opened it to his growing list of names and drew a faint line through each probationary and junior councilor. They'd not be eligible to serve on the Continental Congress. He counted the remainder.

Five senior councilors in Sangal. Two in Beschel. At least three in Renivia Province, between Narona and Masotin.

Those were the councilors she'd had a hand in helping, who might possibly serve in Congress. He didn't know if she had dealings in Garrolin Province or not, but between Delsina and Renivia Provinces she potentially held sway over ten congressional votes. And if he'd been seated, di Les or di Gof could have transferred to Beschel and increased her tally there without diminishing her influence in Sangal.

As he stared at the numbers, he couldn't shake the feeling that they mapped directly toward a single destination.

Why does she care about Congress? Is it the chancellery?

The next morning, Alphonse and the others hitched horses to a logging cart. The animals pulled the cart up to the forest, and with Fred and Manny, Alphonse felled his first ailing tree. They sawed the branches and cut the trunk to lengths. The horses dragged the logs down one by one, and Alphonse's shirt was soaked within the hour.

At midday, Reuben said, "Never said it was easy, but it sells. Every board, it all sells. Best lumber in the belt. You up to it?"

It meant good sleep. "Yes."

The following week they switched to milling. Reuben said, "Moisture'll be uneven if the logs set too long. Boards'd be warped. Fred knows. Been here six seasons."

After milling, they sorted planks by species and cut, and stacked them with crossing slats.

Toward the end of the second week, Reuben said, "All right, boy. You held up. This the sort o' work you want?"

What he wanted was to sort through his mother's actions. This was a good place to do it.

"Yes." The singlemindedness of the work, he relished it. The peace of the forest.

The only awkwardness occurred at meals, when Reuben's wife talked endlessly, stringing together sentences with no relationship to one another. In addition to her verbal disarray, two children ran about the property from suns-up to suns-down. They'd dash into the mill shed or up the logging trail unsupervised, perhaps because of Georgie's morning sickness. Breakfasts were the barest simplicities while she stayed in the back of the house with a bucket.

"Would'ja rather hear that or her gabbing?" Fred asked one morning in a rare commentary.

One morning, as they milled in the barn, a pair of

horses trotted up pulling a carriage. Reuben walked over. "Terrence. Nathan. Good to see you."

"Reuben," the older man said. The three men exchanged a few words and then strode to an irrigation system on Reuben's property line. Reuben spoke to the men while pointing out different parts of the system.

The two children ran over, and Reuben shooed them away, but they went back a few minutes later. Alphonse walked over to retrieve them.

Reuben and the older man were talking. Reuben wore a grin, like he'd won some sort of bet. "Disappointed, Terrence?"

"Disappointed we've another drought. Disappointed somethin' has to give."

"Irrigation would fix it," the younger man said.

"Nathan, we agreed t' see how it holds up." Terrence looked at Reuben, a question in his eyes.

"It takes gettin' used to," Reuben said. "It's sensible, once you get the hang of it. You'd see pretty quick, Terrence. Your crops'd turn around real quick."

Terrence scowled, as though he'd hoped for a different answer. "Can't afford it. 'Sides, pullin' water from the ground could make problems we hain't thought through. And, y'know, Celeste still ain't for it. She's got her reasons."

Chapter Nineteen

Myrta asked Odile to go on a walk after breakfast, like she had every day since Celeste left, because Odile had known the truth about being switched and the reasoning behind it for years. Odile said no, again, and Myrta finally lashed out. "We don't need to spend *any* time together. I don't care."

"It's pointless. Are we supposed to be best friends now?"

Myrta gritted her teeth, thinking if she'd grown up as Odile had, without farm chores, with no threat hanging over her, and interesting people coming through all the time, she'd be content. There were places to shop in Collimais and she might even travel to Beamais. Ephraim went often enough. If she'd grown up at the inn, she wouldn't be self-absorbed like Odile. She'd be happy.

But Odile was angry, especially since the handyman had left. Now she crossed her arms and glared at Myrta.

"What? Stop acting like I'm the annoying one."

Odile's gaze intensified. "You know what? Yes. Let's go on your stupid walk."

They started through the orchard. Here and there missed plums had fallen, brown and limp on the ground, pits poking through the bruises. Warm air pressed against Myrta, pulsing out of the ground like an accusation.

Summertime. Heavy and slow.

"Why didn't Celeste ever tell me?"

Odile snapped a branch off a tree with a loud crack. She broke the stick in two. "You were too little."

Myrta suppressed her annoyance. "I'm older than you, but you knew about it."

"You're older than me? Less than a month." Odile whacked at a healthy tree limb, ripping its leaves. "I asked. It made sense, so I made them tell me."

Myrta stopped. "Why didn't you ever say anything? You could have told me. When was this?"

"I don't know. We were seven or eight. They told me to keep quiet."

All the instructions, as far back as Myrta could remember, to keep her dizzy spells secret. They'd taught Odile to lie too. It sickened her.

Odile tossed one of the sticks back down the path. "Ardelle thought I'd say something, so you stopped coming. And since you never came back, I knew Celeste and Terrence didn't actually want me."

This was the reason the visits ended? Because Odile had figured it out?

"Odile. Terrence never knew. And of *course* Celeste wanted you. How could she not? And trust me, Terrence would have taken you over me any day. Besides," Myrta added, "you knew the truth. I never did."

"So what? You grew up without hearing about Renico every day of your life."

But everything would have been in the open, and that would have been better. It would have kept this anger from taking root. "You could have told me. You could've, I don't know, sent a note with Nathan after Caravan. You could have come to the stead, insisted he bring you. You could've made things better for both of us."

Odile gave her a bitter look. "I had to keep you safe."

"That's scat and you know it. I didn't know any of this. You knew what was going on, you hated it—and you didn't do a thing!"

The way Odile was standing, her angry eyes and crossed arms, tapping the other stick on her elbow, it looked like Celeste facing down an unruly horse and more afraid than she let on.

"Oh, I get it," Myrta said. "You were scared."

"You were too dumb not to see it."

"You knew! And you didn't do anything for what? Ten *years*? You know what kind of person doesn't fix something when it's wrong like that? A *coward*. You're a coward."

Seething, Odile said, "Don't call me that."

"You are. You could have fixed this. Refused to be part of it. Nathan would have."

"*Stop* it."

"Coward!"

Odile threw her stick down and pushed Myrta at the shoulders. Myrta stumbled into the copperwood stump, tripped over her feet, and fell to the ground. "You were afraid." She stood and shoved Odile back.

"You!" Odile said. "Why should I help you?"

"Because what they did was *wrong*."

Myrta was on the ground again, with Odile on top. Rocks and thorns pushed and scraped into Myrta's arms, and she kicked back, scratched at her cousin's face, screaming.

Odile shoved Myrta's head sideways in the dirt. "I hate you," she cried.

"I never hurt you," Myrta yelled back, pushing at Odile and wrestling with her legs to trip her off. "We were friends!"

"I *know* that!"

And Odile stopped, as suddenly as she had started. She just stopped. After a still moment, she rolled off with tears in her eyes.

Myrta's rage evaporated. This was her cousin, her favorite, the other girl.

Myrta said, "I hate this trait. I hate that I can't control it. Ephraim says my muscles are wasted. I'm so angry at him. I'm so angry at all of them. Switching us. The whole thing."

Odile stood and brushed herself off. "You should be." She tipped her head to indicate the trail, and Myrta nodded and stood, and they started up.

"Still," Odile muttered, "at least you had brothers."

Brothers. Running off with Jack. Hiding from Nate. Years of memories with brothers.

Dirt puffed from Myrta's footfalls, the world sneezing dust, too hot. "Did the discerners ever come for you?"

"No. Ephraim saw to it. He took me to see Melville. Said he'd ship me off if I had it, but he knew I didn't." Then she smiled a little bit. "I used to make him tell me the story."

Myrta imagined growing up with a fright story like that to curl into a papa's lap with. A real papa, who would hold her and tell her a story. "Why would they take children?"

"Simple. The younger you are, the easier you are."

She turned Odile's words over. "I'm not sure I understand that."

Odile looked at Myrta with her mouth half open.

"It doesn't make me stupid."

"The auts, Myrta. The exhaust. A child can't see

it yet, so they don't know when someone might be coming."

Oh.

They reached the overlook. It was so dry. So hot. Myrta pulled her hair together at the nape of her neck and tucked it into her collar.

"Anyway, Ephraim cleared my name. Your name, I guess."

Her name, Odile's. Myrta turned that over too. She should have been a Vonard. Odile should have been a de Terr. Aunt, Uncle. Mama, Papa. "I don't know what to call anyone."

Odile was staring off into the distance, her face hard. "It doesn't matter."

"Of course it matters. I can barely use this thing. I can't because of what they did. All of it matters."

The more she said it, the more certain she felt. As far back as she could remember she'd done farm chores with Celeste. Never Terrence, in the fields. How much of her life had nothing to do with tradition—and everything to do with her trait? How much of a papa had she lost? "Everything should have been out in the open, including our names. We grew up with one another's parents. Our whole lives—relationships—it matters."

"It only matters because you want it to." Odile's face looked like Nathan's, the lines crowding her mouth, the hard glare forward. "Well? This is the view. Anything like the stead?"

Nothing like the stead, no. The stead didn't have mountains for one thing, and there weren't nearly so many people there. With a chill, Myrta realized Odile had no idea what that was like.

She's not self-absorbed. She's hurt. Myrta's heart broke at the realization. "Oh, Odile . . . it's beautiful here. The homes, and carriages and fresh bread everywhere. It's perfect. It's a perfect place to grow up."

Odile squinted out over the view.

The pain in that gaze, Myrta couldn't bear it. She began sharing memories. She told Odile about the trees, the goats and chickens, growing up surrounded by the hush of summer wheat and the quiet of winter snow. Family stories, bedtime stories, steader stories. The cave no one knew about but her and Jack.

Odile's face relaxed. Myrta told her about milking and cheese making, about bringing her favorite hens into the house when it was cold. Finding stray eggs days later. Odile smiled, like the storm had passed.

They started back down. She told Odile about Terrence and Celeste watching one another quietly. About hiding from Nate in the distilling shed or in one of the storage silos. All the places he never thought to look. By the time they reached the inn, both girls were laughing.

The meal that night was like supper on the farm. Ephraim didn't speak, just shoveled food in, glowering at the plate as though it had wronged him. Odile dug the tines of her fork into the table top. Ardelle placed her hand on Odile's arm to stop her and tried to start a conversation, but no one was interested.

Afterward, Myrta went to the office with Ephraim. Again. Books were strewn about, most open to charts and columns of words, scribbles and notes. One page showed a face with exposed muscles—surgical?—but Ephraim yanked it away before Myrta could really see. A sheet of paper lay loose on the table. The top read *'Elige trait—Missing'* and it was filled with names. It listed home towns and dates that stretched back to before she was born.

Ephraim watched her as she scanned the sheet. "Your situation is quite serious."

She handed the sheet over, trembling.

He told her to clear some chairs while he shelved more books. "I couldn't find anything useful in any of these. By ten or eleven the trait emerges. Period. By thirteen children control it. There's nothing about atrophy from disuse. I don't know how to get past it." He held two books in his left hand and slammed a third into the case with his right.

"Uncle Ephraim. What would Mr. di Vaun do to me?"

He pushed another book, harder, straight back. "As I said, I don't *know*. I only know protocols from long ago."

"He said there were surgeries. You must have some idea."

His face contorted. "Actually, yes, I do. And of my dated knowledge, you don't need to know *any* of it."

"But I—"

"Myrta, the answer's no." He grabbed more books and shoved them in. "We found passages on tissue modification. The genes, the altered sequences."

"I think I need to—"

He slammed his palm onto the table. "No. There are historical instances of toddlers identifying trace gases. Toddlers!" He shelved more books, and the case tipped back against the wall from the blows. "But is there anything on atrophy? Of course not."

"Papa."

Ephraim stopped mid-push and stood, unmoving.

She didn't know why she'd said it. Maybe she wanted the relationship Odile had once had with this man. Maybe she said it because she hadn't made an impression any other way. Hearing the word from her mouth shocked her as much as it seemed to shock him, but she'd finally gotten through, and so she repeated it. "Papa."

He gently slid the book in. "Yes?"

"It doesn't matter that you can't find me in your books. You know what you saw. Just force it and I'll get stronger."

He dragged out a chair, his face dusty and dry and ready to rest. He folded his hands on the table. "I don't want to."

"I know. But when you sprayed me, I saw colors. Clouds and trails and specks. Everything moved and swirled, and some colors changed from one shade to another."

"The Elige trait is nothing short of astounding. You saw chemicals oxidizing, and others forming free radicals."

"I don't know what those are. You said if I control this, I'll be safe."

He closed his eyes and pinched his fingers to the bridge of his nose. "Safer, not safe. I do not want to force this. I do not want to force *you*." He opened his eyes.

"Would it work?"

"It could."

He was actually agreeing with her.

With a heavy sigh, he said, "We'll start a new regimen. If you can't flip the switch on your own, I'll blast you with carbon."

Chapter Twenty

On a grassy field, life surrounded Alphonse, but not life as he knew it. Giant beasts lumbered across the plain, and a small furred creature scurried into a burrow. There were no flowers in sight, not a single one.

"Where are we?"

"The question is when. We are, roughly, sixty million years into the past."

A forty-foot beast charged them. The carnivore had serrated teeth and forelimbs so small as to seem pointless. Alphonse screamed and the theropod roared, swooping its head downward as if to grab him in its massive jaws. But at the last moment, it veered after a smaller dinosaur.

"Grandfather!"

"It's fine, Alphonse. Look." A pinprick of fire appeared in the sky.

"What is that?"

Stavo remained silent. After minutes, then hours, the point grew, hurtling toward them.

"It's going to hit!"

The meteor struck, and a titanic shock wave knocked Alphonse to the ground. Dinosaurs nearest the strike were vaporized. Others burned. Others ran, screaming and falling over one another in terror. Flames rained down.

Dust filled the air, the planet darkened, and days turned to weeks. The world remained dusty and dim.

The plants died. Then the animals that ate the plants, they too died. And the animals that ate the plant-eaters died as well.

Alphonse turned, and turned, and turned again. "Everything's dead."

Through the haze, Alphonse and Stavo wandered the wasteland, the death-scape of the late Mesozoic. And at last, on the dim little world, as the Cenozoic dawned, they found plants that persisted and small animals surviving on the barest of seeds or leaves.

The centuries passed, and a new regime began. The small feathered dinosaurs, they were few, but their descendants became the birds.

And the small furred creatures who lived in burrows, their descendants rose to dominance. The age of mammals had arrived.

"Think of it, Alphonse. The trajectory of an entire world can be changed by a single event."

Logging on the de Reu stead, Alphonse found satisfaction deeper than anything he'd known in Collimais or Sangal. Whether felling trees in the forest or milling in the shed, his effort became a quantifiable, tangible product—good boards. Planks of oak and pine that would one day become homes and businesses.

He didn't earn much pay, but his needs were met, and the gratification of the work filled him. The only remotely similar experience he'd had was the summer he'd spent waxing carts on the docks, where he'd made a game for himself to be the fastest and best among the wax boys. But there'd been no real fruit to that labor, nothing he could put his hands on and say, "This is the thing I made."

And as he worked, Alphonse noticed two good-sized gardens thriving between the home and logging track. Ripening vegetables, leafy greens, everything healthy and lush. One evening after supper he asked Georgie what she thought about their irrigation system.

"Oh, it's wonderful. Why, when we go to market and I see how small everyone's vegetables are, I'm just so embarrassed that ours are so big. But we aren't selling vegetables after all, so no one knows. I don't say a word. I just keep my mouth shut. It really makes a point though, doesn't it? What a difference water makes!"

"It's amazing, ma'am."

"Of course, the mechanation is loud, and Rudy and Rosa keep climbing on top of it, which they really oughtn't." As she said the words, Rudy ran up to the system and began playing with the knobs again. "Rudy," she called. "Come back here."

Alphonse walked over and brought the little boy back.

"Oh, thank you, Alphonse. I don't know what we'll do when the third one comes. Of course, I suppose it's hard now, me sick all day and not able to watch these two. Sometimes they go straight into the woods. How we haven't lost either one I'll never know."

He wondered if children barely old enough to say

their names should be wandering off, but Georgie always seemed to know where to find them.

She lifted Rosa onto her hip. "Anyway, yes, that's the irrigation. It's made all the difference. Now Reuben wants the other things too."

Alphonse frowned. "I thought the problem was drought."

"Oh, the drought's awful. Irrigation is positively heaven-sent. What would we do without it? Why, when we see some of the other steads, especially the grain farmers, oh, holy heavens. They need irrigation. That would see them through."

She'd lost the conversation again. "Ma'am, you said Mr. de Reu wants other things."

"Oh, there's a milling system. I mean, what you do is so unsafe. I worry every single day that one of you will lose a finger."

"It's not that dangerous."

"Or worse," she continued. "Seeing you out there makes me sick with worry. So, I stay inside and don't think about it. But mechanated milling would be so much safer and quicker, and the boards, well, they say, and please don't be offended, would be more even. Better all around. And then hands like you could hire out somewhere less dangerous."

He looked at the hillside. It was easy to see where they'd worked, healthy and green, all the ailing patches gone. "You'd still need hands for the logging."

"Oh, there's fuel-powered tools for logging too. Really, these devices are amazing. Why, I believe Reuben could clear an entire hillside if logging *and* milling were mechanated." Georgie smiled as though she had a secret. "It would be very profitable."

The light in the sky deepened along the horizon, the suns kissing the world with pink and purple breath from north to south. Alphonse stared at the forest and pictured the hillsides denuded of trees, just stumps left, rows of headstones. "That's a lot of wood."

"Yes. Reuben says we could raise *ten* children." Georgie giggled and kissed Rosa, who was busily sucking her thumb. "Can you imagine?"

One morning, as they stacked newly-milled planks and bundled dried lumber for Caravan, an aut rumbled up to the stead. Alphonse and the others stopped, and Reuben walked over to the vehicle.

Melville di Vaun, the man from the inn, stepped out of the aut carrying a small case. Alphonse found himself staring, astonished to see anyone from the inn here in the middle of the belt. But there was nothing to be done about it and oddly, when Melville's eyes landed on Alphonse, he seemed startled as well. He gave a curt nod.

I could ask him about Renico. Di Vaun might know if the combustion industry was angling for the chancellery.

No. It was too obvious, too frank an approach. It was the way things were done out here but not in the cities—he'd bring too much attention to himself by asking di Vaun so forthrightly.

A businesswoman stepped out of the aut next and immediately said something to Reuben, who replied loudly, "Your prices're too high."

The three came over, the woman taking in the shed's setup in a quick, sweeping glance. "Look at your costs, Mr. de Reu. As they currently stand, you have one worker whose sole job is to guide the log. Planks are cut one by one. One by one. With a mechanated miller, this log would be sliced to thirty planks in a single pass."

"Carmella, due respect, but a machine's got no intuition." Still, the expression on Reuben's face was strained, as though he was working through the numbers and not liking his own conclusion on the matter.

"The savings in time offsets that."

"I'm not sayin' no. I'm sayin' for your price, there'd ought be no down side."

Carmella set her briefcase on a saw brace and opened it. "You asked about a package sale. I've cleared that. We'll give you a break if you take the fieldaut, mechanated saws, and miller."

Reuben scoffed. "Listen up. I'm pushin' your business to anyone payin' mind. Tell you what. You bring in your mechanation, cover the cost, and fix it if it breaks. If it's good as you say, I'll turn profit to pay the package price—after *next* year's Caravan."

Carmella pulled a notepad from her case and made some calculations. "Yes. I'll adjust the contract."

Reuben scoffed again. "Brought a contract? Bit sure of yourself."

"It'll be ready by lunch."

Alphonse, Fred, and Manny worked through the morning. Near lunchtime, Georgie ran out of the house, hair mussed, dress buttoned unevenly and a wild light in her eyes. "The children—where are the children?" That timbre to her voice. It was the tone his mother's voice held the first time she'd physically hurt him, the time she'd pushed him and he'd fallen into the glass table and broken his nose. Georgie sounded shocked. Panicked. Alphonse ran to the door of the shed, but the children were nowhere to be seen. Georgie was crying for them past the house now, and

Reuben was jogging over from the property line where he'd been talking with the neighbor, Claude.

Georgie wailed, "Reuben, I don't know where they are. I can't find them! I can't find them, Reuben. Where are they? Reuben, help!"

"Georgie, focus."

With her eyes clinging to his, she calmed. "I've lost the children."

"Are they inside?" he asked.

"No."

"In the woods?"

"I don't think so. Their shoes are by the door."

Reuben scowled. "Are they at Claude's?"

"They never go to Claude's. He's an old *man* to them. You were just right there!"

"Settle down." When her breathing steadied, he said, "What happened?"

"I lay down like I do every morning. I'm getting sicker, Reuben. I don't remember either pregnancy being like this. I mean, of course, I got sick both times, but this time it's so bad. I'm running to the bucket all morning—what if I lose the baby?"

"Georgie. Focus."

She looked straight into his eyes and grew still. "I fell asleep. When I woke, I couldn't find the children."

Reuben looked around the property. "Rudy, Rosa!"

Georgie went into the shed. "Are you in here, angels? Are you behind the lumber?"

They weren't—Alphonse had already checked. "I'll see if they're up the log track. They might be playing woodcutter."

"Oh, yes, if you wouldn't mind," she said distractedly. Alphonse started past the vegetable gardens when activity caught the corner of his eye. It was di

Vaun, coming out of the bunkhouse. Rudy ran madly in front, screaming and red-faced. Rosa whimpered under one of di Vaun's arms, twisting, kicking, her cheeks wet.

"Here they are," Melville called.

Georgie rushed over and threw her arms around Rudy. "Oh, you sweet angel, oh, dear heavens. Why ever were you in the bunkhouse?" Taking Rosa too, clasping both children close, she kissed them over and over, crying. "Oh, Mama was so scared. Don't ever give Mama a fright like that again. Oh, you sweet dears." She kept kissing the children and crying, and they were crying too and clinging to her from either side. She called, "Reuben, we found them!"

Melville di Vaun said, "You never know what trouble children will get into. Fortunately, they're fine." He took his case to the aut.

Chapter Twenty-One

For more days than she cared to count, Myrta needed Ephraim's gas to trigger her vision. He'd spray her; she'd fall in a fit of vertigo and do her best to contract the muscles he said were so weak. Ardelle insisted on being present every single time.

As soon as her vision shifted she'd feel well again, and the office air transformed into colors.

Pale green, like springtime grass, suffused every corner of the room. According to Ephraim, this was nitrogen gas. Mixed with this was pale red, like the horizon at second sunset. That was oxygen. Silver, like suns-light glinting on a frost-covered field, edged through and settled in a mist. Argon.

These—green and red and silver—made up the space around her, but they were faint. The barest trace of any other chemical blazed through in brilliant intensity. Carbon dioxide hung in cobalt blue around everyone's face, pulsing from noses and mouths. Water vapor, purple, lay on their breath too.

Ephraim sometimes played a game with her. He'd spray his different canisters of gas into the air and she'd learn each one. Methane, ozone, and too many sulfur gases to count. She learned all of them by sight.

After weeks of this, one morning Myrta managed the switch on her own, painlessly and without any need for Ephraim's gas. "Oh!"

Ardelle stood abruptly from the desk. Ephraim

snapped his attention from his case to her temple. "You did it." There was no uncertainty in his voice, none at all.

She laughed. She'd finally done it on her own, just tightened the muscles *there*, and her vision flipped.

He snapped his case shut and put it away. He strode over and felt the sides of her face. "Switch it off."

She did.

"Your muscles are stronger." He chuckled low. "Turn it back on."

She screwed up her face and flipped it, and the air shifted again. She couldn't stop laughing, and Ardelle smiled too, big and beautiful.

Myrta stuck her head into the hallway. "Odile, I did it!" All on her own, she had flipped the trait on.

Behind her, Ardelle murmured to Ephraim, "It's just the first step. And it's taken too long. We're in a stuffy little room."

Myrta turned back to them, switched her trait off and on again. It was easy. "Why does this help me again?" Then she waved her hand through her breath, entranced by the blues and greens swirling around her fingers and didn't care why—air was gorgeous, filled with every color she'd ever seen, shifting and mixing and changing right in front of her eyes.

Ephraim leaned back against the desk and crossed his feet. "Imagine, Myrta. Imagine you know the position of every person standing in a five-mile radius, in a *twenty*-mile radius, simply because you see the pulses of their breath. From twenty miles. Imagine you know which shops in Collimais are running mechanation and which aren't because of their fumes. Picture yourself in the hills and able to spot the chemical signatures of lakes, herds of animals, stretches of forest—because of the changes they make to the air—from twenty miles or more. Everything on Turaset has a gaseous signature. You read air. You can read the behavior of any living or mechanated thing on this world."

In disbelief, she stared, the power of her trait dawning.

Ephraim turned to Ardelle. "Patience. There are more than a dozen duplicated muscle groups, and we can't risk taxing any of them. But we'll get there. We walk, then run."

"It's too slow," Ardelle insisted. "You've never even taken her out of the office. You've never once so much as opened the curtains. How far can she see? Eight feet? If the discerners show up, that won't help."

Later, in her room, Ardelle's words played in Myrta's thoughts and she altered her vision again, thrilling at doing so on her own. Her breath was deep and rich, cobalt, like velvet. It diffused in a plume, steamy blue breath-fog. Everything in the room was a tapestry of swirling and magical chemistry.

How far can she see? Eight feet? Ardelle's words rang in her thoughts, and Myrta turned to look out the window and, dismayed, she sank to the floor. The air outside was not shades of reds and greens, but an ugly brown that became thicker and more disgusting the further out she focused. She tried to pull the colors apart, see each one, but it was no good past a few feet. Ardelle was right—she'd taken one step, no more.

Myrta began flipping her vision back and forth as often as it occurred to her to do so. She gauged how far she could tell red from green, how far she could see her breath, five feet or ten. Some nights she fell asleep with her lensing altered and woke the next day to find it still locked in place, with a burning sensation in the middle of each eyeball and a dull ache around her sockets. Occasionally her trait shut down while she used it.

More weeks passed, but she didn't progress, and Ephraim grew impatient. Working with his gases in the office was one thing, but the briefest look out the window and the air muddied. "No one could make sense of it, Papa. There are too many gases."

"Not true. It's a matter of focus."

One morning he took her to the orchard, saying a change of scenery might help. "These trees make oxygen. Try to see that."

Brown. Everything was brown, except her breath.

"Try harder." Tension wove through Ephraim's words. "We're in full suns-light, right next to the trees. They're making oxygen—"

"Red is *faint*. I see your breath. It's blue."

He exhaled loudly and turned away. "Yes."

They stood like that, the wall of his back to her, the expanse of his shirt blaming her, the linen whiteness of it like something she could scrawl her failure onto.

"Trees are supposed to be easy. They're stationary and they make oxygen. Look at the leaves."

"Red is *faint*." The backs of her eyes pulsed in painful waves that wrapped around to the front of each. She didn't want to be here, not like this. Anything would be better, milking a goat would be better. Planting crops would be better.

After a moment he turned back, his eyes wet. That wasn't fair. She was trying, and he ought to see it. He ought not cry. And the fact that he made no acknowledgment of her effort didn't help either.

"Focus in and out."

The carbon near his mouth was blue, sort of. She

focused away from him slowly. But she couldn't see anything but brown past five or six feet. Without a doubt she was weaker. Her lower lip began to tremble.

"Sweetheart," Ephraim said quietly. "Turn it off. Rest your eyes. You have an amazing ability. I don't have it. Your mother doesn't. Very few people can do what you do."

I know.

He sat under one of the trees and patted the dirt next to himself. She brushed the ground and joined him, mumbling, "I don't know why mechanation's so bad anyway."

"It isn't." He picked up a stick, rubbed the bark off, and began scratching the dirt. "It's the fuel."

He drew a circle and pointed at its top. "Imagine if we relied on nothing but trees for energy. Over our lifetimes we might harvest a forest and use the wood for warmth, for building things, and for power."

He moved his stick around to the bottom of the circle. "The trees would be gone, but we'd replant them, and the forest would grow back. In a sense, they'd grow back in synch with our own lives. They'd grow and they'd pull the carbon back out of the air, and our children would have a new forest to harvest. That's a complete cycle." He was pointing at the top of the circle again. "Are you with me so far?"

"Yes." Of course. Growing and harvesting and starting over was like anything else—like a good night's sleep or winter before spring.

"Here's the problem. The combustion industry doesn't use trees to power its devices. It digs into the planet for a different fuel, a different source of carbon. Archaic carbon. The carbon in coal and oil hasn't been in the air for a very long time. It's been in the ground for hundreds of millions of years. When that fuel is burned, the carbon goes into the air and overwhelms the natural carbon cycle. The trees can't absorb it. They can't cycle it all back. It takes far too long. And as a result, the carbon in the air increases. That puts the entire global climate at risk."

Ephraim stared at the circle and drew a decisive 'X' through it. "But archaic carbon is fantastic energy. You, sweetheart, you see carbon in the air, you can see it increase year over year, and in a nutshell that's why Renico finds you problematic."

"Because I see carbon."

He squeezed her hand. "Because that threatens profits."

This thing she could do—it should be *useful* to Renico. They ought to be able to work together somehow, find pollution and clean it before it became a problem. Something.

He stood and helped her up. "I have a meeting in Beamais. Rest. Rest your eyes."

Mulling over it, Myrta went around to the front porch, broke a sprig of jasmine from one of the bushes, and sat, twirling the flowers between her fingers. The industry had its own ideas about her; in a way, like everyone else had, her entire life. Myrta rolled the stem back and forth. Her life should be hers to decide.

The perfume from the jasmine, the scent from the blossoms, it was strong enough that she could see it with her trait. The scent was a gas, and it jiggled, like a shimmer, around each little white bloom. It definitely had carbon in it, but the carbon in breath didn't jiggle like that. Puzzled, she squinted closer at the carbon oils wafting off the jasmine. Definitely jiggly.

The carriage pulled around. Ephraim waved as he drove out. He did a double take and reined in the horses. "What are you doing?"

She flicked her trait off.

"Myrta? I asked you a question." Ephraim climbed out of the carriage.

"Nothing."

He strode over, his expression intensifying. "How much practicing have you done outside of our lessons?" He stood in front of her now, glancing from one of her eyes to the other. "Go to the office. Now."

She went inside, and Ephraim stormed in a moment later. He grabbed his case and slammed it on the table. "I told you to rest."

"Mama said—"

"Ardelle does not have this trait."

"Neither do you."

He opened his mouth, then closed it and yanked out his scope. "Look at me. I said, look at me."

The command in his voice terrified her, like Melville di Vaun saying, *We'll take you with us.* She did as she was told.

He grabbed the side of her head, easily wrapping three fingers around the top and jamming her left eye open with his thumb and forefinger. He pushed her head backward and examined one eye, then the other. His breathing grew louder and his hands rougher with every passing second. She choked up, shaking against his hand, trying to breathe.

Finally, he pulled away from her with a roar. He hurled the scope across the room. It crashed against the wall and the eyepiece broke from the handle. He went to the desk and pulled out the whiskey.

Ardelle rushed in. "What's going on?"

"You," he yelled. "She overworked her muscles."

Ardelle blanched.

He filled the shot and downed the drink. He

pounded the glass onto the table saying, "Congratulations, Myrta, you've lost ground."

Myrta looked at them in stunned disbelief. "This is not my fault. You don't *explain* anything."

Ephraim laughed bitterly. "This is why you've stalled. You've overworked the ciliaries. Do not use your trait. Do not turn it on. Do not so much as think about it." He left.

Myrta ran out of the office and up to her room, pulling the door hard. Right behind her, Ardelle knocked.

"No," Myrta yelled, grabbing a pillow and falling to the bed with it. She beat at it two-fisted, her thumps pummeling into her chest, her anger dissolving into frustration and confusion. She sobbed until nothing was left but a stinging, swollen wetness. With a shuddering breath, Myrta pushed her hair back and sat.

Outside, Odile was hanging laundry. Piece by piece in a tidy row, neatly, like she did everything. Odile never messed up. Sniffling and wiping her nose, Myrta went down and outside.

Odile's eyes widened. "What happened to you?"

Abashed, she said, "I strained something. In my eyes."

"Oh. Wow." Odile stood there, fiddling with a clothespin, like she was caught and might rather just be dealing with laundry. But after a moment she took Myrta into an awkward hug. "Do you want to talk?"

"Yes."

They went through the orchard. The trees were reddening and declining into autumn. Once at the bench, Odile blurted out, "I'm leaving."

"What? Where are you going?"

She sat. "Narona. I'm going to work there, get inside Renico. Change things."

"*What*? You can't. Do Mama and Papa know?"

Odile pulled her skirt up between her fingers. In and out, one hand then the other. "They said to ask Celeste. I did when you first came, but she said no."

"And you're going anyway?"

"You ask a lot of questions."

This needed questions. "Everything you've said is that they're dangerous. You've pounded it into me."

"I want their records."

"Their *records?*" The breeze kicked up, swirling leaves around the bench. Myrta pulled her hair away from her face and tied it behind her head. "You're not making sense. You have to tell Mama and Papa. Talk to them. You can't just run off to Narona."

Although it happened. Steaders went to the city for work. She'd even had the thought herself. With a start she realized Odile was plenty old enough.

"I don't feel any obligation." Odile stood, went behind the bench, and stripped a handful of splotchy leaves from a branch. She ripped them apart and threw the bits down.

"They love you."

"Renico pollutes. Proving it is literally all I care about. I'd die to prove it."

Incredulous, Myrta said, "*Die?*"

"It's why there's a drought. It's why the stead needs irrigation. You can pretend their pollution doesn't matter, but it does. And if me going makes you think about your situation any harder, that's good too." She slumped forward, onto the back of the bench. "Anyway, that's why I'm telling you. The problem's bigger than you, and you should think about more than yourself. When the handlers come at Caravan, I'm leaving. Keep this between us, Myrta."

Standing and going around the bench, Myrta took Odile in a hug. A real and true hug, caring and warm and soft. Odile had always been the other girl, her cousin, the one who made sense in a way brothers never did. "You can't leave. I won't keep it secret."

Odile hugged back, harder than Myrta expected. "You have to. If you can't, it justifies everything they did. It justifies their choice to not trust us with secrets. If you tell them, they'll know they were right to keep our real birth parents hidden from us."

Chapter Twenty-Two

Buzzing and hooting filled the forest. Apes lumbered by. Other primates swung in the trees. Alphonse and Stavo walked further in to a clearing where gorillas sat and groomed.

"How long ago?"

"Three million years. Sink into it, Alphonse."

He was the silverback. The females were his—they relied on him and bore his offspring. His purpose was to protect them.

Another male entered the glade, enraging him. He stood and roared, baring his fangs and pounding his chest. The intruder howled back, posturing and thumping.

Alphonse rushed him. His arms were longer than the other's and he used them like bludgeons. Howling in fury, he pummeled away. They wrestled and roared, Alphonse protecting his group as the other male swung and loped and growled. Then, in confused amazement, Alphonse saw the other lift a branch, giving it the greater reach. The ape clubbed him, and he sank.

"The dawn of tools. The intruder thought beyond himself to control his environment. It is a way of thinking we have inherited."

The days grew warmer and drier, and Alphonse, Fred, Manny, and Reuben logged early and milled during the heat of the day. Reuben eyed his withering stands and muttered about wildfire. "It's pests. A healthy tree can fight 'em, but these're sick. Pests brood twice a year now. Too many of 'em."

His words hung like a death shroud. The trees failed because of the pests, the pests were brooding because of the warmth, and the warmth was because of the changing climate. Odile said *that* was because of combustion.

Tightness in his chest had returned without him realizing. One evening Manny asked if he was all right, and with a start, Alphonse found himself pulling a hard breath. The same constriction he'd had at the inn and after failing on Tura. The way he'd felt after political events with his mother. "I'm fine."

Soon, the fuel-powered devices arrived, and everyone gathered in the shed to have a look. Reuben tested settings on the mechanated saw. He sliced a two-inch slab from a log, turned the device off, and stared in wonder at the round on the floor.

Horrified, Georgie said, "Oh, Reuben, that's not right. Why, Renico didn't say anything about how dangerous the saws are. How could they sell us something like that? We can't have those on the stead, not at all. What if little Rudy learned to turn one on? Those are death traps." Rudy and Rosa were clinging to Georgie's legs and crying.

Reuben muttered, "That's power."

"Reuben. They're louder than the irrigation and much more dangerous. You know how the children get into things. I won't have it."

He shook his head and tried another cut, laughing at the ease of it.

Fred spoke up. "Ma'am, I agree. I'd be nervous if my young'uns were here." Then he showed her the safety fastener.

"That's a good latch, but my children can't be around such dangerous things. How could Renico not tell us? Why, it frightens me to be anywhere near it." Georgie shooed Rudy back to the house and followed with Rosa.

After learning the settings, they took the saws to the forest and felled and cleaned two trees back to back. The fieldaut pulled both trunks down together, and the mechanated miller screamed as it sliced each log to planks in a single pass.

After a week, Reuben admired his new collection of stumps. "Holy heavens," he chortled. "This'll bring in cash faster'n we thought. Break early, you earned it."

Alphonse scratched his head, bothered by the ease with which they'd cleared the trees. As they walked down the track he asked Manuela, "What do you think about these tools?"

She clapped him on the back. "We have the afternoon off. I think it's great."

"But we cleared a big patch. We milled all of it. We could work the hillside in a season."

Manny laughed good-naturedly. "Yeah—and we'd sell more lumber, get bigger paychecks, and have afternoons off. More lumber means prices come down, so I get into construction with fewer costs. You don't think that's good?"

"Look. Besides the fact that we'd run out of trees, what happens in ten or twenty years? If the steads are mechanated, they're more like cities."

"The problem with cities is they don't have enough

space. There's no air to breathe." Manny spread her arms wide. "Here, there's space. Space and convenience? Sounds great."

"But the math is wrong. Eventually there'd be as many people out here as in the towns."

An image of the combustion industry stretching across the land flashed through Alphonse's mind. Power lines, like arteries coursing into the foothills, creeping into the belt, a serpentine web covering the continent.

"That's way in the future," Manny said. "We don't need to worry about it."

Unsettled, Alphonse hiked up into the hills. He slumped against an oak and closed his eyes. The roughness and warmth of the trunk pressed through his shirt. Odile had said Renico would destroy the culture of the belt and that steaders and foothillers didn't want any part of it, but Reuben seemed to.

There, on the hillside above Reuben's stead, the view shifted, or maybe time did, and he saw the belt not as rolling hills of trees and lakes but a resource. He saw it cut down and dug into. He saw rutted roads replaced by paved streets, manpower replaced by machines, and forests replaced by rows of buildings and streams of auts.

His breath caught, and he saw a polluted city. Blinking and shaking his head, it was tree stumps again, and far below him, Reuben held Rudy on his shoulders and pointed at the hillside. Little Rudy pointed too.

Alphonse tried to take a breath, but it turned to a sob. His choking anger became a seed, planted itself, and sprouted. Alphonse stood and hiked away from the stead. With each footfall he thought of the people his mother had placed, the laws they had passed, regulations stripped, money taken and shifted according to greed; the change to Sangal, to Beschel, Narona, Masotin. The change underway in the belt, and his mother's march toward the capital city of Vastol and the Continental Congress for some reason he still didn't understand.

His feet hit the ground harder and his fury built. His boots ripped the ground; he pushed tree limbs aside. Then he broke into a run, fast. He crashed through brush and over roots, hurdling logs and running, screaming; he pelted through dry creek beds, under branches, past brambles, yelling, bolting through the forest until his body collided with dirt.

Alphonse hit the ground again, this time with his fist, harder and harder, shouting his impotency at the sky, the world, until he was spent. He fell into a void and nightmare images, arteries and powerlines—snakes?—beset him. Black ropes circling his body, twining into the land, ensnaring him to the continent. The very world became a serpent, coiling round and round into a giant ball, and he stood upon it and gazed into its eyes. It hissed, *You cannot destroy me. I give you the distillate of time.* He screamed, and with his knees to his chest, waited for morning.

Chapter Twenty-Three

Two weeks of eye exams, every day, with Ephraim's broken scope taped around its middle—Myrta suffered through it all silently, him swearing at the scope and the days passing. Caravan drawing near.

This whole problem was his fault. Why in the name of either sun above hadn't he explained that *using* her trait could damage it? She wanted to tell him he should have been clearer, should have explained that she might hurt herself, and, oh, by the way, did he know Odile was leaving? She could tell him *that*. Anyone else probably would. He'd probably have something to say about *that*. She almost told him twice, just to see the look on his face. Here was something *she* knew, and what did he think about that? But she held her tongue. Because Odile had made a fair point.

Ardelle was so wretchedly nervous that Myrta wanted to lash out at her too.

Odile kept to herself. Of course she did.

Myrta endured the exams and kept her trait off.

Finally, the morning came when Ephraim told her to turn it on. Her palms clammed up, and her nerves pricked away. It would've been easier if he wasn't so obviously anxious. But she took a breath and turned her trait on, expecting mud.

The office air swirled again in reds and greens. Relief flooded through her. "Oh, thank all the five heavens, it works."

Ephraim's face eased, and he brought out his gas canisters again. After another few days he said it was past time to work on distance. They hiked up the path behind the inn.

Caravan wagons would soon pull into town. According to Ephraim, so would the discerners.

"I don't understand why they care about Caravan."

"It's the numbers."

"But why—"

"You know all you need to." He was breathing harder as they climbed. "They'll be in town, and we'll keep you safe."

"Why won't you tell me?"

He stopped. "Because. On top of Mel coming, and on top of Ardelle's anxiety, and Odile's obstinacy, the way she trivializes everything we're up against, I cannot take one more variable. I will not inject any more *fear* into this household."

And suddenly, all the recent little random comments made sense. That winter couldn't come soon enough. That Ardelle might feel better if she'd go buy herself something nice. That Odile should help Myrta practice.

Ephraim's feelings on the matter were crystal clear. To him, she was like the farm was to Terrence. These days they were living through, it was like Terrence when the droughts kept rolling in, when the heat of summer had baked the dirt and he'd head to the trickle of stream past the property with a bucket, as if a bucket would help.

Ephraim was desperate for some speck of control.

Well, so was she. "I want a knife."

"Excuse me?"

Sweat ran down the middle of her back in a punctuated trickle, down past the little gap in her waistband.

"You won't tell me anything, and I don't feel safe. Give me a knife." Nathan carried one. He used it for everything—tightening screws, measuring things. Ripping through the soil after conjunction and cleaning the dirt under his nails. Lots of things.

Ephraim's breath had steadied, but his hair clung to his forehead and his face was moist. "Fine. We'll get you a knife."

They hiked up for over an hour. When they finally stopped, the homes and shops were tiny, a little gameboard in browns and faded green. The air was clear from one edge of the sky to the other, and hazy patches of dust hung low in the belt. Even out past the belt, to the uninhabited stretches, the view was unbroken.

Ephraim sat on a flattish boulder, leaned on his knees and stared outward. "I'm sorry, Myrta. I shouldn't have lost my temper."

She sat next to him. A pebble pushed through her skirt, and she shifted and brushed it away. "I'm sorry too, Papa."

And that was that.

"All right. Let's check your vision."

She dreaded the words, dreaded the mud she'd see. "Myrta?"

"It won't work. It's going to be brown. Everything's too big here. Let's go back to the office."

"It will work." He held out his hand, palm up, waiting for her with his kind of hug, not Celeste's wide-open arms, nor Ardelle's sideways comfort. Ephraim's hugs were always a hand, held open.

She grumbled and took it, and it was warm and strong. "Well, at least when I fail I can say I told you so." She pulled her hand back, turned to face straight down, and flicked her vision on. The colors captivated her again, reds and greens. Blue pulsed into the space between her nose and lap. "Everything's fainter here."

"The higher you go, the less gas there is." Then he said, his voice quavering, "How far can you see?"

She turned her trait off and pursed her lips.

"Sweetheart." His eyes had gone wet again. "Have faith. Try."

Nervous, she turned it on and traced along the ground, outward, toward the side of the path. She saw the air, so beautiful, and the soil below. She worked out seven feet, eight. She startled.

"What is it?"

"There's a . . . a halo of red by the creosote bush." She leaned toward it, staring intently. It was making oxygen.

Ephraim inhaled sharply and began to chuckle. "Plants are supposed to be easy."

"It's plain as day. I see it, Papa. It's breathing." She stared more closely. Besides the oxygen, oils came off the creosote. The scents, they were carbon compounds evaporating away in shades of blue. He was talking about something, but she didn't listen. The scents shimmered in the air like the jasmine had. Her breath never jiggled like that.

"Myrta, are you listening?"

"What?" She turned off her trait.

He sighed. "What is so fascinating about the creosote bush?"

"Some gases jiggle."

He gave her a long look. "Yes. Some reportedly 'jiggle.' A fact you would know if you'd studied the chemistry book I gave you."

That book was impossible. Full of words she had no good reason to learn, diagrams of circles and dots.

"Read it. Ring compounds, like creosote oils, shift between different stereoisomers. They 'jiggle.'"

He seemed to expect her to respond, but what could a person say to something like that?

"All right," he said at last. "Distance. How far can you see?"

She turned her trait on again and followed the slope down to the inn, to the shops in Collimais, the distant stretches of the belt and beyond. In disbelief, she focused further and further out.

There was no mud. Only color, everywhere. Every beautiful shade imaginable, all the way to the horizon. And everything shifted, near and far, and she could see all of it.

Air is so beautiful.

She stretched her arm out and waved her hand through the colors, fingers moving like the gesture of an ancient priestess. She smiled, pushed gases back and forth, like water. Like swimming in a lake and moving the cool water into the warm water, only this was color.

Focusing on any one signal dampened every other one around it, and she could zoom in, see the individual particles, the ones near and the ones far away. The colors didn't blend at all. There was no brown, only swirling rainbows from one edge of the sky to the other.

Ephraim watched her intently. His voice was quiet. "What do you see?"

"Papa. I see all of it. I see all the colors. Every single one. I could work out who's using their stove. Papa, I could find the bakery from here."

The smile started at the corners of his mouth, then crept up, reached his eyes, and he laughed, straight up to the sky. "They say Old Steader Elige could never get lost."

Her attention snapped to the middle of Collimais. "There's a blue cloud moving through town."

He braced backward on the boulder, his weight on his hands. "That, my dear child, that is an aut. More precisely, the carbon dioxide from its tailpipe. I cannot see it, but you can." With a curious expression, he said, "Are there any in the belt?"

She scanned again. Air was so pretty. Layers, she saw layers of it in the sky, and some areas had more carbon dioxide and some had more oxygen. "No. I see carbon, though. A cloud of it there." She pointed. "It's not moving, but someone's burning fuel. Maybe Mr. de Reu running his irrigation."

In that moment, the landscape shifted into a story of interconnected lives. A story Myrta could tell with a glance. She felt a strange release deep in her awareness, as though something pushed and expanded. Like some place inside of her awoke. Like a bird cracking its shell, taking its first breath.

The wagon grounds were cleared, and the shops were stocked and freshened for Caravan. One evening, the family took dessert in the office to discuss keeping Myrta safe. Ardelle handed a bowl of plum crumble to Ephraim. "There's no question. I'll take the girls to the stead. You stay and manage the inn."

Odile took a second bowl. "I'm not going to the stead."

Ardelle dished up a third bowl. "You should visit at least once in your life."

It seemed like a good idea. If they went, Odile

wouldn't have the chance to rustle up any handlers and leave for Narona. Myrta took her bowl of crumble. "It'll be fun. I'll show you—"

"The inn needs me." Odile was glaring at her.

Ephraim chewed at a bite of dessert, frowned at the bowl, and set his fork down. He pushed the bowl away. "We're agreed as far as Myrta's concerned. Take her, come back in two weeks."

But Odile would be gone by then, with the handlers. "Papa. Let's say you're wrong. Mr. di Vaun expects me in the belt anyway. He's probably found the stead and goes there all the time thinking he'll find me."

"*Melville* doesn't think at all."

"Odile," Ephraim said, "not now. Myrta, the reason your trait protects you is because the belt is wide open. There's no easy way for any aut to get close without you knowing, not if you're paying attention. He knows that. And he's strategic. He'll be in the foothills because of the crowds. You're safer in the belt."

Myrta imagined Odile at Renico, surrounded by mechanation and discerners and carbon and who knew what else, getting worn down day after day. No—she wouldn't leave Odile. "You can't send me away every time you're afraid. I'm staying." He studied her and she tensed under it. "Unless Odile goes too."

Ephraim said slowly, his eyes locked on hers, "I don't know what you have in mind, Myrta, but I think I will insist."

"Papa! If my trait had stayed quiet, I'd be matched by now. Probably married and pregnant. And you're treating me like a child. This is my risk, and it's *my* decision."

His gaze bored into her. "What exactly are you planning?"

"Why don't you trust me? *Uncle Ephraim*. You gave me *away*."

"We kept you alive," he roared.

She stood, her chair falling backward. "By pretending I didn't exist! And now you want to send me off because it's convenient? I'm staying." She gave each of them a hard look. Odile's eyes had flown wide, and Ardelle was resting her forehead on her fingers and shaking her head.

Ephraim was back in his chair now, shaken and pale.

"Maybe if you told me what he'd do to me, I'd want to leave."

Ephraim's expression was one of near-breaking desperation. Another drought settling in and all he had was a bucket and a trickle of creek to fight it with. He breathed out in defeat. "We'll all stay. We'll take it as it comes."

Chapter Twenty-Four

Lightning guttered from lowering clouds like a flicking mane of hair, the ends brushing the savannah.

"The world looks like it should."

"Every age looks as it should, Alphonse. But now, we are a mere three hundred thousand years into the past."

Lightning struck, setting a shrub ablaze, and a group of people emerged from the forest. Not quite people. Hairless apes with furs around their middles carrying clubs wrapped in greasy leaves.

Stavo smiled. "They'll enjoy a fine feast tonight."

Alphonse watched them encourage each other. One collected fire from the bush onto his club-end, and they all ran back to the forest, transferring the flame from club to club as they went.

And Alphonse was there too, a boy in the forest clinging to his mother as the men returned and lit the wood in the pit. The fire blazed to life, crackling and hot, and his group cheered and danced. He cried in fear, but his mother held him close. The mustiness of her, the scent he knew, it wrapped him up. She taught him

*to be safe as they cooked their meat. She taught
him that fire kept them warm. She taught him
that it served them.*

*From somewhere nearby his grandfather
said, "Coal and oil are the fuels we burn now,
and we'd be pressed to survive without them.
What is lost, I wonder, with fire gained?"*

They sorted boards, and Fred tied them into stacks,
leaving Manuela and Alphonse to load the wagons. Each bundle fell with a thump onto the bed.

Alphonse pushed the heels of his palms into his eyes
as they went back for another load. "Manny. What do
you know about the prime chancellor?"

"How do you mean?"

He stretched his arms behind his head one by one,
bending them at the elbow and pushing down. Insomnia. Since that moment of double vision, seeing the
belt as a polluted city, he'd not slept well. "Didn't we
learn about it? Doesn't the chancellor keep order in
Congress?"

"I think he moves the agenda."

"It's not very much power." He'd always felt that
way, that holding the top political position on the continent didn't seem to have much going for it. "He gives
up his vote."

They hefted another stack, oak, heavy, and carried
it sideways to the wagon.

"Yeah, that sounds right. I wasn't really a very
good student."

Manny would have taken civics, though, and she
might remember something Alphonse had forgotten.
He shifted his hand, trying to get better purchase on

the wood. "It seems like even a probationary councilor would have more power than the Prime Chancellor."

"Maybe it's an honorary role."

"Maybe." They dropped the stack and pushed it against the others. The wagon was full. They slatted up the rear and started back.

"He can name a province."

Her words fell into place and Alphonse stopped. It was the piece he needed. He turned, looking to the forest and hills beyond. The chancellor could name a province, unilaterally. It never happened, but technically, yes. He could name a province. Provincial law would immediately apply, including not only things like wage requirements, but also the industry's right to prospect for reserves.

Manny stopped too. "I remember that. Our instructor was this guy named di Ren. He kept telling us Renivia Province was named after one of his great grandfathers. The story got real old, real fast. He said every first son ever since was named Rene to keep the connection to the province. It was the only thing he wanted us to learn, that Renivia Province was named after someone in his family."

Miere. The last province named had been Delsina, eighty-some years ago.

A parcel of land had to be a certain size and a certain population. The marshals conducted the annual census during Caravan, and the only individual who could call for provincial status was the prime chancellor.

His mother wanted the belt named. He had to stop her.

There were eight wagonloads of lumber for Caravan. Over supper Reuben chortled that the coming season would see twice as many. "We'll need hands just t' build more wagons."

In the mornings, Rudy stayed with the hands more too. Fred asked Alphonse to keep the boy away from the power tools, and so he sat outside the milling shed while Rudy played.

"Make boards?" Rudy ran back and forth, trailing a stick in the dirt behind him.

"Fred and Manny make boards." Alphonse watched him, this little man who would take the stead one day. Rudy might not ever consider anything else, belt culture being what it was. It was a moment for Alphonse, a view to another life that could have been his but wasn't. If Marco had stayed, Alphonse might have been drawn to his father's work. It happened sometimes. Maybe he'd have gone into architectural design with Marco.

"Boards? Fred and Manny?"

"Yes, Rudy, they're making boards. Look how fast they are—we need more trees." Alphonse yawned.

"More trees?"

Alphonse stood and jumped a few times. "Do you like trees, Rudy?"

"Yeah. Like trees." With his mouth wide, the boy held his stick up, then tilted it and it fell to the ground.

Georgie walked over, Rosa on her hip. "You're a sweetheart to talk with him. He's such a good boy, isn't he? You'll be a good father someday too, Alphonse. It's nice that you listen to him. I mean, Reuben listens, but you're right here, spending time with him. It's nice like that."

"Rudy's a good boy."

"He's an angel. Reuben wants him learning now. You know, finding the right trees."

"I don't think Mr. de Reu's finding the right trees anymore. He's taking all of them."

"Oh, well, he's excited. He's got new toys, you know? New toys are like that. I remember when Reuben bought the stove. What fun I had! I must have cooked every recipe I knew. Anyway, if Reuben clears a hillside, he can plant it back up."

Alphonse scrubbed at both sides of his head and tried to focus. "How deep are the roots?"

"Oh, you know. They're really deep. Mostly they are. Sometimes you pull down a tree with shallow roots. And you wonder, 'Why are the roots so shallow?' But you don't wonder long, because there's another tree right next to it."

"They find water?"

"There's not much water. It's the drought. But yeah, the trees find it."

Rosa began to squirm, and Georgie set her down. The little girl chased Rudy, and they ran toward the house.

Alphonse said, "What if the young trees can't?"

"What?"

"If Mr. de Reu plants small trees, their roots might not go deep enough to find the water."

Georgie's brow furrowed. She cocked her head to the side and slowly walked back to the house after the children.

That evening, he sat in the middle of a cleared patch of stumps, watching his final night on the stead draw to a close. First sun was setting and the light visibly dimmed, the magic of the moment as strong as ever. Everything bright and double-shadowed one minute, then well-lit with sharp edges the next. Tradition said the shift brought clarity.

On this night, as first sun set, the weight in his chest eased.

I failed on Mount Tura, but I tried.

Surely the effort to summit was worth something.

His mother—she had deeper ambitions than he'd ever imagined, and he didn't know how to reach her. But he could try.

The second sun settled, kissing the hills with pink.

Reuben's eight wagons left for Collimais where they would join Caravan. They camped the first evening. The new hands, hired to help drive, told stories that Manny, Fred, and Alphonse hadn't heard before. Even Reuben shared tales, and the evening was rowdy.

The next day they pulled onto Collimais' wagon grounds, on the western edge of town. Alphonse suggested to Manny that they grab a bite. They found a café on the thoroughfare and took a table in back.

"Great to be around people again." Manny grinned at the other patrons.

Alphonse wasn't sure. Odile might still be in town; might walk by. Or she might not. He didn't know which he'd prefer, because if he saw her, she might have nothing to do with him. He hadn't said goodbye, and that had been a mistake. Anyone who had grown up here would have shown courtesy enough to say goodbye. He should have. He glanced out to the street. "Do you miss the cities?"

"Nah. I mean, you know. They have a lot going on, but the air's better here." Manny leaned back and winked at one of the wait staff. She came and stood close to Manny, asked if she needed anything. Manny told her to check later, and the waitress brushed her hip against her and said, "Sure will, honey."

Foothillers passed by outside, enjoying the fine autumn afternoon. Alphonse didn't know how to approach his mother, to change her mind on something she'd spent years working toward.

"Those wagons ahead of us," Manny was saying. "Did you see their load?" Alphonse shook his head and she grinned. "Let's just say you can *smoke* it. We should buy some. Take a little trip without leaving the grounds."

Alphonse laughed, and everything turned around then. They talked about cities, steads, and normal things.

Chapter Twenty-Five

Myrta moved into Odile's tiny bedroom, next to Ephraim and Ardelle's on the inn's lower floor, under strict orders to stay put.

She'd memorized every square inch of the space within fifteen minutes. "Isn't there anything to do in here?"

"Leave," Odile replied, which she promptly did.

Myrta stayed.

She experimented with her vision, flipping it on and off and spelling words in the air with her breath. She ran in place and watched her breath grow deeper blue. That held her interest, but after a few minutes Ardelle knocked and said to keep quiet.

There were eighteen wrinkles in the wallpaper, if you counted the small ones that might be the edges peeling. Six cracks in the ceiling. Odile had four pairs of shoes and an unpaired sandal.

Three days in, Odile snapped, saying there was enough to worry about without an uptight cousin too. Myrta said cabin fever wasn't *her* invention. Odile said to stop griping since all she did was sit around and look at air anyway.

Myrta sucked in a lungful. "At least you can go out." Odile glared, and Myrta hissed, "*None* of this is my fault."

"We know, Myrta. Literally all of us know." But

the anger in Odile's eyes faded. "Come on. We're going outside."

They went out the back, where even the morning heat was welcome—she was out of that room.

Odile strode ahead of her through the orchard. "Hurry. Ephraim will have a fit if he sees you."

Myrta ran to catch up. Once at the overlook, she shaded her eyes. The spread of wagons outside Collimais dwarfed the town, and she gasped. "There's hundreds. Holy heavens, that's a whole season of goods."

"Of course. What'd you expect?"

"Doesn't anything get pilfered?"

"You're kidding, right?"

"It's everything they grew."

A breeze blew up, carrying yells and stakes hammered into the ground. Steaders, at the end of a growing season. An unexpected ache started in her chest, the harvest she'd missed by being here. Myrta pinched her lips thinking of the harvest meals Celeste made. Late nights putting up food; the smell of hay everywhere. Maples turning red.

"Myrta, if anyone stole anything they'd be shunned. It never happens." Odile sank to the ground. "I mean, there're the marshals. They carry doses of pacifon. If a fight breaks out, they take care of it."

There'd been a marshal at market a few years earlier, not in any official capacity, but it had caused a stir. Such an official-looking person out in the belt. "They put people to sleep?"

"They're mostly here for the census. But they carry pacifon, so I guess they're keeping order. No one steals anything. There aren't many fights."

Horses were hitched up on the nearer side of the grounds, and one of them looked a little bit like Rennet, but it was too far to be certain. "Is Jack here?"

Odile leaned back on her elbows. "Yes. He and Nate got in two days ago."

Myrta studied her cousin's profile. Her strong nose, straight hair. The blouse and skirt in a green deeper than the sagebrush around them. Odile was watching the thoroughfare, then looking out to the wagon grounds, then back at the thoroughfare again. She belonged here, Myrta thought, right here. "Please don't go with the handlers."

Odile crossed her ankles. "I'm not. You're right, it would be too hard on Ardelle and Ephraim."

Myrta took a deep breath of relief. "Thank heavens. Oh, thank the holiest heavens above, Odile, thank you."

She didn't respond, just kept watching the thoroughfare and the grounds. The breeze swirled up again and Myrta shifted her lensing.

"What do you see?"

Odile could always tell when Myrta was using her trait. Ephraim, Odile had said, had explained it years ago, how the muscles shifted near the temples. And, she'd said, she'd read the books in the office.

Myrta said, "It's busy. All the stovepipes are going. All of them. There're more auts than normal." She squinted out at the wagon grounds. Black fumes swirled near the hitching posts. "There's methane. I guess it's the manure."

Softly, Odile said, "What's it . . . Myrta, what's that like?"

She looked over. Odile never sounded shy, except she just had. It was odd to see Odile so vulnerable, and Myrta felt gentle suddenly, like the difficulty between them had turned upside down, leaving her, oddly, more knowledgeable than her cousin. She thought of the pain she might feel if things were reversed. "I wish you had it, Odile. The air's beautiful. The lenses in my eyes can do something if I squint, where I see the particles, the molecules, each one of them." She pointed out to the distant pastures. "I can see the breath from each ox in that field. It's like a flower blooming from their nostrils and then fading, again and again. Some of them are mouth breathing."

She looked south. "There are three auts coming from Beamais and one going there. There's some water vapor above Beamais' lake, even though we can't see the town from here and I've never been. Out there," she said, pointing to the belt, "there are more lakes. It's like reading a picture. It's beautiful, and I wish you had it. I wish it was something we could share."

Odile was staring at her toes, her face still. Her face sad. "I used to wish that too." After a while she stood and brushed her skirt off. "We should go back."

They neared the orchard, and Myrta stopped. An aut stood in the lane, the green one, the one di Vaun had driven after market. The one she'd first put her hands on, back at the de Reu stead all those months ago. Alarm filled her, but Odile grabbed and pulled her across the yard, into the inn and toward the bedroom. Once inside she closed the door to a crack. Voices from the front carried.

"I'm sorry, Mel. We're booked."

That was Ephraim.

"You promised a room."

And that was di Vaun, sounding annoyed.

Myrta fell to the cot, her fear giving way to fury. Ephraim hadn't breathed a blessed word about holding a room for that man. It shouldn't surprise her anymore, his inability to provide the most basic information. But holy heavens.

Odile shot her a warning look, shook her head, and went out.

Ephraim's voice sounded pleasant, almost friendly. "Ardelle double booked. When we saw the mistake, we needed your room, but the lodge is nicer anyway. Stay on the thoroughfare. We'll cover it."

"We aren't staying at the lodge. Move one of your guests."

"A settled guest? I don't think that'd work." Then Ephraim added drily, "We have a pallet in the hayloft. Odile could make it up for you."

Odile's voice was next, sounding bored, like she'd just been working on the accounts instead of spending time with Myrta. "The lodge has nicer rooms, and the food's better. Ephraim, we should bring their food in."

"Odile. Mel wants a room, not supper."

Another voice, a new one, chimed in. "The others are staying at the lodge."

"Close off your front room," Melville said. "We'll sleep there."

Myrta dug her nails into her palms. Surely he wouldn't sleep right across the hallway from her.

"I can't see that working. The guests use that room. If you truly enjoy our company, you could always dine with us."

Myrta was sweating.

The other voice said, "The lodge seems nice, sir."

"Mel. It's best. Bigger room, better food, and it's closer to the thoroughfare. You'd be right in the heart of, well, everything."

There was more grumbling and more arguing. That man. His voice.

Ephraim repeated his suggestion, ending with, "We'll make it up next time."

The front door opened and shut. A moment later,

Ephraim barged in, eyes blazing. "I want you in this room."

He was angry at *her*?

Odile was back too, and she dropped onto her bed. Ephraim pivoted to her. "What possessed you to take Myrta out?"

"The hills are as safe as the inn. Melville wouldn't go back there." She pulled her shoes off and dropped them to the floor.

"He might!" Ephraim swung back to Myrta. "You're confined. Here."

"Seriously? I've been stuck in here for three days. It reeks!"

"I don't care," he said icily. "Do not test me." He left.

Myrta fell against the back wall.

After a moment, Odile came and sat next to her. She pulled off her dirty socks, tossed them on the floor with some others, and crossed her legs. Her ankles were filthy. "He's overreacting."

Myrta pulled her blanket away from Odile's feet. "I should've stayed in."

Odile didn't respond, just sat there with a thoughtful expression. After a few moments, a wicked smile flickered around her mouth. "Do you want to know what Melville does to people like you?"

Myrta looked over sharply. "I thought you didn't know."

She laughed soundlessly and raised her eyebrows. "We know what they *used* to do."

Myrta forced herself to breathe. "Tell me."

Odile leaned over, and in a lilting voice, said, "He wants to slice into your face. He wants to cut into you so he can look at your muscles. And he wants you wide awake while he *dissects* you."

Myrta's stomach twisted. That couldn't be right. There'd be no purpose to it. It would make more sense to kill her outright, blind her or take her ovaries, something like that.

Odile ran her fingers back from her own eyes as she spoke. "He likes peeling the skin back. Real slowly. And then, he likes watching your muscles *contract.*"

"Stop it. I don't believe you."

"He makes you *use* your trait while you're bound and gagged and sliced wide open." Odile stood, taking up all of the free space in the room. She threw her arms out, flailed, and cried, "He likes the screaming."

"That's enough." Myrta put her hands to the sides of her head and closed her eyes.

"First on the *left* and then on the *right.*"

"Stop. Stop it!" Myrta pulled her legs up.

Odile leaned over and hissed, "Then he goes inside your eyeballs. With needles."

"I said stop. I don't need to know any of this!"

"Oh, fine." Odile sat. "The point is, you *don't* know. It's beyond stupid that you're sitting here when there's so much going on out there."

Myrta stared up at the crack in the ceiling. "Di Vaun gets in my head, like a song I can't stop hearing." *We'll take you with us when we leave . . . I understand she's here . . . You promised us a room . . . I understand she's here . . .*

"Melville's a worm. A disgusting, filthy worm with bad breath who wants to carve you up." Odile sat without moving. "You know what? I'm going to find Jack. Do you want to come?"

Myrta glared at her. "No."

"Suit yourself. Enjoy . . ." she looked around, "the bedroom."

After Odile left, Myrta rolled off the cot and kicked

Odile's dirty socks under her cousin's bed. Then she cracked the window and looked around again. She picked through the stack of books on the nightstand. One was a drug manual. A few pages were earmarked, with notes scribbled in the margins. There was a book on the global environment. And another, worn and smudged. *Anatomy of the Genetically Modified Human Eye.*

She took that one to the cot. Half the words made no sense, and the diagrams brought Odile's words back. . . . *while he dissects you* . . . Nauseated, she closed it and lay there.

After a while Ardelle opened the door. "I brought supper."

"Can you bring me a candle? I want to burn something."

Ardelle frowned and set the tray down.

"Mama, I've been stuck in here for years. Shouldn't I practice? I think I should."

Ardelle glanced around the room, her expression softening, and she went back out. She returned with a candle.

The meal was roasted vegetables and sauce, buttery and smoky, like it had all been cooked on a wood fire from one of the carts on the wagon grounds. It tasted like the outdoors, fresh and sharp, especially the tomatoes. It tasted like harvest, like Celeste's meals back on the farm. The belt had a rhythm Myrta understood, all the details in place, neat and tidy, even who you'd marry was all figured out. Celeste had said she could go back someday. Maybe doing so made sense. She understood the belt. Renico? Not so much. "Renico targeted Great-Grandpapa."

Ardelle's eyes turned tired, like the skin around

them wanted to fold right over. "Yes, they did. But they never caught him."

"Tell me about him."

"Sweetheart. I was small." Ardelle put her plate on Odile's nightstand and stood to open the curtains wider. "Mama and Papa fought whenever Grandpapa came, that's all I remember. Mama didn't want him living in the mountains, because he was getting on, but he always went back after his visits."

"Stop. Why did he live there?"

"Well, Papa said the mountains were safe because people with other traits live there. It seems . . . I don't know, it's hard to believe that there are people there, but Grandpapa certainly was. Ephraim thinks it could be true, some group in the mountains. But if it is we shouldn't know too much about them. That if there are . . ." Ardelle fiddled with her fork, "if there is a pool of genes, forgive me, that's very clumsy, a group of people with certain genetics living there, then *not* knowing about them keeps them safer."

Living in wilderness. It would be more isolated than the stead. "You're saying people live in the mountains just to be safe from the combustion industry."

Ardelle seemed so tired. Her shoulders, her hair, even her clothing seemed to drag down. "It's possible. He left a few letters. I have them somewhere. Sweetheart, there's something you need to know. This inn is part of a network. We give refuge to anyone who needs it."

"Mama. How can that be? Mr. di Vaun stays here."

"Only when we let him. As they say, pen the fox to save the chickens. Yes, he knows we shelter people. Ephraim suggested that we send you to Arbremais right now, since Melville is here, but it's so far away, and you had no intention of leaving."

"Mama."

"I know it's a lot."

Myrta sighed. She looked around, as if something new would pop up in this little hole. For all the dirty socks on the floor, Odile's bed was tidy. Her nightstand was stacked neatly with those books, and the dresser sat square against the wall.

Odile knew the family history and had for years. She'd had time to make peace with it.

I wish I'd known . . . But it didn't matter. It was time to catch up. "How can a whole network exist for a few people?"

Ardelle fiddled with her fork again, pushing her last bite of food around. "It's more than a few."

"What do you mean?"

"There are other traits.[3] Different combinations, like we've said all along. Different abilities. The marshals, they have altered myostatin. They're very strong. That's common, as these things go. We think they have a second mutation linked to myostatin to draw them to law."

An odd thing happened at Ardelle's confession. Between one moment and the next, the idea of being born wrong fell away. It just fell away. Myrta's trait was a combination. Like height. Like hair texture, or skin tone during conjunction. Her trait was normal, a combination of genes, and everyone had their own combination. She was just like everybody else.

Ardelle said, "Some believe that aggression was removed from our genes after we landed on Turaset. Our ancestors may have been much more violent than we are. And of course, the colonists didn't have secondary skin pigments."

---

3   A list of fictional genetic modifications is described in Appendix 3.

The words barely registered. Myrta was normal, just a different normal.

"There were so many challenges in the early years. The founders—according to the stories, the founders needed to make very difficult choices to survive."

There was nothing wrong with her, and she wasn't born wrong any more than anyone else. "Thank you, Mama."

Outside, the light was almost gone and Ardelle picked up the dishes. "I'll be in the kitchen." On her way out, her eyes fell on the candle. "Please don't burn down my inn."

Different combinations. Different genes. Different traits.

Myrta lit the candle. Carbon plumed away from its flame in brilliant blue and she looked around for something to burn. There wasn't much to choose from—dirty socks, tracked mud.

Books.

She idly ripped a corner off a page and put the snippet in the flame. Blue carbon flickered outward and yellow streaks of soot drifted down. She burned another corner. One by one she incinerated her way through the corners of the book.

Then, using the knife Ephraim had picked up, she carved splinters out of the windowsill and burned those. They didn't catch as easily as the paper.

Minutes passed.

Someone tapped the window and a muffled voice said, "Myrta."

"Jack!"

There he was, grinning, outside.

She ran to the back door to let him in. He looked the same, clean shaven, even his head bald like he did sometimes. She said, "You smell like horses. Come into the bedroom."

She threw a pillow from the cot and sat, suddenly nervous in a way she hadn't expected because this was Jack. She said, "I don't know if you're still my brother. I mean," she swallowed, "you're kind of not my brother anymore, and we didn't really talk about it."

He sat next to her. His lips thinned and his eyes were just a little moist, but he was smiling too. "I think I always knew something was off. Look at Odile. Look at Nathan, and how much the same those two are. But you—Myrta. You'll always be my sister."

Jack always made up his own mind. Maybe he'd be newly bald, like he was now, and she'd wonder if that really was about keeping the dirt down or if there was more to it because no one in the belt was ever bald except for Jack. And he'd say tradition was fine for what it was, but someday he'd be somewhere else.

She hugged him. "Well. Good. Yes, I always will be."

"Listen, Myrta. I only have a second before Nate wants me back, but Odile said you're dying in here. Come to the grounds. Come visit. The wagons go on forever. There's food, entertainers—everything."

"I can't leave."

"What, your legs don't work? Just come. I'll be there. It'll be fine."

She started to answer, but he stood and ducked back toward the door. "No. Come. Come visit. I'm not taking no for an answer. I will see you. Goodbye."

By the end of the next day, ash covered everything in the bedroom. Odile walked in, stared at the coating, opened one of the books on the nightstand, and raised her eyebrows at the missing corners. "Learning much?"

"Socks don't light."

"Mm." She pulled a sweater from her dresser and went back out.

Myrta fell asleep at odd hours and lay awake into the nights. Even cleaning would be better, and Ardelle brought her a pail and washcloth. Myrta lugged the dresser out, wiped the floor behind it, then worked her way under the cot and around to the next section of wall.

Cobwebs clung to the nightstand, she wiped them off. As she tipped the stand to get at the feet, something jostled.

It was another book, this one strapped to the underside of the nightstand. Myrta fell back against Odile's bed and pulled it out. It was a journal. It smelled like old saddle. She stared at the spray of flowers carved into the leather.

She really oughtn't read it.

On the other hand, she'd been cleaning for five minutes at least.

The first page had a beautiful inscription, written in cursive. "Dearest Odile, for your dreams. Love, Mama Ardelle."

Blocky words filled the next page, misspelled with letters sloping down. It had been Odile's sixth birthday and they'd had chocolate cake. She'd wanted a visit from the de Terrs.

The next pages described days at the inn, a visit from someone or other, going somewhere in the carriage.

Rapt, Myrta turned page after page. She came to a childish picture, eight stick people, the Vonards and de Terrs holding hands and standing in front of the inn. Faces looked out every second-story window and two suns shone in the top left. Myrta remembered that visit. The inn had been full.

She read more, and as she read, she recalled her own childhood in the belt, running in the fields, playing in the forests, being five, being six, being seven. She turned the pages, thinking about the girls they'd been.

On Odile's eighth birthday Ardelle made carrot cake. Odile's writing was better, with fewer errors and small, even lettering.

Then Myrta came to a section with no pages, just remnants of paper clinging to the spine, memories ripped away. Myrta looked under the nightstand, but there was nothing. The pages were gone.

Past the missing section, the handwriting was the slanted hand Myrta knew from some of the inn's receipts. The diary ended with, "I don't have a mama. I don't have a papa. I'm a placeholder."

Shaking, Myrta closed the book and tucked it away.

The next afternoon Myrta was working through the last chapters of a textbook, one even thicker than the beginning chemistry book, and the entire thing, from the first page to the last, described sulfur-containing gases. There were far, far too many.

Odile came into the room and Myrta rolled onto her back and groaned. She dropped the book to the floor where it hit squarely with a thump. The impact reverberated through the cot frame and into her. Even the floor didn't like the thing. "You've been smiling all week. It's driving me nuts. Stop being happy."

"I'm not happy, I'm resolute." Odile hummed as she rifled through her closet.

"Stop being resolute."

Odile pulled a skirt out, folded it, and set it on her bed. She glanced around the tidy room. "Nothing else burns?"

Myrta didn't answer, just waved a sheet of paper that had fallen out of the textbook. It was the sheet she'd seen weeks earlier, with "Missing" written across the top. Circumstances surrounding each disappearance and "di Vaun" scribbled along the margin.

Parts of it were in Ephraim's handwriting and parts in Odile's. One of those had a small heart inscribed.

"This makes everything so real. The danger."

Odile took a pair of shoes from her closet and put them next to the skirt on her bed. "I asked Jack to come back."

"Thank you."

"I don't think he can. Nathan wants him talking with the other growers. Tonight's your last chance. If you go, he's in the closest row near the northern edge." She piled toiletries with her other items. "Don't wait up." She left.

Myrta lay flat on the cot and pushed the bedsheets down with her feet.

She could do as Odile suggested. She could visit Jack and get her mind off that stupid list of names. She'd been in this stuffy little room all week. This room where no one else spent more than five minutes. For all she knew, Melville and that other man might be gone by now. No one would have bothered to tell her. She kicked at the sheets again, and the list of names fluttered off, out of sight, like a sign.

She stared at the rumpled bedsheets at her feet, a mass of peaks and valleys and ridgelines and canyons.

She nudged at the edge of the bedsheets, traced up one of the creases with her toe. Before she could change her mind, she jumped off the cot and ran out the back of the inn, heading up to the overlook.

There were at least twice as many wagons as before. More than that. They spilled past the edges of the grounds and into the streets of Collimais itself. Animals, goods, people—in a heartbeat she knew. No one could find anyone in a crowd like that. And all of those people were steaders. Her people.

Myrta smiled, and a breeze blew straight through her. She breathed it in, beautiful air blowing the week away. She held her arms straight out sideways, closed her eyes, and laughed into the wind. She'd visit Jack, tonight. She'd see him, and the wagon grounds, and all of Caravan. Tonight.

Chapter Twenty-Six

Herds covered the plains. Horses and bison, sloths and camels. Grazing. Migrating. The air smelled of tar.

"It's cold," Alphonse said.

"The glaciers advance."

"Is it the blue-green bacteria?"

"No. This time it is the world's tilt and orbit. The forces that allow life, Alphonse, extend past the planetary boundary. Solar activity, variations in the orbit and ecliptic. The physics are not hard to understand, but we're not here for that. Live the age, Alphonse."

Alphonse fell to all fours, he was a dire wolf bounding through the Pleistocene, with strong forelimbs and stronger hindlimbs. With his pack, he drove a group of pronghorns. He and his closest pack-mate separated a doe from the herd, and it dashed over logs and between shrubs, toward the acrid petroleum pits.

Running harder, faster, they closed on the prey, and leaping, Alphonse sank his jaws into the animal's hip. Blood spurted into his mouth in salty, hot victory. The animal kicked him in the chest, then landed a blow between his eyes; it was dragging him. He wrenched it side to side, his pack-mate at its forequarters now, *and together they overpowered the doe. He yanked the hip with a pop; his partner was at the animal's throat.*

They tore into the stomach, to the sweet entrails. Glorious rich fat covered his face, intestines dangled from his mouth. Alphonse lapped it up, mouthful after mouthful. He attacked the rear haunch again as the other wolf ripped fur and flesh from the shoulder.

As his hunger eased, Alphonse pushed to stand, but his hind foot mired into the sticky, black ground. He pulled harder. Yipping, struggling, he found himself trapped. Before an hour had passed he was too weak to move.

"When we lose foresight, we risk our very lives. Keep reason close, always. It tempers our instincts as we fight to survive."

Half of Reuben's wood was sold in Collimais. The remainder included a load of burled black sweetnut, a rare tree unique to the belt. Alphonse and Manny unloaded planks of it for a woodworker from Terremais.

Reuben chortled, "None o' the other loggers had sweetnut. She's been lookin' all week."

"It's beautiful, sir." Alphonse lugged more of the boards off the back. The wood, with swirls of black checker marks against a white grain, was like an intricate piece of art. It reminded him of the table in his mother's study.

"Beautiful nothin'. Fetches twice when no one has it."

Manny and Alphonse loaded the woman's vehicle

as she settled with Reuben. Then he released them for their final evening in Collimais, and they walked to the thoroughfare. Another impromptu party was forming in the Grand Square.

"You want to check that out?" Manny was eyeing one of the food carts. From the smells, the vendor was roasting raptorfowl.

"No, I'm beat." He hadn't slept. Couldn't sleep. He yawned, the strain pulling against his mouth.

But despite his exhaustion, the evening was fine. Friendship with Manny had no taint of politics; they simply got on well, and Manny suggested one of the pubs. They took a table in front, one that looked out to the thoroughfare. This particular pub, in fact, faced the very hardware store Odile had shown him so many months earlier.

Manny went for drinks and returned a few minutes later, humming happily. The yeasty smell of her ale infused the air, blending with ciguerro smoke from a nearby table. Handing a mug over, Manny said, "Civilization, yeah? Love it."

Maybe. He needed to get home. Provincial governance of the belt would destroy it.

"Yeah, I need to get home. You're coming back with Reuben, right?"

"Right, yeah. There and back, whatever he needs." Froth hung on Manny's lip and she licked it off, sighing and grinning.

Alphonse rubbed his forehead, worked his fingers to the top of his head, scratching his hair, oily and rough. With his arms up, he realized more than his hair was dirty. "Regular bathing'll be nice."

Manuela laughed.

"So what'll you do after? You know, back in Narona."

She'd finished half her pint already and settled back in her chair and propped the mug on her stomach. "Carry packages. See the coast. Find places to build."

She had a clear shot to her future. Alphonse nodded. He couldn't see his own. Townsfolk, steaders, by and large they didn't seem to want a province. Prime Chancellor Nabahri hadn't ever named it, no doubt there'd be a revolt if he tried. He yawned again and grabbed a handful of nuts from a passing waitress. "Look. If you make it up to Sangal, let me know. We'll grab a bite."

Manny shifted. "Uh, well. I do sometimes, and don't get me wrong, it's a nice city."

"You don't like Sangal?"

Manny stared out to the street; she raised her eyebrows and tilted her head sideways and back. There was an awkward, long silence. "Oh, you know. I mean, it doesn't smell like Narona, so that's a plus."

No way was Sangal sub-par to Narona, of all places. "But?"

"I avoid Sangal. Unless there're packages going north, because then it's on the way. Hard to say no if you've got a job up the coast, but I ask for the southern route, down to Granvil."

Granvil was an arts community, a bunch of painters with canvases and brushes. Drugs, bad music, and the highest poverty rate on the continent. Manny preferred that to Sangal? "What's wrong with Sangal?"

She'd had most of her ale and was loosening up, but still she grinned and shook her head no. Alphonse waved the server over, ordered two more pints and waited while Manny wandered around in conversation through her next drink. Family, school, old girlfriends, the works. Another round of drinks, more conversation, and Alphonse asked again.

Manny leaned over, her eyes flashing around the room. She murmured, "Look, Narona's a dive. For sure. But the government isn't killing people, you know?"

Is this about Grandfather? "What do you mean?"

"Come on. You have to know about this."

"I'm not sure." Alphonse kept his voice low.

The neighboring tables were celebrating a week of hard selling, so this conversation needn't attract any attention at all. As busy as the pub was, no one was likely to notice their conversation. His mother used to say anywhere could be private.

"All right. I used to deliver there. Anything that needed to go. Books, papers . . . whatever. Sometimes things went *back* to Narona. And those packages? The ones sent back? They'd start to smell, and I know all the normal smells, if you know what I mean. Sometimes the packages *leaked*."

Alphonse stared at her, his fatigue now gone. "Manny—"

"It gets worse. The packages would come from some little nondescript place in the middle of Sangal. Like, you wouldn't know who it came from, but there were rumors."

She had to be pulling his leg. Alphonse had never heard anything remotely like this. "Who sent them?"

Manny looked around the pub again and began to chuckle. "They didn't *label* it, Alphonse. Some of the couriers say it's the government. Someone with the government."

"That's crazy. They—what, you mean they're sending *body* parts? Why?"

"Keep your voice down. They went to Renico. Renico sent these nice tidy envelopes to this place in the middle of Sangal, and there'd be a . . . package to go back. At first I thought it couldn't be anything real. I thought I imagined it, but you know, over a few years, it happened a couple more times. I asked the other couriers and they said no one stays on that route for long. They give it to new couriers."

It had to be her imagination. Alphonse would have heard something—there'd have been gossip, some tipoff. Fierno—his mother would have found out and used the information.

"Yeah, that kind of stuff never happens when I go to the southern cities. Not saying they don't have their own problems, but you don't want that kind of thing in your aut."

After the pub, Manny left Alphonse and went to meet her waitress friend down at the café. Alphonse walked back to the grounds. She couldn't be right about the packages.

Autore, Grandfather's casket was closed.

Odile was there, on the grounds, facing away, talking with two men. Alphonse flushed. She was still here, in Collimais. She hadn't left, hadn't gone any-where. He could talk to her, *should* talk to her. She deserved that. She might even know something about what Manny had said.

She nodded to the men, then turned and her gaze fell straight on him. Her eyes hardened and there was a slight shake to her head.

Or not. Fine. He didn't need to see her. He hadn't wanted to anyway; still didn't want to. He strode past the group toward the far side of the grounds, yanked his tent flap open and tied it to the corner. Heat and staleness wafted out. He didn't need to see her at all.

His flash of anger faded. Except, he'd missed her. He'd missed Odile's passion, her insight. He'd missed everything about her.

"Thank you, Al, for going wide."

He turned and there she was, and her eyes weren't hard at all. She looked how he remembered, the only difference being the purple undertones in her complexion—her secondary pigments beginning to show. She was so pretty. Her skirt fluttered around her shins. Her blouse, worn and wrinkled, and her eyes like mountain granite.

"Odile. Your family opposes Renico, right?"

She drew in a sharp breath.

"Right?"

She looked at the people nearby. "Walk with me."

He did, and they passed the fenced oxen, more tents, and a few food carts. Odile walked without speaking, purposefully, the wind pushing her hair back. They reached the dirt road out to the belt, and she kept going, no sign of slowing.

"It's one thing to talk at the inn," she finally said, still striding along. "It's another to blurt out something like that in a crowd."

There was something so innocent about it, that the people at the tent seemed like a crowd to her, and he smiled as they kept going. "Odile. A friend I've been logging with, she carries packages. Says the government murders people, chops them up, and sends parts to Renico."

Odile burst out laughing, but she didn't seem surprised. "You and Ephraim should talk. I told you, it's profit."

"Is it true?"

She didn't really answer. She frowned, faced away, wouldn't look at him. She said at last, "They claim to improve lives, but it doesn't hold up. Not when you think about the droughts and the cyclones. I mean, holy heavens, in a bad year a thousand people or more die in those storms. So, yes, of course they kill."

That wasn't what he meant, and she knew it. He waited, and after a few more paces she said, "Ephraim killed."

Now it was his turn to laugh. "Yeah, highly doubtful." The man wrote protocols. His mannerisms, his meticulous nature—none of it was that of a killer. He was a medical aide, a technician, something like that.

She stopped walking and turned to face him. "How is it that I know more about your grandpapa's death than you do about the Vastol Vendetta?"[4]

"The Vastol . . ."

"Vendetta. The two councilors murdered in Vastol, I don't know, twenty years ago. Ephraim was there."

Alphonse had been a child, barely old enough to speak, but a memory surfaced. *There's been a backlash . . .* His grandfather's words floating up the stairwell. Alphonse remembered hugging his stuffed lion at the top of the steps. Someone yelled, something crashed and broke. His mother's voice. *You're going to get us killed!* The vendetta . . .

Two councilors in Vastol, the capital city and home to the Continental Congress, had drafted a bill requiring the combustion industry to publicize certain data. But before it passed, those councilors were killed, their corpses found days later in the river, eyes removed, faces sliced open.

Their seats had gone to investors with Garco, the subsidiary of the industry in Garrolin Province.

Alphonse reeled, his foot caught on a lip of dirt, and he fell back and down. It was incomprehensible,

---

4   These events are described in *The Vastol Vendetta*, a short story found at pltavormina.com

that this plot his mother was caught up in might trace back so far. Had she been involved with combustion even while her own father was alive? No, she must have been brought in.

The wind picked up, blowing along the hillsides and through his shirt, a low, soft howl. "Odile." He searched her face, latched onto her cool, gray eyes and tried to ease the ache in his heart.

Her face shifted to patience, then to a soft smile. "Don't be too hard on Ephraim. There were circumstances. It was a long time ago, and I truly don't know the details. He's made amends for whatever role he may have played." She looked off to the side, to a copse of copperwoods. "Holy heavens. *I'm* the one who's hard on him. He's found people up and down the foothills, organized us, gotten us to decide for ourselves if modernization is what we want. He's done that almost singlehandedly."

"Ephraim *killed*?" It stretched Alphonse to the breaking point and made Manny's claims quaint by comparison.

"I don't know the details. He was there."

Dust imps blew down the road, her skirt blew up, she pulled it snug against her legs with one hand and held out the other. He took it, pulled up, and gestured to the copperwoods. They went into the windbreak, and she stood nearer than before. The tilt of her head, her eyes searching him, it was like a salve.

"Odile, what does Ephraim know about Vastol's Council? How many delegates would vote to replace Prime Chancellor Nabahri?"

She scoffed. "I doubt he knows *that*."

The smell of her was the same as he remembered, spices and herbs. She'd been cooking. He inhaled quietly, stretching the breath out. She smelled right. He didn't know when he'd learned it, the earthy tones of her underneath the spice. He inhaled a second time, taking this breath longer, pulling the air deep into his chest.

Odile let go of her skirt. "Do you believe your logging friend?" She was close enough that she needed to tip her head to look at him. She was close enough he could put his arm around her and grab the trees on the other side.

"I don't disbelieve her. I'll ask around."

The wind blew through the branches overhead, not a wail but a hush. She leaned into him. "It's really windy. This windbreak is too small to—"

He kissed her. He wrapped his arms around her and pulled her in. She held back, caught off guard maybe. But then, she opened up. And she was so soft, her mouth yielding, her body fitting. She smelled so good, and her passion . . . she kissed him, with her lips and her tongue and her arms around his back.

Odile had been his introduction to all of this. His gateway to the belt, its sensibilities. And this wasn't her first kiss, and that excited him too.

She was so slender. His arms could probably go around her twice. How had he never noticed? It must be her drive, or else her clothes were too baggy. It didn't matter. He pulled her closer, her mouth tangy. He kissed her cheek, her neck, under the ear where she'd rubbed something. Her head tipped back. He couldn't get enough, and her breathing grew louder. He didn't know what this kiss was, a beginning or a goodbye. He wanted her, wanted this, this life, all of it.

"Al, I want you—"

"I want you too, Odile," he murmured into her hair, grabbing handfuls of her blouse into his hands, aching to feel the small of her back, warm and soft, delicate. Pulling her, needing her.

"I want you," she breathed, "on the Council."

He stopped.

The wind blew through the branches, louder. His arms were tangled around her, still caught up in the cloth of her shirt. Her words hung in the air. He couldn't *un*hear them. He stepped back, away from her, this young woman with ideas about his future. "What the fierno?"

She pulled away too and pushed her hair from the side of her face, the side moist from his affection. She swallowed, wiping her mouth with the back of her hand. Even her breathing was steadying out. "You can make a difference. A real difference."

He couldn't get his mind around it. His heart pounded, blood sang in his ears, and he needed something right now, but not politics.

He jammed his hands in his pockets. "I actually wanted *you*, Odile. Nothing of you, just you."

The kiss, in that moment when she kissed back, it had been a connection, a confession between them, the family he'd choose, and for a fleeting moment he thought she would too. Maybe politics *was* the core of power. Maybe he was naïve to think otherwise.

"Don't be stupid. It makes no difference what you want. It's *never* mattered what I want."

This life, he'd come to love all of it, and for a moment Odile seemed like his harness here outside the cities, an anchor to hold to. But this anchor bent downward. He couldn't trust it.

There was no family here. Back home there'd be only dysfunction. His mother had raised him to see people's motivations before they knew those things themselves, and he had completely, utterly botched seeing that in Odile. If Manny knew his name, if Reuben did, they'd play him too. "Forgive me for being stupid. I guess I thought I mattered to you."

Her hair blew forward again, and frowning once more, she pulled it behind her head. "In fifty years or a hundred we'll be gone, and it won't matter one whit if we cared for one another or not. The *only* thing that matters is that you can be on the Council. Take charge, make the system better. Heavens above, we need it. *Turaset* needs it."

Any life here was slipping out of reach, but as soon as his anger filled him, it drained away.

Because this was Odile. Her expression. Her beautiful face so full of passion, so full of a belief in a better future, even at the expense of herself, her own feelings, and he wanted that too. Here she was, asking him to fight for the future. How could he say no? She'd probably do it herself in his place. She'd storm into Governance Hall and spark a revolution if she could.

He said quietly, "It's not that simple. Combustion owns Sangal's Council, and there's no easy way for a dishonest boob like me to make any real difference."

He said it without thought, without recalling that they'd never actually spoken of those careless words she'd dropped back when he started at the inn. He'd never admitted that he'd even overheard their conversation that night before closing his window. But the look on her face now—he hadn't meant to shock her. Not Odile, the woman who in this moment he'd trade his past for. "I'm sorry, Odile. I—"

"No. No, I'm the one who's sorry, Al. It's possible . . . you know what, it's possible I was wrong about you."

Chapter Twenty-Seven

The inn settled down. Ephraim went out for the evening and Ardelle turned in. Quietly, Myrta left the inn and made her way to the wagon grounds, which were loud enough she could have found them with her eyes closed.

Inner ring, northern edge.

She found Terrence's wagons. These were his, there was no doubt. She'd helped repair the rails a few seasons earlier. But there were hardly any grain sacks and no tobacco. A few whiskey barrels stood on the second wagon.

The yields must have been horrible.

Jack jumped down from the whiskey wagon and called over the noise, "Hey! You made it."

The other wagons had their own horribly scant yields.

"It's louder than I expected," she yelled.

"Let's go out a ways. I'll tell Nate." Jack jogged around the second wagon.

Movement on a neighboring wagon caught her eye, a couple involved with one another in an intimate way. She flushed and looked down. Jack returned, and they made their way down an aisle.

She raised her voice again. "Is it like this every year?"

"Yeah."

A steader going the other way grinned at them, and

Jack raised his hand at the man. It was no one she recognized, but Jack always made friends.

Ahead, a fiddler played a market song. Jack nudged her and pointed at two men in front of the fiddler. They were dancing to the tune and using identical footwork. The musician played faster and faster. They kept up, focusing on their feet, keeping the pattern.

One of them was Emmett, the cotton steader's son, wearing a richly-dyed tunic and vest. He was tall, that was plain even as he half-crouched for the dance, and he was handsome enough, but so old. She might have married him, if her life had gone differently.

Myrta tore her eyes away, and they walked past the dancing game. "Is Nate selling? The wagons were empty."

"It's the drought. We won't recover costs, but he's made new contacts and we might plant more acreage. Depends if we buy the irrigation." The noise tapered a bit as they walked outward. By the edge of the grounds there were fewer lanterns, a handful of people and some food carts. Jack bought her a candied apple and they took the next aisle back in.

She licked caramel from the apple's fat middle. The sweetness coated her mouth, gooey and thick.

She pulled her hair back. "Jack. You don't want to be a farmer. Why do you do all this?"

He grinned and looked away. Sometimes he was like that; he'd take a few minutes to answer. She focused on the apple. Freshly dipped, the caramel warm, the fruit cracking as she bit into it. Tart juices slipping under her tongue.

"You know, it's not forever. Nate'll start a family someday."

They drew near the innermost ring. It was loud again, and they cut through wagonloads of poppy pods to the next aisle. Caramel was coating her fingers now. "You'll leave the stead?"

He smiled a little half smile. "I'll do something."

She looked at him more closely. It seemed pretty clear he had an idea. "What something?"

"Something." He grinned, and they kept walking.

There were fewer people as they went out; the people had all congregated at the inner ring with the lanterns and music.

"That's it? Something?"

"Yeah." He was beaming now, and it was odd, him talking about not being on the farm, but not talking about it at the same time.

"You aren't going to tell me," she said. "Fine." They drew near the outer edge. The tents were out here, where it was quieter.

A small group of people stood past the wagons, in shadows amongst the tents. She pulled Jack back. "Look."

Odile was there, with four others in city clothes. They were handlers, scouts. They had to be.

"She *lied* to me, Jack." Myrta cupped a hand behind her ear.

". . . overnight . . ."

"I'm ready to leave."

". . . indenture . . . three months."

Odile said, "That seems fair."

"We can't let her." Myrta ran out.

Odile saw her and yelled, "No," just as one of the others turned.

It was Melville di Vaun.

Myrta turned back in panic and slammed into Jack. His face lit. He pushed around Myrta, went straight for di Vaun, and pulled back to slug him.

Melville grabbed Jack's arm and forced him to the ground. "Floyd, grab her."

Myrta ran toward the wagons, but Floyd was on her, pinning her to his side. She screamed. He hauled her up and clamped his hand over her lips. It stank of ciguerros. The filth on his hands got into her mouth. Odile was yelling too, held fast by two men. They dragged her off.

Jack was on the ground, unmoving. Myrta flailed, pulled at Floyd's fingers, tried to get them out of her mouth. They tasted vile and it wasn't just ciguerros. She bit them as hard as she could and he yelped. Her neck grew damp from his breath.

"Myrta."

She froze. Melville was inches from her. He gestured behind a tent, and Floyd dragged her back, kicking, with Melville right behind.

Melville took a knife and flipped it open. He ran the sharp edge along the side of her face. The blade was warm. It scraped her skin. Her heart pulsed in her ears. Sweat drenched her. She tried to scream, but Floyd grabbed her hard.

Melville smiled, and even in the low light his dimples showed. "Don't need to examine you at all."

A shudder ran through her and she twisted harder and freed her mouth. "Help!"

"Hold her," Melville roared.

Floyd wrenched her sideways. "Yes, sir."

Melville's grin was wolfish. His voice was cold and detached. "You're developed."

She squeezed her eyes shut, twisting from the blade again. He put the knife on the other side of her face, turning her head square to him. "Good specimen."

Against the back of her head, she felt Floyd swallow.

"Floyd. You're overdue on fieldwork." Melville handed his knife over. "Think about the anatomy. Give the extra-orbital muscle group a warning tap."

"Yes. Yes, sir." Floyd swallowed again.

Myrta struggled and a sharp pain jabbed out from her forehead.

"Too high," Melville barked. He grabbed the blade and gouged straight into her temple and she screamed. Pain wrapped down her cheek and around to her ear. Nauseous, hot, she fell over Floyd's arm, retching.

"Stop!" Ephraim was pelting over with three steaders.

Myrta struggled to stand and Floyd smacked her temple.

Ephraim's eyes were desperate, and he said to Melville, "Please, Myrta's my daughter. Let her go. I'm asking you. By Autore, we're *friends*."

Melville looked at her again. Something new lit in his eyes, a reckoning. His expression grew deadly serious as he turned to Ephraim. "You know the first lesson. My family, your family, a stranger's—it makes no difference."

At those words, Ephraim lunged straight toward di Vaun's stomach. Melville wrestled back easily, like someone half his age. He shoved Ephraim into a tent, toppling it. Ephraim pushed up, yanked a stake from the ground, and smashed it against Melville's head. Melville went for Ephraim's stomach with the knife.

Myrta kept screaming. She wrangled her foot around Floyd's ankle, and another steader was on his back. They all three fell and she twisted away, but Floyd still had her by the arm.

More angry shouting came from the wagons. A heavily-muscled woman on horseback rode up with more steaders racing behind.

The marshal slung off of her horse, it reared and raced to the tents, snorting. The marshal yanked Floyd's arm back with a sort of strong grace, and citing regulations and codes of order, pulled a syringe from her holster and injected him. He sank and Myrta was free. She scrabbled away, then ran to Ephraim who was clutching his stomach. She tried to hold him. "Papa, Papa," she cried. Blood was everywhere, soaking his shirt, the ground.

Meanwhile a few others were on Melville, and the marshal settled him with a second dose of pacifon.

Ephraim's head lolled to the side. Myrta cradled him and tears streamed down her face. A few feet away, Jack was groaning.

Two steaders transferred Ephraim onto a wide plank and carried him off toward the town clinic. Sobbing, Myrta followed. Jack too.

A nurse at the clinic opened the door. She ran her eyes up and down Ephraim and said, "Put him in the first room." She pulled supplies from a cupboard and sent one of the steaders for the doctor. Then she inserted a tube into Ephraim's stomach and put some sort of medicine straight into the thing's other end.

Tears streamed down Myrta's face, but she couldn't tear her eyes away. "Is he going to die?"

The nurse swabbed around the tube again and again. "Oh no, honey. He got a bad slice, but he'll be fine."

She took Myrta by the chin, tipped her head, and cleaned the cut on her temple. "You'll be fine too."

Someone pounded on the door. Jack left and came back with Ardelle.

"Ephraim," Ardelle cried, rushing to his side. "Cordelia, how bad?"

"He'll be fine. We'll start regeneron as soon as Doctor orders it. Ephraim's fine, honey. I promise."

Ardelle looked back and forth between Myrta and Jack. "What happened?"

The anxiety in her mama's voice pushed Myrta to panic again, and she choked out, "It was me. I was supposed to stay home. I thought it would be safe because there were so many people."

Then the other part came back. "Mama! Odile was there. The scouts took her. I tried to stop her—"

"Calm down." Jack was trying to put his arm around her, and she shrugged it off.

It was unfathomable. "We have to help her. We have to go to Narona and find her."

Ardelle wiped Ephraim's hair away from his forehead. "Cordelia. He's going to pull through?"

"Yes. He'll need a few weeks."

The doctor arrived and ordered regeneron, and Ardelle helped Cordelia with the first dose. Seeing Ephraim treated was a new level of horror for Myrta. He writhed and screamed while the two women braced him against the bed.

Quaking, Myrta backed against the wall, and for a moment, she stood outside the entirety of it all. Between village and city, tradition and modernization. As Ephraim's cries faded, she saw her vision trait as one small piece of a much larger puzzle. She saw the other people, other issues, joining together or lining against one another. Ardelle and Ephraim. Odile. Everyone back at the stead. Even Renico.

Each with their own idea of right and wrong and which way to turn next. Her choice to go out that evening had hurt the people she loved, and worse, Renico now knew Ephraim was her papa. He'd been the one to admit it, but that admission traced back to her choice.

She'd been so selfish, thinking she was the only one who mattered.

Later, back at the inn, Myrta realized she wanted to claim her side in the fight. Holiest of heavens, she shouldn't be *hunted* simply because of her genes, and the first order of business was to not put a single person in danger by her mere presence.

With growing clarity, Myrta found her knife and a change of clothes. She wrote a note that she'd go back to the stead. Pressing her lips together, she wrote that she'd be safer with Terrence and Celeste.

It didn't need to be a lie, not necessarily. She might go back there someday.

Myrta left the inn and stole back to the wagon grounds, quieter now. She climbed onto one of the de Terr wagons, worked between some sacks of grain, and fell asleep.

Bumping woke her at dawn. Wheels creaked and men shouted, as one by one the wagons filed out of town. With the motion, and the grain cocooning her, she slept again.

When Myrta woke a second time, the bags were damp from her sweat and she pushed them away and peered over the rails.

Nathan. She slumped back down. The wagon bumped along through grassy hillsides. One of the sacks jostled against her, and she pushed it back, worked the fastening loose, and took a handful of wheat berries.

He'd better not tell her to walk back.

After a few hours the bumping slowed and stopped. Nathan was climbing down, and he went to talk with the driver behind—Jack. Myrta took a deep breath and crawled out.

A grin spread across Jack's face.

She climbed off and straightened her dress. Jack chuckled, like they'd pulled a prank. "Didn't know you were coming."

Nathan stared at her. "You don't belong here."

"Really, Nathan? You know what, I don't belong anywhere."

"We're working."

"I know how to work."

"I don't want you here."

"I didn't hop on the wagon for you."

He went to the side of the road, lowered his trousers, and relieved himself, dirt splattering onto his shoes. Jack put his arm around her shoulders and turned her away. "Caravan culture."

"Think I should join him?" She had a mind to.

"Not if you want him to settle down." He touched her temple. "How's your head?"

She felt at the scab, about a half inch long. "Everything still works. I'm okay."

Nathan stalked back, buttoning his trousers. "You going to cook?"

She crossed her arms. "I didn't plan any of that out after Jack got slugged and I got jabbed."

He took off his hat, thwacked it against his hand, and a cloud of dust puffed out. "Caravan's business. Why're you here?"

"Nate, if you need me to cook, I'll cook. If you need someone on the teams, fine. Put me to work."

He turned to Jack. "She's riding with you." He put

his hat back on and left. Jack looked at her and rolled his eyes.

Wagons spread along the roadway as far as Myrta could see, front and back. Lined up as they were, there was no end to them. Men and women were stretching their legs; oxen snorted.

The de Reu group was behind them, with four wagons and extra hands. It looked like Fred was logging again. One of the other hands was limping up to Fred, and she squinted.

It was the handyman from the inn.

"Jack?"

He was adjusting the bows on his team's yoke. "What?" he said without looking up.

She went to him and lowered her voice. "Who's the man? On Mr. de Reu's crew. The one with the limp."

"Is he limping? That's Alphonse. I noticed him too." Jack watched Alphonse as he went to one of Reuben's lumber wagons.

"I know him. I mean, I recognize him."

Alphonse had avoided her at the inn, at least it felt that way. He spent time with Odile, who said he was from the cities. A stab of suspicion hit Myrta. Why would anyone from the cities take work at a little inn, or in the belt for that matter? She quelled her paranoia. "Does he seem strange to you?"

Jack frowned. "No. Why?"

It was probably nothing, but that man had grown up with mechanation every day of his life. And thinking back, Ardelle had told her to give him his space. Then he'd left, and that part hadn't mattered anymore. Now he worked with Mr. de Reu, who did business directly with Renico.

If he'd been friendlier at the inn she might feel less wary. Or, she thought wryly, if she hadn't been attacked last night. "Well, he worked for Mama, and then he disappeared without saying goodbye. Why do you think he's with Mr. de Reu?"

"I don't know. Lots of people move around."

She climbed up onto Jack's wagon seat and stared at Alphonse. Odile was right. She needed to learn to read people.

Chapter Twenty-Eight

They stood in the midst of snow-covered huts. Pack animals filed past.

"The rise of commerce."

Wearing layers of rags, Alphonse trudged next to one of the beasts. His fingertips were blackened with rot. He had hunger so great he felt only dull acceptance in the pit of his gut.

A woman behind him led a string of animals piled high with furs. Around her neck hung coins. She yelled at him to move faster.

With those coins he might buy fire. Food. Survival.

Alphonse turned and grabbed her, wrapped his hands around her throat and throttled her. She choked, she fought back, but he forced her down. Desperate, he wrenched the necklace of coins from her throat, the chain drawing blood as it broke free.

Stavo's voice went almost unnoticed. "Money. These tokens. They come to underpin society itself."

A few days into Caravan, Alphonse was pasturing the oxen when Reuben came up. "You might want a walk. You ain't been since Collimais."

Alphonse had thought he wouldn't have the opportunity. He'd assumed any solitude in the wilderness was over. A walk? Yes—certainly. Laughing, he grabbed Reuben by the arms and took him in a quick hug. Reuben pulled his head back, eyes wide, and Alphonse laughed again and thanked him. He found his line and hooks and told Manny he'd be back with supper.

He hiked in, the scent of pine and sage welcoming him. Soon, Alphonse found a pristine mountain tarn tucked against dark granite walls. The lake was clear, and ripples slip-slapped on its shore.

Two people, a slight girl and a bald man, dangled their feet in the near end. The man looked familiar. Alphonse had seen him with Nathan de Terr on Collimais' wagon grounds. Alphonse went wide to avoid them, past a thicket of trees to a spot near a two-hundred-foot cliff face on the far edge.

Light danced on the water. Alphonse smiled at the thought of a bath—but first, the stone. He hugged the cliff and with the warmth of it seeping into his chest, the months fell away. Caravan fell away. The botched kiss with Odile fell away. Even the weight of returning home fell away. He *was* home. He breathed in moss and sulfur.

I am rock.

Relaxed, he sat and dropped a line with fifteen baited hooks. The voices from those two steaders at the other end carried. The man said seeing air could be helpful to Nathan. Useful to the farm.

The girl said something about water vapor being purple.

Whatever they were talking about, it sounded like nonsense. Alphonse turned his attention to the mountains around him, ranging in grays and greens. A cloud drifted by.

Studying the cliff again, he massaged his thigh and thought this wasn't Tura, not by a long shot, but it was probably part of the same formation. He might not have another chance to climb, and so, deciding, he stood and took hold of a frag overhead. He found a toehold crack and stepped up, and his heart sprang open in joy.

There were plenty of frags and none looked sharp. He found a finger hold and pulled. The rock was solid, as solid as the Prophets, and there were no anchors. Just good face. He was twenty feet off the ground, free climbing, his hands and feet fusing to the stone. Encouraging him. Begging him.

Those two at the far end of the lake were still splashing, the girl going on about seeing everything in the air as colors. She sounded crazed, but neither of them seemed to notice him. They seemed more interested in splashing their feet.

He splayed his hands around any good piece of rock. His legs were strong and loose. At eighty feet his biceps began their familiar burn; his right thigh, the regenerated one, did too.

Testing you out, buddy.

He pivoted and swung from grab to hold to crack, the rhythm, the zone, the focus, the harmony of flesh and rock.

Halfway up, he stopped for a moment. A patch of green rippled below, and a memory tried to surface, something about time and chemistry and carbon, but he couldn't place it. He found more frags and continued.

Without warning, his right thigh shuddered, sending his foot hammering against the cliff. "Don't start." He shook the leg out.

The steaders were gone now. Alphonse was alone in the ranges, alone on all of Turaset—he had the world to himself and there was only this perfect cliff.

At a hundred and fifty feet, his thigh spasmed harder.

He anchored his thoughts into the rock again, into the eons within the mountain, within him.

At a hundred and eighty feet, his right leg went off yet again. "Autore, miere!" The spasms pounded his leg, his knee, his hip into the cliff, over and over. He swore with each blow and waited as the regenerated muscle took hold of the entire lower half of his right side and slammed him into the rock like an accusation, that if he'd never sought Arel he wouldn't be here now, hanging on a cliff with no line. He blocked any thought of Tura, any acknowledgment that his fall there would have been fatal without rope. Glancing down, he quelled his anxiety, focused on *this* moment, not that disaster so many months back. He breathed in actinomycetes and mosses. Good soil, the smell of time.

There was another crack, he grabbed and pushed up. His right leg massively revolted. "It's three more feet, you Autore*malde*, piece of *miere* muscle!"

Another foothold, another handhold, he gambled on luck and slung his arm over the top. He pushed up and threw his other arm over.

Sucking in deep breaths and sobbing tears he didn't know he had, Alphonse rolled away from the edge. He cried and choked. He opened his eyes, and his sobs transformed to laughter. He couldn't stop—he laughed in relief, he laughed at success, he laughed on top of a cliff he'd climbed free without falling, on a muscle that had never trained for anything remotely like this.

With tears flowing, the realization gave him hope that he might convince his mother to change course. He stood and screamed, victorious, until his chest ached.

The cliff wasn't Tura. It didn't matter. He edged back to the lip and looked down to the lake below.

"I love you," he screamed out, to the lake, the cliff, the entire planet. It filled him, the euphoria and victory, it was all the same and it was love and it was this perfect moment, alone on a mountain.

Then, still laughing, still crying, he scouted down the back of the cliff and picked his way back to the lake. He bathed, pulled in his line, and returned to the wagons with a dozen fat quiverfish, clean, content, and companionable.

Fred helped filet, Manny started the fire, and Reuben complimented his haul. Alphonse sat, welcoming the fatigue deep in his thigh and watching the flames climb the wood like the perfect cliff.

The de Terrs came over, including the bald man and the crazy girl from the lake. But the girl, she wasn't really a girl, just very slight, with a guarded look, something in her eyes like a rabbit.

Nathan said, "We boiled some wheat, happy to share. Reuben says you have extra fish."

"Help yourself."

The last four quivers sizzled in the pan, lost their orange, and began to flake.

The bald man smiled in a forward way and said in a deep voice, "I'm Jack. This is Myrta. You had better luck than us." Jack sat next to him.

The girl, Myrta, sat on the opposite log. She had a scab above her cheekbone on the side and it was bruising. Whatever had cut her, she'd been lucky it missed her eye. She said, "Where did you go?"

She sounded nervous and looked it too. He didn't want to be around her, not after hearing what she'd said about air. He had enough on his mind. He certainly didn't want her to know he'd overheard her bizarre claims, so he tipped his head opposite to where they'd all been.

A funny thing happened. She looked where he pointed. She squinted, stared at the air *above* where he pointed. "Are you sure there're lakes over there? I've never seen any."

Nathan sounded exasperated. "You've never been here."

"I've never *heard* of lakes over there. How far was it?"

Warmth flushed through Alphonse. She thought he was lying, and he was. Somehow she was onto it. But what she'd said about seeing air was absurd. "Two, three miles."

"That's far, there and back with so many fish."

She was right; it sounded ridiculous.

Reuben walked over grinning. "Alphonse, that was real good. Nice treat." The man sat next to Nathan. "Nate. I talked t' the others. They're goin' in on the irrigation. Tell Terrence, get in now. Renico'll haggle."

"Sure," Nathan said tersely.

Jack and Myrta exchanged a glance. Myrta said, "Nate—" but he stood and stalked off, and Alphonse wondered if anyone's family was easy.

The following evening he was unyoking his team when Myrta approached. There were only a few days left before Sangal, and he didn't want to spend time with this girl. He pulled the animals to the pasture.

"Wait," she called.

He slapped them in and closed the gate. "What?"

"I want to talk to you."

She was such a little thing, dark hair and slight, every bit as nervous today as before. He pushed by her toward the road.

She followed. "Why are you working with Mr. de Reu?"

He went toward the hills on the other side without breaking stride. Why should she care? "Just a job, miss."

She was practically running to keep up. "You had a job. You worked at the inn."

He stopped, recognition hitting him. This was that guest. She was so easy to forget, but in hindsight she'd looked the same back then. Coarse clothing, sturdy shoes, hair knotted back.

She threw a glance over at the wagons where her brother—was it Jack?—watched them. "Why did you quit?"

"Look, no offense, but we don't know each other. I'd like to be alone." He started up the slopes, grasses brushing his trousers.

"Let's try this," she called, scrambling after him. "I'll leave you be if you tell me why you lied about the lake."

"Seriously?"

Her expression firmed, her little jaw thrust forward. "Do you work for Renico?"

Autore. Even here. Even here on the wagon train everything was about combustion. It owned the continent. "No."

"Then why did you lie about the lake?"

"Look, miss. I imagine it takes courage to walk up to a complete stranger and ask questions out of the blue." He'd give her that. She might be loose in the head, but she had fortitude to be so direct, and she'd caught onto his lie when no one else had. "The truth is, I have a lot on my mind and I don't have time . . ." He waved a hand, searching for words. ". . . to make friends. No offense."

He pushed around her and continued into the hills. By some grace from the powers above she didn't follow, and after a while he collapsed under a sandsap and dug his fingers into the soil. Ignoring the burrs and prickles, he closed his eyes and turned his thoughts to his mother.

For all the decisions she'd made through his life, money was usually part of the calculation. Becoming a funder and working with Zelia for so many years had probably strengthened her financial instincts. And she was drawn to power too. That was probably why she took a job with combustion in the first place.

Mechanating the belt would be easy if it was named as a province, and mechanation meant profit, more money for her to work with. But naming it could lead to a revolt—which would undermine the entire continental economy. She stood to lose money if that happened. Not to mention that naming a fourth province would weaken Delsina's power in Congress directly, from a third of the votes to a quarter.

And in that light, he wondered fleetingly if his assumptions were correct. Any personal power she might hold in Congress would be diluted by a fourth province. Some part of the puzzle still eluded him.

That's why I'm going home. To speak with her. He'd never seen her willingly give up power. He'd add that to his argument. She stood to lose power both directly and indirectly. Less overall influence in the Congress and undermining goodwill with the belt. Maintaining goodwill as a type of power. That framing—it felt like something his grandfather would have argued for. It felt right.

His case against her began to take shape.

Another day passed, and another, and he ran through his final argument early one morning as he rolled up his tent. Three things drove his mother—money, power, and family. The continental economy, that was the money, and this plan was hostile to it. Maintaining goodwill was a form of power.

That left family. *She loves me.* More than any other piece of the puzzle, he was certain of that. She'd raised him through the hard years and the wealthy ones. They'd always been together, since he was a child, for better or worse.

The suns crested the range, pulling the autumn bite out of the air. He gathered his things and took them to the wagon.

Myrta came up. "Good morning, Alphonse. I'm with you today." She threw a blanket onto his seat.

"What? No, you're not."

"Yes. Mr. de Reu said."

He threw his things in back and went over to Reuben, who was talking with Nathan and Jack. Reuben scowled as he walked up.

"Sir, is Myrta on my wagon? I think it's better if I drive solo." He had nothing against the girl, but also no reason to want her around.

Reuben crossed his arms. He gave Alphonse his complete attention. "That's my lumber, them's my oxen, and you been fallin' asleep on the job. You need a partner."

That much was true, and Alphonse closed his eyes.

He exhaled and opened them again. "Have another hand drive the wagon. You have enough people, sir."

There were bags under the man's eyes, and he spread his feet and squinted straight at Alphonse. "This ain't up for debate. You near pulled off the byway yesterday. Myrta's ridin' with you and that's final."

Chapter Twenty-Nine

Using her blanket as a cushion, Myrta sat far back into the corner of the seat. She watched Alphonse, tried to figure him out. She kept one hand on the folding knife in her pocket, determined to learn what she could about this strange man.

It was why she'd convinced Reuben to let her ride with him.

Alphonse was such a strange man. A city man. She knew so few people from the cities. None really, except Ephraim who was more of a foothiller now.

He seemed so private. She waited for him to say something. Anything. But the miles rolled by and he didn't. Even Nathan would say *some*thing.

After a while, the narrow band of coastal plains came into view, and the ocean. She'd never seen so much water in her life, all the way out as far as she could see, out to the very horizon. She threw a glance over, but Alphonse was still staring straight at the byway and still not saying a word. Myrta put her hand along her cheek and switched on her vision.

Above the ocean, water vapor went up to the sky in purple spears, like a grape taffy-pull, drifting into the clouds, *becoming* clouds. Brilliant, dense purple, lobed balls of colored cotton in the sky. Some of the clouds were drifting over land, where a haze of misty purple rain fell.

Water, everywhere. So much of it.

Ahead, two smudges of gray lay along the coast. Cities. Each blanketed in blue. Blue carbon. And outside each city, stronger and angrier, bruises seeped out of the ground, black and blue. She altered her vision to normal and saw nothing but the gray-smudged cities. She flicked her vision on again and there it was, carbon bleeding from the ground. *Outside* the cities. Methane, ethane, carbon dioxide, straight out of the ground. "Holy heavens."

He glanced over. "What?"

She glanced back. He'd spoken! At last. She pointed at the distant carbon seeping. "What is that?"

"I don't know. The gray blotch is Sangal City."

Surly, that's what this man was. He looked enough like a steader, unshaven and trail-dusty, but no steader would be so contrary.

On the other hand, him being so withdrawn didn't feel much of a threat. "Next to it. Left. North."

"North is Delsico and a few oil extractors. You can't see them from here."

In a heartbeat, Myrta understood, and not just in her head but in her gut. Seeing that carbon bleeding straight out of the ground was something the industry didn't want *anyone* to know about any more than they probably wanted her seeing the aut exhaust. "Is Renico bigger than Delsico?"

He scoffed. "That's one way to put it."

"Holy heavens. You don't *see* that?" But of course he couldn't. She didn't see the carbon herself without her trait turned on.

And he didn't answer anyway. Like a closed book, one with a hard spine, that's what this man was. If he'd been a steader, he'd talk. She'd say "drought," and he'd say something about profits, or next season, and they'd go from there. It was easy to talk with a steader.

Then Myrta remembered that Odile used to talk about the handyman. She used to talk about *this* man. "Odile's my cousin."

Alphonse looked over sharply. "What?"

That worked.

"We're cousins." Myrta took off her shoes and tossed them under the seat.

"Autore. That explains a lot."

"Odile cares about pollution. She cares about *that*." Myrta pointed again. "She's obsessed with it. With the industry too."

He slammed the seat between them, the boards jumped and Myrta did too. He said, "I wouldn't work for them. Ever."

She planted her backside back where it'd been.

"I want you off my wagon. After the break, you're off my wagon."

She fisted her hands and took a deep breath. "You probably think I'm crazy because what I said back at the lake, about my eyes. Well. I'm not crazy. But, imagine how *nuts* it'd make me feel if someone like you talked about what you heard. Imagine how insane I'd get, knowing you're out there, somewhere, telling people that this girl you saw on Caravan thinks she can see air!"

"Autore, calm down. Why would I do that? I don't care about you."

"Exactly. So, you have no reason to protect me. Why do you think Jack and I waited until we were at the lake to talk about it? Did we sound crazy?"

"Yes!"

She inhaled sharply. "Have I talked about it anywhere else?

"I don't know."

"I'm not *crazy*."

They rode in silence, and her worry grew. There was an expression in the belt, split the milk between the pails—but convincing him of her ability was the only pail she had. "There's a river ahead. It's big, and it's going north to south."

"Can you *hear* it?"

"No. I *see* it. I see the water vapor. There're rapids. It's a *huge* river, running north to south."

He glared straight ahead again. She cried out, "Why don't you believe me?"

"Why do you *care* if I believe you?"

Never had she felt so completely at the mercy of another human being as she did now, admitting her trait—her vulnerability!—to a stranger. "Because there are people *after* me. How do you think I got this?" She pointed at her scab. "Melville di Vaun, from *Renico*, did this."

His mouth fell open. It hung there like truth to a lie. She snapped, "You *know* him? Great. Fantastic." She pulled out the knife, unfolded it, and gripped it hard.

"Whoa, put that away. Look, Myrta, I swear I'm not with Renico. And no, I've only met the man. I don't know him at all."

She pointed the knife toward him and leaned closer. "Let's pretend you're telling the truth. Now imagine, as a person who is definitely not with Renico, that someone you cared about was attacked by them. Wouldn't you want to protect that person?"

"Stop talking about it!"

She roared in frustration and turned away.

And Alphonse just sat there, yelling at the team and driving them all wrong. "Come on. Yah!"

He was such a total rube. "You're holding the lines too tight. You're hurting them."

Groaning, he loosened his hold and called out to the team again. Myrta turned back to the hills, not knowing why she'd even bothered to correct him, except the oxen didn't deserve this man's ignorance any more than she did.

"Look, Myrta." His voice broke in what sounded like pain, and somehow that was more comforting than his actual words. "I won't tell anyone. About your . . . eyeball thing. I promise. It doesn't matter if I believe you or not. I wouldn't want—look, no one should be hurt by that industry. Your secret is safe."

She watched him for a long time. His face was haunted, but it was the caving of his chest that convinced her. She folded her knife. "Thank you."

The groans and whines of the wagon were punctuated by steady hoof strikes. Lowing from the teams, yells on the wind, all of it blended into a sort of out-of-tune trail song. Myrta pulled her hair back and shoved it down into her collar. Dust had caked onto her neck, was inside her nose, on her wrists, everywhere. The dirt was so thick she could probably flake it off in chunks.

They continued on like that for a while, and the train finally broke in the late morning. She got down and slapped her trousers, slapped the dust out. Alphonse pulled out his line and hooks from the back and came around to her in a halting way. He fidgeted with his gear. "Um. I'm wondering. Are there any lakes around here?"

She stared. In disbelief she stared at this strange city man, this surly man asking her to find a lake, for him. Then she faced up to the sky, and laughter spilled out of her. "Yes." She wiped her eyes with one hand and pointed with the other. "Half mile that way."

He grimaced awkwardly, maybe it was supposed to be a smile, and headed off.

She unyoked the team, still grinning. He believed her. He seemed nice even, under that hard spine of his. She led the oxen to the water barrel on the side of the road. They started lapping, their spittle floating off in white bubbles, and she wondered what had made him reconsider.

She pulled burrs off one of steers and scratched its crest. Its eyes were deep brown, the lashes long, curled and black, darker than its coat. There was something about cattle that reminded her of calves even when they were fully grown. They were gentle, and their ears so soft. Their eyes so trusting. Alphonse had a good team.

A man walked up with his own oxen. Tall and well-dressed, he stood closer than customary. "Myrtle."

She startled as she recognized Emmett, standing there as fresh as a market morning. His face, his hands, even his clothing—he looked immaculate. Emmett must have brought a change of clothing for every single day. She wondered how he found water to bathe. Surely, she thought, he wouldn't use the drinking water. "Hello, Emmett. It's Myrta."

"Myrta." His gaze travelled down her body, then he met her eyes.

She took a step away, toward Alphonse's nearer ox who was still lapping noisily. Emmett's animals stood on the other side of the barrel and drank just as thirstily.

"I trust you're well." She willed Alphonse's animals to hurry.

"Terrence says you left the stead."

"That's right."

"But you're here." His eyes ran down her body again. She found herself bunching her shoulders forward.

The oxen drank and drank, and there was barely enough room for all four. His team . . . She did a double take. Both stood with their backs arched and their tails between their legs. Either of those were bad signs, and his animals showed both. She stared harder. Were those welts? Strips of raw flesh showed through the dirt on their rumps. His team had sores along their haunches and backs, as though they'd been flayed hard. Some of the sores festered, and a fly landed on one.

She looked away and told herself he hadn't beaten his animals. She told herself she didn't feel ill.

He stepped closer. "I expected to father children on you."

She swallowed and crossed behind Alphonse's team to the far side.

"I turned down other options."

"Excuse me." Myrta pulled the team away, and her revulsion gave way to a bizarre mix of feelings. Disbelief, realization, and underneath those a strange sense of something else—gratitude. It couldn't be plainer. Emmett, of all people? She could never make a life with a man like that.

Myrta put the oxen in and pulled the gate shut. On the heels of her relief, dismay crowded in. She'd had no idea Terrence would match her to someone abusive.

The possibility of life on a stead was more outlandish than ever.

And then, as quickly as the dismay had filled her, it faded again, and a strange new sensation filled her chest, one she didn't recognize at first but felt she ought.

Freedom.

This was what Terrence meant when he talked about loving the belt, that an opportunity to find one's own way, as uncertain as it was, was beyond any price. To not be bound by others' expectations.

A hand fell on her shoulder. She jerked.

"Jumpy much?"

"Jack, I'm sorry. I just saw Emmett."

Jack grinned. "Ah. My old ex-future-brother-in-law. How is he?"

"We didn't talk. He just sort of measured me. With his eyes."

And he freed me from agreeing to any *match, ever.*

They were underway again, and Alphonse kept looking at her. Past her, actually, morosely toward a mountain with spires on top. Above those, Bel and Letra were drawing close to one another.

"Conjunction's coming, I guess." She said it to get him talking again, even though everything about conjunction was silly. Plenty of steaders stayed indoors when Bel'letra formed, thinking the single sun would eat their soul. "I wonder if anyone'll hide. You know, under their wagon or something."

He didn't say a word. Tentatively, she said, "Do you want to talk about it?"

"No. No, I do not want to talk about it."

His eyes were moist, and his face looked like the end of the road, the world too big and everyone in it too wrapped up in their own worries. That's how he looked in this minute. Right now, he looked like death, all withdrawn and miserable.

"Whatever it is, it's bothering you. Was it bad?"

"Is there a problem with your hearing? Drop it."

She blinked. "Did someone die?"

He threw her a hard look. "Like your eye thing takes up too much brain space and your ears don't work."

"I'm sorry. It seems something bad happened, and you keep looking at that mountain like it's to blame. You have a perfectly nice person sitting next to you offering to listen, but I'll leave you be."

She did, and they rode like that. Out of the corner of her eye she saw him fidget, and he kept looking at that mountain and occasionally glancing at her too. She turned to him. "I'm keeping quiet. I'm not asking."

He jerked his head a few times like he was trying to shake something. But then his expression changed, and he went all open and earnest. He had a kind face, she thought, when he allowed it.

He said, "Have you ever felt like everything was coming to a head? Like everything you ever wanted was coming together and you have *one* shot to get it right. It could go either way, and however it goes—that'll be how it is for the rest of your life."

"Like a crossroads?"

"More like a bullseye." His voice rose. "That peak is Mount Tura. There's a legend. A man named Arel was killed up there. The legend says he wanted something for his people—something his leaders didn't want. Arel was an upstart, a visionary, and he tried to change the way things were done because he thought it'd be better. So, they killed him. And his spirit is up there. If you find him, he gives you wisdom."

She didn't say anything. In part, the fact that he'd opened up so completely made the whole conversation bizarre, and the wild notes in his voice were disturbing in their own way.

"People who summit shape the future. If you reach the top, you earn insight. Wisdom beyond your years. You set destiny."

He sounded fanatical.

He looked at her, and his face grew sterner. "Don't look at me like that. It's a serious climb. Most people can't do it. Call it whatever you want, but if you make it? It *changes* you."

She took a breath and held it. "So did you summit?"

"No. I didn't make it. If I had, I'd know how to fix . . . I could convince Mother . . ." He gave an inarticulate howl. "Never mind. You wouldn't understand."

Understand *what*? Finding your way in the world? She saw herself through his eyes, a dusty farmgirl riding on a wagon. And here he was, a city man.

"Alphonse. There's nothing—" Her voice was trembling, and she looked to the side for a moment. How dare he? "There's *nothing* stopping you from setting destiny."

"Look—"

"No, you look. They would've *married me off* to someone who beats animals. I didn't even know that until today. I don't know *him* at all. They had me marching into that box, and I would've spent the rest of my life inside it. Then this happened," she pointed at her eyes, "and now I don't know where to go. I'm being hunted. You're going home. To your family. You're setting your destiny. You don't need a mountain for that."

His lips were curled back. Well, she was ready. She had a few choice thoughts when it came to destiny, whatever ridiculous all-encompassing scat he might say. Maybe he'd say she shouldn't have dreams of her own. She should just have children by some random man who beats animals.

She was ready.

Before he could say anything, calls came from behind to hold up. Alphonse looked back with a roar, and fuming, she turned to the hills again.

A man trotted up. "Lamed steer. Gotta break."

"What?"

"One lames bad, best t' butcher it. You set up at the river. We'll be there 'fore long." The man trotted on.

And as soon as the river was in sight, she jumped down and walked, still furious.

Jack was at his wagon, pulling his tent out and she grabbed his blankets and hammer. She followed him and started pounding a stake into the ground even before he'd unrolled his tent.

Jack grabbed her arm. "Whoa."

She threw the hammer down. "That Alphonse is griping about destiny." As if she hadn't thought about her future in a dozen different ways and still didn't see a good one.

"Myrta," Jack said softly. "Calm down. No one's going to force you to do anything."

"Why am I on Caravan, Jack? Why under the holiest of all five heavens am I here?"

"Easy. You're keeping Ardelle and Ephraim safe."

"But what'll I do in *Sangal*? Stay there? Will I go back to the stead? I'm not marrying Emmett. Ardelle said there's people like me in the mountains. People *hiding* in the mountains." .

He laughed. "Well, that's not your destiny. We barely tolerate the farm."

She pursed her lips. "If it weren't for discerners, I could live anywhere."

They finished pitching the tent and walked back. The mood at the wagons was dour. After a week on the byway, everyone—the men, the oxen, even the air—sweated in grim determination.

Reuben was speaking with Nathan. "Why'd'ja decide against it? Your stead'll go down."

And Nate's expression, well that was just plain rotten. "Cost is too high."

Nate didn't mean the money; he meant her. Her trait. The family curse he might carry and pass on to his own children. The genes Renico wanted gone.

Reuben was frowning at Nate and shaking his head. "Cost'd pay back right quick—two seasons, maybe three. You'd best think about it good and long, son. The math ain't hard on this one." Then to Jack he said, "That's one o' Claude's steers what lamed. You build up the fire, we'll get you top cuts."

Jack thanked him, and Reuben walked off.

If it wasn't for the discerning program, Myrta thought, Ardelle and Ephraim would be safe. And the stead could have its water.

Everything she cared about was strangled by that obscene program. All of their problems, every last one, boiled down to it. She said quietly to Jack, "Odile's right about records. Not just pollution. If people knew about discerning, it'd have to stop, and then the stead could get its water."

She'd talk to Nathan about it. He had a stake in this too.

Chapter Thirty

"The time for remembering is close, Alphonse."

Their surroundings were pleasant. They stood in a room of golds, browns, and blues. Around a raised dais, a hundred desks arced, and a pale, dark-haired man addressed the assembly. He did not pound his podium as Stavo might have done, but his passion was unmistakable.

"Where are we?" Alphonse asked.

"Listen to the senator."

The man spoke of damage in the atmosphere. He argued for cleaner air. He said the science and the law were clear, that life itself hung in the balance. Punctuating his sentences by slicing the space in front of himself, his voice rose with each cut of his hand. He tipped up onto his feet. "Why do we not protect the global environment?"

The senator wanted to limit the use of ozone-destroying chemicals.

The assembly listened and took notes. Hearts shifted, not through artifice or deception, but because of common ground.

The vote was unanimous. The chemicals would be outlawed, and the air cleaned.

And then, Alphonse and Stavo were outside

of the planet, above a hole in its layer of ozone. Too much radiation from the planet's single sun passed through the hole, making the world's inhabitants sick. But now, through shared effort, the chemicals that destroyed that ozone would be controlled.

Years passed. The hole stopped growing. It began to heal.

"People and shared purpose. Human will-power. It's a force as strong as any other in nature." [5]

At the river, Alphonse stretched his arms, popped the joints in his spine, and climbed down from the wagon. The stink of the animals clung to him, blending with his own odor. He needed another bath.

Dried grasses carpeted the hills around the camp like the tawny pelt of a wild beast, and standing there, next to the wagon, he closed his eyes, imagined solitude, and for a split moment stood in two places. Here with the river's roar, its spray dancing onto him, and somewhere else too, another world, a private place.

After a few minutes he settled the team and pitched his tent. Myrta and Jack were building a fire nearby.

That night, the steaks were thick and juicy. He'd never had meat grilled over a wood fire, and sitting with the others, the tang of the meat, the community, shared purpose—he soaked it up. He was a tree, his roots sank deep, finding what he needed, right here.

Reuben's neighbor, Claude, joined them, and

---

5   Senator Al Gore's comments to the United States Senate, e.g. https://www.c-span.org/video/?24137-1/senate-session.

Nathan tapped one of the whiskey barrels. Alphonse took a large shot of the stuff. He was here, in the mountains with the evening breeze and good friends. He sank into the embrace of alcohol. Manny was on her third shot and lighting a ciguerro.

Alphonse laughed. "You a smoker? I would not have guessed."

Manny tossed Alphonse the pack and said, her voice huskier than normal, "Only when I drink. *Some-times* when I drink. Bad habit."

Alphonse put the pack on the log between them, next to the empty flask. His head, his mind, seemed to float. *Malde.* He was already drunk. It never took much, and sometimes he considered taking up drinking, just so he could enjoy a few shots on a night like tonight without losing his better judgment.

Manny leaned on her knees and grinned for all the world like a kid. "Beats the city, huh?"

The evening breeze kept kicking around. Myrta and Jack stood off a few feet. She was doubled over, chortling. The wind shifted, a few words carried, ". . . Nate never looked in the silos . . ." and Myrta was laughing, slapping the air in front of Jack and shaking her head like she couldn't stop.

Manny stood, arched her back, and lit another ciguerro. "More whiskey." She wandered over to Jack's wagon with the flask, humming, gait unsteady. She leaned up against the back of the bed, ciguerro planted in one side of her mouth. She opened the tap to fill the flask and launched into an off-color sailor song, then tottered back.

Fred held out his cup.

"Oh, sure," Manny complained with that same grin. "I get myself a nice flask and now I'm 'spected to share." But she poured into Fred's cup. Reuben held out his, and Manny topped everyone off.

She said to Alphonse, "They're always taking advantage of city folk." She wove back to the wagon and grumbled loudly, waving her hand over her head.

"What's that?" Reuben called.

Manny took her ciguerro out. "Tap leaked. Whiskey on the bed. Straw got most of it." Claude threw her a cloth and she pushed the packing straw away from the barrel and swabbed the puddle. The ash from her ciguerro fell and she threw the butt to the ground. She filled the flask again and came back, taking a swig. "I closed it tight."

Reuben asked Manny to sing some more, and she did, off key, about the sailor who found a tentacled sea maiden, a girl of the okeafolk. The girl wooed him to her watery home. Once there, she wrapped herself about him and pulled him apart limb by limb. Fred was chuckling by the end of the second verse, and even though Alphonse knew the song, Manny's drunken version took enough liberties with the sailor's anatomy that he was soon laughing too.

Reuben sang the complementary song next, of the woodland horseman who courted a farm girl. She straddled him, and they galloped into the forest to live among the hickory trees. Reuben kept crooning along when Fred bolted upright.

"Fire!"

Flames blazed under the whiskey wagon, and the grasses had caught. The fire was creeping up the side of the wagon, toward the rails.

Nathan yelled to the men to grab shovels. Jack threw a pail to Myrta. She ran to the river with some others.

The side rails burned, and the flames tracked along

the pathway of whiskey to the damp bed and packing straw. The alcohol flared, setting the bed alight. Embers floated on the wind.

Alphonse stared, transfixed. Rooted to the ground, he saw the wagon blazing, and he saw something else, more primal, more elemental.

He saw the red-hot sea of Earth's Hadean.

Steaders screamed, shoveled dirt on the wagon bed and on the blaze underneath. Others doused their campfires and yoked oxen with no regard to whose team they had, struggling with the animals to pull the wagons to safety.

Popping sounded over the flames, bungs coming loose. Nathan called out. He rushed around the wagon, pointed at barrels, and steaders threw dirt straight onto them. The hoops split on two of the casks, and the staves collapsed. Blue flames shot skyward. More flickers of ash drifted.

The molten sea raged, and the brightness seared Alphonse's eyes like a nuclear blast. Some corner of his mind, some stretch of engineered DNA thousands of years old insisted he had no understanding of a nuclear blast, and he sank to his knees. He knew only that this was unbearable. His lungs burned. He moaned, flowing into the ground through knees and shins.

Jack's whiskey wagon creaked. One wheel was collapsing, and the barrels jostled sideways. Another barrel split and flared.

The molten sea was everywhere; Alphonse floated in a red-hot sea on primordial Earth. He fell sideways onto the log, and barely feeling it, rolled off toward the campfire. He was the molten sea.

A burst of new panic screamed around him, fifty voices in concert. The blaze had escaped to the hills, and a brush fire flared in dry scrub behind him.

Now he was the violent landscape, meteors crashing down. He couldn't breathe. There was no air; he needed no air.

Jack yelled at him. He didn't know what the man was saying. The words were meaningless. The man yelled again and pointed. Alphonse lolled on the ground, not even a whimper escaping. The thing, the ape, the being that would not exist for over four billion years grabbed him under both arms and dragged him from the growing brush fire.

Screaming something, the ape-thing yanked Alphonse up onto a wagon. Someone yoked a team and pulled it across the bridge. Alphonse was gone.

Chapter Thirty-One

Every last inch of her body ached with fatigue. Her clothes reeked of smoke and her eyes itched. Myrta pushed through the jumble of wagons looking for Nathan, who must be somewhere in this mess. All night, as the fire had burned up the slopes on the far side of the river and the loss of the whiskey began to feel real, through the whole night all Myrta could think of was that Nate would have kids someday, and he should want to end the discerning program too.

She found him, working, moving the few salvaged barrels of whiskey onto the grain wagon. Less than a quarter of it had survived, and Jack's wagon was entirely gone. Manny had taken responsibility for the fire and promised to make up the loss. It was a lot of money. Myrta didn't see how Manny would ever pay for it.

The wildfire had burned toward the treeless peaks of the Martire Arels. It would leave a scar up the slopes for years.

Nathan was busy, stacking bags on his wagon and wedging them in with barrels. He kept at it, like he always did, in his dedicated way.

Regret flooded her without warning, for the missed opportunities. A brother, one who might have been as close in his own way as Jack. "I'm sorry, Nathan." She climbed up and pulled a sack toward him. The burlap scraped. She winced when he flipped to check it.

He threw it up and lugged another barrel into place. It had survived better than most, with no singe marks, just smudges. "Don't worry about it." The back of his shirt had a line of sweat down the middle, seeping outward.

She pulled more grain over. "I know we don't get along."

"Don't want t' talk."

"Okay."

He was like Rusty, when the field was partly plowed, and the bigger horse took the lead and kept going even after Rennet was ready to quit.

"Steading is work," he said, all thorny. He hefted another sack. "We're planning next season. Five months away. Every day on Caravan, I been checkin' with growers and buyers. Every day. What to plant, how much, which field. Which fields t' leave fallow. Which cover crops. We just lost a wagon! Most of the whiskey!"

He rattled everything off grimly. "We don't make a lot of money. I been workin' with Pa since I was five. Five!"

It felt suddenly as though he spoke a language she'd never truly learned.

He lugged another barrel, and a wedge of charred wood cracked off. He swore and stopped, and a bead of sweat dripped off his nose. He carefully eased the barrel into place against the grain.

"I didn't mean to upset you. I was just trying—"

"I know the problems. Frost, we protect the crops. Late spring, we plan for it. Pests, gettin' the right hands, figuring the futures, amount to ferment, sell, findin' customers. All in a day's work."

"You do a lot." She'd ought to leave, talk with him later.

"Now add on, because that ain't enough, add on that *all* the other growers are gonna have water. How am I supposed to compete with that? How am I s'posed to grow food with *that*?"

"Nathan, I never asked—"

"It's not *you*. Get over yourself. Half a dozen things could take the stead down. And now, we got bad genes? That's all you are. One more problem to manage."

"That's all I *am* to you?" Myrta stared in astonishment. "I'm *bad genes* to you? That's just plain cruel, Nathan."

"That's straight up. Steading is work."

Her mind flashed to a day when she was nine and he was sixteen, and she'd been weaving clover chains in the alfalfa. He'd seen her and yelled, "Get outta here. Git," and she'd run off, telling herself he'd given her permission to skip chores. "You wish I'd never been on the stead at all."

"Woulda been easier."

"*Easier*? What about Jack?"

"He works." Nathan nudged another barrel back, grunting. Dark circles had formed under his arms.

"So do I."

"You did. Sometimes. You're pullin' a few bags. Maybe you feel like it. You're like a crop that's s'posed to give a bushel per acre but only gives half. Why would anyone plant that?"

Myrta's breath caught.

Nathan wiped his forehead against his sleeve and muttered, "Least you're gone now."

Her rage boiled up, and she didn't try to stop it. "Nathan."

He faced her and she punched him, as hard as she could, imagining her hand clear through his skull. The blow landed directly under his eye, and he fell back with a groan.

Her knuckles stung, and she threw her fist into the bags and said, "Some things don't grow in *fields*. Some things aren't even food." She jumped down and stormed back to the pasture, barely able to see where she was going.

Somehow Jack was there. He was supposed to be talking to Manny, but here he was, and he was looking at the wagon, at Nathan struggling up. He let out a low whistle. "Did you sock Nathan?"

She fixed him eye to eye. "I did."

The wagons worked down the east-facing flank, and she drove the team because Alphonse couldn't do any more than huddle in the corner of the seat. The acrid tang of smoke coated her sinuses, her throat.

Her blanket was gone. Someone must have used it during the fire. She'd gotten choked up; it had been the last piece of her life from before.

She wanted the blanket and instead had a knife.

Alphonse shifted his weight onto her, leaning against her with his eyes closed and mumbling about lava, saying fragments of things, about his home and serving on a council. It made no sense. But the feeling of trust in how he leaned on her was a comfort. Myrta put an arm around him.

They reached the narrow flatlands in the early evening. She helped Alphonse off the wagon and he sat quietly while she pitched his tent. She told him to wait, that she'd bring him water and something to eat, but when she returned he was asleep inside.

Chapter Thirty-Two

Alphonse stood on the edge of a bustling city under a single sun. Far away, rigs pulled oil from the ground. "They're taking all the carbon."

"Earth spent a long time storing that."

"I remember."

"There were many forests. Many microbes. Ten percent of planetary history."

"Yes, yes. I know. They're burning it too quickly. It's going into the air too quickly. Don't they see the risk? Don't they remember the blue-green bacteria and the trees? Volcanoes? Don't they understand atmospheric chemistry or planetary physics?"

Stavo's voice was heavy with grief. "Some do. Others . . . others know only that they grow rich."

Alphonse stood in a bustling city, on a distant world called Earth.

No, he lay flat on his back in a tent on Turaset.

The bustling city remained with him, as did the tent. City odors stung his sinuses, and he leaned over to smell the canvas, but that wasn't it.

Years earlier, in school, one of his teachers had described a mental state. *Sensato*, one of the ancestral genetic modifications engineered into human DNA. It was supposed to record history, or access time, something like that, through base methylation or epigenetic inheritance. There had been too many modifications to learn, and he hadn't paid close enough attention.[6, 7] His mother had called most of them nonsense anyway. But now, Alphonse stood in a city under a single sun, even though Turaset had two.

Then, his childhood dream of the library surfaced. The memory from so long ago, when he stood in light with his grandfather.

One by one, every sensato dream came back to him.

Alphonse was cold and hungry, trading cloth during the rise of commerce, willing to kill to survive. He was a young hominid at the discovery of fire. He stood on Earth when a meteor destroyed two thirds of its large species.

The trees and giant insects. The age of plants. Alphonse felt again the pressure of granite and the millions upon millions of years to form petroleum. He remembered starving, floating, dehydrating, and evolving as a single cell, and he saw the whole world frozen because of him, a blue-green bacterium.

Alphonse saw back to the beginning, when the

---

6   A wide range of real-world applications of CRISPR-mediated genetic modification is described in Nature Biotechnology, volume 34, pages 933–941 (2016).

7   On Turaset, genes responsible for certain traits (e.g., left-handedness) have been lost from the population altogether. Nasoirian schoolchildren find it remarkable that some ancestors on Earth used a dominant left hand, for example. A fictional list of traits engineered into the human genome is provided in Appendix 3.

planet was lifeless and meteors bombarded its molten surface.

The memories ran forward then, and he recalled in perfect detail the story of the planet's formation, the origin of life to the oxygenation of the atmosphere and formation of ozone. He knew every cycle, every step of evolution's march, each cause for each effect.

Alphonse became planetary history.

And in the last pulse of his heart, humans rose to dominance. Within that short span of time, in the last moment, they found coal, and oil, and gas. They pulled it from the ground and burned it, releasing the massive tonnage of carbon and time back into the air.

The weight of history crushed him, epochal change ripping apart his own life; it was too much, and he became a speck, whirling away to nothingness. No one could survive the knowledge, the context, the immensity of time. He disintegrated. He was detritus in an ocean of events, atoms cycling and swirling.

His consciousness unraveled, words abandoned him, then space, then meaning, then awareness gone . . . and he was *not* . . . and . . .

A thread wrapped itself around the nothingness, the cloud of un-being that could have been, in another universe, a sitting councilor writing legislation to drill the ranges. The thread found him and anchored into him like a line.

Stavo was there. Standing with Alphonse through all four-and-a-half-billion years, laughing and encouraging. It was the barest of glimmers to cling to, a hint of a path through the wilderness, the abyssal depths. It was a mere filament, the possibility to spool his sanity together, the chance that perhaps his experience meant . . .

"Grandfather?" he croaked in the tent.

The story is not over. The thought faded.

Still, he could not fix on this moment, this place of being.

He struggled to emerge from the tent but couldn't open the flap. *I am the chimney. I am the world. I am a cell.* He tried to assimilate the knowledge, the billions of years. He stumbled out among the tents in the gray morning, and his mind zeroed back. For a moment he was Alphonse again. Out and in, through the past and present, the planet in its iterations. *Cycles.*

He was disassembled thought. Alphonse couldn't find himself. He was time. He was a planet. He was history.

Awareness centered somewhere near his head, but also extended to the oxen and trees, the rocks and dirt. There were cells there too . . . He tottered around in the hazy dawn. "Grandfather, where are you?"

A steader yelled, "We're tryin' t' sleep!"

This is insanity.

Alphonse climbed into the corner of the wagon seat that morning, hunched. Myrta took the lines and drove without saying a word. The day rolled by in a haze.

They pulled into the outskirts of Sangal in the late afternoon. He couldn't unfurl. He smelled hints of sewage and oil, and pulled every part of himself closed.

"Are you okay?" Myrta asked quietly. Gray and brown smudges dirtied her face, her hands, her clothes. "You should lie down again."

"No." His tongue was too thick. His skull buzzed with electricity. *My fingers aren't in my hands.* "Need to go home." Panic fought up and confusion pushed down, and through it all was a profound desire to cease. *I . . . can't . . .*

Myrta's hand was on his shoulder. "You look horrible."

He slipped off the seat and caught himself on the side rail, shaking his head. Eons stretched through him. He stood next to a city, a forest, a lifeless cliff.

Alphonse stumbled through the wagons, to the edge of them and into the city. Back on paved streets. Back among shops and businesses.

Sangal.

The smell of exhaust, putrid and sharp, enveloped him. That smell, carbon, powering the tools and the auts. Alphonse floundered in four-and-a-half-billion years of climate matching the movements of a single sun, the tilt of the planet's axis, the actions of life.

People are another cycle.

He sat, suddenly, on a curb outside a random storefront and stared at nothing. *We're changing the air. We are like the trees. The volcanoes. The bacteria.*

After minutes or hours, he stood, steadier, and walked to his mother's street, to her door.

The high ceilings. The elaborate draperies and chandeliers. They were the same negligent display of wealth they'd always been. Only the unread society magazines on the front table had changed. He leaned against his knees. He tried to recall his argument against naming the belt and slowing combustion.

'*A beginning,*' his grandfather said.

Alphonse startled at the voice, but the front entry was empty. It must have been some memory of his grandfather in these rooms twenty years earlier.

He went upstairs. His mother faced away, working at her desk next to a narrow, stained-glass window.

Memories stared back. Her erect posture as she wrote something. The scent of perfume in the air. He used to think the scent was her, and he remembered the day he found it in a bottle.

Two walls of the room had been papered, if one

could call it that, in leather, with elaborate murals carved into them. A horse pulled down by lions on one side. Wolves taking a tusked moarab on the other.

Awards of recognition stood on a low table in front of the divan. He used to do his school work there, on that very table of burled black sweetnut. The black-and-white grain swept him back to the age of trees, and he stood in a forest. He fought his way back to the present.

"Hello, Mother."

She turned and her eyes flew wide. "Alphonse. Oh, thank Autore. You've been gone too long." Standing so quickly her chair fell back, she crossed to him in three steps. Her face was haggard; her makeup poorly applied. She took him in a long hug. "You've lost weight."

Tears welled up in him, in both of them. It had been years since she'd given such a strong sign of affection, of acceptance. Too many years spent scheming. All the personal touches swept to the side. Concern for one another's welfare pushed down.

She took in his face again, and he hers, which was worn, but in it he saw the mother of his childhood, the woman whose laughter had always been a warm summer's day. That lay there underneath her thinning skin and creased lines. She said, "You look barbaric."

He laughed. He probably did, but suits and cologne made no sense in the belt. "I'm not sleeping. Can we talk? We need to discuss what you're doing."

He set her chair up and noticed a small statue on the desk, an award he hadn't thought about in a long time. It was to his grandfather, in recognition of council service. She once said it helped her focus on the choices he'd made. Alphonse touched the small statue.

"Do you remember how things were when . . . when I was little? You used to sing lullabies."

"Of course." She gave a puzzled shake of her head.

Something hot, a tear, tracked down his cheek. This was hard, opening up to her. She seemed confused at his display. *But governing the belt, it can't—I won't.* "I miss that."

"Autore, Alphonse, you're a grown man."

History flashed through him and he wasn't a grown man at all, but an ape-child. His mother held him close, told him the fire wouldn't hurt, that they used it, like they used the tools.

'*We must ask if combustion is still our servant.*'

The voice startled him again, and Alphonse glanced around the room. After a moment, he turned back to his mother. "Look. About your plans, for the Chancellery, we need to talk."

Her eyes locked onto his. Her face was still.

"It's . . . an extraordinarily bad idea to name the belt as a fourth province."

A calculating frown appeared on her forehead, one that he knew too well. She was looking for the pressure point. It chilled him to see the expression directed at him.

"Why is that?" she said coolly.

He paced to the divan and back. "Mother. Autore. I'm not your adversary, I'm your *son*." She was in there. He'd seen it. She had missed him; he'd bet his life on it.

Her face smoothed at his words.

And he knew three things that she responded to. He'd take them in order. "Putting the belt under provincial law would fundamentally change the continental economy, and not in the way you hope. The belt's unregulated except by nature. They're proud. They choose it. They like the rhythm, and—"

"They benefit from profit as much as the next person."

He snapped, "If you cared about strangers' finances you'd have helped the line workers years ago. Naming the belt as a province will create enemies. And you'll undercut trade."

She regarded him without saying a word. He waited, still she said nothing. "Do *you* need money? Do you not have enough money? Is that the driving issue here?"

She scoffed. "I've provided for you since Marco left. I've been mother *and* father to you. Look around."

"Why the belt? Is it influence? You're begging for a revolt. They're the ones with the bargaining chips, not us. They'll withhold lumber. Food. The cities will starve if you force this. What can we withhold—oil? They don't need it."

She sighed, watching his face but not seeming to focus upon it.

He said in a whisper, "You used to say I was all you had."

"You were."

The cold and callous way she said it chilled him and he choked out, "We're family. Please. Just come back. I miss you."

The look of bewilderment on her face was so complete he wondered if he'd read her wrong.

"I don't have time for this. Alphie, truly, I'm glad you're back. But things are moving, and I need to focus on the Congress." She sat, turned to her notes, and picked up her pen. "You'll feel better in the morning. There's an event tomorrow. I want you in a new suit. Gray."

He whispered, "I just got back."

"Wear the black loafers."

Planetary history flashed through him with a vengeance, and he wasn't in the room at all. He was in a forest, on a plain, he wasn't Alphonse but a molecule at the dawn of time melting into a raging inferno.

What is this?

Stavo said, '*The beginning of order.*' Alphonse braced himself against the wall.

His mother scratched out a column of numbers, saying, "Have your hair cut and styled." She glanced at him. "Shave."

Rage compressed his chest. He sucked in as much air as he could. There was no oxygen.

"And take a bath. Immediately."

Rational thought abandoned him. He held himself by force of will, as pressure pushed him smaller and smaller in the deep ocean.

"Autore, you smell like a common laborer."

His punch flew hard and fast—and it was only at the last moment, in the midst of the throw, that he pivoted, putting his fist through stained glass instead of her. The window shattered, and pain flew up his arm. A purple shard jutted from his knuckle, which now bled. He pulled the jagged glass out in astonishment.

His mother stared at the hole he'd made. Her eyes blazed. "What the fierno was *that*?"

"Common laborers are the backbone of the economy. Grandfather worked for the people. Not for himself, but for others."

Her eyes narrowed, focusing the blaze. A pinprick of light hurtled toward them from the heavens above. "Yes, his entire life. Writing laws for others, working late hours, and serving others. But not this person. How this detail always escapes your notice is beyond me. He did not help *this* person, not when I was small nor as I grew."

She spoke forcefully, stabbing her finger at the door and hallway beyond. "I adopted every thought he ever had, every philosophy. I cooked meals for him. I gave him a son-in-law, and I gave him a grandson."

The pinprick of light grew larger and brighter.

"And when he planned law? With other women and men, downstairs? He relegated me here, to the upper floor, to tend to you with lullabies and rhymes, away from them, the ones with power, while they ate the food I prepared and talked about the importance of people. But not *this* person. Still, I laughed, and I smiled, and I agreed. And none of it *mattered*." Her eyes strained wide.

The strike was imminent.

"And after that, a lifetime of absence from him, isolation from him and his mission, in the end—my father? Was killed *because* of the choices he made, serving others. He was a weak, impotent, ineffective little man who did not change one thing."

The meteor struck, and the era shifted, the old regime obliterated. Ejecta rained from the sky.

She barreled on. "Change requires strength. My approach, by the way, *includes* you. I bring you into every effort because you are my child and I love you."

Stavo's voice was a mere hint. *'I thought it a small choice, to spend so much time in the Council. I did not know it would have such . . . far-reaching consequences.'*

Alphonse came back to the moment, standing straight. "Mother! Grandfather's ideals stand on their own merit. A good government, driven by the people, is an expression of our best selves. You've tried a different way—you've tried it this way my entire life. And people work longer hours, with fewer safeguards, while you grow richer. It confirms everything he said. It shows he *did* make a difference. Now you work to establish a new province? To expand combustion? Why?"

"To prove he was *wrong*!"

Alphonse was a trader freezing in a village. In front of him stood another, her beast piled high with furs. He was starving, he was dying, and she had wealth around her neck. He threw his hands to it, grabbed at this stranger's throat, this person so different from himself. If he could separate the wealth from the woman, he might survive.

Alphonse was back in the study, his hands around his mother's neck, pulling at her sapphires. She sputtered and her face was turning an unhealthy shade of blue.

Shaken to his core, he threw his hands back. "Mother. Autore, Mother! Are you all right?" He backed against the far wall, horrified and out of reach of her. He couldn't be here, with her. He wasn't in his right mind. He wasn't in this age at all.

Still, the blood from his hand stained her throat.

"Where does it end?" he whispered. "You've taught me to use people, to manipulate them. I needed another way, and I've *found* it, but I love you, and I miss you. How do we get past *this*?"

She looked at him with guarded eyes. "There is nothing to get past."

'*We hope for change.*'

He didn't bother to question the voice. Change was the word. Alphonse closed his eyes, seeking the zone and giving up his final shred of hope for a different future in a different place. Like the last leaves falling from a sugar maple, the sweet possibility of life elsewhere faded.

He roped in for the longer route, the one he'd avoided since leaving Sangal months earlier, the one with cologne and wingtip loafers. "I'm running for Council in the next open election."

"It's too late. The seat's gone."

"I said I'll run."

She stared past him. "I very much doubt you'd win without my help. We'll write a law. You'll run unopposed."

Her vise clamped straight onto him and instinctively he pulled a breath. And . . . his chest relaxed. It was a strange thing, like water rushing down a mountain canyon. He breathed, deep beautiful easy breaths, fresh air from the passes. "Listen. I'll run fairly, on my own message."

"It's easy to add a rider. The Council's in session."

'You could cooperate,' Stavo suggested.

Alphonse shook his head.

'Then adversity.'

Ivette watched him. She smoothed her dress, and her eyes were no longer wide. His blood on her neck had lost its bright tint. "We'll find a way to weight the vote. My councilors do know why they hold their seats, after all."

'She doesn't understand the scale of her actions, not at all.'

She continued, "We'll find a way to seat you."

'Pay attention to the scale.'

You already said that.

'It sometimes needs repeating. The time scale, pay scale, power scale. The scale of carbon released from combustion. By any scale, we're out of balance, Alphonse. The scale is important.'

Alphonse and Ivette faced off at their perpetual impasse. He ached, losing her, for what might well be the last time, and gently said, "It's wrong to use power as you do. You've become the tool. For combustion."

'One event,' his grandfather nudged.

"And they murder people. They murder innocents." He watched her face, as intently as she'd ever taught him to do. He knew her better than anyone. Surely she hadn't known this. He still doubted Manny's story was even true.

But her face held indifference. "Yes, they do."

He swallowed, hard. He took another long breath of mountain air and wondered how closely she might have been involved with the killings, what exactly she'd known, and when. He wondered if he'd ever seek to find out.

"My father had all of Sangal behind him. And even so, one single industry detained him and beat him into nothing. Delsico, Garco, and Renico—they are *relevant*. They're more important than politics ever has been. I'm not the tool, the government is, as I've told you a thousand times. Whoever *holds* that tool dictates terms."

Tremendous pain filled his grandfather's voice, *'There are many who have inherited this way of thinking. She ... Alphonse, she's very rich.'*

It didn't matter. "I didn't understand power, or scale, before. I see it now, what needs to change. Power must return to the masses."

Stavo seemed to smile.

"What are you saying?" Confusion lit his mother's eyes, and something else. Alarm. "Alphonse, what do you mean by that?"

"Goodbye, Ivette."

Chapter Thirty-Three

Myrta pulled up onto Nathan's wagon bed. Jack was there, checking the stitching on some of the bags. One of the reasons Terrence sold grain instead of flour was because when the stitching came loose it was easier to set right.

She outlined her plan to him.

"We're farmers, Myrta. You're talking about taking on a huge industry."

"If we can find a house of refuge, things will line up." She swallowed and forced cheeriness into her voice. "We start by getting a message to Odile. We need a house of refuge, that's all we need to start with."

"Odile told you about those?"

He hadn't been listening. "No. Mama told me. So, I find one, and whoever lives there gets a message to Odile. From me. Then when she gets the pollution records, she gets me the discerning records."

"Mmm." He was re-sewing the end on one of the sacks. She scooted over to help.

"I want their financial records."

Startled, Myrta looked up. It was Alphonse, with blood on his shirt, on his trousers, and along his arm. "Did you cut yourself?"

He looked at his hand. "I don't remember."

She hopped off and took his hand. The gash was clean, like a knife cut. "What's going on with you? You need to lie down."

"Don't worry about it. Look, I have a friend in the industry. He'll have ideas, how to get at financial records. I thought they might also have records of what they do to people like you. Do you want to come?"

She smiled at Jack. "See? We've got friends inside the industry."

The next afternoon the three of them walked into Sangal City. Buildings rose on either side, sooty gray brick. Tall. Taller than anything in Collimais, than anything in the belt. The sidewalks were hard, and the people passing them kept their lips pressed tight. More auts than she'd ever seen, with streams of carbon billowing out. Myrta pulled her collar over her nose.

They turned to a side street. Alphonse had been rattling off what all the buildings were—this was a museo, that was a mail center, there was a bank, those were legal offices. She hadn't expected how busy everyone would look. How does a person look busy by walking?

They eventually reached some homes. Some of them could really use cleaning up. Tires and things that looked like old tools lay in the yard of one. They stopped in front of a little house with a cracked window. Alphonse knocked and yellow paint flaked onto the stoop.

"Who is it?"

"Eduardo, it's me."

The door opened, showing a sliver of a face, then it swung wide. A middle-aged man grabbed Alphonse in a one-armed hug. His other arm was in a sling, and he had stubble on his chin and a smudge of black sauce, like they'd caught him eating.

"You came back." He said it into Alphonse's shoulder with his eyes closed.

Alphonse held the man awkwardly but firmly, and he was blushing. He was such an odd one, Myrta thought. So hard so much of the time, but it was plain he and Eduardo cared about each other.

They went inside, through a cramped hallway to the kitchen, and it was all rather depressing. Faded wallpaper, a can of baked beans open on the stovetop next to a piece of partly eaten toast. A teeny window to gray brick outside. She tried to see it all as charitably as she could. It was a home.

Eduardo cleared off a few chairs. Some of his things lay on top of a counter, and the smell of the room was pungent, like the inn's generator fuel. Myrta altered her lensing. Ring compounds like the ones off the creosote plant, those were everywhere. The air was filled with carbon rings, benzene and such. And there was a cloud of blue around Eduardo's sling, like breath, but from his elbow.

She whispered to Jack, "His arm's rotting." Jack looked at her sharply.

Alphonse introduced Myrta and Jack, and then said, "You're hurt."

"Accident. One of the wellheads blew."

"Autore. What happened?"

"You know what happened. They took shortcuts, skipped guidelines. They want the oil, end of story. We've known the valve couldn't take the pressure. Did anyone care? It's cheaper to keep pulling. There must've been eighteen or twenty citations, and they ignored all of them." Eduardo wiped crumbs off the counter without speaking for a moment. His face drew down. "The blast killed eleven of my people. I can't stop thinking about them. I just wanted them safe."

"Have you been to a doctor?" Jack asked.

"There's no insurance."

Myrta stared harder at the blue cloud around his arm. It didn't come off in pulses, like breath, it just hung there, near the fleshy part of his forearm. It had to be rotting. "You might lose it."

Alphonse looked at her, and she screwed up her face, looked at him, then tipped her head at Eduardo's sling. It was *rotting*, too much carbon coming from it. She could almost smell it.

Alphonse said, "Yes, you need that treated."

Eduardo shook his head.

"Look, Eduardo. I almost lost my leg a few months ago. Even in the foothills you could get that seen to. Don't just swallow this like some kind of misguided hero." Alphonse pulled a piece of paper from the pile and wrote down a name and number. "Ivette's doctor. Give them this account and her name. They'll see you."

"I can't take your money."

"Take it. You know where she gets it."

Eduardo stared at the paper for a moment, then nodded and tucked it into his shirt pocket. "I'll go first thing in the morning. What can I do for you?"

"Tell us about Delsico. The plant. The refinery."

"Why?"

Alphonse's jaw went tight. "I thought the workers' issues were bad, but it's worse. Their plans are bigger. They cover everything, the whole continent. They've got plans to change up the chancellery, the foothills, all of it. Whatever you can tell us about Delsico's layout, operations—it'll help us come up with a strategy."

Eduardo let out a long, slow breath, and his eyes unfocused. "All right, but I'm mostly on the extractor these days."

"Whatever you can tell us, it'll help," Alphonse repeated.

"Yeah, okay."

Eduardo used his free hand as he spoke, gesturing, mostly pointing. "So the extractor's a couple miles out. Pipelines bring the crude in to the refinery, on site, north of the city. The generator burns it to power the city and the manufacturing plant."

Alphonse looked over. Myrta nodded. It made sense.

Eduardo continued, "Pretty soon, not just the city. New lines are going in. Out to the foothills."

Jack whistled. "The length of those lines—how's that possible?"

"Di Vern's promoting it. He says it makes jobs." Eduardo rubbed at his bad arm. "He's right. But it won't be quick, and his actual goal is holding his seat."

Alphonse leaned back in his chair. "Wiring the continent. That sounds like it could be Ivette's idea."

"I don't know. Di Vern, he always has his own motives. He has a habit, you know. He always has, saying one thing and meaning another. I don't know, Alphonse. It sounds like his idea to me."

"Do the foothills want wired electricity?"

"Not as far as I know."

But none of what they were talking about had to do with the discerning program, and none of it would get them any proof of it, at least Myrta didn't see how. She said, "If someone was recruited to work for Renico, is there a way to speak with them? Is there a way to visit?"

Eduardo frowned and shook his head. "Not easily. Recruits sign a financial obligation up front, a sort of indenture to cover training and supplies, that sort of thing. They're sequestered until that's paid. It takes a while. Longer than you'd expect."

Alphonse leaned toward his friend, his face intent.

"There's a girl. Young woman. New recruit. She wanted to work in records, wanted to get at the pollution data. She said she knew how to get assigned there. She'd be safe enough, right? It's not like she's on an assembly line."

Eduardo was shaking his head slowly. "Recruits are assigned based on what they can handle. She won't pick her assignment." He said to Myrta, "Is she young, like you?"

Myrta nodded.

"She'll go on the line. No question. She'll do a simple task ten hours a day. She'd only go to records if she had a physical disability, like she was unable to stand."

Alphonse raised his voice. "But she said she knew what to say. She said she'd be in *records*."

His face was breaking. It looked like his very heart was breaking.

Holy heavens, he cares for her.

Thinking back, of course he did. That's why they spent so much time together, back at the inn. Why Odile was so angry after he left. They were in love. Myrta found herself smiling. In a strange way it helped, knowing Alphonse cared for someone in her family.

Eduardo shook his head. "She's on the line."

On the line. If Odile wasn't in records, she couldn't just walk into some room somewhere and poke around for information. Myrta mulled it over while the men spoke. Maybe Odile had met someone in records, or maybe Eduardo was wrong about the assignments.

He slammed his fist on the counter, bringing her attention back.

"—every year. Now, if a new recruit is connected to someone important, say you, Alphonse. If you went to Delsico, you'd go straight to sales. You'd have an office in the city and not know anything about what goes on at the plant."

"That's not all the assignments," Jack said. "What about handlers and discerners?"

Eduardo raised his eyebrows. "How does a farm boy know about discerners?"

"There were two in Collimais." Her words came calm, and Myrta realized she must have come to terms with things. Melville didn't frighten her as much as he once had, probably because she was finally doing something about it all. "They've been out to the belt too."

Eduardo rubbed his face and forehead. "Sounds like they're ramping everything up." He pushed away from the counter, began to clean up the beans and toast on the stove. Myrta went over to help. He said quietly, "A long time ago my mother was on the Council. That's how I met Alphonse, because of his grandfather, Councilor di Gust. My mother worked with di Gust before he was locked up."

Myrta looked over to Alphonse and wondered again who this handyman, this logger, this city man was. But he was holding his face in his hands.

Jack looked perplexed, and Eduardo sounded none too solid himself. "The way they brought di Gust down. Jailing him on bad charges, wrapping it all up in legal talk about the economy when anyone with any sense could see that protecting those ranges is better over the long term. When I was young I thought I'd go into politics, but it started to look like a bad career. You write good law and someone sends you to jail for it. As crazy as it sounds, going into combustion started to make more sense. You know, like if you want to change things maybe it's best to go to the heart of the problem." He laughed without humor. "I thought I could make the industry accountable from the inside. I started in sales, managed the line for a while, then the extractors. But I was wrong. I was wrong about changing any of it."

Alphonse moaned quietly.

Eduardo had more to say, and Myrta wanted all of it. He was giving the sort of open-book accounting she'd always wanted from Ephraim.

"Discerners," Eduardo said morosely. "You know. I started hearing the rumors. About what they do to the people they find. They take their eyes. They cut out their bloody eyes! And when you hear that from enough people in enough places, you start to wonder. You can't help it. And then you start to believe it. At this point, I've come to believe they'd cut the eyes out of combustion science itself if they could. They'd make the whole world blind sooner than take responsibility for the harm they do."

His words fit everything Odile had said.

"Some of the payouts from the company don't add up. There're a few buildings on site that no one has access to, things like that, and they make zero sense. Eventually, discerning was the simplest explanation."

Alphonse's voice was rough. "Why didn't you tell me?"

"Alphonse. You had a hard time believing the little things. And discerning sounded like a myth at first. When I . . . learned." His head tipped down, making it hard to hear. "It's just that . . . people have a remarkable ability to ignore all sorts of atrocity. We always have, back to the beginning."

After a still moment, Eduardo took another deep breath. "My mother put everything into di Gust's defense. Everything. All her money, any favor she could call in, all of it. In the end he died, and she was voted out, penniless. Di Les holds her seat."

Alphonse's head was twitching, back and forth. Eduardo went around the counter to him and pulled up a stool. "Alphonse, what they did—"

But he just shook his head and sat straight. "Who's picked for scouting and discerning?"

"Well, the scouts, the handlers, that's a good promotion. You get off the line that way. Discerning . . ." He shook his head. "If a recruit's strong enough, if he's motivated, smart, he might be picked. There's psychological conditioning. There aren't many candidates."

Too many questions wanted to spill out of Myrta. This man knew so much. "How many discerners are there? Altogether?"

Eduardo frowned. "I don't really know. I'd guess, based on what I've heard, maybe five or six. People whisper. Most recruits don't make it through the training. Some get out, leave, once they realize it's their soul at stake."

Alphonse seemed to have recovered some of his composure, and his voice was stronger. "Can you take us to the plant?"

"To Renico?" Eduardo's gaze intensified.

Alphonse grinned, and he looked like a hound coordinating with a packmate. "Just Delsico. Close enough to see the layout."

"Why?"

"We're making plans." Then, with a glint in his eyes, he added, "You should join us."

Later that evening, the four stood on a rise outside the city, overlooking an enormous complex of buildings.

Eduardo glowered into the distance, and Myrta followed his gaze to the bruise pulsing from the ground. He said it was where the oil rig had failed.

A few feet away, Alphonse and Jack spoke softly to each other. Myrta joined them. A maroon haze of ozone enveloped the perimeter fencing like a slim vertical halo. Inside, squat gray structures crowded every bit of space.

Eduardo came over. "The central building—that's manufacturing."

Carbon was pluming out of its stacks, brilliant blue. She asked, "Which are the barracks?"

He pointed to a side cluster of buildings with narrow doors and high windows.

She studied them. Each building was large enough that probably dozens of people could stay in them. "They kind of look like everything else."

"No reason to make them different." His voice smoldered.

Alphonse wobbled next to her and she grabbed him. He leaned against her. "Where did the dinosaurs go?"

Myrta stared at him. His eyes were unfocused, and his hair coiled damply on his forehead. Something was very wrong with him. She took him by both arms. "Are you feeling all right?"

"Never mind." He shook her off and stood straight. "Delsico's bigger than I expected is all."

Eduardo was tapping his foot now. "The electrified fence doesn't help morale, that's for sure. They say it keeps the property secure."

Aha. Myrta's thoughts fell back to the old chemistry book at the inn. Ozone—the maroon haze around the fencing—from the electrical current. "Could we get in if we needed to?"

"No. Guards round the clock."

"Is Renico the same?"

"Everything's bigger. The plant . . . the accidents." There was unmistakable anger in his voice, and he planted his feet wide. "Most of my people were married, had kids. I'm glad you're back, Alphonse."

He grinned, focused and clear-eyed again. "We could use a ride to Narona."

Chapter Thirty-Four

The oil was burned, the planet grew warm, and systems fell like dominos. Seas rose. Wildfires raged. Animals migrated to new homes; others went extinct.

"I don't understand." Alphonse's words came in agony. He couldn't conceive of it all—the collapse of Earth—he could barely watch it, the death around him, the end of the most diverse and beautiful biosphere humanity had ever known.

"Try."

Alphonse turned his thoughts to the people. The mothers, fathers, and children. And he saw they were like him—these ancient ancestors in Earth's Anthropocene. Each wanted comfort, opportunity, freedom, and the possibility to have children of their own. And on the warming planet, Alphonse also found hope, like a flower, hiding. He found that among the people, many faced the threat with courage and tried to steer their world toward a solution, as generations before had understood their own threats in their own times and found their own ways forward.

He saw, in a moment of pure beauty and truth, that every person down to the last one cared. A pang of recognition filled him. "They are good people."

"Yes."

The next afternoon, Eduardo pulled his aut onto a quiet street on the northern side of Narona, the part of the city nearest Renico's refinery and plant. Myrta had promised she could find them a safe place to stay, something about people in the same movement as Ephraim. At this point, the idea of an underground against the industry was no stranger than anything else Alphonse had seen. Myrta said a house of refuge would be marked with lavender.

"So I'm just dropping you off in the street." Eduardo sounded irritated. He massaged his treated and freshly-bandaged arm.

Alphonse opened the aut door. "Look, you can't risk your job over this."

"It's okay, Eduardo." Myrta sounded eager. She opened her door and got out with Jack. "No one ever died from walking. It's nice outside."

She was right, the day was pleasant, and a breeze was coming off the ocean. But the petroleum fumes were harsher than anything in Sangal. Narona's reputation held up.

"Look, we'll be fine. What I need is for you to challenge di Gof for his seat."

"I told you yes, Alphonse. I'm in."

"Just wanted to hear it again." Getting onto the Council would be a climb every bit as hard as Tura. He needed a partner, someone on the ropes with him.

They said their goodbyes, and Eduardo pulled away.

Houses lined the streets, set close with cramped yards. Jack wiped his hands on his trousers. "It reeks."

It did. The scent tugged at him, took him to a long-ago plain and herds of pronghorn. Asphalt oozed into him, into every cell. He blinked, but it was hopeless. He was buried, dead; he was darkness and time and he stretched into infinity. He came back to find Jack holding him up.

"You okay?"

"Yeah, fine." These distortions had to stop. They were killing him. For three days he'd gone in and out of time, his mind trying to span all of it. Somewhere in the mess lay a memory from Stavo, saying he'd hold all of history in a thought. But whatever this was, it wasn't that.

"There's lots of benzene here," Myrta was saying, squinting at the air. "It's a ring compound. They jiggle."

They started walking, and auts passed from time to time. Myrta sighed. "Nobody grows anything."

It felt that way; the trees were spindly. Some grass, a few potted plants, not much else.

On the next street opposite them, a pale blue aut with rusted wheel wells slowed and stopped. The driver was grizzled. He stared straight at them. A dog in a studded collar jumped in the back seat, thrust its snout out of the cracked-open window, and snarled.

It wants to hunt pronghorn. Alphonse shook his head. That was twenty thousand years ago.

Myrta was yanking him to herself and pulling him along. The aut turned in the street and followed at a crawl, then it was ahead of them and stopped again. Myrta whimpered.

"They're staying in the aut, Myrta. They're both mammals."

Jack came around and held his other arm.

Myrta made another sound and pointed, past the aut to a house. A straw wreath hung on the door and tucked into the wreath were faded flowers. "I think that's it."

But the smell of tar.

They passed the aut with the dog; his hackles were up. Alphonse did not growl back. Instead, he fell to the ground in front of the house and sat there, his mind running backward to the Pleistocene and forward again. He grabbed up a handful of soil and looked at it. Myrta and Jack were at the door.

The barking grew louder, and he turned to the animal. "Settle down. We tamed you. Remember?"

The dog snarled and wrangled its head, trying to force the window glass downward. Myrta was knocking on the door. A pale woman opened it. Pale, like the people on the eastern continent.

Frothing at the mouth, still snarling, the dog worked its front foot out of the window. Its body contorted, hips swinging. The woman exchanged a long look with the driver.

Myrta made a scared and panicked sound, her eyes glued to the aut. "We . . ."

The dog had forced its shoulder out and now clawed at the air. There was a lot of wolf in the animal, even after all that selective breeding. Alphonse wondered how things would have gone if they'd tamed foxes instead. "Now, now. Is that how a best friend behaves?"

"We like your wreath," Myrta cried out.

The woman fingered the petals, tucked one in more firmly. "I should make one fresh. These flowers are old."

Strange thing to say. Flowers were recent.

Across the street two doors had opened, and the mammals in the doorways stared.

The white-haired woman looked Myrta up and down, then glanced at Jack. Then she studied Alphonse for a long moment. Too long, but he didn't care. The past tossed him around, played with him. He was a plant. He was a dire wolf, and he stood, turned to the dog, and growled.

Jack was at his side again. "Come on, buddy."

He shrugged Jack away. The barking from the aut grew more raucous. The dog had forced its second shoulder out of the window. Now it hung halfway out, frenzied lust on its face.

The woman said, "Is it for the wreath that you stop?"

"Yes," Myrta said quickly. "Yes. Yes."

The dog had pushed the window down. It fell out, scrabbled in the dirt, and bounded straight toward them, barking madly.

Alphonse lunged, he was bigger, his bite more powerful, and he pulled his lips back. He leapt—but the two apes had him again, were dragging him across the yard, away from his prey, into the house. The woman slammed the door, and the dog landed with a thud against the outside, its claws rasping.

The woman said calmly, "I grow the plants in back. Come, see."

Jack muttered to Myrta, "Is any of this safe?"

Alphonse was still snarling. There was a fight outside, but the apes were pulling him past a narrow staircase into a living area. A purifier whirred in the room, fresh air from its top, and with that, time wound forward to the groggy present.

The woman was studying him with interest. "Sit. I am Ralen." She continued to a separate room.

He did, and the fog in his mind cleared. They were surrounded by furnishings and decorations from the eastern continent. And this woman's features were Deasoirian. In disbelief, he muttered, "We're staying with a Deasoirian? Was that really the best you could do?"

"It's a house of refuge," Myrta whispered.

She seemed to think that was good enough. She and Jack were on a long white sofa. Lamps with colored shades on either side, and a green and yellow carpet on the floor. Some of the décor—all of it really—reminded him of that awful childhood trip with Ivette.

Ralen returned with a platter. She placed it on a low table in front of the sofa, and with formal and ritualistic movements poured each of them a glass of water.

Myrta took a glass. "Why do you grow lavender?"

Ralen paused, appraising each of them once more. When she turned to Alphonse, she tipped her head down and drew her eyebrows together. "To honor the memory of my father."

Myrta looked puzzled, but after a moment her face eased and she said softly, "If I understand, then I'm sorry to hear about your papa. We need a place to stay—"

Ralen interrupted. Coming from a Deasoirian that wasn't too surprising.

"What do you think of Narona?" Ralen's face was still, and the whirring from the air purifier stopped as well.

Alphonse set his glass down. "Narona? It stinks. Myrta says there's benzene in the air."

Panic shot from Myrta's eyes.

"What? You did. You called it a ring compound."

Ralen's eyes widened. "That is most interesting.

What else, Myrta, is in our air? What is there, that would not be somewhere else?"

Myrta shot another look at Alphonse, but he shrugged. This house was her idea after all. She looked out the window. "Carbon disulfide. Methylene chloride. A few polycyclic—"

"That is enough." A smile spread on Ralen's face. She inclined her head to Myrta. "You bring honor. I have not hosted an aerovoyant in quite some time. My guest room has two beds, one sofa, and a washroom. The windows face Renico, but you may close the drapes if you like."

The next morning, Alphonse went to use the washroom. His head was still clear. The others woke, began talking.

"Odile's here, in Narona." That was Myrta. Jack had asked how she was feeling. "It helps to think about her being, you know, here. I'm okay, Jack. You didn't have to come along, you know."

"Course I did. I did. This city industry wants to lay line past the ranges, drill the farmlands. Deadly hells—they want to *take* you. Where would they stop? If I was inconvenient to them, don't you think they'd want me gone too? How far would they go? How many people would they kill?"

Alphonse dried his face and went back out. "We just need to see Odile, whether she's working with the records or not, and go from there."

They found Ralen setting a tray of biscuits out downstairs. "Good morning. Eat."

The biscuits were flaky, with butter melting into

each. Food. It hadn't really been on Alphonse's mind since the fire. He devoured one and grabbed two more.

Ralen laughed. "I will make more."

Shaking his head, Alphonse said around a mouthful, "We need to talk with a recruit."

The woman's face grew serious. "A bad idea. Training is to instill loyalty."

"Loyalty to what?" Myrta said.

Alphonse replied, "To their idea of how the world works, most likely. Look, Ralen, she just joined. We think they put her on the line, but she wants to get at records."

"I sympathize with your friend. I do not think a new recruit would gain access. The vault is locked and also guarded—"

"He's right. We need to get a message to her."

Alphonse stared at Myrta, at the strength in her voice.

Ralen said firmly, "It is not safe, not for your friend, nor for—"

"But there are people," Myrta insisted. "Right? In the network. You know people inside, and you're in the network. All we need is to see her. We need to make sure she's all right and give her a message. That's all."

Ralen held Myrta's eyes with her own until at last, she softened. "If you must see her, yes. Yes, we can deliver a message."

Chapter Thirty-Five

That night, Ralen drove them to a service road that ran near the recruit barracks, where she said Odile would talk directly with them.

Myrta was sweaty-damp from a case of nerves and the warm sea air. She flapped the edge of her blouse. Her breath was like a winged thing trying to escape.

Ralen pulled to a stop. "The barracks. Do not touch the fence. I shall wait."

They got out and walked over. The extractors thumped in the distance. Myrta could almost feel them thumping through her feet.

People in this enormous place were tracking her, a farm girl. It wasn't just wrong, it was abhorrent. She was no one. And if they hadn't targeted her, she'd have done nothing with her eyesight, ever, that mattered to these people at all.

They waited near the fence, outside the yellow glow that more or less defined the property's boundary. They sat. Rocks pushed through her trousers, little pricks of hardness, and she shifted her weight and leaned onto Jack. He and Alphonse were speaking in low tones about the industry, details, work shifts, things Alphonse had gotten from Eduardo during the ride down.

Jack woke her with a nudge. "She's coming."

Odile was on the other side of the fence. "Al?" She sounded surprised.

Jack murmured, "She calls you Al?" They stood and walked to her.

She wore miserable gray coveralls and she twitched, like she hadn't slept. "Myrta? Holy heavens. You need to leave."

"I'm taking a stand."

"A *stand*?"

"Yes. I don't want you on the line—"

"I'm not on the line."

Myrta's heart skipped in hopeful dread. "You're in records?"

"No. But I will be."

Hope faded, leaving a sinking feeling as Eduardo's words came back. *Strong... drive and intelligence* ... "Odile. What did they recruit you into?"

At the same time Alphonse said, "What do you mean, you 'will be'?"

A small moth blundered into the fence and crackled, falling downward in a cloud of brown dust.

"Odile," Alphonse said more insistently. "Are you in records?"

The dread in Myrta's chest turned to a lead weight and her knees buckled. Jack caught her. Everything distorted, and Odile's face looked nightmarish. Alphonse seemed to be running through the same logic that she was. His face flicked from anxiety to disbelief to something closer to horror.

He lashed out, "Really? Discerning? What about *records*?"

Odile blinked angrily. "Stop it. I know what I'm doing."

"How could you possibly?"

"Ephraim told me—"

"How would he know?"

"Ephraim and Melville were partners."

Myrta collapsed into Jack. "*Partners*? And you didn't tell me? Bel above, you're worse than they are."

Odile said to Alphonse, "I'm making the difference you refuse to make. I'm going to get access to the records vault, even at my 'ripe old age.'"

His voice rose. "Odile, no. Give me a week. I'll speak with Ivette. We'll get you out."

Her lips thinned, hard. "I'm not going to argue."

Myrta said, "But they shouldn't want you in their program at all. You were at Caravan when Melville attacked me. He knows we're related and that you care about me. This doesn't make sense."

Another moth fumbled into the fence, brown powder.

"Myrta. Melville's the person who *most* wants me trained. He thinks it'll bring Ephraim back into the program, to keep me safe or something. But you need to leave."

Her rage built. How dare they. How dare combustion destroy her family? "No."

"Myrta, *yes*. Look where I'm standing and think about this for one minute."

"No. *You* think about it. The stead is parched. You're throwing your life away. Papa's hurt. And why? Because I *exist*?"

No one said anything. Of course they didn't—there was nothing to say. Her rage pushed any last bit of anxiety away.

"Odile," Alphonse said at last. "We need you out. How do we do that?"

"You don't."

"Why? What are they *doing* to you? Autore, look at you."

"Well, Al. I'm medicated."

"That's how they train you?"

She looked away, grimly. "The training's mostly dissections, but yes. And if we're lucky," she added sarcastically, "they find someone like Myrta, so we can learn this particular trait on a living specimen."

Jack moved his arm around Myrta, but she pushed it off. He was glowering next to her, like Nathan did sometimes, like Terrence. Jack looked like he might erupt. "You can't do this."

Unfazed, Odile went on. "We're learning facial measurements. Those change when the muscles develop. We learn how to recognize someone using it."

"You could already *do* that." Myrta forced her voice back down. "You could."

"Ephraim taught me. Then there's field work. You know."

They stood in silence, the anger prowling between them. Beyond the plant, extractors kept thumping.

Alphonse's next words came soft. Dew drops, a mist on the fields. "Odile. Sweet Odile. I don't want you to do *any* of this. Odile, I want you back." Silent tears were streaming down his cheeks.

Her face broke. "Oh . . . Al. I know. But I'm not going anywhere."

She seemed to soak him in, every bit of him, from his scabbed hands to his tear-streaked face. Her gaze landed on his eyes, stayed there, and he returned it, unspeaking. For all the world, it was like watching Celeste and Terrence.

But it was impossible, that after everything they'd been through, especially since Caravan, that everything had led here—to Odile joining this abominable program.

Myrta clenched her fists and said angrily, "We can't have come here for nothing."

Odile nodded. "Right. Take some information back."

That wasn't what she meant.

"Those are the barracks. That's the cafeteria. We work in a trailer on the other side—you can see the corner of it. Melville and Floyd are with us in the afternoons."

The trailer was about fifty feet inside the fence. Odile waved her hand toward the middle of the complex. "Management and finance are in a building over there. It's white. Records are underground. Myrta, there's another thing I should've told you." She lifted her shirt. There was an incision and a tube, a port like the one Ephraim had gotten the night Myrta left Collimais. Odile said, "If Melville comes after you, or Floyd, go for the stomach. This is for the drugs. Grab and yank."

Repulsed, Myrta closed her eyes. "Odile . . ."

She lowered her shirt. "So don't count on me. They've got me on some pretty strong stuff."

Myrta paced from one end of Ralen's guest room to the other, with all the deadly hells of Odile taking on Melville's role torturing her thoughts.

Alphonse stared out of the window. "I want her out."

He'd been saying it all night.

There wasn't enough air. Myrta needed the belt, somewhere big. She went to the washroom and splashed her face.

Odile, being drugged through that tube. Odile jabbing at people like her. Using knives and needles to torture. Her papa doing those things.

Shaking, she pushed away from the sink and sat on the floor. After a few minutes she got up and went back out.

Jack was talking. "... funds. The indenture."

Alphonse scoffed. "I doubt that program has an indenture period."

"Maybe Ralen's connections," Jack said. "Get to Odile through them."

Alphonse smacked his forehead. "Ivette."

"Who?" Myrta said.

"Ivette. My—my mother. She introduced me to people inside—I know people inside Renico."

Myrta stared at this man, who was suddenly strange again. He might as well have claimed to head the whole industry. "You *know* them? You said you didn't. You said you'd never work for them."

Alphonse shook his head. "Odile said records are below finance. I'll set up a meeting."

"A *meeting*?"

His eyes were lit.

"Yes. With Zelia Naida. Her name doesn't matter. I can get in. I'll tell her . . . tell her we can put the belt under provincial governance immediately. It's what Ivette wants. Probably Zelia wants it too. I'll tell her we can buy your support—steaders' support—with irrigation. That the belt will ask for provincial status if it gets them water. She'll take the bait. That's how we get on site. It's how we get to Odile."

It was hardly a plan, and Jack didn't seem impressed either. He said, "Alphonse. There's no way we go in and walk around that place. How about this. You go in, meet your friend. Get whatever you can, get out. I stay here with Myrta. We're done. Odile becomes a discerner."

No—Odile would never become a discerner, not if

Myrta had anything to say about it. "If you get in, Alphonse, you might find the files I need. The files my family—*Odile's* family—needs. On discerning. No one would let it continue." Myrta's stomach lurched again, and she heard hysteria creeping into her voice. "Not if there was proof. They'd have to stop it, including the training, and then Odile wouldn't be trained. We have to break this into pieces. We can't do it all at once."

"We can if we all go in together. There are three of us. Do the math!"

"What *math*?"

In the distance, the complex glowed. Alphonse stared at it, then crumpled and sank onto the couch with his head in his hands. "Never mind."

Myrta ran through the pieces again. Alphonse knew someone in the plant—he could get in, but he wasn't really himself. Odile had told them where the records were kept. And they all wanted her out.

"Jack, he's right. He can't do any of this alone. I'm going with him."

The next morning, Ralen showed them a room, her papa's, she'd said, filled with his things. Pieces of coral, strange tools, stones, artwork.

A painting of a blue and green world with a single sun hung on the wall. "Is that conjunction?" Myrta asked.

"It is one of my father's visions, during *sensato*." She opened a wardrobe.

Alphonse seemed uncomfortable at her words and fumbled through the suits, settling on a tan one. He went to clean and shave. When he returned, Myrta's breath caught.

His trousers fell straight, the seams were sharp, and every physical attribute a person earned in the belt—strong shoulders, richer skin tones—all of it was accented by the fine city suit. Alphonse was a business-man, and he was intimidating.

The entrance to Renico was a small double gate. Metal, with wire around the edges and a guard house with windows at the side. Myrta had expected something bigger, people coming and going, mechanated devices doing mechanated things. But this, which Odile said was the main entrance, was no more than a metal gate.

Inside the guard house, a man dug around in his mouth with a toothpick. Another rocked on his feet, hands in his pockets, looking out. His eyes tracked her.

Alphonse strode straight up. "I'm here to see Zelia Naida."

She startled at his tone. He sounded arrogant.

The guard was still glowering. "Ms. Naida doesn't take meetings."

"I'm Alphonse Najiwe. I trust you recognize the name."

The guard studied him more closely. The second one stood and said something, but Myrta couldn't make it out.

Alphonse insisted, "Call Zelia. We have a time-sen-sitive opportunity in the belt."

He sounded powerful. Commanding. She felt smaller.

The second guard shook his head slowly back and forth.

Myrta crossed her arms and forced herself to look straight ahead.

Alphonse put a hand on the window frame and leaned in, inches from the glass. "Call Zelia. Tell her things are moving in the belt and I need a meeting. Now."

The guards bent their heads together. They spoke quietly and glanced out from time to time. After a few moments, one picked up a distavoc and made the call. The guard grew attentive and hung the receiver back. "Ms. Naida will see you."

"Thank you." Alphonse went to the gate, and Myrta followed with Jack. This place had worked itself inside every inch of her family, and a case of nerves sprouted at the thought. This . . . *place*, all gravel and fencing, defined her life, wrapped around her family, around the generations, around people she'd loved, and people she'd never even known.

The doors opened. Inside, one of the guards climbed into an aut. Alphonse joined him in front, and she and Jack sat in back.

The man drove, and Alphonse spoke in a constant stream in that same compelling voice, implying that he, or his mama, had helped Renico. The guard seemed more and more submissive.

Around them an occasional person passed by. A vehicle stacked with crates pulled away from one of the larger buildings.

They stopped somewhere in the middle of the place, in front of a whitish building. Alphonse got out, waved for Jack and Myrta to follow, and told the guard to go back to the gate. After a moment the aut drove away, and Alphonse was himself again—an awkward man with a limp.

She said under her breath, "That was very truly weird, what you did with your voice and all."

He shook his head. "Cheap tricks."

The steps and walls in front of them were made of a faintly-streaked stone. The upper floors were mostly window. Alphonse said, "So, I'll meet Zelia. You two, go find the trailer Odile showed us. Knock her out, whatever it takes. I want her out."

"Whoa, hold on there, city boy," said Jack. "That is not the plan. We're with you."

"Jack's right. It doesn't make sense for us to be here on our own."

"Look, Myrta. Today is simple. We get what we need and leave. We need one, records, and two, Odile."

"We stay together," she insisted.

"Myrta. This isn't some big heist. No one is paying any attention to us. They all have jobs. The *gate* secures the place. We're past the gate."

Myrta looked around. He was right about one thing, no one was paying them any mind.

Alphonse repeated, "Getting in was the problem. Now we're in. See? We've done the hard part."

He seemed to think so. It felt odd, but everything in the cities struck her that way.

"Look, the records are what Odile wants, and she wants you safe. So, you find her. If she sees you're here, she'll want you out. If she learns I'm taking care of the files, which I am as soon as you let me, she will agree to leave."

He seemed certain, and clear-headed, but he'd been going so funny lately. "Odile said she wouldn't leave last night."

"Because she wants the *files*. When you explain I'm getting them, she'll agree to go."

Jack looked doubtful. "Something has to be better than two steaders wandering around Renico."

Good point.

"Look, do you have a better idea?"

On the other hand, she thought, Alphonse knew city people, people here, even. He'd been right about getting in, and he was right about what Odile wanted. And Odile said the discerners weren't with them in the mornings anyway, so they should go now if they were going to go at all. Myrta turned to Jack. "We'll be done quicker if we split up. Come on."

Chapter Thirty-Six

Stavo looked around wistfully. "What these people could teach us."

A woman in glistening fabric passed them and walked through a lipped doorway into a room with rows of metallic cabinets. Each cabinet had keypads, gauges, and illuminated readouts.

"I don't understand."

Stavo smiled. "We orbit Turaset. It is the founding."

Alphonse placed his hands upon a cabinet, confused by the indicators, so foreign to anything he'd ever seen. The woman stood in front of a screen. "She seems to know what's going on."

Alphonse became the woman, using the computer interface to check the fecundity of innumerable plant seeds and animal embryos stored within the freezer cabinets. Entire ecosystems waited because the people who built this spaceship knew that systems were necessary for survival; that one part relies on every other part. And so, banks of plants and animals—the producers and consumers, the predators and prey, the foods and pharmaceuticals—waited.

One freezer was entirely dedicated to genetically altered human embryos, intended to help the colony live wisely. Another was filled with plant seeds and fungal spores engineered to produce remarkable medical compounds. Colonizing a new world would bring new challenges.

This vessel, from Earth, was part of a diaspora in search of new homes. It orbited a binary star that periodically emitted unusual radiation. Surviving that radiation would be the colonists' first challenge.

The woman prepared the seeds and embryos for revival.

Alphonse asked the building attendant for Zelia's office and was directed to a corner room on the second floor. He stopped halfway up the stairwell, leaned back, and exhaled. He'd fallen so easily, back at the gate, into the old habits learned at Ivette's side. He'd thought he was done with all of that, but here he was, wearing a suit for the first time since—*Autore, since the gala.* Manipulating those guards wasn't how his grandfather would have done things. But his grandfather never tried to get records from Renico's vault.

He continued up. Her door was open. He knocked.

"Alphonse!" Zelia, all energy and color, stood from her desk.

"Zelia."

The walls of her office were a shade of yellow so intense it verged on orange, and suns-light streamed through a bank of windows. Her desk was tidy, with a few worksheets out, financial from the look of them.

Outside, the surrounding buildings spread out blocky and gray. Past them, the ocean.

Nice view, actually.

She indicated a small leather sofa and sat next to him, her knees inches from his own. "How's Ivette?"

"Excellent, thank you. She's good."

He felt he stood on a mountain ridge. To one side lay the ethics of the belt—a goal, a product, honest effort. He'd found Odile there and the possibility of a different future. On the other side lay his past, peppering the ridge like flinty outcrops. Tools of flattery, innuendo, weaving the barest suggestion of threat into language—the parts of his upbringing he'd so consciously moved away from. But the tricks Ivette had taught him—those were still within. He wondered if he'd ever be free of them. "The line expansion is moving forward." His words came unbidden, like an old habit.

"Everything's falling into place." Zelia's manner was easy, comfortable, and so was her smile.

With a jolt he realized he'd duped her into sharing something she knew. He teetered on the edge of the ridge.

"Alphonse, can I ask you something?"

He nodded. A debate tossed within him. Exploiting a person's weakness—it wasn't illegal. Today was an opportunity and something he'd aimed for. He'd already done the hard part, getting into the facility. And the belt was at risk. Surely the ends justified the means. But it meant deceiving Zelia.

"About that gala, last spring. I've been curious, and Ivette's kept quiet. Everyone thinks you simply lost your temper with di Les."

He unbuttoned his suit jacket. The ends were important. The *belt* was important. There were thousands of people living there, and, in fact, in that moment he saw how to spin that gala. Pushing absent-mindedly against his thigh, he said, "Confidentially, Mother and I staged that. We wanted to get the attention of the minority caucus."

She cocked her head, frowning. "Why?"

He committed to the lie. Doing so was distressingly easy. "To establish a narrative. That I'm willing to join that caucus and work against her. Against *you*. I'll announce my candidacy and find support in the working class. I'll win, Zelia, and when I do, I'll claim to carry on Grandfather's fight."

Her expression shifted from uncertainty to interest. "Working with the minority caucus. But *why*?"

Yes, it was a lie, but one with a large dose of truth, and the ends mattered. Outside the windows, activity grabbed his attention. Guards were dragging Myrta and Jack away.

His stomach turned to lead. He'd been so certain there'd be no guards on the grounds. At the gate, yes, inside some of the operational facilities sure, and in sensitive areas like records—but not strolling the grounds.

Focus. The first goal was records, now with more urgency. "We think we'll swing a few of their votes if they believe I'm on their side."

She seemed to consider it. "You're talking about ancient councilors who won't serve much longer anyway."

"It's an edge. We'll take it, use the narrative to move a few early bills." Leverage works both ways, he thought. Sliding the pivot was the key, and he shifted the balance of the conversation to a new fulcrum. "Imagine if opening the Martire Arels to drilling topped the agenda."

Zelia smiled slowly. After a moment she laughed. "We appreciate any help you can offer."

She believes every word I'm saying.

"Listen, Zelia, the reason I'm telling you is because a new path to the chancellery has opened."

She looked at him curiously. Gullibly. And not at all surprised by his words.

"We've worked for years to put the belt under provincial law."

"It's been a long haul."

He kept his face blank and gambled. "To install di Les as a new prime chancellor."

She nodded.

Prime Chancellor di Les? Like fierno. "Here's the thing. We don't need a new chancellor. Nabahri's wanted more direct oversight of the belt for years. He's only held back because the steaders would revolt if he so much as hinted at naming a new province."

"Yes. We need di Les. He'll order the marshalry—"

"No, we don't need him. We don't need Congress at all. The droughts, Zelia. They work for us." Alphonse waited a moment to let that sink in, then tilted his head sideways and smiled. "You'll never believe how I spent the summer. Look at this."

He held out his hands and she took them. Hers were smooth and soft, the opposite of his—dark, calloused, and nicked from one side to the other, including the scabbed gashes from Ivette's window two days earlier.

"Autore." Her eyes grew wide, and she turned his hands over and back again, wincing at the scabbing. "What happened?"

"Manual labor. I worked in the belt, even grew a beard. Mother and I needed a read on these steaders— miere, Zelia. They've got no water. They're *dying*."

Her words came out in a breath. "Because of the droughts."

"We need two things from them—to request provincial status and to follow continental law once they do. Period. And the first naturally leads to the second."

She looked out the window, her eyes flitting back and forth. "That's right. If they request it, Nabahri would agree. We make them request it. He'll name the province."

Alphonse flicked a smile at her. "Can you think of anything that would encourage the belt to request provincial governance?"

She smiled back. "Can I offer you a glass of water, Mr. Najiwe?"

He laughed. The ease of deceiving her revolted him. There should be a better way, a way to meet minds with this woman, open a debate, work on areas of common ground, as his grandfather would have. In this moment, he didn't see it. "We are going to get the belt, and all the oil underneath. No more waiting. If steaders think of opposing any point of law that allows you to drill, you raise their fuel prices."

She ran both hands through her hair, her eyes still darting back and forth.

"You get your wish. The Prime Chancellor gets his. And we'll convince him that new tax revenue from the belt is a good rationale to offset *your* rate. He'll put corporate taxes on the agenda. It stands a decent chance of passage. Mother has ten votes in the Continental Congress already." Alphonse considered Odile's comments about the Vastol Vendetta and gambled again. "Or twelve."

"Thirteen." Zelia leaned back. "But the other provinces won't want to dilute their control. That was one advantage of the long path. It gives legislators in each coastal city time to come on board with the idea."

"Renico is the sole economic power in Renivia Province. You call the shots here. Mother will sell the idea in Delsina Province. Chancellor Nabahri can convince the Assembly in Garrolin Province."

She stood and paced between the sofa and her desk. "Provincial status. Those steaders get testy when it comes to their land. They'll block exploration."

"The timing, Zelia. The minute the belt's named, you're free to drill. They'll be too busy electing a council, choosing a seat of governance."

She leaned back against her desk. "This plan—it all uses rather a lot of blunt force. More than I personally like. Still, the board might agree with you."

"They will."

"Forgive me, Alphonse, but I remember you as more interested in policy than in Renico's needs."

Her full attention was on him. She was really listening, offering her thoughts in exchange for his. In a flash, Alphonse saw Zelia not as an adversary, but as a person whose goal was financial success for the industry. And that was all. His grandfather surely would have debated this woman, tried to shift her priorities ethically.

There was still no time for debate. He stood and joined her at her desk. "I've become more interested. The only point Mother and I are unclear on is the population of the belt. Do you have census information?"

"Yes, certainly. In the records vault."

He smiled.

They went down the stairwell to the basement. She unlocked the door at the bottom and led him into a small windowless room with yellow lights overhead.

A man with knobby bulk sat inside, paging through

a log book of some sort. Beside his desk was a heavy door.

The man nodded to Zelia and handed her the log book. She wrote her name and Alphonse's, and the guard unlocked the vault.

It was enormous, extending well past the periphery of the building. With sinking realization, Alphonse's eyes fell on row, after row, after row of shelving. He'd need to find information on pollution, the line expansion, discerning . . .

Zelia turned back to him and seemed to register his dismay. "Right. You've never been."

It was an absolute maze. "No, I haven't. You know, Mother and I could plan strategy more easily if we had a better handle on your resources." He pulled a file off of a nearby shelf as he spoke. It was from the industry's counterpart in Deasoir.

Zelia gave him a small smile. "That's a good idea."

She led him to the central corridor, her heels clicking underfoot. Small aisles branched off every few feet.

"Everything is sorted by topic and year. It's not hard to find something when you understand the organization. Each section of the vault has an overarching purpose." She pointed to one portion of the room after another. "Mapping and reserves, research, personnel. You get the idea."

He drew a map in his thoughts as they walked. She described new extraction techniques, horizontal drilling, solvents to release more carbon from the ground. Alphonse listened, absorbing what he could, running the flat of his hand along the documents.

Deeper into the maze, they reached the section on finance, her specialty. Files on managing the market through supply, or political pressure, through trade practices between the provinces and with Deasoir.

An entire eighth of the vault stored data on the accumulated effects of combustion on health.

'*Alphonse,*' he thought he heard, '*the scale of their impact.*'

Deeper yet, she showed him protocols. Recruitment methods, training methods, medical procedures to identify genetic traits within the population—the vision trait and dozens of others by the looks of the tabs.

How many are there? he wondered, and his grandfather laughed. And for a brief flicker Alphonse was a strand of genetic material recombining and altering in a thousand different ways.

He swayed and held the stacks. Seeing it all in one place, documented and categorized. "Zelia."

She stopped and turned. "Yes?"

"This is stunning. I need a minute." He leaned onto his knees, breathing slowly, running his thoughts through the mental map he'd made and solidifying his understanding of key areas of the vault. This was a climb. He needed the zone.

As his breath steadied, he remembered Odile arguing about pollution. Jack's willingness to risk himself for Myrta, who might be dead right now because of a combination of DNA she'd inherited. He thought of his own grandfather dying alone in prison because he fought this industry's too-rapid growth, and he thought of Eduardo and his workers on that rig. Of Ephraim Vonard and his dedication to justice.

He tried to comprehend the vastness of this vault, tried to pull the layout of it into a single coherent thought, and at that moment, the stacks flickered into trees with yellow light streaming down. He was an ape child. No, he wasn't. He was a fully grown ape deep in a forest, and his job was to protect the others.

"That's better. I'll just make sure I'm all here." He straightened and paced a few feet down the aisle and back, into the past and back to the present, time tied together in the ape and the man, funneling into a primal rage. Alphonse felt an overpowering urge to bare his fangs.

He came up from behind Zelia and landed a bludgeon-blow behind her ear where his distant ancestor knew it would have the greatest effect. Zelia let out a small crying moan and crumpled to the floor.

He stared at the woman unconscious at his feet, horrified that he'd fallen so fully into putting his own ends before hers. Surely there was a better way to change the industry than through physical assault.

'Now is not the time, Grandson.'

He turned, ran down the aisles, and pulled records. Summaries of pollution, of proposed expansions and anything to do with the belt. Files on public policy, influence into politics, the courts, law enforcement.

He took files on profit margins and investments. On health. On spills and leaks. On genetic variants like Myrta, and on discernment. He took maps and census summaries. Racing through the maze, he pulled anything that might be of use to Odile, to Myrta, to Ephraim, to himself.

Finally, breathing hard, he reached the door and set the folders down to straighten his jacket and tie. He picked up the stack and stepped through. The door clicked shut behind him. He set the files on the desk as if it were perfectly normal to carry out so many. "Ms. Naida's faint. She'd like some water."

The guard eyed the files.

"We're working on the belt expansion." Alphonse fought an urge to bolt up the stairwell. He looked for the next grip up the cliff.

The guard stood and poured a glass of water. "Everyone gets faint in there. It's too stuffy."

He needed to take this man out too.

He pulled back and threw a punch, but the guard ducked, dropped the glass and hit back, catching Alphonse on the chin. His head spun, and black spots filled his vision. He lunged toward the man's legs, toppled him. Wrestling, they slid into the water.

Sinking into a sea of history, Alphonse was a blue-green bacterium, floating. He made sweet, sweet sugar from carbon dioxide . . .

'Now is not *the time.'*

Fighting back, his own past enveloped him. Alphonse's hands wrapped around the guard's throat, and he yelled, "You didn't help Grandfather. You tried to *buy* him, and you never helped him!" The guard tugged mightily at Alphonse's hands, sputtering, but Alphonse forced the man's head back against the floor twice. It was enough.

Staring at the man, lying there like Zelia inside the vault, Alphonse rocked back onto his heels.

This can't be right. Assaulting living, breathing people because they stood in his way. He felt a fleeting moment of identity with Ivette's passions. Sickened, he stood and grabbed the stack. He dashed up to ground level and left for the training barracks.

Chapter Thirty-Seven

Myrta came to consciousness on a hard surface. A thick strap bound her chest and upper arms; another bound her stomach and forearms, and a third, her thighs. Her feet and shins tingled, and pain throbbed from the back of her skull.

People were speaking nearby. Cracking her eyes, a light overhead blazed. She jerked from the glare, but metal clamps held her head in place. Panicked, she groped at her pocket for her knife. It was gone. Oddly, other blades lay within reach, pointing upward from a tray.

Three of those knives were long and broad. Five were short, with blades no bigger than her thumbnail. There were two syringes with short, wire-thin needles beside the knives.

Five people stood across the room, including Odile and Melville. Floyd. Two others.

Slowly, she moved her hand toward the blades. She wrapped her fingers around a short one, pulled, but it held.

Bile came up and she swallowed it. She reminded herself that the only way out was to *move*, to find the resolve to do that, like Odile always did.

She needed to fight. She turned her attention to the voices.

"... incisions kept shallow ... everything functional."

The recruits—their expressions were unnerving. One kept clenching his jaw.

"Acuity," Melville said. The three fiddled at their sides, and then they all—all of them—their eyes fell on her, and it felt like that first day in the back office at the inn, when she saw herself as a mistake. Odile's expression was worse—she looked like Celeste did when it was time to butcher a goat. Grim, with empty terror filling her eyes.

Melville's breath brushed her face. "Hello, Myrta." She struggled against the strap at her legs, but it held fast. If she could get her fingers to the fasteners, she might be able to work it loose.

Melville turned to the side. "Floyd." The younger man came over, swallowing nervously, beads of sweat on his lip. He lifted a body off the floor, limp and gagged.

Jack!

Melville flicked his head upward, and Floyd pulled Jack to his chest.

Then Melville wheeled a cart over. It held canisters like the ones back in Collimais. Her head swam, the room unfocused, and she whimpered at the thought of Melville having canisters like the ones Ephraim had; the reason Ephraim might own such canisters falling into place.

"Ah. You're familiar with these. I'd hoped Ephraim might have played this game with you." He picked up a canister and sprayed methane.

When had her vision turned on? She switched it off.

"What gas is that?"

This couldn't be true, where the game had started.

"She'll tell us." Melville flicked his head at Jack again, unconscious against Floyd's chest.

Floyd pulled a knife, *her* knife, from his pocket.

He put the blade on Jack's forehead. She switched her vision on again—Jack was breathing.

Melville sprayed the canister again. "We're waiting."

She couldn't get air. Floyd pressed the point of her knife into Jack's scalp.

"She needs encouragement."

"No!"

Melville put his hand up. "That's fine." The tension in Floyd's grip released, and the dimple of pressure against Jack's forehead disappeared.

Melville strode up to the table, released a syringe, and before she knew what was happening, he stabbed it straight into her right temple. She screamed, not from pain but shock. He released a scalpel and pushed the blade against her eyelid. "Tell me the gas."

Her right eye was numbing, growing cold.

Melville turned to Floyd and roared, "Cut him."

Floyd gashed along Jack's hairline, and Jack was awake and howling through the gag.

"Methane! Don't hurt him."

The recruits turned to her in astonishment. Even Odile seemed stunned.

Melville spun on his heels, eyebrows up. He looked at the canister's label and then said to the three recruits, "She's right. Eight to go."

Jack struggled against Floyd, but Myrta focused on Melville. He sprayed a second gas.

"Oxygen," she sobbed, and Odile looked intrigued again, which made no sense, and Myrta's heart was breaking. Her family was breaking.

Melville sprayed gas after gas, and Myrta choked her way through them. He brought the recruits up next.

"You control her." In their eyes, she saw glimmers—it seemed the idea of power twisted alive in their thoughts, and somehow she understood at a deeper level that these recruits were learning to feel repulsed by her from the simple demonstration of her ability.

When Odile stood with the final canister, Myrta murmured, "No," but her cousin looked like the others. "Carbon dioxide," Myrta whispered. Underneath her despair, anger rose. No one even treated an animal like this, not like *this*.

Melville pushed the cart away, and the recruits turned to him. He handed Odile some colored pens. "Diagram her anatomy."

Odile stared blankly.

Melville repeated, "Draw her alterations on the side of her face. Just draw it. All of it."

Odile studied the pens in her hand. "Yes, sir." She turned to Myrta, tilting her head as if in thought. She began to draw.

Odile was being abused too. The thought added to her fury, that this way of thinking that Melville had, that it was being propagated, like a crop, into a new generation.

With her head clamped, her feet asleep from the too-tight straps, her right eye unable to focus, Myrta saw abuse as an idea passed down.

This idea needed to die.

Odile drew around Myrta's temple and eye socket, she used color after color. She used the entirety of the left side of Myrta's face, all of her forehead, her cheek, her chin, down her neck.

When she stepped back at last, Melville nodded approvingly. "You know the tissues." Odile pushed something against her waist and her face flushed.

Melville's eyes raked Myrta's face. "I keep a

tradition for aerovoyants like you. Anyone old enough to understand why your trait risks us all. I doubt you have any idea how we lived before we harnessed archaic carbon. Do you know Turaset's history, Myrta? The millennia after the founding? The centuries we spent dying? Ephraim would have us on wood fires and stone knives. We would not be able to feed people without oil and gas. We would not produce the medicines that save lives. Archaic carbon is why we *survive* on this world.

"Today's a simple thing for you. You end. Much harder for us, for me. I've given my soul for this work. For advancement. Health. Food. This—" and he waved his hand at the table and blades, "today is easier if you understand."

He watched as though hoping for her permission, but his words fed her rage.

Sighing, he walked away.

The place inside her, the one that opened on a hillside over Collimais back on the day she pinpointed signals all the way out to the horizon—she remembered that place. A place of knowledge, of knowing more of the world than anyone around her could possibly understand.

She turned her sight on again.

Traces from Melville's game lingered, including the sulfur compounds that anyone ought to be able to smell. She'd acclimated to the odor but still saw the sulfur.

Cobalt clouds surrounded everyone's face, drifting in and out of their noses and mouths, little pulsing plumes of carbon and water. Life. Her own face had the cloud. Melville had the cloud.

She stared. But his breath was different. It had sulfur and traces of complex compounds.

That's why he smells. Methylamines, ketones, she saw them all in his breath.

His lungs were rotten.

Melville spoke to the recruits, explaining that they would cut into Myrta's temples, peel the skin and learn the musculature, then remove the eyelids and dissect her eyes. "I'll make the first incision."

"No." Odile released a scalpel from the tray.

He turned, eyebrows up. "Wonderful morale." Odile pushed at her waist and her face flushed again.

Jack struggled against Floyd, moaning through the gag.

Melville roared, "Stop interrupting my class," and slammed his fist into Jack's stomach. Jack doubled over, unconscious and on the floor again. Floyd came to the table, sweat glistening down the sides of his face. "Take a scalpel, Floyd. Autore, Odile has more courage than you."

Floyd nodded quickly and released a second scalpel.

Odile took the flat of hers and pressed it on Myrta's temple, a cool pressure.

Myrta saw more gases from Melville's mouth than before, and the cloud was going in and out harder, faster. His eyes were harder too. His arousal, her terror, they tied together inside her, into a knot. She whispered, "Please, Odile, stop. Please." But Odile just stared at the side of her face, studying it.

The recruits were close enough that their breath, warm and heavy, pulsed on her arm, matching her waves of fear and rage. Jack was curling into himself.

Odile said, "We should increase acuity, memory, and pleasure."

Melville nodded. "Get on with it. Do it."

Odile looked up at Melville, her face almost languid.

"You believe in me. No one else ever has. You really believe in *me,* like a proper papa. Thank you, Papa."

She said it like a forlorn child.

Confusion clouded Melville's face. "Odile . . . girl. I'm your mentor, not your father."

Her face—the grief, the emptiness. "In a way, you are. You're like a papa to me. You are."

In that bizarre moment, as he stared uncomprehending, and Odile seemed to hold his gaze and neither looked away from the other, Myrta heard a ripping sound near her legs and felt the straps loosen. Blood rushed to her feet, painful needles, knives, she almost cried out, but she bit her tongue and the fleshy part of her cheek. She shot a glance down. Odile had sliced the binding. The straps on her chest loosened, and the clamps against her head clicked.

"Get up," Odile yelled. Then she grabbed one of the recruits around the middle and jabbed upward into his stomach. He flailed, bizarrely uncoordinated, and she threw her other fist into his jaw. He was down. He was out.

"Myrta, get up," she yelled again as she grabbed the other recruit.

Myrta twisted her legs off the table, her feet hammering with the rush of blood. "Jack!" She stumbled off the table and lunged at Melville, who had Odile around the middle. Myrta threw herself at his back, got a leg around him, and grappled at his stomach. He let go of Odile and wrenched her off, gripped her wrist so tightly that something crunched, and pain shot into her hand. She clamped her other arm around his neck, and they toppled over. She twisted to break the fall with her shoulder, but her head still hit the cement and her ears rang.

Somehow Alphonse was there, and papers were

sliding across the floor. He was on Floyd, and Jack was coming to.

Odile was going for Melville's stomach now, grabbing at it. The man's shirt was partly open, and the drugs were there, strapped to him. Odile pulled tubing off in pops, and Melville slugged her, pushed her, and began reattaching the tubes. Myrta got up. Her right eye refused to focus, and her hand pulsed in pain. She kicked. Her foot connected with his stomach, he fell, wheezing and coughing. Odile got on top of him and slammed his head into the floor with a loud crack. He passed out.

Breathing heavily, Odile pulled his shirt open.

Melville's chest was wrinkled and shrunken. This man was so sick.

"We have to reconnect these." Odile untangled the tubing and matched ends on his drug manifold.

Myrta scooted back. "Connect them? You want him back? No!"

"Myrta," Odile hissed. "He's unconscious right now. Help me connect his tubes."

"Why?" Myrta cried, pushing further away, toward Jack and Alphonse. They'd handled Floyd, and Alphonse was binding him with strapping from the table.

"We can use the drugs to make him remember anything we want." Odile removed her own drug pack and shunted that into Melville's manifold too. "Al. Come here. Tie his hands."

Alphonse frowned, but cut off more strapping. As he bound Melville's hands and feet, Odile went to the other recruits and adjusted their drug ports. They were out.

Then she was back on Melville, dosing him, and he groaned alert.

Pressed back against the exam table, Myrta cried out, "Odile," but her cousin ignored her.

"Ephraim taught me the drugs, *Mel.*" Odile checked each connection on the manifold and the strapping now binding his wrists and ankles. "He told me all the details of the first person you killed."

Myrta took a sharp inward breath.

Odile adjusted a port and dialed up a knob. "Do you remember Jose?"

The names on that sheet in Collimais came to Myrta's mind. There'd been a Jose.

Melville was watching Odile's hands on the manifold. He didn't move his head at all, only his eyes, which looked like those of a snake. Unreadable. "Stop that. I'm not your monkey." Then he gasped, and pain flashed on his face.

Odile had done something. "You sound afraid."

He stared at her finger, at the port on the end. A drug from her pack, not his. A pain drug. From her pack. He said in a panicked voice, "Stop. Yes. I remember—" But his gaze dragged down, and he coughed.

"What?" Her finger hovered over the port. He didn't respond, and she pushed at the drug port.

"I didn't want to!" He was trembling violently. "I didn't want to hurt Jose. It could have been Ephraim's job, but they thought I had more promise."

Odile scoffed. "Wrong. They could manipulate you. Tell me about Jose."

He looked over to Floyd, unconscious next to Myrta.

Odile pushed the button.

"Oh," he cried, doubling around himself, wheezing. "I remember. Jose was my uncle."

"Your uncle?" Her eyes roved back and forth over

the drugs and she pushed two in concert. "Tell me about that."

Melville's eyebrows drew close. He seemed unfocused. "I was his favorite nephew . . ."

Odile gave him more pain, and he groaned and stared at her, wide-eyed.

"Why were you his favorite?"

Her cousin was treating this man like some sort of sub-human thing, like a machine, the drugs no more than dials to tinker with. "Odile stop it!"

Melville snapped his gaze to Myrta, his eyes focused like a predator's, his gaze roving to her temples. She cowered back against the table legs.

Odile glared at her, then returned to Melville, dosing him with each word. He groaned, punctuated, every time. "Why. Were. You. His—"

"Because I heard things!"

Odile pushed a different drug and his face lit with pleasure. Flushed. His expression almost heavenly.

His words sunk in. *I heard things.* There was moisture in his eyes, and he shuddered with each breath he took.

Odile moved her hand to the end again and he cowered. "Don't—please, Odile. I'll talk. I heard more frequencies. I was audiovoyant. The world, it was music. Life was music, and you don't hear it. I could. I heard angels, harmonies everywhere . . ." He began to sob, curled around himself.

"You had a genetic variation from the founders."

It was unfathomable.

"I didn't know my uncle had the vision trait. I thought it would be a stranger. I didn't know, didn't know."

Odile remained stony-eyed. "But you hurt him anyway."

"They *made* me."

"Coward!"

"I had no choice," he screamed back. "They drugged me. Like you. I fought, said no. And they—" The scars around his malformed ear were red. "They took it. My hearing." He curled around himself, moaning. "I cooperated . . . to keep the other ear." Myrta could only just make out his next words. "It doesn't work with one."

Odile doubled two of the ports.

"Stop it!" Myrta couldn't take her eyes off of the man. His face streaked; his body convulsing.

"Get it through your thick skull, Myrta. He wants to kill you, and Ephraim has always wanted him out of this place."

Myrta's head swam, every part of this was wrong.

"Melville," Odile said, "remember Jose's face." The man contorted, and Odile continued, "I'm dosing you with suggestibility and emotion."

He said, cheeks wetter than before, "Why? Please don't. Please stop."

"Oh, believe me, this is for your own good. Are you going to cooperate?"

Melville shook.

"I want you to remember cutting Jose."

Melville moaned.

Odile's voice was razor sharp. "The person feeling the dissection is you."

A cry tore from Melville's mouth in another man's voice, "Melville, stop!" and Melville arched on the ground, his head flung back.

He went silent, staring straight up. Except for the faint carbon pulse around his mouth, Myrta would have thought him dead.

Odile rocked back and took a long breath. She

rolled her shoulders, stood and stared at Melville, studied him like Nathan might a field.

He was so small, bound like an animal.

She walked around him, lying unconscious, and said to Myrta, "Jose was first. Ephraim has said for years that if Melville faced his past, he'd leave discerning."

A new spike of dread pierced Myrta. "How many were there?"

"Thirty-eight. On the second, he started and Ephraim finished." She sat again and reached for the stimulant port.

Myrta lunged, grabbed her arm. "You can't do this. You're hurting him, and he's *dying*."

Odile shook her head and started in. Myrta scooted away, stumbled back to Jack, hands over her ears, trying not to hear Melville's pleas.

Ephraim's name came up again and again. Myrta was sobbing, rocking against Jack, who was too weak to do anything but rest his arm around her shoulders. Alphonse was muttering about radiation and petroleum, adversity and cooperation.

With each name that Odile forced, Melville grew weaker.

And Myrta's life flashed through her mind. The decisions others had made to steer her, mold her. Her parents sending her away. Celeste withholding the truth. Terrence shaping her into a steading wife. Emmett planning his children through her. Melville seeing her as some sort of threat to the entire continent. People controlling people from beginning to end.

She wrenched her thoughts back and threw herself in front of Melville, who was unconscious again.

Sweaty, Odile panted, "Get out of my way."

Myrta held her ground between them. "He's help-less."

"He wants you dead."

A discordant sound, like a squeaking hinge, whim-pered behind her. Myrta whipped her head around. But Melville was no more than a husk now, his eyes hollow. "I'm sorry," he said, his face open.

Odile grabbed her arms and pulled. "Get out of my way."

Sobbing, Myrta yanked away from Odile and drew Melville to herself. He was so light. So wasted. So sick. His breath full of the wrong things. He smelled horri-ble. He'd lost control of his bowels, but she held him. This frail man, with her papa, oh, what they'd done. Odile had suffered too. It had all been ripped from her journal, the years lost, the absence of her life.

This, now.

"Odile. You matter. You've always mattered. You're my cousin, we're family, and I love you. You're not a *placeholder*." She pulled Melville closer, unwill-ing for this brokenness to continue one more second.

Odile's stony eyes morphed from dispassion into something else, hot and flayed wide. "Did you read my *diary*?"

Movement broke out across the room. Floyd was out of his bindings and lurching toward the knives in the tray. Screaming, Myrta released Melville and scrabbled back to the wall. Floyd howled, his eyes strange, and he lunged.

He plunged the knife straight into Melville's chest and yelled, "You killed *me*!" He pulled the knife back out. Blood spurted twice, three times.

Melville's blue cloud vanished.

Floyd turned the knife on himself and plunged a

second time, straight under his ribs. He fell to his side, as blood soaked his clothes and pooled on the floor.

The room fell silent. Odile stared at the death. The other recruits still lay unconscious.

Alphonse pushed up and began gathering papers. "Can we leave? Can we leave now?"

Odile turned to him, and her eyes grew wide as they landed on the papers. She picked up one sheet, then another. "You got all of these? *You* got these?"

He didn't answer, just kept gathering. Myrta went to Jack. He was pale, but his bleeding had stopped. They stood and left the trailer.

Outside, the shadows were crisp and vehicles drove in the distance.

Jack leaned against the wall of the trailer, panting. "How do we . . . get out of here?"

Alphonse gripped a share of the files with one hand and Odile's arm with the other. "We walk out the front when everyone leaves."

Jack breathed his next words. "You're really . . . not all here . . . are you? Odile's a recruit. Myrta's marked up . . . like a book. I'm bloody." He tipped his head at the files. "And these."

Myrta clutched her share of them to her chest. It had been Alphonse's connections that had gotten them in. "What about Zelia? Can't you do something like you did before?"

He looked at her like she was the addled one. "No, Myrta. Not after the records vault."

"We go to the . . . loading dock. Go out with . . . shipments." Jack was very pale.

Odile shook her head. "The cargo's checked at the front gate."

Myrta scanned the grounds. There had to be a way out. In the distance, the extraction rigs pounded away.

But Ephraim was right—closer on the property, she could track people by their breath, and there were no puffs of breath anywhere nearby except for their own.

She looked out, past the fence, out where they'd stood the previous night. Stunned, she focused on the wires wrapping the fence rails. There was no haze of maroon at the fence. There was *no* halo. No oxygen radicals, no ozone . . .

The others kept arguing as she focused in and out. No ozone . . . those wires were as dead as a shovel. "The fence is off."

Jack was leaning against Alphonse. Odile kept putting one hand to the side of her head and reaching for something at her waist. Then pulling her hand away and looking irritated.

Alphonse muttered, "We find somewhere to hide. Wait until dark and leave then."

"When the floodlights are on? It's never dark and the gate's always guarded."

"The *fence* is *off*," Myrta repeated.

"All right. What do you suggest?" Jack breathed, his face gray.

They weren't listening. They could leave this minute. She grabbed Odile's shoulder and pointed at the fence. "It's off!"

"It is?"

Myrta ran to it, grabbed it with her free hand. The wires were dead. Like a shovel. She started climbing.

Alphonse glanced up. "Conjunction. It must have fried the wires." Odile passed the files to Myrta and followed her over. Alphonse helped Jack. They fell to the other side and ran.

Chapter Thirty-Eight

Two suns blazed overhead. Stavo's face was leathery, eyes pounded into it deep and dark.

Strange plants surrounded them, gelatinous and furry at the same time, with downward hanging limbs that plumbed the ground. Under these red and purple tree-like plants, wide pads lobed with brown and orange riffles spread along the ground. A single spiceberry shrub grew, and ramshackle buildings dotted the crest of a nearby hill.

Stavo's voice was thick. "Turaset was founded. It was not an easy path."

They walked up to a few sad metal huts. A graveyard lay beyond, stretching down the hill and up the next. Overcome with grief, Alphonse barely managed to speak. "So much death."

"People." Stavo leaned onto his knees, squinting at the rows of grave markers. "Livestock. Each life was so precious."

Meager patches of crops—rye, poppy, a few he didn't know—grew between the shacks. A sickly mare and an emaciated foal grazed in a pen.

"I don't know these plants."

Stavo hesitated. "Turaset, Grandson. Turaset had its own ecology. We brought

Earth's. We had little choice. We cannot eat sandsap."

"We can eat spiceberries."

"Not many."

Two people made their way from one building to another. They were thin and pale-skinned, and their clothing was torn and frayed. One held her stomach, the other put a hand under the woman's arm. Both had blisters on their faces.

"How did we survive?"

Stavo turned to him. "We learned. We adapted. We evolved."

Three Months Later

Most of Renico's files were released and published throughout the cities. Prime Chancellor Joshi Nabahri ordered a temporary freeze on oil exploration and extraction and an immediate investigation into the practice of discerning. Seven councilors resigned, others drew intense scrutiny, and emergency sessions of Congress began untangling the full influence of the industry on the councils and the courts.

Alphonse pulled into the lane alongside Ardelle's inn. The plum trees rested bare, snow rimming their branches like piped icing, and one of the horses in the barn whickered. The inn was as he remembered, only now ashy smoke spilled out of the chimney, sinking along the roof and down to the ground. Crisp winter air, with wood smoke lacing through, pulled it all together into the life he still wished for.

The back door swung out and Ephraim trotted down the steps. "Al. I'll get your bags."

They went in. Ephraim tipped his head at the dining room and continued up the stairs.

Myrta rose from the table and hugged him. "Thank you, Alphonse." Ardelle came from the kitchen with a platter of sandwiches. Four. There should be five. He wondered if Odile was here, wanted desperately to see her.

"For what?"

"Running for Council."

Ephraim's steps plunked back down, and he came into the dining room. "You're all set. First room." Then, chuckling, he pulled out a chair. "'Councilor Najiwe' will have a nice ring."

"Don't count on that happening. Di Les has held that seat for years, and Ivette won't support me. They both play dirty."

"Your Grandfather's name . . ."

It touched the sore spot, the node in his heart. Anger had grown in Sangal over the past three months.

"Isn't enough to get past Ivette's. She's wanted me on the Council for years. When the files went public, the money she received from Renico, the councilors she backed, everything fell into a very straight line. I'm not trusted. And the way we got those files broke a few laws. Even with Nabahri promising pardons, even with the necessity of what we did, this race is all uphill."

Ephraim's eyes were warm. "But not impossible."

The man was good. It didn't fit his history, and Alphonse thought of Ivette, wondering if anyone's story was ever complete. "Eduardo's challenging di Gof. If we can knock off both of them, we'll have a toehold. Your help's important."

"You have a room here whenever you need it. And we've gone through the records again, this time with an eye to Renico's timelines. The proposals they've developed for the foothills—Al, it's remarkable. Those files have energized people. The network's expanding."

Myrta sat peacefully, her hands folded neatly on the table. "That little taste of their vault makes me want more."

He'd never seen her at such ease. "You look rested."

"I am. I enjoy not being afraid. I have everything I wanted. Plus, you're going to win, so things will get better and better."

That seemed a bit optimistic.

"The records, one of them says our ancestors used my trait to find game herds. It's how we survived." She smiled, and it lit her face in a way Alphonse had never seen before. "And I finally know where I want to go."

He was shocked at her words, but a pleasant kind of shock.

"I want everyone who has anything like what I have to be safe. I want each of us to see one another."

Alphonse tensed. It felt like a challenge, direct to him, to speak openly about his time-knowledge—what Ralen had called time-binding and said her father had also had. He wasn't ready.

"Take Jack, look at his selflessness. Look at Mama and Papa, their resilience. Melville had a gift to hear things that none of us can imagine. How much better if he'd been encouraged instead of having his ability used against him like it was."

He couldn't talk about it, his life as a planet. Myrta should understand, she was close to this kind of thing, what it was like to wrestle with something so freakishly bizarre.

She continued, "Everyone has something. If anybody's living with anything like me, I want them to know they can talk about it." Her gaze suddenly reminded him of Ephraim's. Intent and focused. "There are people *suffering* because they have a certain combination of genes. And if I help you win your race, then I'd have a friend on your Council who understands. Alphonse, I want to go to Sangal with you and work on your campaign."

After lunch, Ephraim and Alphonse met in the office. Odile was nowhere to be seen, and no one had mentioned her. Maybe she'd gone to the belt.

Ephraim pulled out a copy of the records and took a ledger from the desk.

Alphonse sat, craning his neck to see the pages better. "We need to think about all of this. The economics of the industry. Jobs. Carbon and climate. We have to balance *all* of it. Ephraim, I don't know how to do that."

The whirl of time pulled at him, the efforts of past civilizations down through the ages trying to balance resources with wisdom, sometimes succeeding and sometimes failing.

"Just go slowly and pay attention. If you make a mistake, pick yourself up and keep going."

Today's goal was finalizing a foothill response plan

to the possibility of provincial designation. A slate
of leaders in the towns and belt had been identified
through Ephraim's network, and preliminary bills
had been drafted to prevent oil exploration. The only
question remaining was where an assembly could be
seated, if Nabahri named the province.

After a time, Ephraim leaned back and ran his
hands through his hair. They'd been at this for hours.
"Have you been sleeping?"

Alphonse scratched the back of his neck. He'd been
spending most nights trying to get his head around
sensato and how to control it. Ephraim didn't need to
know that. "Not really. Working with Ivette all those
years and trying to leave behind everything she taught
me. Knowing it *works*. It messes with me. Sleep's a
casualty."

Ephraim's face, and his tone too, were kindly. "We
all have a past that messes with us. You saw Mel. You
saw what Odile brought out in him."

Maybe she'd gone back to Renico. No, that didn't
make any sense.

"In hindsight, I shouldn't have ever hinted we try to
pull him out." The man's face was empty and full, like
a cemetery, things hidden, precious and sad. "You saw
Mel face his ghosts. I've never faced mine, not like he
did. If you're haunted by your past, well son, you've
got company."

"You left that business. Melville didn't."

Quietly, Ephraim said, "That's a bit harsh. There
were so many others, especially Ardelle, who saw to
it that I got out. I failed to help Mel. Autore knows
I tried. I knew him before he became so ill. We were
good friends, once."

If Ivette could feel any of that regret . . .

Ephraim stood and replaced the ledger onto the

desk. "My memories from that time had a life of their own. Discerners, they . . . *we* . . . were taught to believe the program advanced society. With every victim we learned to feel some level of righteousness at the thought of improving life for the masses. Improving the future. There is profound satisfaction in believing you make the world a better place."

"You left that life and built a new one. It had to be hard."

"Sure, okay. But I'm telling you, it's not that simple. Habits develop a life of their own. It took a long time to detangle the memories, to put the horror into its place, and pull the . . . sense of righteousness elsewhere. After a time, the nature of my torment changed, and now, for better or worse, in a way I rely on the horror. It reminds me what I'm capable of, the human drive that puts numbers ahead of the individual. What we're fighting."

Ephraim turned to the window and murmured, "What he might have been rescued from." He stood stock still, solid, like an ox in a morning moment of stillness. His shoulders lifted and fell and he turned back. "Your experiences are part of you, telling you what's important. They're your signposts. Odile says—"

"Where is she?"

Ephraim stared, his eyes changed after a moment and lined with understanding. "Oh, Al. What she did came at a cost. It's taking a while for the drugs to clear."

"She wasn't medicated."

Ephraim frowned, and he looked down, rubbing the toe of his shoe along the edge of the carpet. "Odile's as cool as they come, son, but no good human being could torture another without aid. She needed to remember the names and details of every person that Mel took over the past forty years."

Alphonse blinked. *Miere.* She'd been a machine that day.

"Memory enhancement, acuity, emotion-numbing medications, all at full strength, maybe double strength knowing her."

Groaning, Alphonse put his head in his hands and rubbed his forehead. He knew some of those drugs. Ivette had joked about them often enough.

"She watched Mel experience each death he caused, and she knew that she was forcing that on him. When the drugs wore off, there was something of a backlog. Mostly emotion, and she couldn't help but remember *all* of what she did to him. Every last detail of how she inflicted . . . how she tortured him."

He'd been in the shadows, lost in history, not really present at all.

"She knew she was responsible for Mel's pain. She'll remember that day for a long, long time."

"Ephraim. Did she truly mean to become a discerner?"

Slowly, sadly, he shook his head. "I thought—*she* thought she'd get straight at the data. Go in and get out, that was her intent. But, she's always known that I wanted Mel out of that program, and she's always known he'd be a powerful ally if he chose to. No, Al, she wanted the records, that was all. When they put her into that training, she must have seen a way to get at them."

"I didn't—"

"Of course not. We all make sacrifices. Possibly she's at the overlook."

Alphonse hurried up the trail. As he rounded the top, he stopped in shock, three months of willful ignorance draining from him. He'd been too busy planning his campaign, and she'd been so clear she didn't need him here.

Odile sat hunched, her hair lying flat and limp, her body too small in the heavy coat she wore. A shudder seemed to pass through her.

"Odile," he said softly.

She startled and looked around at him.

Autore, her eyes—they're so pained.

He went to her and sat, unspeaking, the way Eduardo had done when Alphonse was small. He simply sat with her, breathing the same air. Being.

Another breath rattled through her. He wanted to take her hand, her whole body, but she was barely there. She seemed to have forgotten him.

"I didn't know."

Her nose was red, her eyes bloodshot. Minutes passed. "It doesn't matter."

But it did. *She* mattered. He sat next to her, unspeaking. He sat with her as Bel and Letra lowered in the sky. He waited with her as first sun set and hoped for the focus it could bring, for her, but it didn't come.

Alphonse ached for the determined, fiery woman he knew. He'd give anything for that woman to have a lifeline that might bring her back. A whisper of a thread through the wilderness. He'd give anything; he'd give the thing he held dearest.

"Odile," he whispered. "We are part of Turaset. We are. It's not a thing to be used. We need this planet. It can exist in any number of ways and it has through time, but we . . . can't, and we need to understand the scale of our actions. I . . . what I'm trying to share with you, it's important."

She turned to him, the barest light in her eyes.

He hung onto that light, clung to it, and he cracked open a door he wouldn't close again to let her know that *he* knew that she'd always been right in her passion. He said simply what was in his heart. "We need to feel the things that came before. We need to *know* the things that have come before. We need to understand that we're changing our home."

A tear stole down her cheek. She leaned against him and trembled through another long breath. "Thank you." She said the words, but any emotion behind them was unapparent.

Tentatively, he put his arm around her. "I'm worried about you. I want you to be better."

She shuddered, another breath. "Al." Her frame was so still, so frail, slight, and frightened, and the silence hung between them again. "This is . . . better. I'm getting better." After another long moment she said, "Trust me."

"We can talk about it."

"No." She pulled away, and the chill in the air sank in. He crossed his arms, hugging himself. Eventually, Odile leaned on him again. This time, something of her old self came through. An awareness, a watching of the things around her, of Alphonse. The slightest pressure against him, the faint substance of her, the warmth and trust—it was a step. He put his arm around her shoulders again. He pulled her jacket around her a little more snugly. He thought of the future, the march of time, possibility and growth, change, and cycles— and he smiled.

THE END

₰PPENDICES

1. Timeline
2. Cultural conventions
3. Known genetic variants
4. Political structure of Nasoir
5. Glossary

1. BRIEF TIMELINE OF COLONIZATION OF TURASET.

The collapse of civilization on Earth in the late twenty-first and early twenty-second centuries resulted from two things—a rapidly warming climate and an exponential rise in computer sentience. In parallel, advances in molecular biology, most notably gene-splicing technology (CRISPR), enabled radically new gene-engineering strategies of crop plants, livestock, and humans.

Within this milieu, dozens of ships from numerous space agencies fled Earth determined to start over and, once established on new worlds, avoid the lure of advanced technology. The ships' cargoes held genetically modified seed and embryo banks. While diverse and extensive in scope, these banks did not include all the species Earth had to offer. Species with no obvious value (e.g., *Varanus*), disease vectors (e.g., *Aedes*), and parasites (e.g., *Giardia*) were not included in the cargoes, for obvious reasons.

Of the fleeing ships, six arrived at Turaset decades later. As a planet in the "Goldilocks" zone of a distant star system, Turaset first appeared to be an ideal, if tiny, new home with a breathable atmosphere and no initial evidence of intelligent life. The day length (27 hours) and orbit (420 days) were Earth-like, and water covered eighty-eight percent of the planet's surface.

The touch-down site was named "Good Air" (later, Gaderr). Although the ships were not designed to launch back into space, they could manage travel between land masses. Such travel was intended and expected after the colony took hold—an estimated five to ten years' time. This time frame was thought long enough for the colonists to develop agriculture suited to Turaset and to begin having children.

However, three months after landing, the rotation of Turaset's two stars aligned with the planet in the celestial arrangement later known as Conjunction. The colonists grew sick, as a previously-unrecognized form of cosmic radiation hit the planet's surface. The first instance of this event killed seventy percent of the colony and was called the Great Death (later, the First Great Death). Crops and livestock were similarly devastated.

The mission at Gaderr became feeding and housing survivors and finding a means to survive the radiation. This state of affairs lasted for close to a century, and the goal of dispersing to other sites was forgotten. Scientists and engineers looked to Turaset's brightly-colored native species, which were immune, and reasoned there must be a biological solution—pigmentation genes—they could force into humankind. Many generations passed before the pigment genes were adequately expressed in the human form.

Roughly five hundred years later, the colony at last took hold. Gaderr achieved Earth-analog status, and dispersal to secondary sites began.

Approximately a millennium after landing, multiple outposts across Turaset (including all four major land masses) were largely self-sustaining. This was a turning point in history—Earth-like agriculture had blossomed and trade began. This expansion era continued for many generations. Turaset had been tamed, and the founders' vision realized.

The Second Great Death, biological rather than radiological in nature, occurred during the second millennium. One theory holds that the transport of goods across and between continents trafficked disease organisms. A second theory speculates that silent DNA, inadvertently introduced at Gaderr alongside the pigmentation genes, had been activated. Some argue that the combination of these factors precipitated a pandemic. Sixty-five percent of the human population died. Several staple crops and animal species (e.g., soybean, dromedary) were lost.

During this period, any remnant of ancient recorded history from Earth was scoured for techniques to fight plague. This effort led some Turasetians to argue that the Second Great Death would never have occurred had their world hewn to more technologically-advanced practices. They claimed that the agrarian lifestyle adopted by the colonists (part of the founding precepts meant to avoid a second rise of computer sentience) lay at the root of the Second Death. They said more advanced technology was necessary going forward.

In particular, one woman (Betha O'Mardon B'Ger-Fra) became a vocal critic of the rustic path humanity had chosen. It was clear, she insisted, that agrarian living was fraught with risk, and that trade by its nature promoted homogenous thinking and prevented the development of diverse societal approaches that might benefit humanity over the longer run. The loss of "idea diversity," she said, was to everyone's detriment. She began a movement toward isolationism. The concurrent cessation of trade (intended to help end the pandemic) led to some settlements perishing while others began to grow.

Regional traditions took hold. Distinct cultures formed. Some settlements, especially those influenced by Betha B'GerFra's adherents, eventually re-developed more advanced technologies. Over time, fossil fuels (called archaic carbon) were discovered on Turaset and technologically-inclined settlements embraced them.

Eventually, trade was established once more and intermixing of cultures and ideas began again.

Approximately three thousand years after humanity left Earth, the global population on Turaset surpassed one million. Cities dotted the coast of Nasoir (the largest continent in the western hemisphere) and Deasoir (the largest continent in the eastern hemisphere).

The events of *Aerovoyant* occur at roughly this point.

2. CULTURAL PRACTICES ON NASOIR.

2A. SURNAME CONVENTIONS.

Following the First Great Death, rapid reproduction was mandated. As part of the effort to prevent inbreeding, surnames derived from a child's parents' and grandparents' given names. A child of Mary and John, for example, who were themselves the children of Frances and Michael or Yvonne and Francis, would have the following surname: *of MaryJohn by Frances-Michael and YvonneFrancis* (abbreviated to o'MarJoh b'FraMicYvFran). While bulky, this convention did limit interbreeding. Over time the convention simplified.

On Nasoir:

1. Partners take a unique surname at marriage which derives from the given name of the member in higher business standing. If this partner is a woman, the prefix "Van" (coastal, urban) or "Von" (inland, rural) is added. If the partner is a man, the prefix "di" (coastal) or "de" (inland) is used. Thus, the surname conveys a general geographical location of the family and relative business standing of the respective partners. E.g.:

    a. Ardelle and Ephraim Vonard: This couple lives in a rural region. Ardelle has higher business standing than Ephraim.

    b. Lesteri and Marja di Les: This couple lives in a coastal city and Lesteri has a higher business standing than his wife.

    Children are given this surname until their own marriages. For example, in the event that Odile Vonard takes a business and marries, her surname will change from Vonard to Vonod, unless her spouse holds higher business standing.

2. In cases of divorce or death, surnames can be changed to remove implications inherent in the traditional construction. Typically, the prefix

"Na" or "Pe" is appended to a chosen word. Children take the new surname of the parent with whom they remain. E.g.:

a.   Alphonse Najiwe: As a child, Alphonse's last name was di Marc. His mother, Ivette, changed her last name to Najiwe in order to convey "by (na) stone (jiwe)," or "by hardness," which is how she envisioned surviving following her father's death and husband's abandonment.

2B. MATCHING AND COURTING.

Marital practices vary by region.

1. **In cities: Formal education (and larger populations) promotes socializing between peers.** Attachments between young men and women naturally form. Self-matching is typical. Parents are rarely consulted in any decision regarding marriage.

2. **In agrarian regions: Interactions between peers are less common.** Consistent with managing an isolated family stead, parents seek suitable matches for children. A match can be initiated in either direction.

3. **Marital practice in the foothill villages lie between these extremes.** Parental matching occurs in villages, especially if a match would promote the family business. For example, if the son of a weaver is expected to take over the family business, a sensible match is with the daughter of a

dressmaker. However, it's not unusual for village youth to self-assort. Parents may be consulted in these cases.

Courtship traditions exist in the villages. For example, if a person initiates courting and the recipient is disinterested, the courted individual will insist the two are strangers. On the other hand, if the courted individual welcomes the courtship, they will give their name whether the two have previously met or not.

2C. BUSINESS.

Generally, any individual on Nasoir is free to pursue whatever business interest they wish.

1. **Manufacturing drives city economies.** The idea of a family business is irrelevant in Nasoir's cities, where industry (energy, pharmaceutical, etc.) employs most people. Family-run businesses in cities represent a small percentage of the economy, and it's common for city youth to try a number of various jobs before choosing their individual career paths, which may or may not follow their parents' paths.

2. **Family businesses form the economic backbone of the agricultural belt and foothill villages.** Apprenticeship to the family business is common in rural areas. Even more than formal schooling, children learn to take what their parents have built.

The net-positive birth rate in the countryside

leads to surplus labor, and some claim holdings in the agricultural belt—for mining, farming, logging, ranching, or, in some cases, construction and artistry.

3. **Pay Gap:** There is a pay gap on Nasoir opposite to that which existed on Earth. Nasoirian women earn almost twice the pay that men receive, for equal work. This gap traces to events during colonization including a loose interpretation of one of the founding precepts. Over the centuries, women came to be seen as more valuable members of the work force than men for the following reasons:

   a. The life span of women averages six years longer.

   b. Similarly, retention of mental executive functions averages eight years longer.

   c. On the whole, women are more risk-averse and suffer fewer injuries in their adolescence and young adulthood. This translates into fewer job-related accidents and fewer ongoing liabilities.

   d. Women tend toward relational interactions. Relational interactions are seen as more beneficial to business than hierarchical interactions.

   e. Hiring a woman often enables two jobs— one for the woman and one for whomever she hires to care for her children. Thus, a fraction of pay for hiring mothers goes toward childcare. (This allowance can be made for men under analogous circumstances, but it's more common for women to hire care for their children.)

Certain careers, such as political posts (for which pay is internally determined), are more likely to approach pay equity. Livelihoods requiring physical strength are biased toward men, but income from these jobs often depends on product to market. The idea of a pay gap doesn't apply.

3. PARTIAL LIST OF MODIFIED GENETIC TRAITS AMONG TURASETIANS.

During the CRISPR frenzy on 21st-century Earth, myriad genetic modifications were introduced into the human genome. These modifications included duplication and specialization of tissues, introduction of genes from other organisms, and computer-based prediction and *de novo* synthesis of genes with novel function not previously extant in the biosphere.

All manners of new abilities were designed.

Once landed on Turaset, colonists engineered additional traits in a more *ad hoc* fashion toward survival. However, the ship-board technology to manipulate DNA was eventually lost, and this engineering ended.

Over the centuries, the frequency of any particular trait began to vary by location—the result of genetic drift and selection. During the events of *Aerovoyant* and its sequels, differences in allelic frequencies are most pronounced when comparing between continents. Below, an approximate global frequency is provided for each trait.

Some traits, such as modified genes conferring resistance to radiation, are carried by everyone. (They are universal; the allelic frequency is 100%.) The origin of each human trait (Turaset or Earth) is also indicated. Plant-based and fungal-based gene modifications will be described elsewhere.

1. **Aerovoyancy** (rare; Earth origin): Duplication of visual cortex tissues to allow perception of atmospheric chemistry. In essence, this trait is a biological encoding of a technological tool. More broadly, conversion of technology to genetically-encoded function was part of a trend to send technology to space in human form.

2. **Audiovoyancy** (common; Earth origin): Duplication and specialization of aural tissues to allow perception of sound above and below the normal human range.

3. **Barometrics** (believed extinct; Earth origin): Barometrics tolerate rapid shifts in pressure with no ill effect. Based on marine animals that transit vertical depth routinely and easily, the ability was reverse-engineered into humans and augmented.

4. **Chronovoyancy** (rare; Earth origin): Individuals capable of marking time to a remarkable degree of accuracy and precision. The ability stems from changes to cell cycle proteins. Pairs of chronovoyants can separate from one another and synchronize their behaviors over minutes, days, months, and years.

5. **Docility** (universal; Turaset origin): Genes linked to aggression were pruned out of the genome in an effort to limit human-on-human death in the early generations. Turasetians are gentler than their Earth ancestors.

6. **Dowsers** (somewhat common; Turaset origin): Specialization of tissues in the hands toward the detection of moisture. Dowsers detect groundwater through handling soil.

7. **Elysians** (rare; Earth origin): The ability to host foreign plastids in dermal tissue; specifically, the ability to ingest an algal meal and sustain chloroplasts in the skin. In so doing, Elysians can photosynthesize sugar for themselves from sunlight. This provides an evolutionary advantage during food shortages.

8. **Geovoyancy** ("Time binding." Rare; Earth origin): Earth history was encoded onto the Y chromosome, and a new organ able to interpret the coding was developed in the amygdala. Geovoyants serve as historians on colonized worlds.

9. **Gravimerics** (extinct; Earth origin): Individuals capable of detecting gravitational anomalies by sight. This ability was rumored to play a crucial role in allowing ships to find new homes.

10. **Healer suite of genes** (uncommon; Earth origin): Enhancement of the parasympathetic nervous system, with some duplications in the hands and feet, such that touching a patient allows a healer to assess their physiological state. Healers can

measure pulse, body temperature, blood pressure, and immune system activity through touch.

11. **Insensates** (rare; Earth origin): Extreme down-regulation of nervous system function related to pain tolerance. Insensates are naturally tolerant of pain.

12. **Isotopics** (rare; Turaset origin): Like aerovoyants, isotopics perceive particles down to the molecular level, and some of the same tissue duplication lies at the basis of this ability. However, this trait is specialized toward the detection of elemental isotopes.

13. **Luminescents** (unknown; Earth origin): Bioluminescence was one of the earliest test applications of CRISPR, and that manipulation quickly found its way onto the black market. The desire among some parents to give their children the ability to glow can be thought of as loosely grouping with vanity surgeries, body painting, and so on. The ability made its way to Turaset, but the gene frequency is unknown, as bioluminescence requires a dietary component to activate.

14. **Magnetotactics** (unknown frequency; Earth origin): Enhancement of the organ in the human forebrain that detects magnetic fields. Magnetotactics have a well-developed sense of direction.

15. **Peacekeeper suite of genes** (somewhat common; Turaset origin): This group of genes includes sequences coding for super-strength (augmentation and overexpression of myostatin) and adherence

to order. So-called "peacekeeping" individuals self-select toward law.

16. **Piezoelectrics** (rare; Turaset origin): Piezoelectrics have a third long bone running parallel to the radius and ulna in each forearm. This third bone, the piezus, is specialized to absorb and store piezoelectric energy (generated from mechanical stress). The stored energy can be discharged from the hands and used in various ways.

17. **Pigmentation** (universal; Turaset origin): Pigments identified in Turaset's native fauna were reverse-engineered into the human genome to protect the colonists during Conjunction. Within three generations of landing on Turaset, everyone carried some new form of pigmentation, but these colors varied in their relative efficacy. Over subsequent centuries, evolutionary pressure selected the fittest versions of these pigments.

18. **Skeletonics** (common; Earth origin): Enhancement of the LRP5 allele to promote dense bones. These individuals' bones do not break.

19. **Super-sleepers** (uncommon; Earth origin): Individuals with alterations in the hDEC2 gene, who maintain normal functioning over several weeks at a time in the complete absence of sleep. Super-sleepers were valuable crew members in space, but the gene frequency on Turaset drifted downward over time.

20. **Super-sprinters** (somewhat common; Earth origin): Enhancement of the ACTN3 genes. Super

sprinters sustain a three-minute mile for five or more miles.

21. **Telomerics** (rare; Earth origin): Individuals whose chromosomal telomeres are protected from degradation. The natural lifespan of telomerics measures into millennia, but these individuals often see psychological decline after a few centuries, and some telomerics take their lives before they've reached their own natural middle age.

22. **Vocalizers** (unknown frequency; Earth origin): Duplication and specialization of vocal tissues to allow speech above and below the normal range of human hearing. Selective communication is possible between vocalizers and audiovoyants. Individuals possessing both of these modifications can communicate in a way that mimics so-called telepathy.

4. POLITICAL STRUCTURE ON NASOIR.

Nasoir is ruled by a representational democracy at three levels: city (city councils), provincial (provincial assemblies), and continental (the Continental Congress.) At the time of *Aerovoyant*, three provinces had been designated on Nasoir.

4A. CITY COUNCILS.

Each of Nasoir's six coastal cities are ruled by a twenty-five-seat council.

The five most recently-elected councilors hold

probationary seats. These councilors vote on proposed legislation and can draft preliminary bills but only if they work in concert with at least one other councilor. Probationary councilors cannot call for votes or oppose points of order when council is in session.

Ten junior councilors hold additional powers—the authority to draft bills on an individual basis and to oppose points of order.

Ten senior councilors serve as committee heads, call votes in general session, and serve on the Provincial Assembly.

City councils write local law, oversee local taxation, and manage the budgeting for established and proposed projects, institutions, and policies. Councils steer city goals. A council term is five years, with elections held annually on a rolling basis.

4B. PROVINCIAL ASSEMBLIES.

Each of Nasoir's provinces is overseen by a twenty-seat assembly.

All senior city councilors automatically serve on their respective provincial assembly. Assembly members meet to ensure that the city councils are operating in an equitable way—for example, if one city's council plans a geographical expansion, the assembly judges whether this poses a negative impact to the province as a whole. Environmental impact is a common focus of discussion for assemblies, as is any joint venture between cities that might benefit both simultaneously. Assembly members communicate the outcomes of deliberations to their city councils.

However, the primary role of the assembly is

oversight of interprovincial commerce and any associated collection of tariffs. Funds obtained through tariffs are used to maintain provincial waterways and roadways.

Assemblies elect ten of their twenty members to serve on the Continental Congress.

4C. THE CONTINENTAL CONGRESS.

Ten assembly members from each province serve on the thirty-seat Congress.

Congress sets a continental tax rate (limited to provincial lands) and manages trade between the provinces and the non-provincial agricultural belt. Congress also settles trade disputes between provinces.

One congressmember is elected by the full body to serve as prime chancellor. Principal responsibilities of the chancellery include ordering the congressional agenda, commanding the continental marshalry, and naming new provinces. The chancellor relinquishes congressional voting rights but retains assembly and council voting rights.

5. ABBREVIATED GLOSSARY.

Autore: The singular deified embodiment of the group of scientists responsible for humanity's survival following the First Great Death. Also, a city-based swear word similar to "God." Autorism is a belief structure (a quasi-religion) based on science and technology.

Autoremalde: Loosely, "goddamned." Its most common usage is in connection with any negative consequence arising from science and technology.

Bel: One of the two stellar masses (stars) around which Turaset orbits.

Bristlepod: A shrub-like plant on Nasoir's southern isles. Ripe pods are harvested and pressed for their nectar.

By the code: A swear phrase referring to the power of science. In practice, "by the code" is a throw-away city phrase similar to "by all that's holy."

Byantun: A tree-like organism indigenous to Turaset with features resembling both plants and animals. In some ways, byantun trees are reminiscent of Earth sponges, although they are larger and land-based. Byantuns are sessile and grow in varied forms. They have a "root" system that penetrates the ground, and their "branches" are pad-like and motile. Byantuns are colored and harvest energy from the suns. That energy is stored in their roots as light, to attract sub-surface prey (e.g. worms and grubs). In this manner, byantun trees are predators. Byantun pigments were analyzed and reverse-engineered into the human genetic code during the First Great Death.

Camsin: A hot beverage prepared with leaves of *Camellia siniensis*. Tea.

Conjunction: The alignment of Bel, Letra, and Turaset into a straight line. During conjunction, Bel'letra appears as a single stellar mass and radiation bathes Turaset.

Copperwood tree: The name of this Turasetian plant suggests the wood is valuable, but the soft, fibrous bark is the cash crop. The fiber can be worked and spun, is naturally a pale shade of red, and can be bleached with acid, after which it takes dye.

Deadly hells: Swear-phrase in the foothills and belt.

Distavoc: A device that would once have been called a telephone. When humanity fled Earth, countless measures were taken to avoid communications surveillance by sentient AI. One such measure was to substitute a range of etymological roots into common words.

Fierno: (1)The radiation that bathes Turaset twice yearly, during conjunction. During these radiation bursts, ocean life descends to the benthos, land forms become more vibrantly pigmented, and soils form a leathery crust. (2)(metaphorical/archaic) The fires of purification. (3)A city-based swear word.

Holy heavens: Foothill phrase denoting disbelief.

Lele: A stringed instrument similar to the Earth ukulele.

Letra: One of the two stellar masses (stars) around which Turaset orbits.

Martire: Martyr.

Miere: A city-based swear word meaning excrement. A roughly equivalent word in the foothills and belt is "scat."

Moarab: Tusked, multi-appendaged (up to fourteen-legged) beast, with lizard-like head and skin, roughly the size of a small bear. Moarab are indigenous to the forests of Nasoir and are considered dangerous. Moarab can eat virtually any plant or carcass or piece of debris they find, and they store what they eat as layers of a fat-like substance. They're occasionally hunted, and their meat smoked.

Museo: Museum.

Meldeto/maldeto/maldeta (spelling varies by city): A city-based curse associated with Autorism and derived from the word "malediction." Similar in intent to the Earth word "damnation." In essence, the word implies the degree of suffering that would be associated with damnation. To be in maldeto pain is to be in pain beyond comprehension.

Nanquit: A small animal indigenous to the Singing Sea along the coast of Nasoir. They are comprised of a central mass with four radiating arms and measure eight inches from tentacle tip to tip. They move by spinning through the water (or through the air when the fog layer is sufficiently dense). Nanquits are chemo-attracted to iron and capture small prey with their tentacles, usually fish or mice. They sometimes mistakenly wrap around iron fencing and railings. Baby nanquits are called nanquittens.

Okeafolk: The intelligent life living deep in the oceans of Turaset. Okeafolk are tentacled and beautiful, and their songs enrapture men and women alike. Sea maidens. The okeafolk were encountered after humanity began sailing the oceans.

Quiverfish: Animal native to Turaset. Quiverfish are approximately 12 inches long and resemble small eels. They have six paddle-like appendages along their ventral line. Orange quiverfish pigments were reverse-engineered into the human code during the First Great Death.

Raptorfowl: Beaked animals native to Turaset. Raptorfowl have webbed limbs and can coast for a mile or more following a single leap. Their flight is described as bounding.

Rebla: Standard unit of currency. In principle, one rebla can feed a person for approximately one week.

Sandsap: A tree native to Turaset that grows above eight thousand feet of altitude. The tree retains water but the high solute concentration in the sap gives it a sandy texture.

Scat: A swear word in the belt meaning excrement. The analogous word in the cities is "miere."

Spiceberry: Native shrub of Nasoir. Spiceberries are not true berries but small fluid-filled sacs localized to plant meristems. Spiceberries are sweet and will cause nausea when eaten in large doses.

Spinebark: A low-lying sessile organism, like a carnivorous plant, that camouflages with the surrounding soil. Small animals that run across spine bark fall paralyzed and are consumed.

Tar: Stringed instrument similar to the old Earth guitar.